carrington cove: book four

SOMEDAY YOU *learn*

HARLOW JAMES

Copyright © 2025 by Harlow James

All rights reserved.

No part of this publication may be reproduced, distributed, or transmitted in any form or by any means, including photocopying, recording, or other electronic or mechanical methods, without the prior written permission of the publisher, except as permitted by U.S. copyright law. For permission requests, contact [include publisher/author contact info].

The story, all names, characters, and incidents portrayed in this production are fictitious. No identification with actual persons (living or deceased), places, buildings, and products is intended or should be inferred.

Book Cover by Abigail Davies

Edited by Jenny Ayers (Swift Red Pen)

Proof Read by Emma Cook

ISBN: 9798312758276

Contents

Dedication		V
Epigraph		VI
Prologue		1
1.	Chapter 1	4
2.	Chapter 2	31
3.	Chapter 3	45
4.	Chapter 4	52
5.	Chapter 5	72
6.	Chapter 6	79
7.	Chapter 7	103
8.	Chapter 8	118
9.	Chapter 9	134
10.	Chapter 10	146
11.	Chapter 11	161
12.	Chapter 12	171
13.	Chapter 13	183
14.	Chapter 14	196

15.	Chapter 15	213
16.	Chapter 16	228
17.	Chapter 17	244
18.	Chapter 18	255
19.	Chapter 19	264
20.	Chapter 20	274
21.	Chapter 21	287
22.	Chapter 22	292
23.	Chapter 23	301
24.	Chapter 24	310
25.	Chapter 25	320
26.	Chapter 26	325
27.	Chapter 27	330
Also By Harlow James		333
Acknowledgements		336
Connect with Harlow James		338

This book is for my dog, Daisy Mae, who left us on September 16, 2024.

She gave us 15 years of unconditional love, and sat underneath my feet during every book that I've written so far.

This was the last one she was alive for.

I love you, Daisy. Thank you for being the best fur baby I could have asked for.

"I think the hardest part of losing a dog you love isn't having to say goodbye...

it's the way your entire world changes without them and the emptiness that's left in your heart when they go."

Unknown

Prologue

Parker

Four Years Ago

"You can't make me go!" Sasha screams at me as I pack her suitcase, warring with this decision but knowing it's the right one.

Nothing has been the same these past two years. Ever since she followed me back home to Carrington Cove from UC Davis, I've noticed a change in her, but I didn't want to admit it. I didn't want to see it. But the phone call from the cops the other night was the last straw.

I can't keep pretending she doesn't have a problem.

"If you don't go, we're done," I say, spinning around to face her now as my words hit her square in the chest.

Her chin wobbles as she speaks. "You...you don't mean that."

"I do." I rake a hand through my hair, trying to stay strong. "I can't keep living like this. I can't keep worrying every time I leave the house, wondering if you'll still be here when I get back, or if I'm going to get a call that you've wrapped your car around a telephone pole again."

"It was one time. I haven't done anything like that since—"

"What about the bottle I found under your bed?" I ask, cutting her off.

But instead of being remorseful, she scowls at me and clenches her teeth. "Why are you going through my stuff?"

Ignoring the deflection, I press on. "We don't even sleep in the same bed anymore, Sasha. Is that the kind of relationship you want?" Sasha started coming home late at night from parties with her friends, and instead of stumbling into our bed, she started falling into the one in the guest room. Before I knew it, that's where she was sleeping permanently.

Again, I can't believe we've ended up here, yet here we are.

"You need help."

"No one is going to help me because I don't have a problem."

"If you love me, Sasha, you will do this," I plead, holding back tears as I stare at the woman that captivated me the moment that I met her.

It was the first day of our second year of college. I was technically a senior because of all the dual enrollment credits I earned in high school, but that didn't matter to her. I sat down next to her in our advanced biochemistry class, she leaned in and asked to borrow a pen from me, and the rest was history.

Little did I know that we'd end up here someday, me begging her to get sober so we could spend the rest of our lives together like we planned.

With tears in her eyes, she steps toward me until there's only an inch of space between us. "I'm...I'm scared, Parker."

"Me too."

"I don't want to be away from you."

I swallow down the sharp words on the tip of my tongue about how we've been drifting apart for years, and instead reply, "I'll visit you the second I can. I promise." And I will. I'd do anything for this woman, even sacrifice months of our life together if it means she can get healthy. I've failed her, ignoring what I knew was happening, but not anymore. It's time I be the man I promised her I would be when I slipped that ring on her finger.

I need to give up this need to keep proving myself to everyone.

And what I need Sasha to give up is alcohol.

I might have been absent lately, trying like hell to prove myself at the animal hospital and telling myself it was a good sign that Sasha was making friends and spending more time with them. But the night she got into the accident, I had to snap myself out of my denial.

"You can do this, Sasha. I believe in you. Our future is on the line, and I don't want a life without you in it."

She nods as tears roll down her cheeks. "Okay."

"Okay?"

She nods again. "I want that life and future too."

"Fuck," I grate out as I pull her into my chest. "Thank you. I promise, things will be different. We can get back to us once you're better, okay?"

"Yeah. I think we need that."

When we part, I look down at her and press my lips to hers, wanting her to know that deep down, I still love her—and part of me always will.

But the sharp taste of vodka on her lips should have told me that nothing would be enough to save this woman from herself.

Chapter One

Parker

Three Years Later

"You ready for another busy day, gentlemen?" Dr. O'Neil hoists his pants up on his waist so that they're hugging his protruding belly even tighter, though they're just going to slide right back down in a few minutes. The man seriously needs to invest in a better belt or a pair of suspenders.

"As ready as I'm going to be," I say, stifling a yawn. "The truth is, I'm still trying to recover from yesterday."

An emergency surgery kept me here until well after midnight, but it was worth it just to see the look of relief on the young girl's face when I told her that her puppy was going to be all right. The little German Shepherd got stuck under a chain-link fence and sliced his belly open pretty badly. Of course, the parents were grateful too—until they saw the bill.

"Well, I'm bright-eyed and bushy tailed, ready to be put to work, Dr. O'Neil!"

That's my new colleague, Seth Brown, who has his schnoz shoved so far up our boss's ass that his last name has taken on a new meaning. It's pathetic, really.

Or maybe I'm just too tired today to tolerate his kiss ass behavior.

I take a moment to stare at him, trying to read him for the thousandth time and give him the benefit of the doubt.

Nope. The guy really irritates the shit out of me.

"That's the spirit, Dr. Brown." Dr. O'Neil, who insists we call each other by our rightfully earned titles, slaps Seth on the back while I try to conceal my eye roll. "Glad to see we have a team player on the staff."

Seth has only been here for a few weeks, but it hasn't taken very long for me to get an uneasy feeling about him. The front receptionists adore him, but all I sense is fakeness and an overeager need to get everyone to like him. He's happy all the time, which is a huge red flag if there ever was one. I mean, no one is happy all the fucking time. And the passive-aggressive way he likes to try to correct me at every turn has me itching to take him out back and show him what I can do with a pair of dog nail clippers.

Unfortunately, his services are necessary, given how fast Carrington Cove has grown in the past few years. Dr. O'Neil and I just couldn't keep up on our own anymore. Now, between the three of us, we're able to juggle the workload a bit better, but it doesn't mean there aren't still long and draining days.

Another yawn escapes my lips. "Well, I'm going to check on Chewy and then prepare for the day." Holding up my coffee to the two men, I turn on my heel and head toward the recovery area of the practice, intent on making sure my little German Shepherd pal is doing well so his family can take him home later today.

I didn't always used to be this irritated by everyone and everything. In fact, there was a time when someone might have accused me of being as cheerful as Seth. But life has a funny way of changing you, and not always for the better.

As I check on Chewy's vitals, my boss comes up behind me. "You saved this little guy's life last night."

"He got lucky. He didn't puncture any internal organs, just some deep lacerations that needed stitches and a course of antibiotics."

"Still, Parker. You care. I know we're not supposed to get attached to these animals, but you always put your heart into it. That's what makes you great at this." He clasps my shoulder. "You've come a long way since you were a rookie, always trying to prove yourself." He chuckles, likely remembering all the times he had to rein in my over-eager work ethic. "One day when I finally decide to retire, I know I'll have two sets of capable hands to leave the practice to."

"Two sets of hands?" I say, looking down at my one set.

"Yes, you and Seth."

"Ah."

"Of course, that's if I can ever make that decision. Beth says they'll have to drag me out of this building kicking and screaming in order to make me hang up my lab coat."

I snort. "Sounds about right."

"You get it, though. When you work this hard at something, at a job that feels more like a purpose than just work, it's hard to step away."

I nod, but the irritation simmers beneath the surface. I've given too much to this job—and sacrificed more than I care to admit—so the thought of Seth taking even a piece of that away from me makes my blood boil. If I have it my way, that guy won't be around for long. My goal is to take over the practice as the sole owner when Dr. O'Neil decides to retire, whenever the hell that may be, and I sure as hell don't want Seth to be my right hand man when I do.

The last thing I should feel toward my colleague is a lack of trust, especially when there are furry lives on the line. But the fact is, I don't trust him, and if I've learned anything in the past few years, it's to trust my gut.

I just turned thirty last month, but I'm already further along in my career than most vets my age, and owning my own practice in my hometown would be the icing on the career cake. I finished most of my undergrad work in high school, thanks to dual enrollment classes, which helped fast-track me through vet school. By twenty-four, I was fully certified from the Veterinary School of Medicine at UC Davis and ready to come back home to work in the community that, honestly, I hated being away from.

Dr. O'Neil's father, who ran the practice when I was growing up, knew I planned on returning. But he passed away shortly after I left for school. Luckily, when I came home, Dr. O'Neil was eager to bring in some new blood—especially someone who knew the latest techniques, which worked out well for me.

Dr. O'Neil and I have history, you might say. And you can't beat history.

Take that, Seth.

I have my dream job, I live in a town with front-row access to the ocean and a beautiful cove it's named after, and—even though they drive me nuts—my entire family lives here too. Some would say I have it all. But my personal struggles continue to plague me every day. There are just some things you can't distract yourself from—no matter how good you've got it.

Dr. O'Neil clears his throat, continuing his thought from before. "Although, retirement does sound nice. Maybe then my June Bug will come to visit me instead of the other way around."

"I know that'd mean a lot to you." My boss talks about his daughter all the time, but she's never visited Carrington Cove. Robert only moved back here ten years ago when he inherited the practice, and he never mentions any other family. I found out from one of the receptionists early on that his wife died years ago when his daughter was younger, and not that it's any of my business, but the man has never mentioned dating anyone in the time that I've known him.

He's a lone wolf, a man who is married to his job and prefers animals to humans.

Can't say I blame him, as I find with each passing day that solitude is my preference as well.

"You remind me a lot of my June Bug," Dr. O'Neil continues. "Driven, passionate, and hardworking. A professional to the core. Such a shame you two haven't met, but she's busy taking on the big city, trying to rule the court system, and I can't seem to get her to make time to visit her old man. I think this small town is just too quiet for someone like her."

"Well, I imagine her caseload is hard to walk away from too."

"Yes, I suppose, but that's the life of a lawyer. All work and no play."

I wave my hand around the room. "Uh, can't say our lives are much different, Doc. I was here for fifteen hours yesterday."

Robert chuckles as he takes a kitten out of her cage and holds her to his chest, petting her softly. "Yes, but we get to love on animals all day and get paid for it. That's where the difference lies."

Smiling, I scratch behind the little cat's ears. "Yeah, I guess the job does have its perks."

"Plus, you're going to that dental care conference in Philadelphia next week. You've got to be looking forward to that."

The truth is, I am. Poor dental hygiene in animals is the leading cause of so many preventable health problems. But it's not like I'm going to Vegas. It's two full days of lectures and conversations with people that do the same thing for a living that I do.

I wouldn't necessarily classify it as a vacation, but it is still a break from the hustle and long hours I've been putting in at the practice lately.

I'll take what I can get at this point.

"I'm looking forward to seeing the latest techniques in dental care, of course. I just…"

"Need to have a little fun too?" Dr. O'Neil winks at me as he places the kitten back in the cage.

"Fun is overrated, Dr. O'Neil."

He eyes me wearily. "Parker, you're a thirty-year-old man, and though I know you love this job, it's important to get out and live too. Don't end up like me," he says with a pinch in his brow. "Maybe take an extra few days. Extend the trip and explore a bit. Philadelphia is the city of brotherly love anyway, right?"

I eye my boss, wondering if he's been doused in rainbow dust, because I'm pretty sure I just saw one shoot out of his ass. He's never this sentimental.

Has Seth been slipping him whatever drugs he's on?

"I don't need brotherly love, Doc. I have two older brothers, if you've forgotten. And I much prefer women for any lovin'."

He chuckles. "You know what I mean. You don't want to wake up one day as an old man and realize you wasted the best years of your life. Take it from me," he says, meeting my eyes. "Tragedy can prevent you from truly living if you let it. That's why I pushed my June to make something of herself, and I'm going to do the same for you."

Before I can reply, Dr. O'Neil reaches in to pet Chewy just as the dog stirs awake. When the puppy blinks up at me and I see cognitive response, I know he's going to be okay, and his family will be grateful to have him back.

And just like that, I'm reminded of why I chose this career. We don't deserve pets. The unconditional love they show us is unmatched. They don't give us shit like older brothers, or torture us like ex-fiancées.

They serve as yet another reminder that most humans don't even understand the concept of love, even when it's right in front of them.

Unfortunately, I know that firsthand and refuse to be made a fool of ever again.

***

"Why does it take people so long to get on an airplane?" I grumble to myself as I stand in the aisle, waiting for a few people up ahead to stop arguing about who has the window seat and just fucking sit down already. Luckily, they figure things out, finally allowing me to take the few steps to my seat. I stash my carry-on suitcase in the overhead compartment and plop down into the seat below me.

"More people die in car accidents than plane crashes, Cashlynn. Just remember that." My head snaps to the woman on my right, who's staring out the small window at the asphalt below, muttering to herself.

Jesus. Of course I get seated next to the woman who's talking to herself.

"Although our luck seems to be subpar anyway, which means we could be the one that increases the statistic. Oh God, this is how we're going to die..."

Fuck. This woman is afraid of flying. And even though it's none of my business, if she keeps narrating her death in the third person, I'm not going to be able to ignore her.

The last thing I wanted to do on this flight was strike up a conversation with the person sitting next to me. I was actually looking forward to binge-watching the second season of *Bridgerton*. Hazel, my younger sister, is watching it too, and we are planning on talking about it tonight on the phone once I get settled into my hotel.

But now, I feel an obligation to calm this woman. She's obviously afraid, and the last thing I want is for her to have a fucking panic attack mid-flight. Then someone might call out for a doctor, and I'll be put in that uncomfortable position where—yes—I *am* a doctor, just not for people. And then I'll have to explain why I didn't just help her in the first place and look like an asshole who saves puppies but lets humans freak the fuck out.

"You're not going to die," I say, debating placing my hand on her shoulder and deciding against it.

She pushes her hair away from her face but keeps her gaze locked outside, her hands continuing to fidget in her lap. "I'm just trying to remind myself that the likelihood of me plummeting to my death in this plane is fairly low." She clears her throat. "Sorry if I disturbed you."

I remove my hand from the armrest and start to fasten my seat belt. "The worst part is taking off and landing, in my opinion. Once you're in the air, there's not much to worry about." I snap the belt in place, feeling slightly less irritated now that I've tried to comfort her. But then she blows out a breath and turns to face me just as I lift my head. When our eyes meet, it's like someone just punched me in the chest.

Holy shit. This woman is fucking gorgeous.

Silky blonde hair. Amber eyes that practically glow. Soft, full pink lips.

But her eyebrows are drawn together, every ounce of her fear etched in the lines of her face. My chest does some weird tightening thing and I want to reach out and touch her again.

Fuck.

This woman is exactly the type I should stay the hell away from—the kind that makes me feel something other than just horny. Although my dick definitely has some thoughts about our seat neighbor. Too bad he's not running the show today.

"I just don't do it that often, so when I do, my anxiety builds up, you know?" she says, pulling me back to reality. "For instance, I couldn't sleep at all the last three nights just knowing I had to take this flight today."

"Three nights?" I shove my laptop bag under the seat in front of me, hoping my heart rate will calm the fuck down before I look back at her.

"Yeah, which means I'll at least sleep well tonight when my head hits the pillow."

"That's true." We stare at each other for another moment, my mind and body at war before I finally remember my manners and extend my hand to her. "I'm Parker, by the way."

"Cashlynn."

"Nice to meet you."

"Sorry you had to hear me rambling about dying," she says with a chuckle.

Suddenly, our conversation isn't so irritating anymore. "It's okay. Flying is a legitimate fear."

"I know, but I don't want to be that annoying person you sit next to on the plane and tell your friends about later," she says, just as there's a sudden bang from beneath us. Her eyes widen instantly. "Oh my God! What was that?"

I glance around the cabin, expecting to see something out of the ordinary. "What?"

"That noise!"

My brain catches up to speed. "Oh, they're just closing the luggage compartments." Cashlynn closes her eyes and breathes deeply, in and out through her nose. "Are you going to freak out about every sound on this flight?"

She peeks one eye open. "Maybe."

I huff out a laugh, surprised by how entertaining this woman is. "Is there, uh, anything I can do to help?"

"Do you happen to have any Xanax?"

I pat the pockets of my pants and the one on my shirt mockingly. "Nope, fresh out."

"Not funny."

I twist in my seat, facing her, hating how the more I look at her, the more I find myself wondering what her lips taste like.

Is she wearing flavored gloss? Would I taste coffee on her tongue? Or is she a Diet Coke drinker like...

Nope. Not going there, Parker.

"Then what can I do to help?" Color me surprised, but seeing this woman on the verge of a panic attack is really messing with me. And fuck, she's piqued my interest like no other woman has in a long time.

It couldn't be because she's quirky, sarcastic, and beautiful... Right, Parker?

"Nothing. I'll be okay."

"I don't know if you will."

Both of her eyes fly open now. "Why would you say that?"

"I'm just thinking maybe you're denying my help out of pride, not because you truly don't want it."

"What on earth could you possibly do to help me through this?" she asks, right as the captain comes over the loudspeaker, signaling the flight attendants to complete their final checks. "Oh God. It's coming." She covers her face with both hands, and for the life of me, I'm not sure if I should be alarmed or if she's going to snap out of it once we're in the air.

"I could hold your hand," I blurt, surprising myself.

Her hands fall from her face. "What?"

"You heard me. I'll hold your hand. It might help."

She arches a brow, like she's considering it for a moment, then shakes her head. "No, that's really not necessary."

"It's worth a shot." I shrug. "Plus, I've been told I have very strong, capable hands." I hold them up, fanning them out for her to admire.

"Did you really just brag about your hands?" she asks, laughing. "I'm sure they are very impressive, but I can't ask you to do that."

"You're not asking. I'm offering."

"No." She shakes her head again. "No, it's okay. I appreciate the offer, but…"

"You're seriously denying me the pleasure of holding your hand?" I tease.

"Denying you the *pleasure*? You sound like one of the men from *Bridgerton*."

"Well, for your information, I intended to watch season two during the flight until you started rambling."

She covers her chest with her hand. "Seriously? You watch that show?"

"Yeah." I push my glasses up on my nose. "My sister got me into it, and I'm not ashamed to admit it's really fucking good."

She tilts her head, a small quirk in her lips. "Who the hell are you?"

I clear my throat and offer my hand to her again. "I'm Parker Sheppard, your in-flight companion, and I think you should let me help you get through this."

Her eyes drop down to my hands before lifting to meet my gaze. I can see the hesitation, the way she bites her bottom lip in contemplation. Then the plane starts moving and she lets out a small whimper that isn't meant to make my dick twitch, but he definitely approves.

Before she talks herself out of the innocent gesture, I make one last attempt. "How about I play you for it?"

"For my hand?" Her eyes dart around me, watching the flight attendants check the cabin.

"Yeah. If I win, I hold your hand throughout the flight."

"And if I win?" she asks, the pinch in her brow growing again as the plane starts to roll along the asphalt beneath us while we make our way toward the runway.

"Then you can suffer in whatever way you please."

"What are we playing?" she squeaks out as the flight attendants begin their safety demonstration.

Leaning closer so as not to talk over the instructional recording, I say, "Rock, paper, scissors."

She rears her head back. "Seriously?"

I arch a brow at her this time. "What? Afraid you'll lose?"

"How did I manage to get seated next to you?" she asks rhetorically, but there's a hint of disbelief in her voice.

"Flight attendants prepare for takeoff," the captain says over the loud speakers as the plane continues to roll toward the runway.

"You're running out of time, Cashlynn. Now what'll it be?"

"Fine." She sits up taller in her seat and twists slightly so we can face each other head on. "On three?" she asks as we both poise our hands out in front of us.

"Yup," I agree. "One..."

"Two..."

"Three," I say as she displays a closed fist and I flash my best set of spirit fingers underneath hers. "Ha! I win!"

"What the hell is that?" she practically shrieks. "That's not a rock, or paper, or scissors!"

"Nope. That's fire, baby."

"Fire?"

I drop my hands back down as she follows suit. "Yeah, haven't you seen *Friends*?" I ask, chuckling to myself because only a true fan would know why I knew I was going to win this game from the moment I suggested it.

"The TV show?"

"Yeah. Fire beats everything, at least according to Joey Tribbiani."

Cashlynn blinks at me, still trying to process what just happened, but I reach for her hand just as the plane starts careening forward, the speed climbing higher and higher. She closes her eyes and whispers, "Oh my God, oh my God..."

"Shhh, it's okay," I murmur and squeeze her hand, stroking it with my thumb, and wrap my free arm around her shoulders, pulling her close to me. Big mistake.

Fuck. She smells incredible, like citrus and vanilla, with a hint of coconut in her hair. And the way she leans into me, her breasts press into my bicep, doing things to me that are not at all helpful right now.

"Just breathe, Cashlynn."

"I hate this."

"It will be over before you know it." Just as the words leave my lips, the plane lifts off, climbing toward the sky. Cashlynn squeezes my hand so hard, I swear I hear a bone crack. "Easy there, Tiger."

"I'm sorry..."

"It's okay, I just really need my hands for work."

Her grip loosens slightly. "What do you do?"

"I'm a vet," I say proudly as the force of the plane sends us back into our seats. My ex wasn't as proud of that title, opting to tell people I was a doctor instead—because saving animals wasn't as impressive as saving humans in her book.

Fuck, now's not the time to think about Sasha, Parker.

"That's a pretty demanding job," Cashlynn says shakily as the plane continues to soar.

"It can be, but I live in a small town, so it has busy days and slow ones."

"Where do you live?"

"Carrington Cove. Ever heard of it?"

Her eyes widen slightly before falling to her lap, and I wonder if I said or did something wrong. "I, uh...haven't."

She's quiet for a moment before she clears her throat and asks, "Why are you flying to Philadelphia, then?"

"For a dental hygiene conference."

She snorts, the tension in her shoulders easing just a little. "Sounds like a party."

"Hey, I'll have you know that veterinarians are fun people when we want to be," I say a little too defensively.

"I'll take your word for it." Her lips twitch up with a hint of a smile.

As the plane starts to level out, Cashlynn's grip on my hand finally loosens. "How are you doing?" I ask.

"Can you do me a favor and shut the window thing?" She flicks her head in the direction of the window behind her.

"Of course." Keeping her hand in mine, I reach around her, pressing our bodies even closer together, which doesn't help the tent forming in my pants. Once I've closed the shade, I slide back into my seat. "Window thing is closed."

She leans back and looks up at me. "Thank you."

Our eyes dart back and forth between one another, and neither one of us speaks.

Fuck, her eyes are mesmerizing. They're like warm honey swirled with chocolate, dotted with flecks of gold around her irises. And those lips. Jesus, I'm seriously cursing the man upstairs for putting me in this situation.

My brothers would have a field day if they could see me right now. They'd read me like a book and pressure me to make a move.

But do I want that?

It has been a while since I've flirted with a woman, hoping it might actually lead somewhere. It's not something I actively seek out anymore. After the way my engagement ended, it just doesn't seem worth the risk. I've been in no hurry to put myself in that position again, not that I expect anything to happen with Cashlynn. But there's something here, and I can't help but wonder if I should play my chances and see how things pan out.

Shit. I've been staring way too long.

"Anytime." My voice comes out rough, betraying my wayward thoughts.

Cashlynn looks down at our intertwined fingers. "Do you need your hand back?"

"That's up to you. Like I said earlier, I am fully prepared to spend this entire flight with only one functional hand."

She smiles softly, amusement flickering in her eyes. "I know your hand won't save me if we plummet to our deaths, but...it's nice not to feel alone."

Damn. She has no idea just how hard that hits home.

***

"So how long is the conference?" Cashlynn asks after the flight attendants serve us drinks. I opted for a Coke, my usual go-to, while she ordered a ginger ale. We separate just long enough to open our Biscoff cookies, and once we're done, she reaches for my hand again. I'm surprised by how much I like that she still needs me.

"Friday through Sunday, but I'm staying a few extra days. My boss insisted."

"Sounds like a nice boss."

"He could tell I needed a break. I guess you could say I'm a bit of a workaholic."

She chuckles. "That checks out for a doctor."

I smile. "Guilty as charged."

She licks her lips. "Can I ask why you became a vet?"

Her question feels genuine, the kind people usually ask when they find out what I do. "If I said it's because I've always loved animals, would that just add to my list of clichés?"

She shrugs, but her lips are lifted in a soft smile. "If it's the truth, then I don't see the problem."

"We don't deserve pets," I say, easing into my story. "When I was ten, we had to put down our family dog, Daisy Mae, because of old age. She was the best fucking dog," I say, thinking back fondly to our sweet puggle that gave my family fifteen years of her love and loyalty. "I just remember crying so hard, yelling about how it wasn't fair. That there had to be something we could do to save her."

Cashlynn's bottom lip juts out. "You're gonna make me cry."

I huff out a laugh. "Sorry. The point is, that was the day I decided I wanted to make sure that all animals got to live their best lives like she did." I look away. "I don't know... That moment stuck with me, so I pursued veterinary medicine."

She gently rubs the back of my hand with her thumb. "Thank you for sharing that with me."

When our eyes meet again, something shifts in my chest, and I try to ignore the dull ache building from the memory and from opening up to this woman that I just met. "So what do you do?" I ask, wanting to know more about this woman the longer we sit here, especially given that I've shared more with her than most of my family and friends.

"Oh, I'm, uh..." She looks away from me, biting her lip.

"Did you forget what your job is?" I tease.

"No," she says with a nervous laugh.

That's when I notice the paint under her fingernails. "I'm going to guess artist or teacher."

She looks down at our clasped hands. "What makes you say that?"

"The paint under your nails. I figure that means you're either doing arts and crafts with tiny humans, or you're an artist yourself. Either way, you just became even more interesting to me."

She tilts her head, her lips curving into a smile. "That detail made me *more* interesting? So you were already interested?"

I take a sip of my coffee, my eyes locked on hers. "I shouldn't be, but I am, Cashlynn." I can practically see the wheels turning behind those gorgeous eyes, but she shakes off the thought, saying nothing. "Does that mean that you're *not* interested?"

"No, I am I just..." She sighs. "This is the last thing I expected when I jumped on this flight."

You and me both, beautiful.

I take a sip of my Coke and decide to steer the conversation to safter territory. "So what brings *you* to Philadelphia this weekend?"

"Philly's home now. I flew down for a meeting in Raleigh." She shudders slightly, as if recalling the experience.

"Did your seat mate offer to hold your hand on that one?"

She shakes her head with a grin on her lips. "No, she didn't even speak to me. She was knitting the entire time with earbuds in. I'm pretty sure she was listening to a spicy romance novel."

I raise an eyebrow. "What makes you say that?"

"Well, she would stop knitting and stare off into space at some points. Then she'd start shaking her head and fanning herself, and I mean"—she shrugs—"seems like something was getting her all worked up."

Laughter erupts from me. "Fuck, you're probably right." I swear, I'm having so much fun talking to her that I'm almost wishing we were flying to the West Coast so we could have a little more time together.

"Maybe. Either that or she was having a hot flash."

"Also a valid guess. So, you had a meeting in Raleigh…" I say, prompting her to continue.

"Yes, and now I'm flying back home." She darts her eyes to the side, avoiding my gaze. "Uh, where is Carrington Cove by the way?" When her eyes return to my face, she smirks. "It sounds like a *magical* place."

God, I love that this woman is sarcastic and has a sense of humor. "It's on the coast by Camp Lejeune, north of Wilmington."

"Have you lived there your whole life?"

I nod. "Yeah, except for the time I spent at UC Davis getting my veterinary degree."

"That's a lot of schooling."

I shrug. "I actually made it through in record time. I took some college classes while I was in high school, so I only had a year and a half to spend on my bachelor's before moving on to the veterinary program at the best school in the country on a scholarship ."

"Damn. Smart *and* handsome." She shakes her head at me, the curve of her lips drawing me in even more. "How am I supposed to resist you?"

I lean toward her a bit more. "Does that mean you're trying to resist me?"

Our eyes bounce between each other. "Let's just say that meeting a handsome stranger wasn't expected, let alone one who makes me wish the flight were longer."

I stroke the back of her hand with my thumb. "I'll take that as a compliment."

She chuckles. "You should. Especially since you now know how I feel about flying."

***

"So, you save furry lives during the day, but what about after you leave the animal hospital? What keeps you entertained then?" Cashlynn takes a sip of her drink as we continue to sail across the sky.

"Mostly, I just work out, read, or watch TV. I live a pretty simple life."

"That sounds boring."

"What did you expect? That I jump out of airplanes for fun?"

She shakes her head. "No… I guess I just figured you were more of a social guy."

I scoff. "Yeah, well, the only people I can stand to socialize with these days are my family and a few close friends. Sometimes, even that's pushing it."

"I guess that's normal for a small town, right?"

"I mean, Carrington Cove is more of a tourist town, so there are people to meet and places to go, but that's not really my scene." I shrug. "Never has been."

"So meeting strangers and offering to hold their hands isn't your usual M.O.?"

I look Cashlynn dead in the eye when I say, "Not at all. This is a first for me."

She licks her lips, her eyes lingering on mine. "Me too."

"So if flying weren't an obstacle, where would you want to travel?"

Cashlynn hums as she thinks, and waiting to hear what she says next has become the most unexpected form of entertainment on this flight. "Greece, Egypt, and France."

"Nice choices. Why those specific places?"

"The water in Greece seems unreal, so I feel like I need to see it to believe it. Egypt's history has always fascinated me. And France for the art."

I glance down at our intertwined fingers, stroking the top of her hand again. "So, you do paint..."

"Uh, yeah...you could say that."

"What do you paint?"

"Mostly scenery, sometimes abstracts. I'm more of a mood painter, so I let my brain tell me what to create."

"Have you always been artistic?"

"Yeah. My mom was big into creating art, so I guess I got it from her."

"My mom is a fantastic cook, and luckily, she handed that talent down to me."

Cashlynn smirks at me. "Okay, now you're just not playing fair. You're a handsome doctor who wears glasses *and* you can cook?"

My eyebrows shoot up. "The glasses do something for you, huh?"

She nods slowly. "Apparently so. I think they up your sophistication factor. But then I remember that you made me play rock, paper, scissors, and I'm confused."

Chuckling, I ask, "Why confused?"

"I don't know. You seemed irritated when you first sat down, like there was this cloud hanging over you." *Fuck, she had you pegged from the beginning, Parker.* "But you've surprised me."

I look away from her, not sure how I feel about her accurate assessment. If a complete stranger could pick up on my foul mood that easily, that's telling. I've walked around with this chip on my shoulder for four years, so it's not that easy to get rid of.

But this woman makes you feel more at ease, doesn't she?

I swallow hard and Cashlynn's eyes dart down to my throat as I do. "Do you happen to be free tonight?" I ask, surprising myself but going with this gut feeling to step outside the box for a change.

She tilts her head curiously. "Yes."

"Good. Because I think you could probably use a drink after this flight, and I'd love to buy you one, if you're interested."

"Um..." She bites her bottom lip in contemplation.

"No pressure. But if you're unsure, we could always play rock, paper, scissors again..."

She licks her lips, smirking. "I actually think a drink is exactly what I need."

***

"Fuck," I hiss as I deepen the kiss, pulling Cashlynn closer. I bury one hand in her silky blonde hair while the other squeezes her hip as I draw her closer to my chest.

Suddenly, she pushes me away, her eyes wide and chest heaving, with her hand still firmly planted on my pec as we both struggle for air.

"What floor is your room on?" she asks breathlessly.

"Eleven."

"Take me there."

We abandon our drinks as I take Cashlynn's hand and lead her through the hotel bar to the nearest elevator, hoping no one notices the outline of my cock in my pants. Once we're inside—alone, thank God—I press her up against the wall and bury my hands in her silky strands again.

"Parker..."

"Fuck, Cashlynn. You're sure you want this?"

"Hell yes. Fuck me, Parker. I need it."

I move my mouth down to her neck, kissing and nibbling the skin there as I squeeze her ass in my hands, bringing her hips to collide with my torso so she can feel how much I want her. "You're so fucking gorgeous. You feel what you do to me?"

She pulls my mouth back to hers, kissing me desperately until the elevator dings, signaling our arrival on my floor. With her hand in mine, I lead her down the hall, pass the key card over the sensor, and push the door open just enough for us to slip inside before our hands and lips are back on each other.

When I sat next to a random stranger on that plane today, I never imagined this would be how our night ended. But all it took was one drink for us to realize what we both wanted—and now that my body is primed for what comes next, I'm definitely not complaining.

Cashlynn pushes me up against the door and then drops to her knees, her eyes locked on mine the entire time. Those amber eyes are silently making promises as she pops the button on my pants and yanks down my zipper.

"Fuck."

"I can't wait to taste you, feel you in the back of my throat." Her words make my dick even harder as she pushes my jeans down along with my briefs and wraps her tiny hands around my aching cock. "God, you're thick," she says before licking me from base to tip.

"Jesus, Cashlynn." My hand finds the top of her head as her mouth envelops me, taking me as deep as she can before sucking me back out. With fascination, I watch her bob up and down on my cock, dragging her tongue along my length, swirling her tongue around my crown, and repeating the process over and over again. I love how eager she is, not letting up even as I hear her gag when I hit the back of her throat.

Who knew that showing kindness to a stranger would lead to one of the best blowjobs of my life? This is so much better than watching *Bridgerton*.

"Shit," I grate out as she sucks in her cheeks and pulls me in and out even more rapidly. "You're gonna make me come if you keep doing that."

She immediately releases me with a pop and stands back up. "We can't have that yet now, can we?"

I pull her mouth to mine and back her into the room with my pants still down around my ankles. I help her out of her coat and rip her shirt up over her head, tossing it to the side, revealing a deep emerald lace bra containing her perky and fucking perfectly sized breasts.

But it's her ass that I'm dying to see, preferably with my handprint on it soon. The moment she stood up on the plane, revealing those beautiful curves, I nearly drooled as I followed her down the aisle. She's so fucking sexy and my heart is thrashing at the idea of claiming her.

"Get naked, beautiful."

We don't take our eyes off each other as shoes, pants, and underwear hit the floor. Finally, we're both standing bare, mere inches apart, waiting for the other to make the first move.

My eyes roam all over her body, memorizing the dip in her waist, her rosy nipples, the trimmed pubic hair above her pussy, and those thick thighs I can't wait to feel wrapped around me.

She eyes me appreciatively before stepping up to me and running her nails up and down my stomach, tracing the V of my hips. "God, your body. You must work out a lot."

I chuckle. "I try."

She nods, licking her lips. "Your effort is appreciated."

I whip my glasses from my face and set them down on the dresser. With my hand stroking my cock, I nod toward the bed. "Lie down."

Cashlynn doesn't speak as she moves to the bed, our eyes locked on one another, crawling up toward the pillows as I reach down to my pants and take out the just-in-case condom from my wallet.

I toss the condom onto the bed and begin crawling forward, making my way closer to this woman and the sweet heaven between her legs. I dip my head down toward her pussy, pushing her thighs open with my shoulders to expose her to me, and Cashlynn doesn't even hesitate.

"Lick me, Parker."

Jesus. This woman is something else.

"With pleasure," I mumble against her inner thigh before dragging my tongue through her slit, tasting her sweetness that only intensifies my need for her.

"God, that feels good," she moans as I keep licking her, flicking my tongue back and forth over her clit and sucking the little bud between my lips. "Parker...yes...right there..." Cashlynn guides me to where she needs me most and then stuns me by saying, "Put your fingers inside of me...please."

I suck two fingers in my mouth, then slowly push them inside, watching her pussy stretch around me and suck me in as I stroke her G-spot. God, it's so hot, so carnal, so out of this world that my dick twitches as I go back to sucking her clit and finger fucking her until I know she's close.

This woman is unraveling me and I couldn't even stop it if I tried. Her confidence is sexy as hell, her sounds are like a soundtrack I didn't know I was missing from my life, and feeling her tighten around my fingers makes me feel like the luckiest fucking man on the planet—that this woman is giving herself over freely to me.

Fuck, I'm already addicted and I haven't even been inside her yet.

"Oh, God...right there. Yes, Parker!" On a scream, Cashlynn comes all over my hand, soaking my fingers with her release and bucking herself against my mouth, seeking out the pressure and friction that she needs.

When her body collapses on the bed, I kiss her inner thighs and tease her clit again with my tongue as I reach for the condom. I tear it open, covering myself as I move to hover over her.

Her eyes snap open, meeting mine before she pulls me down to her, swirling her tongue against mine and opening up her legs so I can slide right inside her. It takes a few thrusts, but when I bottom out, we groan simultaneously.

"Jesus, you're tight," I manage to grate out as her pussy squeezes and sucks me in.

"It's been... a while," she moans as I thrust in and out of her.

"Me too. Fuck, Cashlynn. Suck me in, baby." I lift her leg up and wrap it around my hip so I can slide in deeper, making us both moan.

"Keep going, Parker. Harder."

The bed slams against the wall with each thrust as I pound into her. For a second, I contemplate our neighbors on the other side, but the thought is fleeting as I feel Cashlynn tighten around me. Her nails dig into my back as I suck and nibble along her neck, moving down to her breasts and sucking one of her nipples into my mouth, making her moan louder.

She moves her hand down to her clit, circling her bundle of nerves as I pick up my pace, helping her get there.

"Yes, yes...God, yes!" Cashlynn comes again, and watching her beneath me, tossing her head back as her release overtakes her has me finding my own orgasm at the same time.

Completely spent, I roll to her side as we both come down from the high. I lie on my side, facing her, tracing along her collarbone while her eyes remain closed.

I wonder if she's up for a long night of fucking... After having her once, I know without a doubt I want her again.

But before I can say anything, her eyes pop open and she launches herself from the bed, rushing to find her clothes.

What the fuck?

"Uh, is everything okay?" I ask as I watch her naked form dart around the room.

"Yup!" she replies, about two octaves higher than her normal tone, avoiding my eyes.

"You sure?" My dick is still half hard and this woman is acting like there's a fire in the building. Was the sex not satisfying for her? I mean, she sounded like she was enjoying it. Hell, if she was faking it then she must be one hell of an actress.

"Everything is perfect, Parker. I just...I need to get going, okay?" I watch as she puts her clothes back on before I can even process anything, and then she's grabbing her purse and heading for the door.

I jump from the bed, intent on chasing her, but then I think better of it.

That's all this was supposed to be, right? No strings attached sex.

Then why do I feel this overwhelming need to convince her to stay?

"Thanks for the orgasms," she says over her shoulder, taking one last peek at my dick with a smirk before stepping out of the hotel room. I'm left standing there in nothing but my birthday suit, wondering if this is all I should have hoped for—if this is what the rest of my life will be like since I've sworn not to fall for anyone ever again.

Little did I know that seeing Cashlynn again was inevitable—and that when I did, I'd be wishing I never gave in to my attraction to her at all.

Chapter Two

Parker

Present Day

"So, how about dinner Saturday night?"

A woman I recognize from earlier this week rushes up to my car before I can even turn the ignition off.

"What?"

She giggles, tossing her hair over her shoulder. "Sorry. Good morning, Parker. You look extra sexy today with a fresh haircut. I'm Christy. We spoke yesterday and the day before, but who's counting?" Another giggle escapes her lips. "So, dinner Saturday?"

I shake my head as I grab my bag from the front seat and step out, locking my car before heading toward the animal hospital. "I, uh...need to get to work."

Christy scurries after me. "Of course. I just thought since I don't have plans this weekend, we could finally go on our first date. You have to admit, our connection is pretty amazing, don't you think?"

Our connection? This woman must be certifiable because I think I've said a total of ten words to her, but apparently, she is already planning our wedding.

Okay, let me back up.

In the last year, my single status has remained intact, just the way I like it. Watching my two older brothers and my friend Grady fall in love over the past two years has only confirmed that I don't want to end up in that situation again. Luckily for them, they found women who didn't make them question the sanctity of love and marriage, but the vulnerability, the trust, the *work* it takes to be the "best version" of yourself for someone else? No thanks. My issues have been serving me well for the past four years, and I have no intention of changing that anytime soon.

But last spring, I became an unexpected chick magnet, and not in the sense you might think. My brother Dallas and his wife, Willow, noticed a goose had laid some eggs on their property. It didn't surprise me since the gaggle of geese practically became pets after Willow moved into the house she inherited almost two years ago. Willow became a little obsessive about them, texting me at all hours with "prenatal" concerns about the mom's diet and how uncomfortable she looked while waiting for them to hatch.

So, the next time I was at their place, I humored her by giving the goose an "exam." I got on the ground, talked to the geese, checked the nest, and dodged the hissing mom and dad, who clearly weren't thrilled about my visit. I explained to Willow that no, she didn't need to worry about giving the goose a pregnancy pillow or calcium supplements and went over what they should do until the eggs hatched.

Apparently, she'd been recording the whole thing. She posted the video online with the caption: *A man who takes care of animals...And he's single, ladies*

To make matters worse, I'd just come from the beach, so I was only wearing a pair of swim trunks. Now, dodging overly eager women who want to take my last name as their own has become my daily routine.

You'd think the video would have died down quickly, but every time I went to check on the geese, she'd film me again. I had no idea—it took me a while to figure out why random women started throwing themselves at me. Now, it's been months of this shit, and all my siblings think it's a fucking riot.

Thanks a lot, Willow.

As I reach for the clinic's door handle, Christy stops me with her hand on my shoulder. "Parker..."

Inhaling deeply, I turn around to face the woman, hoping that some directness will get through to her. "Christy, you seem lovely, but I'm not interested in dating right now."

Her head rears back on her neck. "But I'm a catch."

"I'm sure you are, but I'm just not available."

Her hand drops from my shoulder as her entire demeanor changes, her eyes narrow, and if she could, I'm pretty sure she'd shoot laser beams at me. "God, you're just like every other guy on the internet."

"And how's that?" I ask, not necessarily eager for her response, but curious, nonetheless.

"You put on a show for the camera and then turn out to be an asshole in real life."

Shaking my head so I don't say something to spur this woman on, I turn back to the door and enter the hospital just as three of the technicians scatter from their post at the front counter.

"Subtle, ladies."

Cassandra smiles. "What level of crazy was that one?"

"On a scale from one to ten, probably a five."

"That's it? I saw her parked out there when I came in at six this morning."

My eyes bug out of my head. "Okay, maybe closer to a seven or eight. She wanted to go out this Saturday."

"Did she start planning your imaginary wedding too?" Kelly, our newest tech, interjects with a smile on her lips.

"I wouldn't be surprised if she did, but I turned her down before she could tell me the colors of our napkins and place settings."

"We have a problem." All four of us spin to find Beth, our lead technician, striding out to the front of the office. Beth has been here since Dr. O'Neil's father was still alive. She practically runs this practice now. Everyone knows you do not want to be on this woman's bad side.

We follow her to the back and join the rest of the staff in a huddle.

"Dr. O'Neil fell at his house this morning," she announces.

"What?" "Oh my god!" Several of the employees exclaim their shock at the same time. Seth and I lock eyes across the room, knowing exactly what this means for us.

In the past year, I've come to respect the man more as a doctor, but we're never going to be grabbing beers together or painting each other's finger nails—not that I do that with other men, but you get what I'm saying. We coexist for the sake of the practice, but that's it.

"Is he all right?" I ask over the staff's murmurs.

Beth nods at me. "Luckily, nothing's broken, but he will be off duty for the rest of the week and part of next. So, that means we're down a doctor."

Robert has only been practicing a few days a week as it is, but on the days when he's here, things definitely run more smoothly. This means that Seth and I are going to have to pick up the slack.

But that's not the only thing on my mind.

Dr. O'Neil is only getting older. I think all of us are wondering how much longer he is going to push himself until he finally realizes it's time to retire.

"Everyone needs to be on top of things this week and communicate effectively. No calling out unless absolutely necessary," Beth says as everyone nods in agreement. "I will be visiting Dr. O'Neil later tonight to check on him and bring him some paperwork." She slides a card out from under the stack of papers on her clipboard. "I thought it would be nice if we all sign this card for him too, just so he knows we're thinking of him."

The staff practically lunges at Beth with their pens poised while I head back to my office to look at the calendar and see what I can move around. I usually take a long lunch on Thursdays at Catch & Release, my brother Dallas's restaurant, but I'm not sure I'll have time now, so I shoot off a text to him while I have a free minute.

Me: *Not sure I'm gonna make it for lunch tomorrow. Dr. O'Neil fell this morning so we're down a physician.*

He responds almost immediately.

Dallas: *That sucks. Is he okay?*

Me: *Apparently nothing is broken, but the man is getting up there in age. I hope he takes this as a sign to slow down.*

Dallas: *You think he might retire sooner than later?*

Me: *Ha...maybe. I'll stop by and visit him this weekend and try to see where his head's at.*

Dallas: *And convince him to leave the practice to you and not Doctor Brown Nose?*

Me: *In a roundabout way...yeah.*

Dallas: *Are you sure? You're already married to your job. There's more to life than work.*

This is rich coming from my former Marine brother who owns his own business. Before Willow came into his life, he was a workaholic too. But love made him change his ways, which is another reason I'm glad I dodged that bullet. I've worked too hard to give up now.

Me: *You found a good woman. Not all of us are as lucky. I'm just fine with my job as my wife.*

Dallas: *Does the animal hospital have devices that can suck your dick for you that I'm not aware of then? Or did you finally buy the breast pump you were trying on for size when we were shopping for baby shit with Grady?*

Me: *I'm going to tell Willow you only keep her around to suck your dick. She'll love that.*

Dallas: *Don't you fucking dare say that to my pregnant wife, asshole. She is very sensitive right now.*

Dallas and Willow found out she was expecting soon after they got married last summer. She's due this May, which is about three months away, and I've thoroughly enjoyed watching him walk on eggshells around his pregnant wife.

Me: *Then stop telling me how to live my life.*

Dallas: *I'm just looking out for you since you're too fucking stubborn to think about the future. It's the curse of being the oldest brother.*

Me: *I do think about the future and I know I'm happiest alone.*

Dallas: *Fine. Text me tomorrow if you can make it in for lunch. You know the boys and I always enjoy your grumpy ass.*

Dallas, Grady, and Penn, my other brother, love to ruffle my feathers at these lunches. But after Penn nearly choked me out one day because I was giving them shit about their relationships, I've learned there are lines you don't cross—even with brothers.

Penn said it was because I was jealous, but that's not it at all.

Would I have been married already if I hadn't forced my fiancée to confront her demons?

Yes.

Would I be a lovesick man like my brothers, attached to a woman because she made my life better than it was before?

Maybe.

Or would I be a thirty-year-old divorcé who's even more bitter after finding out that his wife was a lying, cheating alcoholic that cared more about booze than him?

I'm betting on that last one.

I toss my phone on my desk just as Beth comes into my office with a knock on the open door.

"Dr. Sheppard?"

"Yes?"

Handing me a stack of files, she says, "These are half of Dr. O'Neil's patients for the week. You'll need to become familiar with them."

"Of course."

"And don't bother making any evening plans this week. You and Seth are going to take turns managing our surgery patients until the night shift comes in."

I was already expecting that, but I humor her. "Not a problem."

With a curt nod, she leaves. I place the files on my desk and step up to my mirror. Adjusting my tie and glasses, I give myself a quiet pep talk.

"This is your chance, Parker. Show Dr. O'Neil that you can handle this. Show Beth and the staff that you can juggle chaos and remain as cool as a cucumber. And before you know it, you'll get everything you've been working for. Good things are coming. Just...don't fuck it up."

Famous last words.

***

"A woman just came in who says she wants you to take a look at her goldfish."

I look up from the dog I'm examining, glaring at Cassandra. "Are you serious?"

"Well, I have to say, it's more original than the ones who ask you to look at their kitten." She lifts a brow, giving me a look and says, "I think we both know that's code for pussy."

Emily, the technician beside me, snorts. Sighing, I remove the stethoscope from my ears and hang it back around my neck before I begin running my fingers over the dog's body, checking for lumps. "Can we just put a sign on the door that says *If you're looking for Parker Sheppard, he's entered the witness protection program*?"

"Kind of hard to back that up when you're right here," Cassandra retorts.

I roll my eyes. "I don't have time for this shit. If Willow wasn't my sister-in-law, I'd slap her with a lawsuit for making my life a living hell."

Cassandra folds her arms across her chest. "You're not even going to consider taking advantage of your situation?"

"What do you mean?"

"I *mean*, all of these women are throwing themselves at you. You could be banging a new woman every night, and yet, you act repulsed by the whole thing." She snaps her fingers. "Oh, I get it now! You're gay."

"What?" I practically shriek, and not in a manly way, I might add. Lowering my voice, I say, "I'm not gay, Cassandra. What on earth makes you think that?"

She tilts her head, inspecting me. "I don't know. The glasses? The hair?"

"Plenty of straight men wear glasses, and what's wrong with my hair?" I reach up and pat my short, light brown locks. Everything seems to be in place, and I just got a fresh haircut last week.

"Nothing really, but you also never have a girlfriend or go on dates."

"That's because I prefer being single."

And the last woman I slept with left an impression on me that I can't seem to shake. Not only was she beautiful, witty, and phenomenal in bed, but she sprang out of my hotel room so fast afterward that it shook my confidence a bit, I'm not gonna lie.

"Which would make sense if you were taking these women up on their offers, but you're not," Cassandra retorts.

"In case you haven't noticed, these women aren't after casual sex. They're after a husband. They want to marry the man that Willow portrayed in that video and I'm actually..."

"Old man! Get back here!"

I spin around to find Beth chasing Dr. O'Neil as he hobbles down the hallway, cane in hand. The last thing anyone expected was to see him back here after only one day.

"Careful who you're calling an old man, Beth!" he snaps back. If these two didn't talk to each other like this on a daily basis, I might be alarmed, but Beth can handle Robert.

"You are not supposed to be here!" she scolds.

"Says who?" he fires back, eyes bouncing around the hospital. The entire staff is practically frozen as we all watch Beth chase down our boss. But if it were me, I'd listen to Beth—not just because she frightens me a little, but because she is liable to kick that cane right out from under him just to teach him a lesson.

"Your doctor, for starters."

Robert waves her off. "That man doesn't scare me."

"You're supposed to be resting."

Dr. O'Neil stops right next to me, and I grab the dog I was examining and hand it off to Emily. "Dr. O'Neil—" I start, but I'm interrupted by a familiar voice.

"Oh my God, Dad! What are you doing here? You're supposed to be at home!"

All heads spin to the back door where the beautiful, quirky blonde I swore I'd never see again strides in, hair flying behind her, purse slung over her shoulder, and a look of irritation plastered on her face.

"June Bug? What are *you* doing here?" Dr. O'Neil says, his expression softening.

Wait. June Bug? The stranger I held hands with on a flight and then had one unforgettable night with is the *June Bug my boss has talked about for years? His* daughter?

"Cashlynn?" The surprise in my voice is enough to catch her attention, but her eyes flick toward me for only a second, recognition flashing, before she refocuses on her father.

"You're supposed to be at home resting, Dad."

"I did. And now I'm fine." He waves his cane around in the air as I dodge it and swiftly move to the side.

"I knew this was going to happen. Beth was right to call me."

Robert glares at Beth. "You called her?"

"With good reason. Look at you, you stubborn mule."

"I'm fine!" he bellows, and the staff scatter to every empty space they can find while several dogs in cages start barking. Once the chaos has died down, Robert turns to his daughter. "So it takes me getting hurt for you to come visit your old man?"

Cashlynn's face softens just slightly. "I, uh…" Our eyes meet again and recognition flashes in her eyes for the second time, followed by a look I should have realized was a warning of things to come. "Well, yes, but that's not the only reason I'm here."

Robert sighs and then pulls his daughter in for a hug. "I appreciate the concern, June Bug, but I'm fine. Truly."

"If you say the word *fine* one more time, I'm going to karate chop your leg," Beth interjects.

"Now, there's no need for violence." I step between Beth and Robert while my heart pounds violently in my chest.

Just act cool, Parker. No one needs to know that you slept with Dr. O'Neil's daughter. You can talk to her later and agree to just keep it between the two of you. Easy-peasy.

"So what else would bring you down to Carrington Cove, June, if it wasn't just to make sure that I'm not dying?" Robert glares over at Beth again before focusing back on his daughter.

Cashlynn gnaws on her bottom lip before glancing back over at me. "Well, uh...you see..."

A pinch develops in Robert's brow as he takes a step closer to his daughter. "Is everything okay, June? Are you in trouble?"

Cashlynn's gaze keeps moving back and forth between me and her father. "No. Everything is fine, Dad. I just..."

"You're worrying me, sweetie."

Cashlynn takes a deep breath and then marches over to me, weaving her arm through mine and flashes a bright, suspiciously forced smile. "I'm here to see my fiancé. I believe you know Parker, Dad. I mean...obviously you know Parker."

My mouth drops open as Robert's eyes snaps to mine. "I...I'm sorry," he stutters, "Did you just say...*fiancé*?"

"Uh, Cashlynn—" I start, but she cuts me off.

"Yes. Fiancé." She squeezes my bicep, then presses up on her toes to kiss my cheek. "It was time to stop hiding, right, *muffin*?"

"Muffin?" I mutter to myself, the urge to vomit coming on strong.

Robert turns to me, bewildered. *Yeah, you and me both, boss.* "Parker? Is this true?"

"Dr. O'Neil—" I start, but Cashlynn tightens her grip, practically cutting off my circulation.

Ouch. That fucking hurts.

"It's true, Dad. We're in love, and I'm moving here to be with him."

At that moment, Seth waltzes into the office and stops dead in his tracks as he takes in the scene. "Uh, Dr. O'Neil, I thought you were supposed to be resting…"

"I'm fine," Robert grates out before directing his irritation back at me. "I'm sorry, but I just don't understand how you two are engaged." The skin on his neck is turning red, which can only mean that the yelling is about to start again.

Cashlynn lets out a nervous laugh. "Well, Dad, it's actually quite a funny story…"

"I'm not laughing," he replies, his eyes darting back and forth between us.

Me comforting you on a flight and then fucking you so hard in a hotel bed that we left marks on the wall isn't a funny story, Cashlynn.

Robert narrows his eyes at me. "I have to say, Parker, I would have expected to hear something like this from you, not to be bombarded like this…"

"Don't blame him, Dad," Cashlynn interjects. "It was my choice to keep this from you. He was just going along with what I wanted."

"And why would you want to keep it from me?" His face starts to turn red again, and I brace myself to cover my ears. "If my daughter is engaged to one of my employees, one I practically think of as a son, why would you hide that?"

Seth clears his throat, clearly perplexed. "I'm sorry. Did you just say that these two are *engaged*?"

Cashlynn nods and moves in closer to me. Her breasts are plastered against my arm now, reminding me of what they felt like when she was beneath me that night almost a year ago.

Fuck, not now. I can't get a fucking hard-on during this chaos.

"Uh, Cashlynn—" I start, but she interrupts me yet again.

"Yes, we are!" Cashlynn declares enthusiastically.

Seth crosses his arms over his chest and a slimy smile spreads across his face. "Then where's your ring?"

Cashlynn and I both glance down at her left hand that's wrapped around my arm right now—the one with a very bare ring finger.

"You didn't get my daughter a ring?" Dr. O'Neil inserts himself once more. "And more importantly, you didn't ask for my permission first?" The vein in his forehead begins to pop. "What the hell is happening right now?" His eyes dart around the room, but everyone else is hiding behind machinery and counters, watching from a safe distance.

Smart of them.

Beth chimes in, thank God. "Cashlynn asked him not to say anything, Robert. Remember?" She motions for him to move toward a chair, but he waves her off. "Perhaps you should take a seat…"

"I'm fine!" he yells again as my balls shrivel up and try to climb up inside of my body.

Yeah, not sure how this could get any worse.

"Parker proposed spontaneously, so he didn't have a ring. We agreed to pick one out together when I came down here."

So now it looks like I'm buying a ring, something I swore I'd never do again, for a woman I barely know. Yeah, this just got worse.

"So you're moving home?" Robert asks, looking down at his daughter. "But what about your job?"

"Uh…"

All cylinders finally fire in my brain, catching me up to speed, so I say, "You're going to be working remotely for a while, right, babe?"

Cashlynn looks up at me as a sigh of relief leaves her lips. "Yes, until I can figure out my next move."

Yeah, you might be relieved right this second, woman, but I have a fuck ton of questions and we are definitely having a conversation later.

"Convenient," Seth mumbles so low that I'm pretty sure no one but me hears it. I glare in his direction, but as all of this slams into me, panic rises in my chest.

Needing some fresh air and a moment to freak out, I release my hold on Cashlynn and then glance at the clock. "Well, I think I'm going to take an early lunch. I didn't eat breakfast this morning and now I'm starving." Patting my stomach, I turn to Dr. O'Neil. "Glad to see you're feeling better, sir. When I return, I can catch you up to speed on a few things..."

"Like how you ended up engaged to my daughter without telling me?" The pinch in his brow tells me he's not happy, and honestly, I get it—because I'm fucking irritated in this moment as well.

"Not today, Dad. You're going home," Cashlynn says to her father.

"I'm not going anywhere." Robert slams his cane on the ground. "This is my practice and I have a right to be here!"

"Okay, why don't you at least go sit down in your office if you're so hell-bent on staying" Beth says, trying to diffuse the situation. She and Cashlynn move toward Robert, so I take that as my chance to get away.

I stop by my office, grab my wallet and keys, and speed out of the parking lot toward Catch & Release, needing that long lunch break now more than ever.

The boys aren't going to believe this.

Chapter Three

Parker

"What the fuck just happened?" I mutter, dropping my forehead to the steering wheel. I take a second to catch my breath before heading into my brother's restaurant.

Dallas bought this place from the owner when he returned home for good after serving twelve years in the Marines, and he's created a booming business that is a staple tourist spot in Carrington Cove. Every Thursday, I meet Penn, Grady, and him here for lunch before he opens to the public. Normally, I just enjoy my time away from the animal hospital and listen to them drone on about their love lives, but today, I'm pretty damn sure the spotlight's going to be on me.

I storm through the front door and spot Penn at the bar with Dallas and Grady. Grady's daughter, Callie, is strapped to his chest, sleeping peacefully.

"Uh, you okay?" Grady asks as I approach the bar, tossing my glasses down and blowing out a breath.

"I don't even fucking know," I mutter, rubbing my temples as I look up at Dallas. "Can I get a beer, please?"

He furrows his brow. "A beer? It's noon on a Thursday..."

"Just pour me a fucking beer, Dallas!" I snap, squeezing my eyes shut and pinching the bridge of my nose as the full weight of the past hour crashes down on me. Dallas slides a beer in my direction, and as soon as it's within reach, I grab the glass and drain half of it before saying, "Fuck. My. Life."

Dallas moves from behind the bar to stand by Penn and Grady, all three of them eyeing me with varying shades of confusion and amusement, clearly wondering what the hell is going on.

I wish I knew. Me? *Engaged*? I mean, I've made it crystal clear to everyone since Sasha left that I'm not going through that shit again. Not opening myself up to trust someone just to be let down. I don't need the risk, and I don't want the distraction. So how the hell am I suddenly "engaged" to a woman I barely know? Worse—a woman who happens to be my boss's daughter.

But before I can say a word, the front door bursts open, and I half-expect to see Dr. O'Neil hobbling in to beat the hell out of me with his cane. Instead, Cashlynn comes barreling in—her hair wild, her eyes scouring the room before they land on me.

"Oh my God, Parker! There you are."

"Who the hell is this?" Dallas mumbles to Grady out of the corner of his mouth.

"No idea," Grady mutters in return.

I spin around and meet the eyes of the woman who just inserted herself into yet another part of my day.

Reining in my irritation, I grate out, "Cashlynn, what are you doing here?"

She brushes her hair from her face. "Well, you rushed out of the vet's office so fast that we didn't get a chance to talk."

I huff out a laugh. "I think the time for talking was *before* you made that little announcement."

Behind me, Grady mumbles, "Should we say something?"

"Not yet," Penn replies under his breath.

"I'm sorry, I just..." Cashlynn blows out a breath and then finally acknowledges that we have an audience, covering her chest with her palm. "Oh God, I'm so sorry. I didn't mean to interrupt..."

I resist the urge to roll my eyes. Seems like unannounced interruptions are her MO.

"You're not, although I think we're all wondering how you know my brother here," Dallas says, gesturing to me. "I'm Dallas by the way."

Glaring at Cashlynn, I turn to the guys, trying to be polite even though there's a million emotions racing through me right now. "Guys, this is Cashlynn O'Neil."

"O'Neil?" Grady asks, confused. "Isn't that..."

"As in Dr. O'Neil, my boss?" I nod. "The one and only."

Grady turns to Cashlynn. "So you're..."

"Dr. O'Neil's daughter," I finish for him. I shoot another irritated look at our surprise guest and then say something I'm sure none of them was expecting. "And as of today, my fiancée."

Penn starts coughing, Dallas's mouth drops open, and Grady's eyes dart back and forth between me and Cashlynn like he's watching a championship ping-pong match.

"I'm sorry...your *fiancée*?" Dallas asks, drawing out the last word.

Cashlynn stands tall and rushes over to them, extending her hand like this is completely insane. "Yes! We're engaged. It's so nice to meet you all."

As if it were choreographed, all three guys twist their heads in my direction, looking for confirmation.

"Uh, little brother..." Penn starts, clearing his throat. "When did this happen?"

I snap my eyes back over to Cashlynn. "Today, right?"

She blows out a breath and steps back over to me, lowering her voice. "I know you have questions, and I'm sorry to have blindsided you—"

"Blindsided?" I cut her off, voice rising. "You didn't just blindside me, Cashlynn. You stormed into my workplace and lied to your dad, who also happens to be my boss, about us being engaged! 'Blindsided' doesn't even begin to cover it."

"I know you're upset, and you have every right to be, but—"

"You don't get it!" My hands start shaking as memories push their way to the surface, images of walking away from Sasha, from everything I thought I'd wanted. The last thing I want is to be back in that space. "I am *not* the man who would get engaged—especially not like this."

"Okay..."

Dallas steps in, gripping my shoulder and turning me to face him. "Look, I don't know what's going on, but maybe you should cool off before you say something you can't take back," he says quietly.

I glance back at Cashlynn and see genuine worry in her eyes. But there's something else there too—fear and a look of regret that tells me she knows what a mess she's created.

If she lied about an engagement to her father, there has to be a reason.

And I want to know what it is.

"Your brother's right," she says shakily, trying to keep her composure. "Let's take a little while to cool off and then can we please talk... Later tonight?"

I simply nod, not trusting that I won't lose it again if I try to speak.

"Can I get your number?" she asks. "So I can text you where to meet?"

Penn steps in since I seem to be incapable of speaking. "I can give it to you," he says, rattling off my digits as she enters them into her phone. A moment later, my phone vibrates in my pocket.

"There. Now you have my number too," she says, offering a faint smile.

"Joy," I manage.

"All right. It was nice to meet you, Cashlynn." Dallas says, signaling for her to leave, and thank God she takes the hint, retreating back out the front door as he follows her to lock it behind her.

When he turns back to face me, I feel Penn and Grady's eyes on me too, waiting for an explanation. I pick up my beer, drain the rest of it, and set the glass back down on the bar.

"Pour me another."

***

Thirty minutes later, my second beer is gone, I've brought everyone up to speed, and managed to choke down half of my burger, but only because my older brothers made me.

"So you met her a year ago?"

"Were you not fucking listening?" Glaring at Penn, I toss my napkin on the bar and lean back on my stool.

"No need for the language, dickhead."

Dallas sighs. "Look, I'm not about to break up a fight between you two again. Have some sympathy, Penn," he says, glancing at the more annoying of my two older brothers. "Think about what this means for Parker."

"That he might be engaged to a beautiful woman?" Penn asks with a shrug.

"Yeah, that he doesn't even fucking know," Dallas fires back.

Grady holds a finger up in the air, swinging his hips from side to side as he rocks his daughter still resting peacefully on his chest. "Not to mention, her dad is his boss."

"Thank you all for the recap," I mutter, running a hand down my face. "You're such a load of help."

Dallas grunts, leaning against the bar and crossing his arms over his chest. "Okay, so let me ask you this. Is there a reason she would have lied about something like being engaged to you? I mean, that's a pretty calculated lie, if you ask me."

"I have no idea why those words came out of her mouth, Dallas." My hands are buried in my hair as I lean my forearms on the counter. "She barely looked at me when she stormed in the animal hospital, chastising her dad about being there when he was supposed to be resting, and then before I knew it, she called me her fiancé."

Penn taps his chin with his finger. "There has to be a reason. You need to ask her about it when you talk tonight."

"You think?" I glare at him.

"I just don't think people are going to buy it," Grady chimes in. "I mean, this is Parker we're talking about. He's made it very well-known that the idea of marriage repulses him."

"My thoughts exactly," I say as I push myself off the bar and sigh. "No one who knows me is going to believe this."

"Depending on her motivation, you may have to become a really good actor," Dallas says.

"Why are you encouraging me to go along with this?"

He shrugs. "People lie for different reasons. And the truth is, you do have a history with this woman."

"Believe me, I know."

For the past thirty minutes, all I've thought about is that night—holding her hand while we were flying, her on her knees sucking my cock, and watching her scramble out of that hotel room after life-altering sex.

This woman has been a fixture in my mind on and off for a year, and suddenly she appears out of nowhere. I've got to be missing something.

Penn pats me on the shoulder. "Just hear her out tonight."

"And if I decide not to go along with it? Then I've lied to my boss." I bury my hands in my hair again. "Fuck, he's never going to leave the practice to me after this."

"Shit, I didn't think about that," Grady mutters. "I don't know what's worse—going along with the lie or admitting it was a lie to begin with."

"I can't win." Groaning, I drop my head onto the bar. "Ow."

"Let's not do that then, yeah?" Dallas says, pushing my head up. "Just talk to her tonight and decide where to go from there."

Something tells me I'm about to agree to being engaged, and I vowed I'd never do that again.

But apparently, life—or more accurately, my boss's daughter—had other plans.

Chapter Four

Cashlynn

"Dad?" Walking through the front door of my father's house again makes this seem all the more real.

"In the kitchen, June Bug." His voice echoes through the house, and I know there's no turning back now.

I set my purse on the couch and make my way to the kitchen, preparing to face the music and start putting the pieces of the mess I've created back together.

This trip wasn't supposed to be this complicated. Quitting my job and moving to Carrington Cove was definitely not on my bucket list. Then again, I hadn't expected to feel trapped in Philadelphia, drowning in lawsuits over jargon I'd long stopped caring about.

This isn't the life I'd envisioned for myself. And if I'm going to make a change, I need to do it now. The realization that I'm about to be thirty slammed into me like a freight train a few months ago. It's time I started living my life for myself, but making my father understand that isn't going to be easy.

"Glad to see you made your way back home," I say as I enter the kitchen and find my father making a sandwich, his cane resting against the counter and Johnny Cash playing on the record player in the dining room. I guess some things never change—one of them being my father's obsession with Johnny Cash.

He scoffs. "Well, there's only so much I can do at the hospital with Beth hovering over me and everyone afraid to look at me." Irritation laces his words, but he seems to be in better spirits than when I left him to chase after Parker.

"You're never going to heal if you don't rest."

"I fell, June Bug...It's not like I had my leg amputated."

"I know, but you're not getting any younger, Dad. Beth is worried sick about you, and I think it's time you consider passing along the practice..."

He turns to face me, his eyes narrowing as he sets down his knife. "Is that why you came home? To tell your geriatric father to hang up his white coat for good? Or was it really to see that fiancé of yours?" His words are accusatory, and my stomach twists.

God, poor Parker.

I feel terrible for dragging him into this, but when I saw him, I panicked.

I knew we'd cross paths eventually, but it completely threw me off to see him in that moment—like all the decisions I've made over the past year collided at once.

"I know you have questions..."

"You bet your ass I do." His neck and face begin to turn red—an unmistakable signal I learned early on meant he was about to blow up. "My daughter shows up out of the blue, tells me she's engaged to a man I work with, and—"

I cut him off before he gets too far into that list of grievances. "I haven't been happy in Philadelphia for a long time, Dad."

He reaches for his cane and walks over to the record player to stop the music, then to his recliner in the living room. As he sinks into his chair, he eyes me skeptically while I make my way to the couch across from him. The tense silence resting between us starts to make me squirm. "You're throwing your life away, all of your hard work and a career you've always wanted, for a man?"

"That's not it at all!"

"Then explain it to me," he says, the volume of his voice rising. "Because I hoped you'd come to Carrington Cove eventually, but not like this."

I shift uncomfortably on the couch. I've only been to this town one other time, right after my grandfather passed and Dad took over the practice. I was with my grandmother most of that visit while my dad dealt with the funeral arrangements and taking over a business overnight. Just a few weeks later, I was off to Cornell to study law just like I planned—well, like *my father* planned for me. After finishing law school, I moved to Philadelphia, claiming the decision was because I loved the city, though it wasn't the work that drew me there. But my father has no idea about what really drew me there.

Over the years, he would either visit me in Pennsylvania, or we'd meet up in Raleigh when I traveled there for work—like the weekend I met Parker.

The man my father always spoke so highly of was suddenly right there on the plane next to me. I felt like I'd met a celebrity. Then I realized how attractive, funny, and caring he was, and I slept with him. Looking back now, that probably wasn't the best idea I've ever had, but I don't regret it. That night was incredible. My only remorse is that I left him so abruptly, but I had to. I couldn't take another moment of the lies resting between us.

I take a deep breath of courage before I continue. "I needed a change, and when Beth told me you were hurt, I just reacted. And Parker is here. That job, that life..." I stare off into space for a minute, gathering my thoughts. "It's not what I want."

He frowns. "Yes, it is."

"No, it's what *you* wanted for me."

Our eyes meet and, for a second, I swear I see a flash of remorse in his. But it disappears just as quickly as it came. "I wanted you to have stability. To make smart choices. To build a life that would last."

"I know."

He sighs. "If that makes me a bad father, then so be it." The defensiveness rolling off him is exactly why I've been putting this off.

"You're not a bad father. I love you and appreciate everything you've ever done for me, but you pushed me into a life you thought was best because you didn't want me to end up like Mom."

Just mentioning her has my father going stiff.

Losing your mother at sixteen is something no person should ever have to go through. But growing up with a father who was never the same after she died? That's another experience that can scar you just the same.

He stares across the room for a moment, his jaw tight and his hands balled into fists as he rocks back and forth in his chair.

"But at twenty-nine, I realized that I felt stuck and numb, Dad. You can't be mad at me for wanting more for myself."

His gaze drifts back to mine. "I'm not mad, June Bug. I'm just worried. You come here and announce you're engaged to a man I didn't even know you were seeing—a man I've been working with for the past six years, no less. Forgive me for being a little concerned."

I stand from my spot on the couch and walk over to him, taking his hand. "I'm sorry for keeping things from you and surprising you like this. But when Beth called me, I knew I had to come check on you, and it felt like the right time to tell you about the changes in my life, too."

"I'm fine."

I tilt my head to the side as I look down at him. "I think you've established that. But like I said, you're not getting any younger, and falling is a sign—"

"That what? I'm clumsy? Because that's all it was. I missed a step."

"What were you doing, anyway?"

He darts his eyes from mine. "I was going down to the basement."

"For what?"

"Just...stuff." His evasiveness should concern me, but this is my father's house. He deserves his privacy and now's not the time to push him further.

"Either way, I don't like you living alone."

"Well, I've been alone for the past eleven years since you left for Cornell, and I don't plan on changing that anytime soon. Except you're here now and need a place to stay..."

"I'll be staying with Parker," I say, hoping that once I speak to him, he'll agree and I won't have to go back on that lie. Besides, it's going to be much easier for me to accomplish what I need to without living under my father's nose.

Taking a step back, I push a hand through my hair, hoping he can't see how badly my hands are shaking from my nerves.

My dad leans back in his chair and begins rocking again. "So, you ready to tell me how that relationship came to be?"

Uh, no. I need to make sure that Parker is going to go along with my lie first.

Not to mention, we should get our story straight so we can put on a united front. Having a fake fiancé was not originally part of my plan, but I think it might help me see this through. My father will have something else to focus on while I attempt to figure out my life, and since Parker's not a complete stranger, hopefully it will be easy to act the part.

Yeah, good luck with that, Cashlynn. Try not to remember what Parker Sheppard felt like hovering over you that night while your father questions how the hell you two met.

Jesus, why did I have to drag Parker into this mess with me?

Hopefully, he'll humor me and support me yet again, just like he did on the plane.

"Let's all have dinner together in a few days," I suggest, carefully keeping my voice casual. "I'm seeing Parker tonight, so I'll make sure he's free sometime this week, and then you can ask us both whatever you want." My smile is making my cheeks burn, but I need some time to get my ducks in a row.

"Fine. But that boy has a lot of explaining to do. You both do."

I give his hand a gentle squeeze. "Don't be too hard on him. He respects you immensely, Dad. And…I love him." I reach out to smooth his graying hair as I swallow down the lies that keep spewing from my lips. "If you think about it, our relationship is what brought me here. You can't be mad at him for that."

My father glares up at me from his seat. "I can be as mad as I want, June."

"Your grumpy old man is showing," I tease, leaning down to press a kiss to the top of his head.

He clasps my hand before I can get too far. "I am happy to have you home."

"This is *your* home, Dad. But now, it's going to be mine too."

***

When I walk back into Catch & Release a few hours later, the restaurant is starkly different than before. There's a line of people out the door waiting to be seated, every table and booth is filled, the bar has not one empty stool, and servers are hustling to deliver food and drinks. Nautical décor is everywhere, with fishing nets hanging from the corners and metal anchors adorning the wood-paneled walls. There are anchors everywhere, actually. Must be a thing in this town I missed the first time I visited.

I've read about small towns and I've certainly watched my fair share of Hallmark movies, but nothing could have prepared me for what it feels like to actually be here right in the middle of quaint, small-town reality.

Dallas sees me from his spot behind the bar and heads over, his smile welcoming despite how we met earlier. "Cashlynn, good to see you again."

I hike my purse up higher on my shoulder, smirking at him. "Are you sure about that?"

He chuckles. "Well, you certainly took us all by surprise this afternoon, but I have a feeling this will all work out for the best."

"That's pretty optimistic of you, but I'm glad someone feels that way."

He motions for me to follow him. "Parker is waiting in the back. I'll show you the way."

When I texted Parker to arrange when and where to meet, he suggested coming back to the scene of the crime—well, one of them, at least. Since it's his brother's place, he assured me he'd put us somewhere we could speak candidly and privately to sort out the mess I dragged Parker into.

Dallas leads me to a back room, secluded from the bustling restaurant. "We use this room for staff meetings and large parties, but you two have it all to yourselves tonight," he says as we step inside.

Parker's alone in a booth in the far corner, staring at his glass, fingers trailing through the condensation. His glasses are perched high on his nose, and his gaze is intense and pensive, his mind clearly miles away.

God, he's so hot, in a nerdy-doctor-with-muscles kind of way.

That rush I felt when I met him on the plane comes back to me now that my heart isn't running a freaking marathon along with my mind like it was when I was racing to find my dad earlier.

His light brown hair is cut short and tousled messily on top. He's wearing a solid black T-shirt that clings to his biceps and the muscles that I know he's hiding underneath. He's got on a pair of snug jeans and a pair of brown boots that make him look way more rugged than he did earlier.

He looked so different at the clinic, in a burgundy button-down, gray slacks, and his white lab coat. My dad insists the staff always look the part—sharp, professional, and ready to tackle anything.

It's adorable how seriously my father takes his job, and after hearing his stories over the years that included the man I owe an explanation to, I know that Parker is very much the same.

Yet another detail I have to admit to this man tonight.

"I'll leave you two to it." Dallas gives us a nod and disappears, leaving me standing there, waiting for Parker to acknowledge me. But his eyes remain locked on his glass.

"Hey." I should have thought of something more clever than that, but honestly, I'm at a loss for words right now.

Funny. You had no problem coming up with all kinds of words out of thin air earlier, Cashlynn.

Parker doesn't look up as he speaks. "How the hell did I not know that you were Dr. O'Neil's daughter? I thought her name was June."

"Okay, so we're jumping right in then…" I slide into the side of the booth opposite him.

That makes his eyes lift, at least. "Forgive me for skipping pleasantries, Cashlynn, but you can't imagine what my mind is like right now."

Sighing, I slide my purse off my shoulder and place it on the seat beside me before reaching for the glass of water that I'm assuming is for me. I take a sip and then draw in a deep breath. "You're right. I owe you an explanation."

"You think?" His jaw flexes as he leans back, crossing his arms, and I'm suddenly hit with the memory of that night—of the way he looked when he pressed me against the wall, his eyes dark with need.

God, that night feels like a lifetime ago.

"Your name," he says coolly. "Let's start there."

"My name is Cashlynn O'Neil, but my father calls me June Bug. Always has."

"And why's that?"

I debate how much he needs to know, but at this point, what do I have to lose? "My parents were obsessed with Johnny Cash and June Carter. Dad wanted to name me June, but my mom came up with Cashlynn, so he went along with it but insisted my middle name be June. He's called me June Bug for as long as I can remember." I shrug.

Parker shakes his head. "You never told me your last name that night."

My entire body breaks out in goosebumps from the memory, along with a twinge of regret. "I know."

"Why?"

I sigh, holding his gaze. "Because I thought you'd figure it out."

He narrows his eyes. "That you were Robert's daughter?" I nod, waiting for his brain to catch up. When it does, his eyes widen and he leans in, eyes narrowing. "You knew who I was?"

I lower my eyes to the table and nod. "Yeah. As soon as you mentioned you were from Carrington Cove, I put two and two together. My dad talks about you all the time. That's when I realized I couldn't tell you who I was."

He leans his head to the side. "Why?"

A heavy sigh leaves my lips as I shrug again, but I don't break eye contact. "Honestly? I'm not sure. Maybe I was scared you'd treat me differently. Maybe I figured you already had preconceived notions about me from things my father has said. Or...maybe I just wanted a moment where I wasn't Robert O'Neil's daughter and there wasn't this pressure on me to be the person he expects me to be. The person I've become accustomed to portraying."

His face softens a bit, and suddenly I feel extremely naked. When I was actually naked with this man, I didn't stumble at all. He made me feel wanted, alive, like I could be myself and he didn't judge me at all for it.

And the sex. Fuck, it was so intense, so hot, so effortless, and just what I needed. He just *saw* me. That night, I got to just be *me,* and I can't remember the last time I felt that free.

Honestly, I'm not even sure who I am anymore, but that's what I'm trying to figure out.

"I can understand that," he says, startling me out of my thoughts.

"Really?"

Parker blows out a breath, gaze still narrowed on me. "Let's just say I understand feeling the need to be who everyone wants you to be, and when you aren't, they treat you differently."

"Exactly."

But then he shakes his head, and I brace myself, watching as the warmth drains from his face. "That said, I can't be your fiancé, Cashlynn."

I try not to let my disappointment show. This isn't his problem to figure out. "Why not?"

"Because I'm not the marrying kind."

That surprises me. "That's cryptic. Forgive me, but the man I met on the plane was thoughtful, genuine, helpful, and comforted me when I was freaking out...all qualities that any woman would be lucky to find in a husband."

He scoffs. "Yeah, well, not everyone is destined for marriage."

I cross my arms over my chest. "So that was all an act on the plane?"

Our eyes lock. "Not at all."

"Then what are you saying? I'm sorry, but I'm confused."

He pushes his hand through his hair. "I can't be your fiancé, okay? That's all you need to know."

The pain of defeat rises in my chest, but before I count myself out, I decide to try my backup tactic. I didn't want to have to resort to coercion, but desperate times... "You know, I'm not the only one with something to gain from this ruse."

His right brow lifts. "What do you mean?" I watch his forearms flex and my body starts to heat up, remembering what his entire body looked like naked, the way every part of him flexed when my mouth was around his cock.

Focus, Cashlynn. That night cannot be a memory we revisit while we're here.

"I saw your videos," I blurt out.

His entire face falls and he leans over the table, burying his hands in his hair. "Fuck. I hate the internet."

"Yeah, well, it seems you're quite popular with the ladies now, aren't you?" The number of times women post videos of themselves ogling this man is insane, but I definitely understand the appeal.

He lifts his head and glares at me. "What are you getting at?"

"Beth has told me about your visitors to the animal hospital and how these women are relentless." I begin to draw circles on the table in front of me. "If you were getting married, that would make them back off."

He sits up again, crossing his arms. "Nice try."

I hold my hands up defensively. "I'm not speaking lies here, am I?" I can practically see the wheels turning in his brain, so I press on. "Not to mention, when I was talking to my father earlier, I brought up retirement. You're in the running to take over the practice, right?"

He smirks as he leans back. "I underestimated you, Cashlynn O'Neil."

"Most people do, but that's why I had to have a plan when I came back here, Parker."

"I imagined you did when you blurted out that we were engaged. That doesn't seem like something you'd come up with on the fly."

"Please don't think that I don't know how crazy this sounds and that I don't know what I'm asking from you. I do. But you don't know my dad like I do, how judgmental he can be, and how quickly he can overreact. I needed something to give me time to plan this big life change before springing it on him, and this is what I came up with." I shrug. "Was it the best idea? Well, that's still to be determined."

His eyebrows draw together. "But why me? Why an engagement?"

Leaning forward, I reach for his hand and lock my gaze with his. "You have a lot to lose here too, Parker. I'm literally related to the man who will determine the future of your career. Do you honestly want to work for Seth Brown if my father chooses him?"

"You know about Seth?"

I nod. "Beth and I are close. I know *a lot*."

In fact, I probably know more about the drama at Carrington Cove Animal Hospital than the townsfolk do—and I don't even live here.

Well, I guess I do now, actually.

"If you come clean to him about our lie, he'd almost be forced to choose Seth. And I know you don't want that."

He swallows, his jaw clenching. "I'm fucked either way, Cashlynn, thanks to you." He pulls his hand from mine, and my stomach is immediately in knots again. "You're right. If I come clean now, I'll lose your dad's trust that I've worked hard to build. But if I go along with this and he finds out later it was all a lie, he'll be even more furious with me."

"No, he won't," I insist. "Because this is temporary. I promise."

"It is?" He feigns surprise. "Thank God—I thought you planned on getting married for real!"

"Your sarcasm is a bit over the top, don't you think?"

"We haven't scratched the surface of my sarcasm, sweetheart."

I blow out a breath, fighting the urge to roll my eyes. "Look, I just need some time to get my life together."

He raises an eyebrow. "And how long is that gonna take? Because I gotta say, I'm not too confident in you and your current life choices."

Shaking my head, I fight back the tears that are threatening to fall. I can't cry. I don't want him to see that his words affect me, but they do—because he's right.

God, I'm a fucking mess.

"Look, I don't expect you to understand. You have a career you love, a picture-perfect family and life here, and I'm sure you've made very few mistakes in your life." His face falls a little. "But that hasn't been my path, and for once in my life, I'm deciding to do something that

I want. I'm sorry that I dragged you into this, but I'm scared, Parker. My entire life just went up in flames, and I'm standing here with a fire extinguisher that I don't know how to use." One tear slides down my cheek, but I swipe it away. "All I'm asking for is your help. I need time. I need space to figure out if I can make my dreams a reality. Haven't you ever fallen on your ass and needed someone to help you back up?"

He stares at me for so long that I'm sure he's about to tell me that I have no one but myself to blame for where I've ended up. And he'd be partially right. But when he finally speaks, his words shock me.

"How long were you thinking?"

I blink at him slowly. "What?"

Clearing his throat, he reaches for his glass, takes a sip, and sets it back down. "How long do you need to figure things out?"

"Um, I don't know... Three or four months?"

He nods. "So until June?"

"Yeah...that should probably work." Honestly, I have no idea how long my plans might take, but if that's what he's willing to give me, I'll make it work.

"Okay."

My mouth falls open. "You're...agreeing to this?"

He blows out a breath and shakes his head. "Apparently so."

I jump up from my side of the booth and launch myself at him. "Oh my God, Parker! Thank you!"

His arms instinctively wrap around me as I lean against him, breathing in his scent that's just as intoxicating as I remember from our night together. I immediately melt against him, sliding into the seat next to him.

When I lean back, Parker's eyes are on my lips.

Oh my God. Is he going to kiss me?

More importantly, do I want him to?

Yes, Cashlynn. Do you remember how well this man kisses? Mount him, right here. No one's around. Seal your fake engagement the old-fashioned way.

Neither of us moves. Parker's eyes remain locked on my lips, and my chest rises and falls as I take shallow breaths. Can I really be fake-engaged to this man when I've already slept with him? Isn't that just asking for trouble?

But then, just as quickly, he snaps out of it, releasing me and shifting down the booth, putting a few inches between us. "Look, it's uh...no big deal."

"Yes, it is, Parker. You're a good man, and I owe you so much."

"A foolish man, maybe," he says with a chuckle. "But you seem like you could use a friend right now, and I've been there. Because, despite what you may think, my life isn't perfect."

"I'm sorry for saying that. I just..."

He holds up a hand. "I get it. But if we're doing this, we need to set some ground rules." His eyes dip back down to my lips, then to my breasts, and then he glances away, pushing a hand through his hair. "Maybe you should, uh, move back to your side of the booth."

Even though my pulse is thrumming from our proximity, I return to my seat, fixing my hair and taking a sip of water. "Okay. Rules. What are you thinking?"

"Well, for starters, no one else can know that this is fake besides my brothers and Grady."

I nod in agreement. "Okay."

"And that's only because they were there when you crashed our lunch."

I wince. "Sorry again about that. I just wanted to explain."

"I know." He sighs. "But no one from the animal hospital can know, not even Beth."

Nodding, I say, "Agreed."

"Next, no more lying to me." His words are sharp, but fair.

"You got it." And then a thought comes to mind. "I guess that makes this a good time to tell you my father thinks I'll be staying with you?"

His eyes bug out. "What?"

"I mean, wouldn't it make sense for me to be staying with my fiancé?"

Parker closes his eyes and pinches the bridge of his nose. "Jesus. Yeah, I guess so."

"I also didn't tell him the truth about my job."

His eyes snap back open. "Which is?"

"That I don't have one. You said I'd be working remotely, which was kind of you—but I actually quit."

"That's right, you're a lawyer. Your dad always talks about how proud he is of his lawyer daughter." He shakes his head. "Not a teacher like I assumed."

I nod. "Right."

"Then what was with the blue paint under your fingernails?"

The details of his memory take me by surprise. "You remember the color of the paint under my nails?"

He shrugs, looking away. "Well, yeah. You don't see blue paint under people's nails every day."

"Huh." I lean back and fold my arms over my chest.

"Huh? What does that mean?"

"Can I ask you a question...without you getting mad?"

His brow furrows. "I can't promise that."

"Well, do your best for me then, will you?"

He blows out a breath, his irritation building again. "What is it, Cashlynn?"

Swallowing down my nerves, I uncross my arms, biting my bottom lip as I glance down at Parker's mouth—the same mouth that did magical things between my legs. "Do you...have you...ever thought about that night?"

His entire body goes still, his jaw tightening as his eyes darken slightly. Then, after a beat, he licks his lips and replies in a low, measured voice, "No."

"Liar," I retort, fighting my grin as heat floods my cheeks. And there it is—memories of that night, the way we'd moved together, each kiss and touch like wildfire. I clench my thighs as desire hums through me.

We just sit there, silent, staring across the table at one another. My pulse thrums in my ears, a soft ache building inside me.

"Rule number three," Parker finally says, breaking the silence.

"We're numbering them now?"

"Rules are always numbered."

"Only if you're a rule-follower," I counter.

He sighs, pinching the bridge of his nose as if I'm exhausting him. "Are you going to argue with me about everything?"

"I'm sorry," I say, even though I feel like my point is valid. "Continue."

He locks eyes with me again and says, "Rule number three. No bringing up that night."

I swallow roughly. "Why?"

"Because if we're going to do this, we need to keep it platonic. No kissing, no touching..."

"But we're fake-engaged. Wouldn't it be weird if we weren't affectionate with each other?"

He closes his eyes, takes in a deep breath, and then opens them again. "Only when necessary, and only in front of other people, okay?"

Disappointment settles heavily in my chest, but I push it aside. I know he's right—this has to be strictly business. But the effect he has on me makes it hard to accept. Today has been crazy, overwhelming, and a whirlwind. I'm not thinking straight, so at least someone is.

Parker's right. I need to focus on my goals and not him and his body, and that scar above his eyebrow that I never asked him about, or why he wears glasses and not contacts, or...

"Cashlynn?" Parker says, pulling me from my thoughts.

"Yeah?"

"Did you hear me?"

"Yes." I force a smile, but it probably comes off strained.

His eyebrows draw together. "Are you sure? You look like you zoned out there for a moment."

"I'm sorry. It's just...been a long day," I say, stifling a yawn.

"Yeah, and a wild one."

"It has, but I can't thank you enough, Parker. Truly."

He nods once. "Just don't make me regret this, okay?"

"The only one who can control that is you."

"Excuse me?"

I trace small circles on the table, thinking back to my last memory of my mother. "Regret is a choice, Parker. *You* choose whether you live with it or not."

He studies me for a moment. "Is that what this is about for you? Not living with regrets?"

"Yes." I look him straight in the eyes. "The last thing I want in my life is to look back and wonder 'what if'. My mother lived by that, and it's one of the few things I still remember about her."

His face softens. "Your dad never talks about her."

I let out a short, humorless laugh. "Yeah, that sounds about right."

He studies me again, his look intense. "I feel like I know you, but that you're a complete stranger at the same time. It's fucking weird."

I chuckle. "I feel the same way. Maybe over the next four months, we can actually get to know each other…"

Something flickers across Parker's face, but it's gone before I can fully register it. His gaze leaves mine as he says, "I just want you to do what you need to do, Cashlynn, so I can move on with my life, all right?"

I swallow, a dull ache settling in my chest, and force my voice to stay steady. "And what exactly are you moving on to?"

I can't figure this man out. He's so hot and cold from one second to the next. He's hiding something, or there's something that I'm missing. Maybe living with him will give me the chance to discover more of the real Parker Sheppard, not just the man he portrayed to me a year ago.

Standing, he drains the rest of his drink and sets the glass down. "Text me tomorrow and we can make arrangements for you to bring your stuff over."

I rise from the booth as well, reaching out and catching his arm before he can walk away. "I told my dad we would have dinner with him soon so he can drill us about our relationship."

"Fuck," he grumbles, but nods. "We can talk about that tomorrow too. I need to get home, Cashlynn. It's been a hell of a day and I'm beat. I think I've handled all I can for now."

Releasing his arm, I flash him a tight-lipped smile. "Thank you again, Parker. I'll be in touch."

With a curt nod, he leaves, slipping out of the restaurant's back room as I stand there, watching him go. I slowly let out the breath I feel like I've been holding since I arrived in Carrington Cove.

Tonight could have gone much worse. Parker could have told me to kick rocks and come clean to my father right this instant. But instead, he showed me compassion, which is one of the most vulnerable things you can do for another human.

Now that I know we're on the same page, tomorrow we can come up with a story to convince my father we're the real deal.

And as for Parker's rule about no more lies, that's a promise I plan to keep.

But my father? Well, he doesn't get the entire truth yet. Not until I can make sure that I'm moving my life and career in the direction *I* want.

I just hope he can see past the hurt in the end—because if there's one thing my father has never gotten over, it's losing my mother, and what I want to do with my life involves every part of her she gave to me—talents and all.

Chapter Five

Parker

"Eight," I grunt as I push the bar up off my chest. "Nine." I blow out a harsh breath. "Ten!" The sound of metal hitting metal rings out in my garage as I hang the bar back up on the bench and roll out from underneath it, standing up to walk around while trying to catch my breath.

It's the day after Cashlynn crashed back into my life, and last night I slept like shit. I've been in my garage for the past hour trying to burn off some of the adrenaline coursing through me before I go to work, but I only feel marginally better than I did when I woke up.

Memories assaulted me all night, each one dragging up pieces of the past I'd like to leave buried—pictures of the future I envisioned with Sasha, flashbacks to the day I met Cashlynn on the plane and the night that followed.

She fucking knew who I was. It all clicks now... Her evasive answers and how she kept steering the conversation away from herself. Now I can't help but question if it was actually a coincidence.

If she hadn't been panicking, would we have even spoken? If I had just watched *Bridgerton* like I intended, how different would my life be right now? I'd probably be sleeping better and wouldn't be staring down the barrel of this fake engagement. Funny how life works.

My phone vibrates on the ground, snapping me out of my head, and I'm grateful for the distraction when I see Dallas's name on the screen.

"Hello?"

"Good morning, groom-to-be. How are you feeling today?" The teasing lilt of his voice instantly annoys me.

"Say one more thing like that and I'm hanging up."

He chuckles. "Calm your tits. I'm just messing with you."

"My tits are calm." I stare down and flex my pecs, just to make sure.

"Good. Seriously though, how'd it go last night?" I rushed out of the restaurant so fast that I didn't even say goodbye to my brother, too eager to get home and process the chaos that is Cashlynn O'Neil.

Blowing out a breath, I say, "Looks like I have a fiancée for the next four months."

"No shit. You agreed to it?"

"I don't have much of a choice. There's too much at stake."

"Okay, but what happens at the end of four months?"

I push a hand through my sweat-soaked hair as I take a seat back on the bench. "Cashlynn figures she can get her life together in that timeline, and once she does, she promised she'd come clean to her dad about everything. Hopefully by then Robert either makes a decision about retiring, or he'll appreciate me helping his daughter get back on her feet and still consider leaving the practice to me."

"So, what is she trying to put together exactly?"

"Hell if I know. We haven't exactly covered that part yet. All I know is that she quit her job as a lawyer in Philadelphia and came down here to figure out what she wants."

"Gotta give her credit—that's pretty brave."

"Yeah, until she dragged me into it."

"Was she apologetic about it at least?"

"Yeah, but her relationship with her father seems way more complicated than I realized. Otherwise, why lie to him about what she's doing here?"

"Then cut her some slack, Parker. You know better than anyone how much it sucks to let someone down." My teeth clench in response to his comment. "Did she at least tell you why she lied?"

I stare out at the street as a couple bikes past my house. This neighborhood is farther from the main part of town, so there's very minimal traffic and people, just the way I like it. Most of my neighbors are retirees or quiet couples. It's peaceful and I don't feel like I have to watch my back everywhere I turn like I do when I'm at work.

Thankfully, the crazy women who've been stalking me haven't ventured to my home...yet.

"A little. I don't know, Dallas, she just seems all over the place right now. I don't need another Sasha situation on my hands—"

"Cashlynn is nothing like Sasha," he says, cutting me off.

"We don't know that. I don't know anything about this woman, and she's moving in with me tomorrow. Shit, I thought I knew the woman I was actually engaged to, but that turned out to be a big, fat fucking lie too."

Dallas sighs. "Parker, you've got to let the Sasha thing go."

I scoff. "You act like it's so fucking easy."

"Believe me, if there is anyone who knows what it's like to hold on to shit, it's me. And I'm telling you, little brother, letting go of my anger toward Dad was one of the best things I've ever done for myself."

I swallow hard, the familiar tightness building in my chest. "And how exactly am I supposed to do that, Dallas? I can't just ignore what she did, or how bad I let things get after. You think I haven't tried?"

"You focus on moving forward. And I'm not gonna lie... Willow's a big part of why I was able to finally let go. Also, therapy is a big fucking help. Willow and I both went after our worlds collided, and we still do from time to time. Processing your shit out loud is life-changing. Trust me."

I hang my head, an ache spreading through my chest. "Not everyone gets a happily ever after, Dallas."

"Only by choice, Parker. Believe me, when it's worth it, you fight for that happiness every day."

"Yeah, well, Cashlynn and I are a temporary thing. Let me survive the next four months and then you can lecture me about dating again."

He laughs. "You might feel different after your time with her."

I huff. "You're hilarious."

"Look, you two obviously have a connection if you slept together. Why not explore it?"

"Because she's my boss's daughter, for one. And two, who knows if she's even staying here? Beyond her moving in with me tomorrow, I have no idea what her plans are." I pause, hearing Willow's voice in the background. "Hey, while she's there, tell my amazing sister-in-law she can foot my therapy bills, since her videos are half the reason I'll need it." Dallas laughs as I continue. "Cashlynn was quick to remind me that a fake engagement would get my stalkers off of my back. Funny thing is, I wouldn't have any if it weren't for Willow, so..."

"You should be thanking her, Parker."

"Uh, for what, exactly?"

"For bringing some excitement to your life," he says with a laugh.

"Yeah, well, between those videos and my fake engagement, I think I'm good on excitement for the next year or so."

I hear Willow's voice again in the background, and Dallas covers the phone. When he comes back, he says, "Willow wanted me to tell you that she thinks the geese are getting ready to lay eggs again, by the way."

I do some mental calculations. "Makes sense. They usually start around the end of February, early March."

"Say, why don't you bring Cashlynn over to see them? Willow can film another video and include your fiancée this time. The women in the comments will go nuts, and word will spread that you're a taken man."

Shit. I hate to say it, but my brother might be onto something. "That's actually not a terrible idea."

"Oh my God, Parker! Let's do it!" Willow screams in the background.

I let out a groan. "I've got a million other things to figure out first, okay?"

"You said she's moving in tomorrow?" Dallas asks as I stand from the bench again and reach for my water bottle, taking a long drag. Cashlynn texted me last night asking if Saturday would work, and honestly, I needed a day to brace myself. I still have a full shift today, and I won't even be home till late.

"Yeah…"

"Then you should bring her by Mom's for dinner on Sunday."

Realization slams into me. "Fuck. I have to tell Mom, don't I?"

"Sorry to say it, little brother…but if she finds out about your engagement from anyone else, you know there will be hell to pay."

"She'll never buy it."

"Maybe not, but you know Mom. She might just be so thrilled that you're dating again that she won't question it. She worries about you."

"Right. It's more likely that now that you and Penn are off the market, I'm her next project."

"She's got Hazel, too."

"Yeah, but that won't last long. You know our sister is a hopeless romantic just like Dad was. There's bound to be some guy that sweeps her off her feet soon."

"You know, with the way you two watch *Bridgerton*, you'd think you'd be more open to love."

"That show is a masterpiece, but it's not real life, okay?"

My brother laughs at me through the phone.

There was a time when I was a hopeless romantic too, but then my heart was ripped from my chest, thrown into a blender, and poured down a garbage disposal. Watching *Bridgerton* now just lets me escape from reality and live in a world that's so different from the one I'm living in now.

"This isn't going to end well, is it?"

Dallas hums thoughtfully. "I wish I had the answer for you, Parker. All I know is that I'm really fucking proud of you."

"Why?" I ask, genuinely curious, because I'm not sure what I did to warrant those words. But Dallas has always looked out for me, even when I didn't want him to, and I've always looked up to him. He was never afraid to stand up for what he wanted, even to our own father. He's sacrificed a lot for others, both in service to his country and for the people he cares about. And the love he has for his wife has turned him into a man I respect immensely, even though he still doesn't know how to mind his own fucking business.

I wanted to be that same type of man for Sasha, but that just wasn't in the cards. And part of that was my own fucking fault.

"Because you didn't run from this," Dallas says, bringing me back. "You could have easily bailed and left Cashlynn to figure it out on her own, and no one would have blamed you."

I stare out at the street. "Believe me, I wanted to."

"But you didn't. You're helping her out, and I think on some level, it's because you understand her decision more than you realize."

"What do you mean?"

"You'll figure it out." He says something to Willow again, before coming back on the line. "I've gotta go. Husband duty calls."

"Ha. Better you than me."

"You say that now, but when you get to show up every day for the one person you can't live without, you might just change your tune." With that, he ends the call, leaving me alone with his words.

The thing is, I did have someone to show up for, someone I thought I loved and would do anything for. And I did—at least, I thought I did. Looking back at it now, I can see that even though I gave her everything I could, it wasn't enough.

That's why I have to keep my distance from Cashlynn. I'll count down the days until I get my life back, and I'll keep my heart out of it. Because when you go above and beyond for someone, you run the risk of getting crushed in the process.

Chapter Six

Parker

"Fuck!" Jolting upright, I blink away the memory of the morning my life changed forever. Shoving the blankets off, I swing my legs out of bed and head straight to the bathroom.

I hate waking up before my body is ready, especially when my heart feels like it's trying to break out of my ribcage. I haven't had that dream about Sasha in months, and now my brain decides to conjure it up again?

As I stare at myself in the mirror, the same dread that always accompanies those memories flows through me. And the fact that Cashlynn is moving in today doesn't help. I'm not ready for this.

It's been four years since I've lived with someone else. Four years of keeping my space exactly how I like it, of keeping my life simple and controlled. Sex is one thing, but living with her will be a whole different level. I blow out a breath, gripping the sink to steady myself. I can't let her get under my skin, but I already know that's going to be easier said than done.

After a workout in the garage and a quick shower, I head to the kitchen to make a cup of coffee. I'm dropping a K-Cup into the machine just as the doorbell rings.

Bracing myself and mourning my last moments of solitude, I head for the door. I open it to find Cashlynn standing there in a red two-piece workout set that's practically painted on her skin, leaving little to the imagination.

Fucking hell.

"Good morning, roomie!" she says, way too fucking cheerfully. I'm not a morning person, and the fact that she apparently is might be yet another source of conflict for us.

"Good morning," I say gruffly. I step aside to let her in, shutting the door with a sigh as she breezes past me.

"Oh my gosh! Your house is beautiful, Parker." She sets her duffle bag by the door and starts to look around as I stare at her bag on the floor.

"Is this all you brought?"

"No, I have more in my car." Still taking in everything, her gaze roams over the white kitchen cabinets, the gray countertops, the large center island, and then moves to the living room—black furniture, gray carpet with perfect vacuum lines, and a single vanilla-scented candle on the coffee table in front of the bookshelves flanking the TV. When she's done assessing my home, she turns back to me and says, "It's so…clean."

"I like things clean," I say, not elaborating further. If you ask my siblings, I'm the type-A, anal-retentive one, but honestly, messes give me anxiety. Therefore, there is very little in my home to make a mess of. The walls are fairly bare, everything is always in its proper place, and I always pick up after myself. I like things a certain way—sue me.

"Well, I will tread carefully, then." She drags her hand along the island countertop and before stepping closer. "Thank you again, Parker. I know I'm disrupting your life and invading your space, but I want you to know that I'm extremely grateful. I probably sound like a broken record, but I mean it." She places her hand on my chest, staring up at me with those amber-colored eyes of hers—the same ones I was transfixed by the moment I met her.

"You're welcome, Cashlynn." Needing space from her, especially her citrus and vanilla scent, I take a step back and clear my throat. "Let me show you to your room."

Technically, if we were really engaged, we'd be sharing a room. But, for my own peace of mind, Cashlynn will be sleeping down the hall from me. It's the only way I'll survive the next four months. Plus, it's not like there are fucking cameras in my house to verify our relationship is legitimate.

No. When we're home, we need to keep our distance.

Yup. That's rule number four.

When I open the door to the guest room, I instantly feel uneasy. "I don't have many guests, so sorry that it's not more homey."

Cashlynn steps inside, glancing around at the sparse space—a queen bed with fresh sheets, a single nightstand in the corner—and then spins to face me. "It's fine. I don't need much." Then she turns to the window. "And the lighting in here is amazing." She walks up to the window and stares out at the street with a smile. "Yeah, this is perfect."

I cross my arms and lean against the doorjamb, studying her. She's smiling, relaxed, and acting as if her moving into my home is some kind of vacation, not an upheaval of her life. "Are you always this happy?"

She glances at me over her shoulder and arches a brow. "Are you always this grumpy?"

"I'm not grumpy."

"Ha. Okay." She waves me off with a grin.

"Seriously. How are you so cheery today? We're wrapped up in this lie for months now, and you're acting like today's your birthday or something."

She ponders her next thought as she stares at me. "Not that you'd understand, but I had an epiphany last night while I was lying on the twin bed in my dad's guest room."

"And what was that?"

"For the first time in my life, I don't have the weight of responsibility resting on my shoulders." She sighs, but her lips are curved up. "I mean, I know I have to make things happen starting tomorrow, but *I* get to choose what that will be." She shakes her head, looking at me. "I've never had that kind of freedom before, Parker. And because of you, I get the chance to change the trajectory of my future. So yes, I'm cheerful today. And I'm not going to stop letting you know that I appreciate everything you're sacrificing for me."

When she says things like that, it makes me want to unlock the cage I've built around my heart and maybe even hand her the key. Let her show me what it might feel like to live freely for a change instead of keeping everything in perfect fucking order like I've done since Sasha left.

"By the way, while it's on my mind, I wanted to talk to you about rent," Cashlynn says, pulling me from my convoluted thoughts.

"Rent?" I ask, frowning.

"Yeah. I'm barging into your life and your home, so I want to contribute."

I shake my head, holding up a hand. "That's not necessary."

She crosses her arms, giving me a determined look. "Yes, it is. It's the least I can do. Plus, I'm a pretty good cook. Maybe feeding you regularly will soften you up a bit." She pats my stomach playfully and my abs tense on reflex, triggering the memory of her nails raking down my skin as she sank to her knees that night.

I shake off the thought quickly. "I appreciate that, Cashlynn, but—"

"How about I play you for it?" she asks, cutting me off.

The corner of my mouth quirks up, even though I try to fight it. "You want to play me for it?"

She nods. "Yup. I think it's only fair. But this time, no secret moves." She points a finger at me, narrowing her gaze.

I shrug, pushing off the doorjamb and stepping close, leaving just enough space between us for our hands. "Fine."

She smiles mischievously up at me. "Great."

"On three?"

"Yup." She positions her hand in front of her as I do the same.

"One, two..."

"Three," we say simultaneously as she lays her hand flat, indicating paper, and I show scissors.

"Looks like your money is no good here," I tell her, still smiling. But when I catch myself, I quickly reset my expression to its usual scowl.

"Fine. But at least let me cook for you."

"Sounds like a fair trade."

She rubs her palms together. "Excellent. Now, can you help me grab the rest of my stuff, please?"

"Of course." Trying not to stare at her ass too hard as she walks away from me, and failing miserably, I follow her out to her car where we take turns unloading boxes, bags of clothes, and blank canvases.

"What's with the canvases?" I ask.

She raises an eyebrow, smirking. "Do you not know what canvases are for, Parker? Spent too much time with animals to understand the concept of art?"

"No need to get sarcastic, Cashlynn."

"I thought sarcasm was your language." she teases, dropping the last box in her bedroom before standing tall again, brushing hair from her face that's fallen from her ponytail.

"Just answer the question."

"Well, hopefully I can fill those canvases with some artwork to go in my gallery."

"You have an art gallery?"

She smiles wide and then plants her hands on her hips. "Not yet, but at the end of four months, I'm hoping I will."

Pieces of the puzzle start clicking into place. "That's what your dream is? To open an art gallery?" I ask, trying to wrap my head around it. But Cashlynn must sense the disbelief in my voice because her smile fades and she becomes defensive.

"Look, I don't need your criticism, Parker. I'll get enough of that from my dad. This is what I want to do. I want to help people tap into their creativity, to explore talents and find art that makes them look at the world differently. I don't expect you to understand since your world seems pretty black and white." She spreads her arms wide, gesturing at my immaculate house. "But I have an entire business plan drawn up. I've been thinking about this for years, and I think Carrington Cove is the perfect place for something like this."

"I'm not being critical, Cashlynn," I say apologetically. "I'm just trying to understand."

She takes a shaky breath, her bottom lip trembling. "Well, I don't need you to understand," she says, her voice barely above a whisper. "But at least try to be supportive, okay?"

Before I realize what I'm doing, I'm walking toward her, tipping her chin up so she's looking me dead in the eye. "Isn't that what I'm doing as the fake fiancé?" There's a hint of humor in my voice, and thankfully, it brings a faint smile to her face. "Being supportive?"

She swallows roughly. "Contrary to what you might think, I'm not stupid."

"I never said you were." Our eyes remain locked, but when my gaze dips down to her lips, I instantly take a step back, needing the distance.

Cashlynn inhales deeply and then turns back to her boxes. "I'm going to start unpacking."

Warily, I begin to retreat from the room. "Yeah, okay. I guess I'll leave you to it."

She nods but doesn't look back, so I walk out of her room, closing the door behind me.

"Jesus," I mutter to myself as I make my way back into the kitchen to retrieve my now cold coffee. And I could use a cold shower—because after just thirty minutes of being in the same space as Cashlynn O'Neil, I'm already hot and bothered, and not in a good way.

***

I'm sitting on the couch, flipping through the television channels when Cashlynn emerges from her room a few hours later.

"Hey."

"Hey."

She bites her bottom lip before speaking. "I'm starving. Want me to grab something for lunch?" She juts her thumb toward the front door.

Looking up at her, I shake my head. "Not necessary. I have food here." Standing from the couch, I head into the kitchen, aware of her trailing behind me. When I reach the fridge, I turn around to speak to her and we bump into each other, her breasts brushing against my chest.

"Fuck."

"Sorry," she says quickly.

"I didn't realize you were right behind me," I say, slightly irritated as I open the fridge and Cashlynn peers over my shoulder.

"I was just trying to see inside."

I sigh, pinching the bridge of my nose. "I'm just not used to someone else being here."

She places her hand on my shoulder. "Parker, I'm—"

"I have stuff for sandwiches," I say, not letting her say sorry for the thousandth time.

"Uh, sandwiches sound great."

Cashlynn moves to one of the stools on the other side of the island as I take out turkey, cheese, and the rest of the fixings. As I start assembling the sandwiches, she drums her fingers on the counter.

"So, not to put any more stress on you, but I think we need to get our story straight."

I peer up at her. "What story?"

"You know, the story of how we met, how we started dating...all of that." She taps the counter in front of me. "My father wants to have dinner with us, and we need to be on the same page."

I nod, already knowing this was coming. "Okay. Let's do it."

"Well," she starts, "I think we should stick as close to the truth as possible. Easier to remember."

"Makes sense," I say, turning my attention back to the sandwiches.

"So, we say we met on the plane like we did, skipping the part about the sex, obviously." My eyes dart up to hers, and she licks her lips as her eyes dip to my mouth. And I'd bet good money we're thinking about the same fucking thing right now." "But, uh, maybe we say we exchanged numbers and kept in contact, and that's when I realized you worked with my dad."

Clearing my throat, I nod while silently telling my dick to stand down. *Fuck, this is going to be a long four months.* "Okay…"

"We didn't want to say anything and get him riled up if this"—she gestures between us—"didn't amount to anything. But after you visited me in Philly a few times, we realized this wasn't just some casual thing—it was real."

I swallow roughly. "Sounds good. I've had a few trips out of town here and there over the past year, so that's believable."

"And on your last trip, you popped the question and suggested I move to Carrington Cove to start our life together, and to be closer to my dad." She winks. "I figure it might give you some brownie points if it was more your idea."

I turn and grab two plates from the cupboard, setting the finished sandwiches on them. Sliding one across the counter to Cashlynn, I say, "Not sure brownie points are enough to get me back on his good side."

"My dad's toughest on people he cares about," she says. "Believe me, it's why I'm not telling him what I'm actually up to yet."

I take a bite of my sandwich, chewing thoughtfully. "Let's go back to your gallery idea for a second."

"So you can criticize it?"

"No, Cashlynn." I pin her with my stare. "I want to know more about it. Truly. If you were willing to quit your job and move down here to pursue this, then it must mean a lot to you."

Her eyes fall to her plate, but when she looks up, there's determination in her eyes. "It is."

"So, tell me. What are you envisioning?"

She wipes her mouth with her napkin before taking a deep breath like she's been preparing for this. "I don't just want to open an art gallery or studio, I want it to be a full experience, and maybe even offer design on the side, like for décor or graphic arts. I want it to offer a full art experience—classes for all ages, showcases for up-and-coming artists, a space for locals to sell their own art, paint nights for kids and families, birthday parties, or girls' nights. I want people to be able to come in and tap into their creativity, whether it's through sculpting clay, painting, or just appreciating the work of others. I want to help people find their spark." She finally pauses to take a breath. "I have so many other thoughts, but basically, I want a space that anyone can walk into and find a creative outlet in, or an appreciation for the world around them."

I blink a few times, trying to process everything. "Wow."

She chuckles. "Wow?"

I cross my arms and lean back against the fridge. "Everything you just described is a far cry from practicing law, that's for damn sure."

"Ha. I know."

"But your eyes lit up when you were talking." I tilt my head. "You didn't look like that when you talked about your job on the plane."

She shakes her head, a small, bitter smile playing at her lips. "I was good at it, Parker, but it didn't make me feel fulfilled. Not even in the slightest. My dad wanted that for me, so I did it to make him happy. When you're raised by a single father after your mom dies, there's a part of you that's terrified of disappointing him."

"Why would he be disappointed in you for this, Cashlynn?" I ask, not fully understanding everything. "If this is what you want to do with your life, why wouldn't he support that?"

She takes a deep breath as her eyes fill with tears. "Because my mother was an artist, and it was her love for art that killed her."

"Fuck," I say, my voice low as the last piece of the puzzle snaps into place. "How?"

Her eyes drop down to her plate. "It was a car accident. A gallery three hours away from our home in Florida wanted to showcase her art. She was so excited. I remember her dancing around the kitchen with me and my dad to *The Chicken in Black* by Johnny Cash, joking she'd no longer have to rob a bank for us because we were going to be rich once she sold her art." She laughs lightly at the memory, but then her smile fades again. "She left the next morning...and never made it to the gallery."

I push a hand through my hair, hating that this is something else that connects us, but now's not the time to get into that. "I'm so sorry."

"Thank you. I was sixteen," she says, sniffling as she reins in her emotions. "It was a life-changing moment, for sure. And up until then, I was open about my creative spirit that mirrored my mother's. I was always drawing, painting, or building something with my hands. But when she died, my dad changed completely. He packed up all of her things, including her art, and pretended she never existed. I knew he blamed her love of art for her death, so I hid that part of myself from him. I didn't want him to hurt any more than he already was."

I nod. "I understand that more than you know." She stares back at me, waiting for me to elaborate, but I don't. "So he pushed you to be a lawyer instead?"

"He wanted me to go to college and study something logical, something stable. Basically, the complete opposite of what my mom did. And I was always eager to work hard in school, so it made sense. But I just never loved it. I continued to draw and paint on the side, but over the past few years, I've grown resentful of the career I felt I was forced into."

"So, why Carrington Cove? I mean, you could open a gallery anywhere."

She inhales deeply. "Because no matter how scared I am to do this and what my father might think, he's here. And over the past year, I've researched the town. Beth keeps me in the loop about things too, so I knew that nothing like this existed here." She shrugs. "It just felt right."

"Now that you're here, why can't you just tell your dad?" I think that's the piece I'm having the most trouble understanding. This is her father, the one person who should support her no matter what.

She pushes her plate to the side. "It seems like the logical thing to do, right?" I nod. "But if I don't have something to show him, something he can see with his own two eyes, he's never going to support it. My father is a man who loves hard, but is stubborn about things he believes in."

"Ha. I'm aware," I say, chuckling. I reach for my sandwich, finally taking another bite. "Okay. So, do you even know where to start with this?"

"I have a list," she says confidently. "And I'm starting tomorrow. I need to find a space, first and foremost, and when I was researching the town, I saw several properties for sale, so I'm going to start there."

An idea comes to mind, but I refrain from saying anything. I want to hear what else she has to say. "Then what?"

"Then I need to figure out branding and marketing materials. I'm sure I'll need to renovate the space to make it work with all of my ideas, so some construction will have to happen." She blows out a harsh breath. "There's a lot to do, but I can't do anything until I have a gallery space."

"Makes sense." At least she has a plan. Once she finds a spot, I have to believe the ball will really start rolling.

She picks up her sandwich again, taking another bite. "Okay, so what about dinner with my dad? Should we schedule it for tomorrow?"

I blow out a breath. "I can't tomorrow. It's Sunday, and I always have dinner with my family on Sundays."

"Oh." Her face falls a bit, but she recovers quickly. "Okay. No problem."

"Actually, you need to come with me."

Her eyes widen. "Go with you?"

"Yeah. I mean, it would be weird if I showed up without my fiancée, and I need to tell my mom before she hears it from someone else."

"Oh God." She bites her bottom lip. "Your mom is gonna hate me, isn't she?"

"Are you kidding? She'll probably try to formally adopt you," I say sarcastically.

Cashlynn chuckles, her shoulders relaxing. "That would be weird."

"I know, but I haven't dated anyone in four years, so showing up to dinner with you is going to make her fucking night."

She tilts her head, curiosity flickering in her amber eyes. "Why haven't you dated anyone?"

"I just haven't," I say, shrugging as I grab my plate and head to the living room.

"Does it have something to do with why you think no one will believe that we're engaged?" she presses, following me to the couch and sitting beside me.

"Drop it, Cashlynn."

"I need to know more about you if we're going to make this believable, Parker." She settles in right next to me, not giving me any fucking space. I glare at her as I take a bite of my sandwich. "Am I wrong?"

I have to admit to myself that she's right. But she doesn't need to know all the details. "Fine. I was engaged to someone else, but it didn't work out."

Her eyes widen. "Oh."

"Yeah, and that's all you need to know, okay?" I face the television and finish my sandwich, but I can feel Cashlynn's eyes on me the whole time. Finally, I glance over at her. "What?"

"Nothing." She turns to face the TV too.

"Are you sure? You look like you've got something to say."

Her head spins to me again. "I just..." Her brows draw together.

I'm growing more irritated by the second. "Spit it out, Cashlynn."

She sets her plate on the coffee table and tucks her legs under her, turning to face me with her elbow braced on the back of the couch and her head nestled in her hand. And fuck, she looks sexy—relaxed, open, unbelievably brave. She has no fucking clue how much I envy her courage.

"I guess I just don't understand how any woman could walk away from you."

Her words catch me off guard. "Maybe you just don't know me well enough," I say, swallowing down the lump in my throat.

She smiles as she studies me. "Not only are you one of the most considerate men I've ever met, agreeing to this fake engagement to help me, but..." Her eyes drop down to my lap, lingering there for a moment before lifting back to mine. "There's much more about you to appreciate than just intelligence and a kind heart." Standing from the couch, she looks down and winks at me. "Thanks for the sandwich, Parker."

My dick rises in my shorts as I peer over my shoulder and watch her walk back to her room, shutting the door softly. I groan, dragging a hand down my face.

There's no way I'm going to survive this arrangement—not when this woman is hell-bent on making me question whether I'm losing my mind...or if I actually want another woman for the first time in four years.

***

"Are you sure I look okay? I'm not overdressed?" Cashlynn smooths her dress down over her thighs, sitting in the passenger seat of my car as I drive to my mom's house Sunday afternoon.

"You look great."

Great is not a strong enough word, considering how my body reacted when she came out of her bedroom when it was time to leave.

She's wearing an olive green sweater dress that clings to every curve, paired with knee-high black leather boots. Her blonde hair falls in loose waves over her shoulders, and her lips are painted the same soft pink as the day we met.

Saliva pooled in my mouth the moment I saw her, reminding me that no matter how much I try to ignore it, my attraction to her is still there. It's only been a few days since she came to town, and already, I'm wishing there weren't so many complications between us—her being my boss's daughter, this fake engagement bullshit, and the history that won't stop haunting me. If none of that existed, maybe I wouldn't feel so damn guilty for wanting her the way I do.

Unfortunately, that's not the case.

"So, what should I expect?" Cashlynn speaks again as we close in on our destination.

"Well, my mother is one hell of a cook, so expect lots of food."

She smiles at that, patting her stomach. "I have no problem eating."

I think back to how I watched her devour the tacos she made last night and how much I stared at her mouth each time she licked her fingers clean.

Fuck, I have issues.

"All my siblings will be there, including Grady and his wife, Scottie. Grady is Astrid's brother, and Astrid is married to my brother, Penn, so he's basically family at this point."

"I'm afraid I won't be able to keep all of these people straight. I have no idea what it's like to have a big family. It's been just me and my dad."

The corner of my mouth twitches as I turn on my mom's street. "Well, my family is loud and loves to give each other shit, so don't be afraid to give it right back."

"I am not about to insult your family, Parker."

Parking along the curb, I turn off the engine and turn to face her. "They won't be insulted, believe me. In fact, you'll fit right in." I reach for her hand, trying to comfort her. I shouldn't be touching her, especially since we're alone. But knowing she's nervous is making *me* more nervous. We have to be on the same page for this to work. "You'll be fine. Just watch out for my sister."

"Why?"

"Because Hazel loves to insert herself into my business. Don't be surprised if she pulls you to the side and starts drilling you with questions."

Cashlynn blinks. "Is there alcohol inside? I think I might need it."

I chuckle. "There's always wine. But I promise, tonight won't be as bad as flying."

"That's not funny!" she calls out as I climb out of the car.

I walk around to her side, opening the door and offering my hand to help her out. She takes it, and I keep hold of it as I lead her to the front door, reminding myself this is all for show.

I brace myself for the inquisition that I know is going to come from my mother as I reach for the doorknob. Before I can even open the door, however, Mom swings it open with a borderline terrifying smile on her face. "Parker Eric Sheppard! You brought a date?"

"Uh, hi, Mom," I say, trying to assess if she's mad or elated. "This is Cashlynn."

She turns to Cashlynn and pulls her in for a hug. "You must have a heart of gold."

"And why's that?" I ask.

"Because clearly, she's broken down your walls if you're bringing her here." My mother shoots me a glare and then smiles back at Cashlynn.

Cashlynn darts her eyes to mine, and then smiles back at my mom. "It's nice to meet you, Mrs. Sheppard."

"Please call me Katherine." My mom pulls her inside a little too eagerly, and I follow them. My entire family is all gathered, staring in our direction as my mother announces our arrival. "Everyone, this is Cashlynn."

"We know, Mom. We've already met Parker's fiancée," Dallas replies, and all the women in the room spin their heads to look at me.

"Fiancée?" they echo simultaneously, Hazel's voice the loudest, of course.

My mom studies me. "Wait. You're—you're engaged?"

I stiffen under their scrutiny, but Cashlynn steps closer, looping her arm through mine and squeezing lightly. And thank God she does—because having everyone's eyes on me is making me feel like I'm on stage at a talent show butt-ass naked.

"We are. I'm sorry you had to find out this way, Katherine, but Parker and I met a year ago, and I just recently moved to Carrington Cove so we could be together. My dad is actually Parker's boss."

Hazel's eyes bug out. "You're Dr. O'Neil's daughter?"

"Yep."

Dallas walks over to us and clasps my shoulder, leaning in to whisper, "Better to get that detail out of the way now." Then, he addresses everyone. "Is anyone else hungry? I have a very hungry pregnant wife, so how about we make our way to the table?"

Willow nods and rubs her belly. "I could eat a freaking elephant right now." Then she looks at Cashlynn and smiles. "It's nice to meet you."

Cashlynn smiles in return. "Likewise."

Everyone moves to the dining room, taking their seats at the table and introducing themselves to Cashlynn as we settle in. The kids have their own table off to the side, where Bentley and Lilly, Astrid and Penn's children, sit with Chase, Scottie's teenage son. And even though Chase barely fits in the chairs at the small table, he plays along since Lilly loves having him near.

My sister and mom finish the final touches on the food, and soon we're all digging in, filling our plates with homemade lasagna, salad, and garlic bread.

"So, I think I speak for everyone when I ask, how the hell did this happen?" Hazel says as the clinking of silverware dies down around us.

"It's a long story," I reply, growing irritated. I knew this was coming, but now that it's here, I feel completely unprepared.

"We've got all night, Parker," Hazel counters with a smirk.

Grady, Penn, and Dallas all laugh under their breath, clearly enjoying my discomfort.

Fuckers.

"Parker comforted me on a flight over a year ago," Cashlynn jumps in smoothly, saving me from launching across the table. "I'm terrified of flying and he made sure I was okay the entire time."

My mother reaches for my hand and squeezes. "That sounds like my Parker."

Cashlynn smiles. "And that night we had dinner and really connected, so we kept in touch. It wasn't until later we realized he worked for my father, but by then, we already had feelings for each other, so we kept it between us while we navigated our relationship. We were tired of being apart, and when my father fell last week, I took it as a sign it was time to move here permanently."

"I heard about Dr. O'Neil," Astrid says. "A few customers were talking about it in the bakery. Is he okay?"

My sister-in-law's bakery, Smells Like Sugar, has the best fucking desserts and pastries in Carrington Cove. Willow practically had a panic attack when they ran out of blueberry muffins one day.

"Luckily, he didn't break anything. But it was a wake-up call that I need to be here as he gets older." Cashlynn reaches for my hand and squeezes it. "And Parker being here made it feel like this was all meant to be."

Man, she's laying it on thick.

"So you're engaged now?" Hazel presses.

"That's what we said, isn't it?" I reply, giving her a warning look not to question it further.

"Then where's your ring?" she asks smugly, pleased with herself and reminding me more and more of slimy Seth the longer we sit here.

"I proposed on a whim. We're picking one out this week," I say casually, even though the one I have in my pocket will be on Cashlynn's finger before the night's over. "Anyway, how's business, Penn?" I ask, trying to get the focus off of me and Cashlynn.

My brother wipes his mouth with his napkin. "Couldn't be better."

"What is it that you do?" Cashlynn asks.

"I'm a contractor. Mostly, I flip houses and turn them into rental properties."

Cashlynn leans forward in her seat, eyes lighting up. "So you know your way around a hammer and some nails?"

Everyone around the table chuckles. "You could say that."

"Then apparently, I'm marrying into the right family. I might just need your services soon."

Penn nods. "I'm sure we could work something out. What do you need?"

"Well, I'm not exactly sure yet, but I have a business venture I'm pursuing. Once I find the right space, I'm sure I'm going to need some renovations."

Willow pipes up. "A business venture? Do tell."

"I was actually going to suggest you talk to Willow about your plans, babe," I say to Cashlynn, reaching my arm around her shoulders and stroking her skin as if I do it all the time.

Babe? Where the hell did that come from?

My sister's eyes dart to my hand and then back to me, a hint of intrigue on her face. I slowly drop my arm and return back to my plate.

Cashlynn turns to face me. "Really?"

"Yeah. She owns her own advertising business, so I'm sure she could give you some advice."

Willow chimes in, "Let's talk after dinner. I want to hear all about your plans."

"I would love that, thank you."

The rest of dinner is filled with updates on everyone's lives, including making some last minute decisions for Dallas and Willow's baby shower next month.

Once the plates are cleared, my mom stands up and claps her hands. "Who wants s'mores?"

The kids cheer, and then my mom turns to Cashlynn. "Would you mind helping me grab the supplies?"

"Of course," Cashlynn says, rising from her chair.

Hazel hangs back with me to help clean up while everyone else heads outside to the deck, gathering around the propane fire pit. By the time my mom and Cashlynn join them with the graham crackers, marshmallows, and chocolate, the laughter is already in full swing.

I'm standing at the sink, washing the dishes as I stare out the window that overlooks the backyard, observing my family all smiling and laughing, looking perfectly content in their lives while mine feels like it's unraveling, one lie at a time.

"So," my sister says, breaking my thoughts, "are you ready to tell me what the hell is going on?"

I stare down at the dishes, scrubbing the same pot for another minute. "What do you mean?"

She places her hand on my shoulder. "Give me more credit please, Parker. You expect me to believe that you're engaged to Dr. O'Neil's daughter when none of us even knew you were seeing anyone?"

Damn. I should have known that Hazel wouldn't buy it.

"We told you. It was long distance."

Hazel huffs out a laugh. "You must think I'm stupid."

I sigh, dropping the sponge into the water and turning to face my sister. "I don't think you're stupid. There's just—"

"It's fake, isn't it?" she asks, cutting me off.

For a second, I debate trying to persuade her. But Hazel's relentless, and honestly, I could use her advice. "Not all of it," I admit, trying to gauge her reaction.

Her expression softens, concern replacing her earlier suspicion. "What's going on, Parker?"

I spend the next few minutes filling her in on how everything between Cashlynn and me transpired. By the time I finish, she's smiling at me like this is the best thing she's heard in her entire life.

"Oh, Jesus. This is great."

"Thanks for the support," I say dryly.

Her face softens as I dry the last dish and place it back in the cupboard. "Sorry, but I actually think this might be good for you."

"It's not like that. Nothing is going to happen between me and Cashlynn. This is temporary, just long enough for both of us to get what we want."

Hazel crosses her arms over her chest. "And what is it that you want?"

"The practice," I say, reminding myself of my goal in all of this and not these lingering feelings for Cashlynn that seem to be growing with each day that we're together. "Were you not listening?"

"So after this is all said and done, what happens? You two just go back to your lives like nothing changed?"

Honestly, I haven't thought about that. What *does* happen once Dr. O'Neil knows the truth and Cashlynn has her business up and running?

"Yeah, I guess," I say finally.

"She's really gorgeous," my sister says, raising a brow like she's daring me to deny it.

"I know what you're doing."

Her hands fly up as though she's innocent. "What?"

Shaking my head, I start to wipe down the counters. "You know a relationship isn't an option for me, Hazel."

"But you are attracted to her, aren't you?"

"Of course I am. I slept with her, didn't I?"

"Then why not see if there's something else there?"

"I'm heading outside," I snap, my teeth clenched. I need to get away from this conversation. I'm seconds from escaping out the backdoor when her voice stops me.

"Fine. But if you're not willing to open yourself up again, Parker, you're never going to find the Charlotte to your George."

I whirl around and arch a brow at her. "A *Bridgerton* reference? Really?"

She flashes me a knowing smile. "You know the spinoff of their story was the best."

I sigh and pull my sister in for a hug. "You drive me nuts, you know that?"

"Of course. But I also know I'm right." She leans back and looks up at me. "Cashlynn might have started this charade, but *maybe* it was meant to be."

I shake off her romantic notions as we make our way out back to join the rest of the family. If there's one thing I know about my sister, it's that she has always rooted for love. It's partly why she captures pictures for a living—the hope that one day she'll find someone to look at her the way her clients do on their wedding day or during a family photo session.

And there was once a time where I had that same optimism, but one woman showed me just how ugly love could really be.

As I walk toward the fire pit, I catch sight of Cashlynn throwing her head back in laughter, the glow of the flames dancing across her face as she talks with my brothers and their wives, eager to get to know them.

Fuck, she really is gorgeous—and funny, and smart. She's sarcastic, witty, and makes my blood fucking boil.

But is this really her true self?

That's the thing that's eating at me. Because I've been burned before—by a woman who had demons she never let me see until it was too late.

I'm not sure I could survive another.

Chapter Seven

Cashlynn

"Our dog had babies, but Parker went to school and told everyone she had rabies and he was going to give them to his friends." Penn finishes his story, making everyone around the fire laugh.

Parker comes up behind me, placing his hand on the back of my chair. For a second, I wish he'd touch me again, but I can tell that he's been tense all evening while putting on this act, with the exception of when he put his arm around me at dinner, that is.

A shiver runs through my body at the memory.

Parker adjusts his glasses on his nose as he looks across the fire at his brother. "Ha. Ha. I'm so glad everyone is getting a laugh at my expense."

"It's kind of ironic, though," Dallas interjects. "You ended up being a vet, so I sincerely hope you know the difference between babies and rabies now."

"He certainly didn't know the difference between a human and animal breast pump in the baby store that day," Grady chimes in. Penn and Dallas fall apart with laughter.

"I feel like that's the next story I need to hear," I say, trying to hide my amusement, but Parker glares down at me.

"Knock it off, boys," Katherine admonishes, shaking her head at her sons and Grady, who might as well be one of them.

"Hey, he was laughing plenty when Penn was sharing stories about me to Willow," Dallas whines, sounding more like a child than a grown man.

I guess siblings never stop making fun of one another. I'm speculating here, of course, since I never had this—siblings to tease or to share the heat when you're in trouble. As much as I love my dad, sometimes being an only child sucks. Maybe that's why I can't bring myself to tell him the truth about my plans yet.

Parker flips Dallas off. I reach back behind me and grab his hand, squeezing it while looking up at him and whisper, "I think it's cute."

"The rabies part, I assume?"

Giggling, I nod. "Yeah, but now I have questions about the breast pump."

His eyes dip down and find mine, a soft smile playing on his lips. "At least someone finds it cute." Then he leans down and lowers his voice. "You doing okay?"

Our eyes lock, and for a second, I imagine closing the space between us and kissing him, just to see how he'd react. But I chicken out. "Yep," I reply simply.

"So, Cashlynn, are you ready to tell me about your business idea?" Willow asks as she stands from her chair, rubbing her growing belly and pulling me from my moment with my fake fiancé.

"Oh, uh, sure."

"Let's go inside so we can talk," she suggests, gesturing toward the house. As I stand to follow, Parker stops me, catching my hand.

"Willow is smart and very financially savvy. Don't be afraid to ask her any questions you have, okay?"

"I won't."

He leans forward and kisses me on the temple, taking me by surprise. But then I remember our agreement about touching—only in front of others. I remind myself it's all part of the act. Still, the flutter in my chest feels too real.

"I'll be out here if you need me."

Releasing his grip on my hand, he takes the seat I just vacated as I head inside, willing my heart to slow down. I find Willow sitting on the couch. "I hope you don't mind being pulled away from the fun outside," she says as she eases down, adjusting herself. "The couch is just so much more comfortable."

"Not at all. How far along are you, if you don't mind my asking?" I take a seat on the opposite end of the couch.

"Seven months," she replies, smoothing her hand over her stomach again. "I'm due in the beginning of May, but most days I feel that if I get any bigger, this kid might fall out of my vagina before then." We both laugh. "So, I hope you don't mind, but Dallas told me a little bit about your and Parker's arrangement."

Nerves race through me. "Oh."

Willow holds up a hand. "Don't worry, I'm not judging at all. And your secret is safe with me," she says with a wink. "But when you mentioned a business idea, I actually got really excited. I've invested in a few businesses since I moved here two years ago, and I love supporting other women with great ideas who want to be their own bosses."

I take a deep breath. "Well, I think my idea is solid, and there's certainly a need for what I want to do here in Carrington Cove, so…"

"Then tell me what you're envisioning."

I spend the next several minutes explaining my ideas to Willow. By the time I'm done, I don't recall if she said one word while I was rambling. For a second, I feel like I got too excited, but then she clears her throat, and shocks me. "I'm in."

"What?"

"I love it, Cashlynn." Her eyes light up. "Small coastal towns like this need a space like you are envisioning. I think it's perfect for locals and tourists alike."

"Really?"

She nods. "Absolutely. In fact, I can connect you with Pam over at Cove Realty tomorrow so you can start looking at properties. And you already know if you need any renovations, Penn's your guy. I have a background in advertising and multiple friends in marketing, so we can discuss those things once you have a space."

My jaw nearly hits the floor. "You're serious? You're willing to invest in me just like that?" I say, snapping my fingers in the air.

Willow reaches for my hand. "Yes. I may not know you on a personal level, but I trust my gut. You've clearly put thought into this, and I can tell you're determined. Plus, I could use the distraction while waiting for this baby to make an appearance," she explains, rubbing her stomach again.

I sink back into the cushion, still trying to process my shock. "I...don't even know what to say. Seriously, I can't thank you enough."

She winks again. "I'm just as excited about this as you are." Then her smile falters, and her tone shifts. "Now, what's really going on between you and Parker?"

Before I can answer, Hazel's voice cuts in, startling us both. "Yes, please. I need your version—because the one I got from my brother was full of grunting and denial."

I stare up at the youngest Sheppard sibling. "What do you mean?"

Hazel rolls her eyes and moves to sit on the loveseat next to the couch. "I know my brother well enough to know he wouldn't just show up out of the blue with a fiancé. Although that little display of affection out there?" she says, pointing outside. "That was pretty convincing. Did you have to coach my brother on that?"

I dart my eyes back and forth between Willow and Hazel, then let out a heavy sigh. "It's complicated."

Willow takes a sip from her glass of water. "Cashlynn, if there's one thing we understand, it's complicated relationships. You should hear the story sometime of how Dallas and I met."

Hazel nods. "It's a doozy. And Penn and Astrid take the cake, literally and figuratively, with their unrequited, friends-to-lovers tale," she says through a laugh. "Grady and Scottie weren't much better—surprise pregnancy, her son breaking into his garage..." Hazel shakes her head with a laugh. "Believe me, whatever you and Parker have going on? You're in good company."

I take in her words, stunned by the amount of drama this family seems to attract. Hazel smirks and leans forward. "Now, *me*, on the other hand? I could regale you with terrible dating stories all night. My love life is a dumpster fire." She pauses dramatically. "I've only had one real boyfriend, and he was more into chasing girls at the gym than me."

"I, uh..." Words evade me as I contemplate what to say.

Hazel doesn't let up, though. "Come on. There has to be more than either of you is letting on." She waggles her eyebrows. "You didn't just come here for your dad and this business venture, did you?"

I sigh, pinching the bridge of my nose. "Honestly, I don't know what I was expecting, but it sure as hell wasn't pretending to be Parker's fiancée."

"We know how that came to be, but what about the two of you? I mean, this isn't some cut and dry business transaction. You guys slept together when you met, right?" Willow says. "So, why'd it end there?"

I close my eyes and blow out a breath. "I ran off afterward."

Hazel tries to hide her laugh. "Oh God, I'm afraid to ask because it's my brother, but…was it…bad?"

Shooting up from my seat, I say, "No! Not at all. Quite the opposite actually. I'm not usually the one-night-stand type of girl, and with him, it was…" I glance away, remembering how insane our chemistry was, how strong and viral he felt as our bodies writhed against one another, how he made me feel safe both on the plane *and* in bed.

Willow clears her throat, pulling me from my thoughts. "So, do you want more with him?"

I shrug, not wanting to let on just how much being near him again has stirred up feelings I've been trying to ignore. Denying these feelings has felt more overwhelming than all of the other choices hovering over me. "Parker has made it clear he's unavailable and just doing this to help me, so…"

Hazel scoffs. "Sorry, Cashlynn, but my brother wouldn't even be able to admit to himself if he had feelings for you, let alone anyone else, even if they were holding a match to his balls." Willow snorts. "Has he told you much about his past?"

I look between her and Willow. "Only that he was engaged once and it didn't work out."

Hazel sighs. "Well, at least he admitted that much."

"Is there more I should know?"

Willow looks at Hazel and then directs her gaze back to me. "It's not our story to tell, and I wasn't around when it happened, but I can tell you that Parker was scarred from that relationship. Dallas worries about him a lot—says he's not the same person he was before. If you do want more with him, it's going to require some patience."

I shake my head, not liking where this conversation is headed, letting my guilt for talking him into this consume me even more. As soon as Parker agreed to this fake engagement, I told myself to shove down the feelings I've been denying for a year, especially every time my father brought Parker up in conversation.

I never should have slept with him. I should have thanked him for comforting me and walked away, pretending I never knew who he was. But the second he offered to play rock, paper, scissors to hold my hand, I was powerless over what happened next. How can a man that showed such compassion, humor, and lust-filled need like he did, not see that he's capable and deserving of being in a relationship again?

My focus is supposed to be on my gallery, not my love life. But being Parker's fake fiancée is making me wonder if I could possibly have it all by making this move—the job and the man.

Could Parker and I turn this into something real? Was our initial connection enough to build a relationship on? Or are we better off just following through with our promises to each other and moving on afterward?

Hazel taps her chin thoughtfully. "No, I think patience will get her nowhere. If she's going to make him admit that he wants her, she needs to be a little more...direct."

Willow beams as she looks over at Hazel. "What are you thinking?"

I'm not sure I like where their train of thought is headed. "Look, I know you two are trying to play matchmaker and all, but honestly, I can't afford to push him away. I need him to keep pretending to be my fiancé until my business is up and running."

Hazel leans forward in her seat. "My brother wants you, Cashlynn. It's written all over his face, and don't take this the wrong way, but you look at him like you want to jump his bones. You two have already slept together, so why not make the most of your arrangement?"

Willow chimes in. "Uh Hazel, it sounds like you're trying to pimp out your brother right now."

Hazel shrugs. "I just know what I see. Like with you and Dallas, and Penn and Astrid…" She rolls her eyes dramatically. "Those two gave everyone around them blue balls for years." Willow laughs. "And now Parker is living with a woman he clearly wants and is trying to be this saint when I know he's at war inside. I'm tired of him punishing himself for what happened with Sasha."

"Sasha?" I ask.

"His ex," she clarifies. *And now the ex has a name.* "I'm telling you, she did a number on him." Tilting her head at me, she narrows her eyes. "But I like you. My gut is telling me you've got your head on straight, you're driven, and you can actually take a joke. It's obvious you care about my brother, and sometimes people need a little push to get out of their own damn way."

"I appreciate that, but Parker clearly doesn't feel the same way."

"I can see why you think that, but I'm telling you, I know my brother." She winks at me. "Test him. Do something that you know will get a reaction out of him and see how he responds."

"Like what?" Willow asks before I can.

Hazel hums for a moment and then her eyes light up. "*Accidentally* spill something on his floor, and then whip off your shirt to clean it up."

Willow snorts. "Subtle."

"He might freak out on me," I say. "Have you seen his house? It's so clean, it looks like nobody lives there. He has freaking vacuum lines in his carpet."

Hazel nods, rolling her eyes. "I'm aware. He has always been a little high strung, but it got worse after Sasha... Like he tried to control everything around him because she left him in a tailspin and he didn't know which way was up."

My word. What did this woman do to him?

A slow grin spreads across Willow's face. "Oh my God. You know what you should do? Unplug all of his appliances when they aren't being used. It will drive him nuts."

Hazel tosses her head back in laughter. "Oh fuck, that will send him over the edge, for sure."

"Tell him it helps conserve energy." Willow joins in the laughter. "It's genius."

"I thought we were trying to get him to admit he wants me, not kill me?"

Hazel waves me off. "Same thing. Haven't you ever had hate sex?"

Heat rises to my cheeks and I drop my gaze to the floor. *Yeah, I'm not going there.* "I don't want him to dislike me any more than he already does."

"He doesn't. But getting under his skin is going to make him snap. And once he does, he might finally admit to himself that he wouldn't have agreed to this if deep down, he didn't care. Plus, you'll benefit from his frustration." She bounces her eyebrows again.

"I don't know..."

Hazel throws her hands up in defeat. "Look, do what you want, but I'm telling you, I know my brother." She leans forward again. "And I just want to see him happy."

"Want to see who happy?"

All three of us whip around to see Parker standing in the doorway, his hand on the knob and an unreadable expression on his face.

"You, big brother!" Hazel exclaims, jumping up from her seat a little too enthusiastically. "I can't believe you've been hiding this girl from us for the past year. You two are obviously so in love and I'm happy for you!"

Parker looks at his sister as if she's grown two heads. "Well..."

Willow stands up now, arching her back so she doesn't topple over. "And her business idea is genius, Parker." She winks at him. "Looks like your future wife is beautiful *and* intelligent."

Our eyes meet and I feel my cheeks heat again.

Parker clears his throat as he adjusts his glasses. "Uh, yeah. I told her the idea was good."

"It is. I'm already convinced and told Cashlynn that I'd contact Pam at Cove Realty tomorrow so she can start looking at spaces."

He nods, though his shoulders remain tense, like he's still unsure about the conversation he walked in on.

"I appreciate that, Willow," he says, moving around the couch to me, wrapping his arm around my waist like it's the most natural thing in the world. The warmth of his touch sends a shiver down my spine. "Are you guys done talking?" he asks me.

"Um, yeah."

"Good. I was thinking we could get out of here. I want to show you something."

I catch Hazel and Willow exchanging knowing glances, but I quickly turn my attention back to Parker. "Okay."

Parker turns to his sister. "Tell everyone we had to leave, okay?"

"Sure," she replies, rocking back and forth on her feet. "Have fun, you two. Use protection! No need for babies yet. Or rabies, right, Parker?"

Parker shakes his head as he leads me to the front door with his hand on the small of my back. Once we're outside, he asks, "They didn't scar you for life, did they?"

"How would they do that?"

He keeps his hand on my back as we walk to his car.

"By asking inappropriate questions...telling you more stories about me." He opens the car door for me, waiting as I settle inside before shutting it and moving to his side.

"What kind of stories would they tell?" I ask as he starts the car.

He gives me a pointed look from the driver's seat as he starts the engine. "Nice try," he says, turning onto the road.

I laugh. "They were very welcoming, actually. Your entire family was."

"Yeah, they're not too bad," he says as if it pains him to admit it.

"You're lucky, Parker. You have so many people who love you, who accept you and genuinely want you to be happy."

He eyes me for a few moments, his expression unreadable, before focusing back on the road. He doesn't say anything else as we drive into town. I've only been here once, but as we close in on the cove that gives this town its name, my heart beats faster as I take in the view.

The streetlights cast soft reflections on the water, golden sparks dotting the surface of the ocean. A few people are strolling along the boardwalk, their coats pulled tight against the chill in the air.

Parker stops the car and steps out, moving around to my side. He helps me out and then takes my hand, lacing his fingers through mine as he leads me toward the boardwalk.

"Where are we going?" I ask as he pulls me past a row of softly lit storefronts. Behind them is another row of small businesses—an ice cream parlor, a pet store, and then we come to a small, vacant space with a *For Lease* sign in the window.

Parker stops in front of it, turning to face me. "I think this space would be perfect for your gallery."

I blink up at him and then turn to the empty windows that are, unfortunately, lined with brown paper so I can't see what's inside. "What?"

He clears his throat. "After we talked about your gallery idea yesterday, I remembered this space was available. It's close to the boardwalk, so you'd get a lot of foot traffic. It used to be a clothing store, and from what I remember, there's plenty of space inside. I think you should look at it."

"You brought me all the way out here to show me this space?" I whisper, staring up at him again in disbelief.

He nods. "Yeah, and to give you this." He reaches into his pocket and pulls out a ring.

I gasp and my stomach flips. "Oh my God, Parker."

His hands are trembling slightly as he holds it between two fingers, and I realize how offering this ring to me must make him feel. He never wanted to do this again—be engaged or even consider the idea of marriage—until I put him in this position.

But Parker bought me a ring, a gorgeous princess cut diamond flanked by amber stones. It's stunning, unique, and something I would have picked out myself. And it's too much.

"I—I can't accept this, Parker."

His brow furrows. "Why not?"

"Because it's too much. It's expensive and gorgeous and..." I take a step back from him as my stomach churns and my heart races. "I just assumed we'd pick out a simple silver band that I would pay for since this was my idea."

He closes the space between us that I just created, his jaw tight as he reaches for my left hand and slides the ring onto my finger. "There's no way *my* fiancée would be walking around without a ring. And this one just...called to me. Besides, I don't want anyone to question that this is real, okay?"

I look down at the ring, the diamonds catching the light like tiny stars. This isn't some cheap placeholder. This is a *real* ring—thoughtfully chosen, breathtakingly beautiful, and way too much for what we are.

"Are you sure?" I whisper, my voice barely audible.

His eyes bounce between mine. "It's done. Plus, I can't return it, so you have to wear it." The corner of his mouth lifts, putting me a little more at ease.

I nod shakily. Parker Sheppard, the man who claims to have sworn off relationships, bought me a diamond ring. He willingly picked it out, spent a fortune, and is now sliding it onto my finger like it's no big deal.

I glance back up at him, at the guarded look in his eyes, and it hits me that Parker doesn't do anything halfway. He committed to this arrangement just like he commits to everything else in his life—with his whole damn heart, even if he won't admit it to himself.

"It truly is beautiful. I love the amber gemstones on the sides. It's so unique. What made you pick this one?"

His gaze softens as he reaches up to push a strand of hair behind my ear, sending goosebumps down my neck. "The stones reminded me of your eyes."

Oh. My. God.

I think my ovaries just wept.

I shouldn't be thinking about how badly I want this man or how I'll never forget the way he made me feel that night. How he acts so gruff on the outside but on the inside, he's been hurt so badly that he's determined to keep himself closed off.

But on some level, I feel like he is opening up to me.

"That's either incredibly romantic, or mildly disturbing."

His lips curl up more now. "I thought it was very Bridgerton-like, actually."

Chuckling, I look down at the ring that feels foreign but spectacular as well. "When did you get this?"

"This morning, when I was running errands."

I nod, remembering he was gone for a while earlier today, leaving me alone at his house. I had the strongest desire to snoop but talked myself out of it. I wasn't sure I'd find anything anyway since his house is so bare.

"Well, it's more than I could have ever imagined." I look back up, into his eyes. "I can't thank you enough."

"You've said that, Cashlynn."

"I know, but—"

"I'm in this, okay? I know a thing or two about wanting something so badly you feel like you would do anything to make it work."

He takes my hand and leads me back to the car, effectively ending our conversation. And even though I want to press him further, I decide against it. He may not be saying much about where his head is at, but his actions speak volumes.

As we head home, I stare at the ring on my finger, turning over the possibilities in my mind. Would I be a fool not to explore this thing between us while I have the chance?

What if he doesn't feel the same way I do? What if it ends horribly, and then we have to see each other everywhere in this small town?

But taking risks is why I'm here—risking my career, my dreams, and maybe even my heart.

Maybe Hazel's right and it's time to test the waters. I'm tired of not living, not chasing what I want. So here goes nothing.

Let the games begin.

Chapter Eight

Parker

"Um, what are you doing?"

The sound of a voice coming from my bedroom doorway almost makes me drop the iron on my foot. Unfortunately, I let out an embarrassing shriek instead, lifting my empty hand to my chest to cover my racing heart. "Holy fuck, Cashlynn! You scared the shit out of me!"

She holds her coffee cup in front of her chest, her hip cocked to one side. "I'm sorry. That wasn't my intention. But, um..." Her gaze drops to the ironing board. "Are you ironing your socks?"

I glance down at the perfectly pressed dress socks and then back up at her, catching the way her ring sparkles on her left hand—the ring I gave her last night that made all of this real. Clearing my throat, I try to shake off the burst of adrenaline coursing through me. "Is that a problem?"

Her mouth parts slightly. "Uh, yes..."

"Why?"

This woman is staring at me like I'm some blue alien with the largest dick she's ever seen. "What kind of person irons their socks?"

My eyes dart back and forth between Cashlynn and my socks that are cooling off the longer we stand here. "They're dress socks."

"So?"

"You don't iron yours?"

Her eyes widen like I've just suggested she eat her cereal with a fork. "No, Parker. I'm normal."

Rolling my eyes, I go back to my task, not in the mood to argue with this woman about yet another thing. "What can I do for you, Cashlynn? As you can see, I'm getting ready for work."

She chuckles and then takes a sip of her coffee. "I just came in to say hello."

It's Monday morning. Cashlynn and I barely spoke after we got home from my mom's house last night. After giving her the ring I picked out, my chest felt tight. Once I slid that ring on her finger, I knew there was no turning back from my decision. And watching her with my family last night was something else.

For once, I wasn't the only single person in the room. Hazel doesn't count; she's in a league of her own. But I'm used to being the one everyone feels sorry for. They know why I haven't dated in four years. They know my feelings about being in a serious relationship again.

But last night, I had Cashlynn beside me, and for a moment, I didn't feel so fucking alone.

Then I woke up this morning and went through my normal routine, forgetting there's another person living in my house now. That is, until she just scared the shit out of me and is now judging me for my totally reasonable sock-ironing habits.

It's not that weird, is it?

"Well, hello." I take both of my wrinkle-free socks and place them on the bed next to my button down shirt, slacks, and tie. "Now, if you'll excuse me, I need to get dressed."

Her eyes dip down my body before she begins to back out of my room. "Of course. Sorry."

Heading toward the door to close it, I say, "No problem. I'll be out there in a few minutes."

After I dress, style my hair, and clean my glasses, I find Cashlynn sitting on a barstool by the island, scrolling through her phone, and that's when I finally take a moment to look her.

Her hair is messy—like she hasn't brushed it yet—and she's wearing an oversized T-shirt that barely skims the top of her thighs over fitted pajama pants that showcase curves I can't help but appreciate.

She looks so relaxed and comfortable, but I know what she's hiding beneath those clothes, and that thought has me snapping out of my perusal and heading over to the coffee machine for my second cup of coffee this morning.

"Are your socks nice and stiff?"

"Ha-ha. Very funny."

She chuckles as she turns her screen off and leans back in the chair, assessing me. "Why do you iron your socks?"

I shrug. "I'm ironing everything else I'm wearing, so it just makes sense."

Her eyes widen. "You iron your underwear too?"

"No..." *Fuck. Maybe it is weird.*

She begins to laugh uncontrollably. "Now I get it."

"Get what?"

"Why you're still single." She stands from the stool, drains the rest of her coffee from her mug, and places it in the sink. I glance at the dishwasher, literally inches from where her mug now sits, and bite back the urge to point it out.

"That is *not* why I'm still single."

She rolls her eyes mockingly. "Okay. But seriously, that's some serial killer type of behavior."

"Go check my freezer then," I say, pointing to the refrigerator behind me. "You won't find anything suspicious. I like my socks to be neat. Big deal."

Still chuckling, she pats me on the shoulder. "Okay. Whatever you say. I should probably tell someone, though, just in case I go missing."

I take a deep breath, trying to remember what my life was like before this woman marched back into it.

Quiet mornings free of judgment—that's what I enjoyed before Cashlynn accused me of being a murderer.

I pour my coffee into a thermos and head toward the door. "I'll be home around five-thirty. My late shifts are later in the week. Willow's phone number is on the fridge. Give her a call, if you need her."

"Thank you."

With my hand on the knob, I ask, "Do you have plans today?"

I shouldn't care what she's up to. I'm not her fucking babysitter, but part of me wants to know. I try not to read too much into that.

"Just some phone calls. I'll probably go visit my dad, too." Before I can turn around, I feel her behind me as she places her hand on my shoulder. I spin to face her, her eyes assessing me as I look down at her. "Do you think Friday night would be okay for us to have dinner with him?"

I take a minute to think about if I have any plans, but I'm not sure why. Most of my Friday nights consist of me flipping through Netflix trying to find something to watch, or watching reruns of *Friends* until I can't keep my eyes open anymore. "That works for me."

She reaches up and straightens my tie, the soft brush of her knuckles against my chest sending a pulse of heat through me. "Okay. Friday it is."

My Adam's apple bobs as I swallow roughly. Cashlynn's hands are still on my chest, smoothing my shirt as her eyes dance across my face. She bites her lip, almost like she's contemplating something before speaking again. "Have a good day, Parker," she says in a sultry voice that makes my dick stir.

"Uh, thanks."

Before I can move, she rises onto her toes and plants a soft kiss on my cheek. I stand frozen as she takes a step back.

I feel like I just lived through a movie scene from the fifties: the husband is leaving for work, his wife is kissing him goodbye, eagerly waiting for his return.

She may be my fake fiancée, but I can't deny that knowing she'll be here when I get home this evening has my mind racing with what that will feel like.

If things were real between us, I'd storm into the house, rip her clothes from her body, lay her out on the kitchen island, and ravage her pussy until she fucking screamed.

Jesus, Parker. Get a fucking grip. No touching, remember? That was your fucking rule.

She licks her lips and then turns away from me, heading back to her seat at the island. "See you later."

I don't waste another second watching her. Like my ass is on fire, I escape to my car, gripping the steering wheel so hard my knuckles ache.

This woman is going to ruin me. I just hope my self-control can survive the next four months. Otherwise, my dick isn't the only thing that's going to suffer from this stupid plan.

***

"What the hell is going on?" I smack the coffee machine because, when something's not working, hitting it is obviously the first logical thing to try.

But the stupid thing still won't turn on.

I tilt my head to the right and then the left, looking for any sign of something wrong and that's when I see it—the damn thing is unplugged.

"What the fuck?" I mutter, just as a chipper voice cuts through my irritation, nearly making me jump out of my skin for the second morning in a row.

"Good morning!"

I whip around, heart racing. But this time, I manage to swallow the embarrassing shriek. Taking a deep breath to steady my racing heart, I turn to face her and interrogate her about the machine, but at the sight of her, the words die on my tongue.

Fuck. Her nipples are standing at attention underneath her oversized shirt and a sliver of her stomach is peeking out from the bottom. I move my eyes back to her face, but that proves to be just as distracting. She looks gorgeous in the morning—messy hair, no makeup, completely relaxed. Call me crazy, but seeing a woman dressed down is far sexier than when she's all dolled up.

Don't get me wrong, I appreciate the sexy dresses and heels just as much as the next man. But a woman bare-faced and slightly messy turns me to stone in an instant.

And just like that, my dick is awake as well.

Focus, Parker. The coffee machine, remember?

I clear my throat and remember my frustration. "Good morning? No, it is not a good morning, Cashlynn," I grumble. "Because I came in here after my workout and shower, desperate for caffeine, only to discover that my coffee machine wasn't working. I just discovered that it's been unplugged, and I know damn well that I didn't do that." I arch a brow at her. "Care to explain?"

She stares at me blankly before her lips twitch and she dissolves into laughter, covering her mouth with her hands. "Wow. You are definitely *not* a morning person."

"Cashlynn," I warn, pointing to the offending machine. "Why did you unplug my machine?"

She breezes past me, plugs it back in, and then reaches for a mug before pressing the button to start the machine. "To conserve energy, of course."

My mouth falls open. "What?"

Glancing at me over her shoulder with an innocent shrug, she says, "If you're not using it, but it's plugged in, it's still using a tiny bit of power." She holds her thumb and forefinger close together to emphasize the point.

This has to be a joke.

"You seriously believe that?"

She nods confidently. "They've done studies on it. And I know it's not much, but I really try to minimize my carbon footprint where I can, you know?"

I pinch the bridge of my nose, reminding myself that living with another person means accepting their quirks and weird obsessions. *It's only four months, Parker. You can handle this.*

"Be that as it may, Cashlynn, I would appreciate it if you didn't unplug my coffee machine," I say through gritted teeth, managing to keep my tone just shy of murderous.

She winces. "I mean, I can try to remember, but it's a habit, Parker."

"When you go to unplug it, just remember that it's going to make my eye twitch if I see it, and then you just *don't* do it." I flash her a placating smile.

She shakes her head, picking up the freshly brewed cup and holding it out to me before sliding another mug underneath the drip. "Sorry. It's one of my quirks."

"No, it's weird and unnecessary," I reply, taking the cup from her.

"Not as weird as ironing your socks," she fires back with an amused smile on her lips.

I clutch my coffee like a lifeline and head to my room. "I need to finish getting ready."

"Do you need help with your ironing? I can take care of your underwear for you so you're fully pressed from head to toe!" she calls after me, laughing.

I don't bother responding as I shut myself inside of my room and take a sip of my coffee, promptly burning my tongue in the process.

"Three months and twenty-five more days. You can do this, Parker."

***

By the time I get to work, my mind is still preoccupied by the coffee fiasco.

"Seriously. What kind of person in their right mind unplugs their appliances when they're done using them?"

"Are you talking to yourself?" Cassandra asks from the doorway of my office.

I look up from the client folders I was just reviewing before the practice opens. She's smirking at me. "No."

"Yes, you were. Everything okay, boss?"

"I'm not your boss."

"Technically, you are. You're the man with the fancy Doctor of Veterinary Medicine degree. I'm just a tech."

"Would you want to go back to school and get your license?" I ask as I stand from my chair and button up my coat.

She shrugs. "I've thought about it."

"You know, if you did, you could be my number two when Dr. O'Neil retires..."

"You're assuming he's going to leave the practice to you," Seth interjects, appearing behind Cassandra, clearly eavesdropping on our conversation. "Let's not forget that he hasn't even mentioned retiring yet."

"Beth says he's thinking about it," Cassandra chimes in, always up on the latest gossip.

Don't let anyone fool you—doctor's offices, schools, and hospitals are full of gossip, just like they portray in shows like *Grey's Anatomy*. Although, when you work with animals, some of the stories can get pretty wild.

Seth flashes me one of his trademark slimy smiles. "Then may the best man win." He heads down the hall as Cassandra steps into my office and shuts the door.

"Sorry. I should have shut that earlier."

I blow out a breath. "It's okay. It's not like he and I didn't know that we're the ones in the running."

"Between you and me, if he takes over, a lot of people are planning on leaving."

My heart skips. "Really?"

"Yeah, no one wants to work for him. We tolerate him now, but honestly, he creeps the receptionists out and I hate how fake he is with patients."

Glad to see it's not just me who sees through his act.

"Well, then we can't let him be Robert's choice."

Cassandra nods. "And now that you're engaged to his daughter, you should have the upper hand anyway, right?"

A bead of sweat trickles down my spine as I turn away. "One can only hope."

"Now it makes sense why you weren't taking any of those women up on their offers."

I spin back to face her. "What?"

"The women who've been stalking you from the videos. I didn't know you were dating Cashlynn, so I get why you weren't interested." She smiles. "It's good to know there are still decent, trustworthy guys out there." Before I can say anything, she opens the door. "Diane Kingston and Blueberry are already here, by the way. And Hazel's with them. Want me to put them in a room?"

The mention of my sister snaps me back to reality. "Uh, yeah. That would be great. Thanks, Cassandra."

"My pleasure, Dr. Sheppard."

Shaking off the guilt from the lies I'm trying to juggle, I grab Blueberry's file and head toward the exam room where Diane and my sister are waiting.

"Knock, knock!" I say as I step into the room to find one of my favorite owner-patient duos, along with my sister who always manages to either elevate or diminish my mood. "How's everyone doing today?"

Diane lets out a deep cough as her oxygen tanks hisses. "Doing just splendid, Dr. Sheppard. How are you?"

"Better now that I'm caffeinated. I thought my coffee machine kicked the bucket this morning, but it turns out my fiancée decided to unplug it. So, it was touch-and-go there for a minute." My sister snorts from the corner, trying to cover up a laugh.

I turn my attention back to Diane and her Frenchie, Blueberry. "What cape are we rocking today, Big Blue?"

"He's Superman today. I think he has a new favorite!"

"Batman looks good on him, but I gotta say, the red is doing much more for his complexion."

My sister smiles as she pets Blueberry behind the ear. "I think he looks handsome either way."

Diane leans forward and straightens his cape around his neck. "He is a handsome boy. Aren't you, Blueberry? I think we're gonna need another photoshoot soon, Hazel."

"Tell me when you're free and I'll work you in. You know I love to photograph this cutie."

When Hazel opened her photography studio years ago, Diane was her first official client. She hired Hazel to take pictures of her only child, Blueberry. Since then, Diane has been Hazel's most loyal customer, and Blueberry the most fashionable Frenchie I've ever seen. Over the years, they've also built a strong friendship.

Since Diane's COPD diagnosis, Hazel has been there for her—running errands, driving her to appointments, and making sure she knows she's not alone. This isn't the first time Hazel's been into the animal hospital with Diane, and I'm sure it won't be the last. Diane's health has been declining steadily over the past year, but her attitude is always cheerful. Everyone at the hospital adores her and Blueberry, the caped crusader.

"You know, last time we were here, they tried giving us to that Dr. Brown," Diane snickers as I start Blueberry's annual exam. "I couldn't believe the girls up front had the audacity to try that."

Hazel scoffs. "How dare they?" She glances over at me, flashing me a wink. "Everyone knows that Parker's the best."

Diane nods. "Exactly. And Dr. O'Neil...how is he doing? I heard he fell."

I clear my throat. "Luckily, he didn't break anything. He's at home resting but should be back later this week."

"I heard you're engaged to his daughter," she says as I glance over at Hazel, who just nods.

"Where did you hear that?"

"At Astrid's bakery. Some women were talking about it. They weren't happy you're no longer on the market."

Hazel chuckles, and I glare at her. "Well, they say when you meet the right person, you just know."

Diane looks over at Hazel, assessing her for a moment. "Well, I just love that all of the Sheppard siblings are finding love. Too bad your father wasn't here to see it."

The mention of our father has Hazel and me locking eyes.

"I agree," Hazel says, emotion clogging her voice. "But it's better that my brothers all tie the knot before me anyway."

Diane looks over at her. "Why do you say that?"

"Because they need women to make them see reason," she says matter-of-factly, making me roll my eyes.

"And you don't need a man in order for you to do the same?" I counter.

Hazel crosses her arms over her chest. "Hell no. I'm independent and always have been. The only man I'll ever love is our father, and that's just the way I think it's meant to be. Besides, nothing could live up to the love in books and movies."

Diane hums. "You're only twenty-seven, Hazel. You're too young to write off love completely."

"Most men aren't worth my time," my sister says. "Plus, you never married, right? So you can't blame me for not wanting to settle."

"I didn't marry, you're right," Diane says. "And I don't think there's anything wrong with that. But sometimes, I wonder if I let my pride keep me from opening up to something wonderful. It's not about needing someone—it's about letting them in."

The room falls silent, her words hanging heavily in the air.

"At least you have Blueberry," Hazel finally says, standing from her chair to hold him still as I grab the syringes for his vaccines.

Diane smiles, stroking her dog's head. "That's true. Your dog is your best friend for only part of your life, but you are your dog's best friend for all of theirs. There is something so incredibly special about that honor. I just wish I'd had a human best friend to share this life with too."

Her words almost bring tears to my eyes. Hazel looks down at Blueberry, her expression tight, as if she's searching for the right response.

"Anyone lucky enough to know you—human or otherwise—is better for it, Diane," I say, finishing Blueberry's vaccines and setting him back on the floor.

Hazel attaches Blueberry's leash and places him on Diane's lap with a small smile. "Absolutely. We all adore you, Diane. And I'm not just saying that because Blueberry is the most fashionable dog in town."

"Thank you. That means a lot." Straightening his cape, she chuckles. "He does look quite dashing, doesn't he?"

"That he does," I reply. "Keep spoiling him rotten and we'll see you guys back here for his next checkup."

"Thank you, Dr. Sheppard," she says as Hazel opens the door to make room for her scooter.

Once Diane is out of range, Hazel turns to me. "Well, that got a little morbid."

"Right? She must be having more bad days than good ones lately."

"Yeah... I know her doctor says her labs haven't been looking great."

"How much time does she have left, do you think?"

Hazel wraps her arms around her body. "I don't know, but I fucking hate this. It's like watching Dad deteriorate all over again."

I pull my sister into my chest, wrapping her tightly in my arms. "I know," I murmur.

"I miss him every day, Parker."

"Me too." My eyes start to sting as I breathe in deeply, holding her close as she sniffles into my chest. I give her a moment, my own heart aching. Losing someone you love, whether to death or something else, fucking sucks. And it's yet another reason I haven't put myself out there.

First, it was Sasha. Then, my dad.

But Cashlynn makes you feel things again, Parker.

Hazel releases me a few moments later, wiping under her eyes. "Okay. I didn't plan on breaking down this morning, but thanks for letting me."

"Always. You know you don't have to be so strong all the time."

She holds her hand up to her ear, mimicking a pretend telephone. "Hello, pot? This is the kettle. You're black."

I roll my eyes. "Get out of my office."

She laughs, dropping her hand. "Seriously, though. How are things going with Cashlynn?"

"Did you not hear about the coffee fiasco earlier?"

Hazel covers her mouth. "It's pretty bizarre."

"Very. And she's such a fucking morning person. I know I haven't lived with a woman in four years, but she's something else."

Hazel pats me on the chest. "We women do have our little quirks, Parker. Eventually, they become endearing."

"I will never find someone unplugging my coffee machine endearing."

Grinning, Hazel grabs her purse and opens the door. "Well, I hate to say it, but if that's the first thing to drive you crazy, I have a feeling it won't be the last."

"What do you mean?"

She shrugs and waves at me. "Good luck!"

As I watch my sister walk back to the receptionist area where Diane is waiting for her, a sense of dread churns in my stomach.

What if Cashlynn has other habits that are even worse? What if she's a closet slob or, worse, folds her towels the wrong way?

What if, as the weather gets warmer, she casually mentions she prefers to sleep naked and then I have to imagine that she's behind her bedroom door with nothing covering her silky, sexy body?

I close my eyes and groan. "Just take it one day at a time, Parker. That's all anyone can do."

Shaking off the thoughts, I head down the hospital hallway toward my next client, but as I pass Beth's office, a familiar voice stops me in my tracks.

"It's time to tell them," Beth says, her voice low.

"No. There's too much going on right now. My focus needs to be on the practice."

Dr. O'Neil? What's he doing here? He's not supposed to be back until Thursday.

"I can't keep this a secret for much longer, Robert. Your daughter deserves to know. I deserve that too."

Unfortunately, before either of them says another word, Seth walks by, startling me from my eavesdropping. "Dr. Sheppard, are you just hanging out in the halls now instead of working? That's no way to become the next boss around here."

My spine stiffens as Beth's office door creaks open. She peeks her head out, expression unreadable.

"Parker?"

I force a smile. "Hey, Beth."

She narrows the door's opening until I can barely see her face through the crack now. "Did you need something?"

Before I can decide how to respond, Robert opens the door, standing tall like he has nothing to hide. "Parker," he says gruffly.

I steel my spine. "Robert."

"I hear we have dinner plans Friday night."

"Uh, yes. That's correct."

"I'll see you then." With that, he moves past me, still using his cane for support.

And as I watch him walk away, I can't help but wonder if Cashlynn isn't the only one with something to hide.

Chapter Nine

Cashlynn

"Wasn't your dad supposed to be here by now?" Parker asks as he stirs the pasta boiling on the stove.

I glance at the microwave clock. "Yes. Do you think he got lost?" Before he can answer, the doorbell rings. My stomach twists, nerves surging. "Guess not," I mutter.

Parker and I rehearsed our story last night and again this afternoon as soon as he got home from the animal hospital. While he was at work, I moved my things into his bedroom so that if Dad wants a tour of the house, it looks like we share a room. Parker didn't seem too thrilled about it, but agreed it was a smart move.

"Just breathe." Parker's calm, steady voice cuts through the my building nerves. He gives me a reassuring smile. "Let's go answer the door together."

"Yeah. Okay."

With his hand on the small of my back—a move I'm becoming a big fan of—we head for the front door. We open it to find my father leaning on his cane, a bottle of wine in his other hand.

"Hi, Dad." I step forward and wrap my arms around him, even though his hands are full.

He kisses me on the temple instead of returning my hug. "Hi there, June Bug." When he stands tall again, he glances over at Parker. "Parker."

Parker reaches for the wine. "Robert. Thanks for coming over."

"Well, I guess I should get used to visiting since this is my daughter's home now too." He walks through the front door and shuffles toward the dining room.

"I'm sorry," I say to Parker under my breath.

"What are you apologizing for now?"

"His attitude. I just—"

Parker leans forward and presses a kiss to my forehead. His lips barely graze my skin, but it's enough to short-circuit my brain. "I can handle your father," he says. "I've been working with him for the past six years, remember?"

"Yeah, but you weren't always fake engaged to me."

Parker's expression hardens slightly. "No, but if he's going to have that big of an attitude about it, I can give it right back."

"You're supposed to be buttering him up, remember? The practice? That's why you agreed to this."

"Not if it means standing by while he doesn't support you." He takes my hand and leads me toward the kitchen, my heart thrashing in my chest from his words.

As the days pass and I inch closer to opening my gallery, I'm starting to feel like Parker genuinely believes in me, and I'm not sure why.

Maybe Hazel is right. Maybe there are feelings there that even he's oblivious to.

"Smells good. What are you making, June Bug?"

"Actually, Parker's cooking tonight," I say, retrieving the wine opener from a drawer as Parker moves back to the stove.

"You cook, Parker?"

"I do. My mother always made my brothers and me help in the kitchen when we were young. She said she refused to raise boys that didn't know how to fend for themselves or impress a woman."

I glance back at him and he winks at me over his shoulder.

"Parker's cooking is one of the biggest perks of living together," I say, loving when he gives me glimpses of the man beyond the exterior.

"I imagine it's hard to do much of that when you're in a long-distance relationship, huh?" My father says, a hint of sarcasm in his voice.

I pour three glasses of the red wine my father bought, handing one to Parker before taking the other two to the dining room table. Placing one in front of Dad, I take the seat next to him.

"I know you have questions, Dad."

"You're damn right I do." He picks up his wine glass and takes a sip as he leans back in his chair, his large belly protruding over the waistband of his pants.

"And we will answer them. But do you think you can chill a bit since you just got here?"

His response is a grunt.

"How hungry are you, Robert?" Parker asks from the kitchen as he starts plating the pasta carbonara. My mouth is salivating from the smell of it alone.

My dad pats his stomach. "Don't give me too much, son. I'm trying to watch my figure."

Parker chuckles and plates three helpings of the pasta and garlic bread. He brings them to the table, settling into the chair next to me.

"This smells amazing, babe," I say, catching his eye.

He smiles over at me before reaching for his glass of wine. "Thank you." Then he holds his glass out, suggesting a toast. "To family and the beginning of a new life for all of us."

My father raises an eyebrow before slowly reaching forward to clink his glass with ours. "To family."

The three of us eat in silence for a few minutes, the tension simmering just beneath the surface.

"Who knew you could cook, Parker?" Dad says eventually.

Parker chuckles. "I'll take that as a compliment, sir."

"Sir? Don't start treating me differently now that you're marrying my daughter," he admonishes. "But while we're on the subject, I think I'm ready for an explanation."

Parker's gaze shifts to me, his expression encouraging me to start, like we discussed.

"Okay, Dad. Here's how things happened." I spend the next few minutes retelling our story to my father, emphasizing how crazy it was that the doctor he'd always spoken about with such pride was the man that ended up comforting me during a flight. We talked about how whenever Parker went out of town, he would make sure to fly to Philadelphia to see me. We fell hard and fast, and after months of long-distance, we realized we didn't want to be apart anymore. Moving here was the obvious choice.

"But I shocked him when I showed up earlier than planned," I explain. "When I heard you got hurt, I came down sooner than we'd discussed. That's why Parker was so surprised to see me that day."

"I see." My father finishes his wine, setting the glass on the table. All three of us are finished eating, so the only thing left to do is soak up the palpable tension in the room. "I understand being wary of telling me, but here's my issue." He turns his gaze to Parker. "If you were serious enough about my daughter to propose, why didn't you come to me then? At the very least, you should've asked me for her hand in marriage."

Parker clears his throat. "If I could take that part back, Robert, I would. Truly." He turns to me and places a finger under my chin, directing my gaze to his. "But we were tired of being apart. I knew if I was really going to convince her to make the move, I had to show her I was all in."

Parker's eyes dance all over my face, and if I didn't know that he was acting, I'd believe every emotion his words are conveying right now. His eyes dip to my lips, and before I think better of it, I press a soft kiss to his mouth. It's brief, just enough to sell it without giving my father a heart attack at the other end of the table.

"Well, I have to say, if I had to choose anyone for my June Bug, it would be you, Parker."

I turn to my father as Parker wraps his arm around my shoulders. "I'm glad you feel that way, Dad," I say, relief blooming in my chest.

"So, when's the wedding?"

Parker coughs behind me, apparently losing his composure from before, so I jump in. "We haven't talked about it much, Dad. It's been a whirlwind with the move and everything."

"I see."

"But we did find a ring," Parker adds, reaching for my hand. He brings it to his mouth, kissing my knuckles before extending it to Dad.

My dad assesses the ring. "It's stunning. At least you did right by her in that respect."

"I tried. I knew this ring belonged on her finger the second I saw it."

"You two still have a lot to learn about each other, though."

Parker laughs under his breath as he rises to clear our plates. "Oh believe me, we've been learning plenty about each other."

My father's eyebrows rise. "Oh? Like what?"

"Like your daughter unplugs appliances when they aren't being used," he says, taking our plates over to the sink.

My father looks at me quizzically. "Is that true, June Bug?"

"Um, yes." My words come out shaky. "It helps conserve energy."

My dad scoffs. "I doubt that."

"That's what I said," Parker calls over his shoulder, scrubbing the dishes.

"Yeah, well, Parker irons his socks!" I counter, folding my arms as I bite back a grin.

My father's gaze darts to my fake fiancé. "You do?"

"They're dress socks. It just makes sense," he grumbles as I fight to hold in my laughter.

My father chuckles quietly, which I take as a good sign. "Well, it seems you two are learning a lot about each other now that you're living together, aren't you?"

"We are, and I'm happy here, Dad."

He leans forward in his chair and lowers his voice. "I'm allowed to be worried about you, June Bug. This whole thing is a little out of character for you."

"Well, people change. And what we want out of life can change too, Dad."

He exhales sharply, sitting upright again. "That it can."

"What about you?"

"What about me?" he asks, a bit too defensively.

"Have you given any more thought to making some changes too? Taking better care of yourself?" Parker clears his throat loudly from the kitchen, so I turn to look at him. His eyebrows shoot up, and he tilts his head slightly, as if to say, *Don't forget our deal, Cashlynn.* Subtle. Real subtle.

I turn back to my dad, trying to keep my voice casual. "You know, now you'll have a son-in-law to leave the practice to."

My dad grunts. "I haven't made my decision on that yet. And given these recent developments, I might need to reconsider my options."

Leaning forward, I reach for his hand. "Dad, please don't blame Parker for keeping this a secret. It was my choice, okay?"

"Besides, we've all got our secrets, right, Robert?" Parker chimes in. I look between him and my dad, confused.

My dad's gaze flicks to Parker, and for a moment, something unreadable passes between them. Then he clears his throat, brushing the remark aside. "I just don't get why you couldn't tell me yourself, June Bug."

"You're not the easiest to talk to sometimes," I admit, my voice low.

"That's not true," he replies sharply, leaving no room for argument.

I give him a pointed look that says *Point made.*

His jaw tightens, and for a moment, he looks like he wants to argue further. But then he exhales, shifting slightly in his chair. "Well...at least I know now. I guess I should just be grateful it brought you here."

"That would be nice."

He stands from his chair, leaning on his cane for support as he pulls me up with him. "You mean the world to me, June. I just want what's best for you." He pulls me in for a hug.

"I know."

"I can't lose you too."

I look up at him, his words cutting deep. "You're not losing me."

Brushing my hair from my face, he says, "You remind me so much of your mother sometimes. You're too smart, too driven."

I life my chin. "Those aren't bad things, Dad."

He nods, closing his eyes and kissing the top of my head. "I know. But when I see you making impulsive decisions, it scares me."

Behind me, Parker clears his throat, stepping closer. "I'm looking out for her, Robert. I promise."

My father releases me, and before I can move, Parker pulls me against his chest. His arm circles my shoulders protectively. "I know you didn't find out about this in the best way, but I'm asking you to trust us. Trust that we're doing what's right for us at the right time."

My dad studies us, his gaze shifting between me and Parker. And standing here in Parker's arms under the scrutiny of my father's gaze makes me feel like maybe I can fight for what I want here—as long as I have Parker to back me up.

I love my dad with all of my heart and soul, but he's so stubborn, so hell-bent on what he believes. I know fear fuels so many of his emotions, but until I can show him how successful I can be doing something that I genuinely love, I have to keep him in the dark.

He nods. "I think it's time for me to make some decisions too."

Parker and I share a look, but Parker speaks first. "What kind of decisions?"

"Well, after our conversation the other day, June Bug, and everything that's happened this past week, I think you're right." He takes a deep breath and says, "I think it's time to start considering my retirement. I'm not saying it will happen tomorrow, but it's time to really consider my successor."

I can feel Parker tense up behind me, his grip on my shoulder tightening.

"I'm glad you're going to consider it, Dad."

"I've been thinking about it a lot, and given all of the changes going on, and the fact that you're here now, I think I'm ready to enjoy the rest of my life outside of the hospital."

Parker squeezes my shoulder again. "That place can suck you in, can't it?"

My dad actually laughs. "Yes, it can. And there's more to life than work."

I eye my father curiously. "I'm sorry, but who are you and what have you done with my dad?"

He smirks and starts for the door. "No need to commit me just yet. I said I'm thinking about it, all right? I didn't say it's happening anytime soon."

Parker and I follow him to the door. "Leaving already?" I ask as he reaches the entryway.

"Yes. It's getting late and I hate driving at night." He taps his cane on the ground. "Plus, Beth is taking me for a walk in the morning without this thing, so I need to get my rest. That woman can be a real ball-buster, if you know what I mean."

Parker laughs lightly. "Oh, I'm aware."

My dad leans forward and kisses my cheek. "I love you, June."

"Love you too, Dad."

Parker reaches out to shake his hand. "Thanks for coming over, Robert."

My father clasps his hand, holding it firm as his gaze locks with Parker's. "Take care of my daughter, Parker."

"I plan on it."

The moment the door shuts behind him, I let out the breath I didn't realize I'd been holding. Leaning back against the front door, I turn to find Parker watching my dad through the window as he makes his way out to his car.

"Oh my God..."

"He's gone," Parker says, his voice low, posture still tense.

I take a deep breath and blow it out. "I think he actually bought it."

Parker's jaw clenches and then he turns away from the window and heads back into the kitchen.

"Parker?" I call, trailing after him cautiously. "Are you okay?"

He doesn't say anything. Instead, he grabs the sponge and starts scrubbing a plate like it personally offended him.

"Hey," I say, placing a hand on his forearm. "I told you I would clean up since you cooked."

"It's fine," he replies, his voice clipped.

I take a step back and study him, wondering how he went from acting the part of adoring fiancé back to grumpy old man again so quickly. "Did I do something wrong?"

"No, Cashlynn. I'm fine, okay?"

"Okay...but you don't seem fine. You seem like you're about to go lock yourself in your room and start ironing your whole freaking closet."

He turns to look at me. "Why would I do that?"

"I don't know. Why do you iron your socks?"

He shakes his head and blows out a breath. "Just drop it."

"I don't understand—"

He drops the sponge in the water and hangs his head. "I just have a lot of feelings right now, and I'm trying not to explode, okay?"

My heart thunders in my chest. "Okay..."

His head turns and our eyes meet, his stormy with something I can't quite place. "This whole thing..." He lifts a hand and gestures vaguely between us as his eyes drop down to my lips and then back up to my eyes. "It's just a lot, okay?"

"I get it."

He nods and retrieves the sponge from the water, going back to washing the dishes. For a second, I contemplate pushing him to open up to me, to tell me everything that's going through his mind, but I think better of it. Because if he's feeling even half of what I'm feeling, I'm sure he's overwhelmed.

Every time this man touches me, my entire body ignites, my skin comes alive, and this need to surrender to him fills my veins. No man has ever made me feel as safe and seen as he does. It was instant the first time we met, and as we slip deeper into our parts in this production, the more I crave that side of him again. This gruff man, the one who's probably about to crack a tooth from clenching his jaw so hard? That man is not the Parker I fantasized about.

The only thing I can do is try to remind him of what we shared, of how incredible our connection was and still is—how the sacrifices he's making for me make me want to give myself over to him, mind and body.

"Parker?" I say softly.

"Yeah?"

"Look at me."

He sighs and drops the sponge back in the water, turning to face me. His green eyes meet mine, framed by his glasses, and my breath catches. "What?"

Without hesitating, I cup his face with both hands and bring his lips to mine. He freezes for a beat, but as soon as I swipe my tongue across his lower lip, he groans and opens up for me.

Mother of God. Yes, this is what I need.

Our mouths move together on instinct, nipping and sucking, swirling tongues and swallowing moans as he lifts me onto the counter, squeezing my hips and devouring my mouth. I wrap my legs around his waist, pulling him closer into me, rubbing myself along his erection I can feel pressing against the zipper of his slacks.

I claw at his back, dig one hand into his hair, and pull him in as tightly as I can. He grabs handfuls of my ass, pressing his cock to my center, right where I need him most.

But then, as if someone threw a bucket of ice water on him, he rips himself from me, his chest heaving as he steps back, his gaze locked on mine.

"Fuck," he groans, turning away and running a hand through his hair.

I hop down from the counter, move closer to him, and gently turn him to face me.

"Thank you for tonight," I say simply, pressing a kiss to his cheek before walking away, giving him the space to unravel in private. I can't bear to see a single ounce of regret on his face—I'm already drowning in enough of my own. Regret for lying to my dad, for pulling Parker into my chaos, for existing in this strange limbo between truth and fiction.

But kissing Parker?

Not a single part of me regrets that. Because with every touch, every unguarded moment, every piece of him he lets slip through, I know one thing for sure—I want this man more than just temporarily.

And after that kiss, I'm pretty sure he wants me too.

Chapter Ten

Parker

"And this is where the tables would go." Cashlynn motions to the large open space beside her, excitement radiating from her. "I should be able to fit twenty to thirty people in here for each class."

Willow rubs her pregnant belly and nods. "I love it. And shelves on the wall behind there for supplies?"

"Exactly. We need to order some cabinets for below the counters, but shelves up above." Cashlynn darts to the other side of the room. "I'm thinking a divider wall right here. That way, it feels like two different spaces. The front will be the gallery with the art that's for sale, and then when you step through, it becomes the creative space where we hold the paint nights and classes."

I've been standing off to the side, listening and watching Cashlynn practically prance all over the space she and Willow just signed the lease on—the space I showed her last week. A lot of paperwork this week delayed the process, but in a few weeks, Cashlynn will officially have her very own gallery and studio.

The whole room could be a crumbling mess for all I care. The way she lights up almost makes the turmoil I've been dealing with worth it.

"So, what do you think?" Cashlynn turns to me, bright-eyed and anticipating my response.

"I think it's perfect." My eyes travel around the empty room, and even though it doesn't look like much right now, I have faith that she'll make her vision come to life.

"It really is." She walks up to me and places her hand on my chest. "Thank you again for suggesting it. You saved me a lot of time looking around." She glances back at Willow. "We only looked at two other places, but the location and lighting here are unmatched."

I stare down at my fake fiancée, focusing in on her lips as she speaks—those same lips that were on my mouth last Friday night in my kitchen, where I was five seconds away from stripping her naked and fucking her until she screamed.

"It *is* perfect," Willow says, thankfully snapping me out of my daydream that was about to become a wet dream. "And now that we know what we're dealing with, we can start talking about branding and marketing—my favorite part." She rubs her hands together just as there's a knock on the front window.

"I've got it." I head over to the window, peeking under the brown paper that's still covering the glass to find Penn outside, nose buried in his phone. "We aren't in need of any stripper services," I say as I open the door to find him in his usual construction attire—blue jeans, a plain black shirt, and his tool belt around his waist.

"Jealous that women find my job sexier than yours?" he asks, pointing at my chest and then flicking my nose as soon as I glance down.

"Fuck off." I swat him away as he walks past me, grinning.

"Who invited the dickhead?" I call out to Willow and Cashlynn as Penn strolls toward them.

"Um, I did. And you shouldn't call your brother a dickhead." Cashlynn narrows her eyes at me disapprovingly.

Willow places a hand on Cashlynn's shoulder. "It's best you just stay out of their brotherly love shit-talking. That's what I've learned, at least."

"And by the way, your fiancée *is* in need of my services, little brother, not yours. Unless, of course, she needs a thermometer shoved up her—

"Jesus Christ, Penn." I cut him off, shoving him as Cashlynn and Willow shake their heads.

"Okay, boys. Enough of that." Willow waves Penn over. "Penn, come over here and listen to what we're thinking."

As they head back to the far end of the room, Cashlynn hangs back. "Do you really think it will come together?" she asks, her voice soft, uncertain.

I step closer, my hands settling on her shoulders before I even realize what I'm doing. I know we don't need to put on a show for Penn and Willow, but touching her feels so natural. The memory of her lips on mine five days ago flashes through my mind. I've done everything to keep my distance since then—everything to remind myself that this is fake.

But right now, it doesn't feel fake. Not the warmth of her beneath my hands, not the way she looks up at me, her eyes searching for reassurance.

"I do," I say, my voice low but firm. "You've got this, Cashlynn. Don't let those doubts creep in now."

She huffs out a laugh. "Yeah, that happened as soon as I saw the rent on this place."

"That's what you have Willow for. Be patient. Building a business will take time."

She bites her bottom lip. "I know, but now that I have a space, it all seems so real. What if I fail, Parker? What if my dad is right and trying to make a living out of art is way too farfetched? That having a stable job like a lawyer is best. That's why he pushed me into that career. I mean, I have my law degree still, and I can always take the North Carolina bar as a backup in case this fails—"

Before she can spiral further, I press a finger to her lips. Her eyes widen as I crouch slightly so I can speak to her at eye level. "We have not come this far for you to start thinking about a backup plan," I tell her, my tone allowing no argument. "Remember what you told me about regrets?"

She nods once, her lips brushing against my finger, but I don't let her say one word in response.

"You don't want to live with them, right?" Another nod. "Then manifest this, Cashlynn. Think positive, envision what you want, and then work your ass off to make it happen. That's why you're here. And I'm not going to let you quit."

Her gaze locks on mine, her lips parting slightly as I drop my hand.

If Cashlynn and I don't get what we want out of this arrangement, it will have all been for nothing. And I hate seeing her doubt herself. She did it on the plane, and I've seen her do it too many times since she arrived in Carrington Cove. This woman is a lot stronger than she gives herself credit for, and I refuse to see her give up on herself when her vision is just getting started.

She blinks up at me, as if she's searching for the right words, but Penn's voice breaks the moment.

"Okay, so I don't think what you need done will take longer than a week or two," my older brother says, strolling back toward us like he owns the place.

Cashlynn twists to face him, brushing her hair over her shoulders and walking in his direction, leaving me rooted in place. "Okay. That's not bad at all."

"It should be easy. And then once I'm out of the way, if you need help with decorating, wiring, or whatever, just let me know and I can send Gary, my top guy, over to help you."

"I appreciate this so much, Penn."

He clasps his hand on her shoulder, and even though the gesture is innocent, seeing him touch her makes me want to rip his tool belt off and beat him with it. "Nonsense. You're practically family now, right?" He glances up at me and winks.

Fucker.

"That was some speech," Willow says as she walks up to me. Cashlynn and Penn are deep in conversation now as she talks through the rest of her ideas.

"Well, she needed to hear it."

My sister-in-law squints at me. I glance over at her before rolling my eyes. "What?"

"Nothing," she says, folding her hands across my nephew growing in her stomach.

"Sure doesn't seem like nothing," I grumble. "It seems like you have something you want to say."

She shrugs. "I just want you to know that I'm genuinely amazed at what you're doing for her."

I shove my hands in my pockets. "It's not like she gave me much of a choice."

Willow nudges me with her shoulder. "You could have said no. And you could have had nothing to do with her business venture. You could have *not* suggested that we talk, you could have *not* suggested that she check out this building, and you could have *not* given her a pep talk just now when her self-doubt came up."

Looking at her, I arch a brow. "Your point?"

She rests a hand on my shoulder. "I think she's affecting you."

"Is not," I say, sounding childish even to my own ears.

Willow laughs. "Okay. Deny it all you want, Parker, but this woman brings out your softer side," she says as she takes a few steps forward, then adds over her shoulder, "and I don't hate it."

I watch my sister-in-law join my brother and fake fiancée as they talk about the light fixtures. *There's a sentence I never thought I'd say.*

And that's when it hits me—Cashlynn may have crashed into my life here, but she slipped into it almost seamlessly.

Sasha never did.

Everything with Sasha felt forced, like I was always checking in, trying to make sure she was happy. But deep down, I knew the truth.

You knew she didn't want to move here, but you pushed her to do it anyway. That's why she turned to alcohol, that's why...

"Parker?"

"Huh?" I look up to find my brother staring at me.

"You all right?"

"Yeah, just lost in thought." I clear the ball of emotion in my throat.

"Don't think too hard," he teases, giving me a light shove. "Wouldn't want you to hurt yourself."

"Fuck off."

"No, seriously." He steps closer, standing shoulder to shoulder with me as we watch the girls. "Don't think too hard about it. If something feels right, just go for it." I don't respond, so he continues. "Trust me. I wasted a lot of fucking time denying what I felt for Astrid, wondering if she could ever feel the same way. And lo and behold, we both wanted the same thing. If I had just had the balls to say something sooner, she and I could have been together a long time ago.

"Cashlynn and I are not you and Astrid. This is a business arrangement, pun intended."

He nods. "You're holding on to your pain like it's a shield, little brother. But it's not—it's a wound. And wounds heal if you let them."

As he walks out, leaving me with the woman who's making me question my life choices thus far, I can't help but wonder if he's right. Because that's exactly what my failed relationship with Sasha feels like—a heavy weight I've been carrying for four fucking years.

And the woman standing in front me might just be the reason I finally let it go.

***

"If you're looking for a clean food source, this is the one I recommend." Seth takes a bag of food off the shelf in the reception area, handing it to one of our clients.

"This the best thing I can feed him?" The young woman looks down at her bulldog puppy, who's currently slobbering all over the floor.

"Absolutely."

Her face falls when she sees the price tag. "It's really expensive, though."

Wrapping his arm around her shoulder, he leads her over to the counter to pay. I cannot believe this asshole. "You can't put a price on your puppy's health, right?"

She nods nervously before handing the bag to Victoria so she can ring her up. "Right…"

"Great!" Seth beams. "Then we'll see you back next month for Sparky's next set of vaccines," he says brightly before disappearing down the hall.

Shaking my head, I follow behind. When I catch up to him, I lower my voice so only he can hear. "You know that shit you just gave her isn't the best food we carry."

"So? We make the best commission off that brand, Dr. Sheppard." He flashes his creepy smile as we pass a few of the technicians on the way to his office. Once we step inside, I close the door behind us. He sighs and says, "If you'll excuse me, I'm busy."

Did he really just dismiss me?

"You're worried about commission? What about that dog's health and longevity? What about that young girl's bank account?"

Seth rolls his eyes as he drops into the chair behind his desk. "This *is* a business, Parker. Or have you forgotten that?"

"Of course not. But at the end of the day, we have to do what's best for the owners and their pets."

"No. At the end of the day, we have to keep the doors open." He shakes his head. "Seems to me someone isn't ready to take on the practice after all."

I glare at the man sitting across from me, knowing in my bones that he's the piece of scum I always thought he was. "You're a piece of shit."

Okay, Parker. That was a bit direct.

Seth leans back in his chair, smirking. "Takes one to know one."

Oooh. Good come back, Seth.

I shake my head, buttoning up my lab coat and resisting the urge to throw his stapler at him. "No, because I would never do what you just did to that poor girl out there."

He waves me off. "Again, it doesn't seem like you're ready to run things around here if you wouldn't do what's best for the practice."

Someone knocks on the door, interrupting the tongue-lashing I was about to give him.

"If you could get that, that'd be great." Seth smiles up at me like I'm his fucking butler.

Clenching my teeth, I open the door to find Robert O'Neil standing there, looking between us with his usual no-bullshit expression.

"Gentlemen," he greets us, looking back and forth between me and Seth, who's now standing behind his desk.

"Robert. How can I help you?"

"We're having a staff meeting in ten minutes. I need you both present." Without further explanation, he storms off, no cane in sight.

He's been back at work for a week, and things have returned to normal for the most part. However, there've been moments where I've noticed him watching me from the corner of my eye, or he'll come up and ask me a question about a case, almost like he's testing me. And maybe he is.

I know I broke the trust he had in me by lying to him about Cashlynn, and I don't blame him for watching me more closely now. But I'll be keeping an eye on him, too—because the more I've learned about their relationship as father and daughter, the more protective I've become of her. My father never would have discouraged me from doing what makes me happy and chasing my dreams. He had his faults, but I guess when it was time for me to start figuring out what to do with my life, he'd learned from his mistakes with Dallas and Penn.

I got the father who believed in me and praised me every time I accomplished something I put my mind to and succeeded—which I always did. I had this obsession with being perfect. But over the years, I wonder if that praise for being driven, for never wanting to make mistakes, is what's made my failed relationship with Sasha haunt me for so long.

"That was your cue to leave my office," Seth snaps, pulling me back to the present.

I shoot him a glare before turning and heading down the hallway, where the rest of the staff has already gathered. A quick glance at the clock confirms that it's lunchtime—the brief window each day when the doors are locked and there are no appointments on the schedule.

Robert clears his throat loudly, commanding everyone's attention. "Thank you all for making time for this. I didn't want this to wait until our Monday meeting because I need to be truthful with all of you about something very important."

Murmurs ripple through the room.

Truthful? My chest tightens. Is he going to explain what he and Beth were discussing that day I overheard them? Fuck. Is he sick? Is he about to tell the entire staff before he tells his daughter?

"My fall three weeks ago was eye-opening, to say the least. Lucky for me, I didn't break anything, but it was a wakeup call—a reminder that I'm not getting any younger." A few of the staff chuckle nervously. "With that being said, today I am formally announcing that in three months, I will be retiring from Carrington Cove Animal Hospital."

Holy shit. He's really doing it.

This is really happening.

Everyone starts to speak amongst themselves, but Robert clears his throat again and they fall silent. I glance over at Seth, who has his arms crossed over his chest, beaming like he just won the fucking lottery.

"As you know, we have two very capable doctors here, Dr. Sheppard and Dr. Brown, both of whom I believe would do great things leading this practice. But only one name can be the sole owner, so in three months' time, I will announce my choice of who will replace me as the head doctor."

Seth and I lock eyes, and he's already smirking like it's a done deal.

Robert steps up to me, offering his hand. "You know what's at stake here, right, Parker?"

"Of course, sir," I say, gripping his hand firmly.

"Good." He leans in and lowers his voice. "And let me make one thing clear—being engaged to my daughter doesn't mean a damn thing. If anything, it means you've got even more to prove."

I swallow hard, willing my voice to stay steady. "Yes sir."

Robert nods once, releasing my hand. "Then I expect to see the doctor I've been mentoring for the past six years over the next three months, and hopefully, someone even better than that."

He turns away and walks over to Seth, probably to give him a similar speech.

But my insides are twisting.

This is my chance. This is what I've been wanting since I moved back home to work at this hospital.

I just hope I can hold it all together long enough to make my dream a reality.

Because chasing dreams is fucking exhausting.

***

Hours later, with the weight of the day pressing on me, I finally walk through the front door. I plop down onto the couch, kicking my feet up on the coffee table and stretching my toes out, trying to relieve the ache in my feet.

"I didn't hear you come home," Cashlynn says from behind me. She's fresh from the shower, dragging a towel over her wet hair.

Fuck, I want to dirty her up just looking at her.

I haven't allowed myself to think about that kiss for days because I've been buried in my work. Thank God it's Friday.

"I just got in," I say gruffly, leaning back and closing my eyes.

She steps closer and pushes my hair back from my face. "You look exhausted."

"Well, I'm trying to show your father that he can trust me—with you and his practice—so yeah...I'm beat."

She nods and heads toward the kitchen, pressing a few buttons on the microwave to heat up my dinner. The smell of enchiladas wafts through the air, and my stomach growls. She did the same thing last night, had a home-cooked meal waiting for me when I got home after a long shift. Gotta admit—that's a detail of this arrangement I don't hate.

"When he told me he was going to announce his retirement, I was afraid this might happen."

"What might happen?"

"You running yourself ragged," she says as the microwave beeps. A moment later, she sets the plate of food in front of me and hands me a fork.

"Thank you." I take a bite of the chicken enchiladas as she sits down next to me. "I have to show him how bad I want this, Cashlynn. If I don't give it my all, I'll regret it."

She props her elbow on the back of the couch, resting her head on her hand. "I get it, but I also know my father. He's the kind of man that will find a fault in anything."

"Believe me, I know."

"But he also isn't impressed by flashy showmanship. You're an amazing doctor, Parker," she says, reaching out and placing her free hand on my forearm.

"How do you know that?"

Her lips curve into a small smile. "My father has talked about you a lot, remember?"

I nod, taking another bite of my dinner. "But this is different."

"No, it's not. He doesn't need you to show off. He just needs to see that you care."

I think back to the many conversations I've had with Dr. O'Neil over the years. "Maybe you're right."

"I know I am. But if it helps, I can keep talking you up to him any chance I get."

"That might do more harm than good. Remember, he thinks I'm the man fucking his daughter." As soon as the words leave my lips, I regret them. But when I turn to look at Cashlynn, she's licking her lips and glancing down at mine.

"True," she says softly.

Needing to steer clear of the tension I just created, I take another bite of my dinner. "This is really good, by the way. Thanks."

She pushes herself up off the couch, bending over right in front of me to run the towel over her hair again before twisting it up and on top of her head.

Jesus Christ. Why was that so sexy?

"My pleasure," she says with a wink, sauntering back down the hallway, giving my dick a chance to deflate.

I reach for the remote, intent on watching some mindless TV, but when I hit the power button, nothing happens. "What the hell?"

I bang the remote against my hand a few times and then try to turn it on again, but still no luck. Setting my plate on the coffee table, I grab new batteries from the drawer and try again—nothing. Then I see it—the TV cord dangling next to the outlet, unplugged.

"Mother fucker," I grumble, apparently louder than I intended. Cashlynn reappears from the hallway.

"What's wrong?"

I gesture at the black screen. "The TV? Really, Cashlynn?"

Her lips curl up like she's fighting a smile, but she shrugs. "I told you..."

"What kind of human does that?"

"Well, you barely watch it anyway, and again—"

I hold up my hand. "Okay, this has to stop."

"Why?"

"Because it's driving me nuts!"

"I'm sorry, but this is what I do!"

"Not while you're living with me, it isn't."

We stand there, staring at each other, but Cashlynn shocks me further when she says, "Fine, then I'll play you for it."

"What?"

She steps further into the living room until there's only a few inches separating us. "Are you scared?"

"You want to play rock, paper, scissors to decide if you get to keep unplugging my appliances?"

She nods. "Yup."

I huff out a laugh despite myself and hold up my fist. "You're on."

"One," she says.

"Two."

"Three," we say in unison as I throw up fire—again—and she dishes out a closed fist, showing rock.

"When are you going to learn?" I ask her a little too smugly, but then she opens her fist above my spirit fingers and makes a whooshing sound. "Did you just..."

"That's a water balloon," she says, smirking. And then she hits me with a confession. "You're not the only one who's watched *Friends*."

With a triumphant arch of her brow, she turns and walks back toward her room. "Looks like the appliances stay unplugged, Parker!" she calls out over her shoulder.

And I'm left standing there, flabbergasted and rock-hard.

Fuck. This woman might be the reason I have myself committed.

Or she might be the one who was undoubtedly made for me.

Chapter Eleven

Cashlynn

"You look like you could use another cup of coffee," Astrid says as I walk through the front door of Smells Like Sugar.

"I don't even know if coffee could solve my problems," I reply, stifling a yawn.

"I beg to differ. Coffee is the antidote to some of life's greatest ailments."

"In that case, another hit of caffeine would be amazing. Thank you."

Astrid smiles and moves to her espresso machine. "Coming right up."

I head for a table in the corner of the bakery that should be big enough for me to spread out my laptop, notebooks, and folders for my meeting with Willow. This week I've been working with her friend on branding, and now we're going to start looking at the timeline for advertising and profit margins, as well as picking a supplier.

Just thinking about everything I still have to do is making my head spin. Of course, another reason for the spinning wears glasses and makes my panties wet each time I see him. My defenses against my fake fiancé—and my growing attraction—are wearing dangerously thin. I'm not sure how much longer I can hold out before I start outright begging for him to touch me again.

I know this attraction is mutual. That much was evident when I kissed him the other night and he eagerly kissed me back. The move sure as hell wasn't planned, but it sure as hell wasn't fake either. God, I can't stop thinking about it.

It's not just the kiss. It's the way he's been showing up for me every single day, encouraging me to believe in myself, calming my self-doubts about the gallery, and working his ass off to rebuild my father's trust while proving he deserves to take over the practice.

This is more than just a fake arrangement. Nothing between us feels fake, and it hasn't since he slipped that ring on my finger. The way he looked at me, the conviction in his eyes and voice—I know there's more between us. But nothing I've tried has made him crack yet.

What if I'm just making this all up in my head?

The bell above the door chimes and Willow walks in, wearing soft black leggings and an oversized cream sweater with brown knee-high boots. Some women just radiate when they're pregnant, and she is one of them.

She flicks her blonde hair over her shoulder and when our eyes meet, she heads in my direction. "Sorry I'm late," she says as she sets her large purse on one of the empty chairs and removes a few file folders from it.

"You're not. I just got here. Astrid is making me some coffee."

"And I have a decaf for the mom-to-be," Astrid announces, setting our drinks on the table.

Willow places a hand on Astrid's arm. "I love you, but I'd love you even more if you've got a blueberry muffin back there with my name on it."

Astrid winks at her best friend. "I saved you two."

As she walks away, Willow turns back to me. "Have you had one yet?"

"Not yet."

Willow gasps dramatically. "They're the best thing she makes!" She rubs her stomach as she takes a seat. "I couldn't eat them during my first trimester because I could barely keep anything down. But now, if I don't get my fix, bad things happen to good people."

Chuckling, I say, "Note to self: butter up my boss with blueberry muffins."

Willow smiles. "I'm not your boss, I'm your investor, Cashlynn. This is your baby," she says, placing her hand over mine. "And with the way things are going, I think we might be able to open in two months instead of three."

"Really?"

She nods.

"I can't thank you enough, Willow. Truly."

"I remember what it was like to be the new person in town, and how nerve-racking starting your own business can be. If it weren't for Astrid and her generosity, I don't know that I would have stayed. And I see something in you that reminds me a lot of myself."

I swallow nervously. "And what's that?"

"Resilience. Bravery. One of these days you're going to understand how your doubts can actually lead you to where you're meant to be."

Her words strike a chord. I've been in Carrington Cove for nearly a month now, and the longer I'm here, the more this place feels like home, like this is where I'm supposed to be. Now if only I could figure out what the future looks like for me and Parker.

"Fancy seeing you two here."

Willow and I look up to see Hazel striding over to our table.

"You knew we were going to be here," Willow says dryly. "I told you that when you texted me last night and asked what my plans were for today."

"Was there a Sheppard women meeting this morning I wasn't invited to?" Scottie walks over to us now. "I know Grady isn't a Sheppard, but last I checked, he and I had been adopted."

For a second, I let myself think about how if Parker and I were to actually get married, I'd become a Sheppard too.

You're getting a little ahead of yourself, Cashlynn. Your relationship has to become real first, remember?

Astrid returns, setting a plate with two blueberry muffins in front of Willow. "Looks like the gang is all here this morning." She leans over and hugs Scottie. "Are you here for your weekly apple fritter fix?"

"You know it." Scottie leans over and says to me, "They're the best thing Astrid makes."

I chuckle. "Willow just said that about the blueberry muffins."

Hazel holds a hand up. "Let me stop you there. Try her raspberry cheesecake cupcakes, and they'll ruin you for everything else."

Astrid dramatically fans her face with her hand. "Oh, you girls are gonna give me a complex."

We share a laugh as Willow peels the wrapper from a muffin and takes a bite. "Well, Cashlynn and I are here to talk business."

"Oh, I just wanted to say hi," Scottie says. "I need to work on my lesson plans, but I couldn't pass up the chance for some adult interaction. Most of the time I only get to talk to eight-year-olds and a babbling five-month-old."

"What grade do you teach again?" I ask, slightly embarrassed that I don't remember from the night I met her at the Sheppards' dinner. But there were so many people and it was all I could do to keep everyone's names straight.

"Third. That's the last year where they're still sweet. When they hit fourth grade, the sass kicks in and then I'm out." She slices her finger across her throat dramatically. The girls laugh.

"You know," I say, an idea sparking, "my gallery would be a great place to host a school fundraiser or take a field trip."

Willow's eyes light up. "Oh my God. I love that idea. When did you think of that?"

I reach for my notebook and open it to the earmarked page. "I've been doing research all week on galleries in other parts of the country, and then I saw an idea on Pinterest about water gun painting. I thought that would be something kids would love. I could even bring the supplies to the school and make it part of a field day—maybe tie it in with a color run or something like that."

Scottie nods enthusiastically. "Oh, absolutely. They would be so excited, and it's perfect for the end of the school year when they're going bonkers anyway."

"Yeah, just let me know when and we can schedule something."

"I definitely will. When will you be up and running?"

I glance at Willow. "Well, that's actually what our meeting today is about, so I'll have to get back to you on that. If I had a business card, I'd give you one, but I'm working on that too." Suddenly, I feel inadequate, putting the cart before the horse.

Scottie waves me off. "No worries, I get it. But count me in. My boss will be on board too, I'm sure."

Leaning back in her chair, Hazel says, "Speaking of being on board, how's your progress going with my brother?"

Scottie laughs, giving a wave as Astrid steers her toward the counter for her apple fritters. Willow gives Hazel the side-eye. "Hazel, this meeting is supposed to be about business," she mutters, but then turns to me and waggles her eyebrows. "But that can wait. Spill."

I groan, burying my head in my hands. "Um, well... I don't think it's going very well."

Hazel reaches across the table and pries my hands from my face. "Why is that?"

"I feel like a teenage girl with a crush, doing stupid things to get a boy's attention, but he's oblivious, and I'm even more confused about how he feels about me."

"What have you tried?"

I pick my head up and take a drink of my coffee. "God, this is good."

Hazel nods. "Yes, Astrid makes a fine latte. But you really need to visit Keely's Caffeine Kick. That woman is the master of iced coffee."

Willow rolls her eyes, sighing. "Enough with the coffee! Get back to Parker, Cashlynn."

"So, I started with the appliance thing you suggested, Willow. I unplugged the coffee machine, which sent him into a total tailspin."

Hazel snorts. "I saw him at the animal hospital that morning, and he mentioned it. I could tell his underwear was wedged between his butt cheeks after that stunt."

I laugh. "It definitely threw him off. Besides that, I've been testing the waters—little touches here and there, nothing too obvious. But the night my dad came over for dinner..." I hesitate, glancing between them before admitting, "I kissed him."

Both women's jaws drop. Willow recovers first. "And how did he react? Did he kiss you back?"

I clench my thighs together at the memory. "Oh yeah. But then he jumped away like I'd burned him."

Willow scrunches her nose. "What did you do?"

"I decided to give him space and just went to my room for the night."

Hazel nods approvingly. "Nice. Leave him to stew."

"That's what I was thinking. But the next day, he acted like nothing had happened. For days, it felt like he was actively trying to avoid me—until I took him to see the gallery space."

Willow perks up, reaching for her coffee. "But that day, he gave you that little pep talk when you were doubting yourself. It was definitely something a real fiancé would've have said."

"I thought so too, but he slipped back into a routine of avoiding me...until the other night."

"What happened then?" Hazel asks, leaning in.

"Well, my father announced he's retiring in three months, so now Parker and Seth are battling it out to see who will take over the practice. Parker has been running himself ragged trying to prove himself. He was working late the other night, so I had dinner waiting for him when he got home, and we sat on the couch together and talked. It felt so...normal. And I swear, he looked at me like he was glad I was there. That is, until he went to turn on the TV I forgot I'd unplugged earlier..."

Hazel and Willow both burst out laughing. "Oh my God," Willow manages. "What did he do?"

I chuckle at the memory. "He snapped, saying he doesn't understand what kind of human would do such a thing, and told me I had to stop. So, I challenged him to rock, paper, scissors for it—and I won. Now I get to keep pushing his buttons, one power cord at a time."

Willow tilts her head. "Rock, paper, scissors? That's one way to handle a disagreement, I guess."

"It's how he got me to hold his hand on the plane when we met."

She covers her chest with her hand. "Oh my God. That's adorable."

Hazel chuckles. "Sounds like something the old Parker would've done."

"The old Parker?"

Her expression dims slightly. "The one before Sasha put his heart in a blender."

Nodding in understanding, I lower my gaze to the table. "I just don't know if he's ready to open himself up to me, you guys. I see these glimmers of the man I met on the plane—sweet, funny, a little cocky—but then the closed-off grump comes out, and I feel like I'm getting emotional whiplash trying to figure out how to handle him."

Hazel and Willow share a look before Hazel speaks up. "Besides the kiss and the grazes, have there been any other physical moments?"

I bite my lip. "Not really."

Hazel shrugs like the solution is obvious. "Then you need to step it up."

"I don't know…"

Willow nods. "No, I think she's right. Sometimes men just need to get their pent-up frustrations out to relax enough to talk about their feelings. When Dallas is in a mood, I always initiate sex, and afterward, he spills his guts. It's not exactly moral, but it works every time."

I blink, unsure whether to laugh or take notes.

"Have you taken your shirt off yet?" Hazel asks.

My cheeks heat. "No…"

"There's a reason why sex sells, Cashlynn. I'm telling you…show him some freaking skin."

"You are strangely invested in Parker's love life," Astrid says, reappearing with a plate of raspberry scones.

"It's not just that, okay? Tormenting my brothers is entertaining as fuck, for one," Hazel says, holding up a finger. The rest of us laugh. "But two," she continues, sadness filling her eyes now. "I want my brother back."

Astrid nods in agreement. "I get it. He just hasn't been the same since Sasha."

"Has he opened up to you about that yet?" Willow asks me.

"No, and I haven't pushed him."

Hazel shakes her head. "And now's not the time for that. First, get him to admit that he wants you. Then maybe you can get him to talk to you about his feelings."

"There's definitely something between us. The things he says, the way he touches me in front of other people—like he can't help himself."

Hazel leans forward and places her hand on top of mine. "I know we haven't known each other very long, but I can tell that you care about him."

My heart is hammering so hard that I can hear it in my ears. "I do. More than I probably should."

"All I've ever wanted for my brother is to find someone who understands how incredible he is. Parker is one of a kind, genuine and smart. He treated his first girlfriend in high school like a fucking prize, and I knew I could only hope to find a man that treated me like that one day. But Sasha..." Her jaw tightens. "She didn't appreciate him. He was still the same man, though, bending over backwards to make her life incredible. She burned him—scarred him so deep that it's almost as if a part of his heart died along with the loss of her."

My heart aches at the weight of her words. "I wish he would tell me everything."

"He will, once you get that pent up frustration out." Hazel winks and Willow nods in agreement. "But since you've been here, I've seen glimpses of the old him, so as disturbing as it is to say... You need to fuck my brother, and fuck him good."

I choke on my coffee, coughing as Willow cackles. "Yeah. That *was* disturbing coming from you."

Willow shakes her head, still laughing. "Okay, now that we've established Cashlynn's mission to fuck Parker's brains out, can we get to our business meeting?"

Hazel stands from her chair. "Yup. I'll leave you to it. I have a long day of editing to get through, and I need a raspberry cheesecake cupcake to reward myself with." She waves her fingers at us as she walks away. "Have fun you two. And don't forget, Cashlynn—strategic nudity."

Once she's out of earshot, I lean in toward Willow. "That was a little weird, right?"

She shrugs. "Yes, but she's not wrong. It sounds to me like the only thing standing between you and Parker's feelings might just be your clothes."

Chapter Twelve

Parker

"Fuck." I push the barbell back up far enough to rack it, blowing out a breath. Challenging myself with heavier weight today was my game plan going in, but everything feels really fucking heavy this morning.

The elephant sitting on my chest isn't helping either.

It's been an entire month now that Cashlynn has been living with me, and with time, I was hoping it would get easier to be around her. But it's only gotten harder to ignore how she makes me feel.

When I get home from work, I genuinely look forward to our conversations about our days. She fills me in on her progress with the gallery, and I tell her about my patients—and the daily battle not to level Seth out in front of everyone at the practice.

"How early do you get up to work out every day?"

I twist my head to the doorway and stop cold. Cashlynn's standing there, her hair thrown into a messy bun and her body poured into black spandex—the smallest fucking pieces of spandex that must exist in the world.

Holy shit. She might as well be wearing a bikini.

I gulp down the knot in my throat. "Five."

She covers her mouth as she yawns. "I thought so."

"What are you doing up this early?"

She walks further into the room, and that's when I notice she's carrying a mat under her arm. "With everything going on, I've let my morning yoga routine slip, and I was really good about it back in Philly. I figured I'd get back into it now that things have settled. It keeps my mind centered and my body flexible."

She rolls her shoulders back, arching slightly, and it's all I can do not to groan.

Fuck me. As if I needed more fuel for my already overactive imagination.

"It might be quieter in the house," I say, wanting nothing more than to watch her bend herself into all sorts of positions, but knowing that watching her do so will be fucking torture.

"I don't mind the noise. This is your gym, right?" I nod. "Then this is where I'll work out too."

Resigned to my fate, I lie back on the bench, gripping the bar like it's the only thing keeping me tethered to sanity. I stare up at the ceiling and curse myself, knowing that if I don't control my imagination here, Cashlynn will get a front-row seat to my cock standing at attention under my gym shorts. The mesh does nothing to contain an erection, that's for damn sure.

Gripping the bar above me, I lift it off the rack and do my next set, breathing out hard as I push close to failure. Racking the bar again, I sit up and find Cashlynn bent over right in front of me, her shorts doing nothing to hide that ass I know I shouldn't have memorized like I do.

"Jesus," I mutter.

Cashlynn peeks at me from between her legs. "Is something wrong?"

"Nope." I stand, avoiding looking in her direction, and walk over to the free weights where I grab the forty-pound dumbbells for some bicep curls. Staring at my form in the mirror helps for about three seconds—until I glance toward Cashlynn again and find her still bent over, watching me.

"You have an incredible body, Parker." Straightening, she brushes loose strands of hair from her face and lets her gaze roam up and down my bare chest. Then, as if the torture weren't enough, she licks her lips.

"Thank you," I manage, my voice tight.

"You're welcome." She smiles and then goes back to stretching, moving down to her mat and starting a pose. Her body stretches flat to the mat, then shifts as she starts to arch and flatten her back. With each movement, I think about what she'd look like on all fours, bowing her back like that as I fuck her from behind.

Jesus Christ. This is torture.

When she stands, she rolls her neck and reaches behind her to fiddle with her top—which let's be honest, is basically a sports bra. Between the shorts that barely cover her ass and this top that is straining to contain her breasts that I remember vividly, Cashlynn's body is entirely on display, and I'm struggling not to appreciate it as she did mine.

She scrunches her nose. "This top is digging into me. Could you adjust it for me, please?"

I place the dumbbells back on the rack. "Uh, yeah. I can do that."

"Thanks. I think the straps are just too tight."

I walk over to her and when she turns her back to me, my eyes involuntarily trace the curve of her waist, remembering what her hips felt like in my hands, thinking about how easy it would be to push her forward onto the bench and have my way with her.

Focus, Parker.

I grip the metal piece that slides along the straps and pull it down, releasing some of the tension.

Cashlynn lets out a sigh of relief. "Oh my God. Thank you. Can you do the other side too, please?"

I repeat the process, making sure the two sides are even. The smell of her coconut shampoo hits my nose with each passing second, and that smell…does things to me. It makes my dick stir, and just as I feared, my shorts start to tent.

I turn around quickly, adjusting myself, and go back to the free weights.

"Thanks, Parker."

"No problem."

Cashlynn drops back down to her mat and I try with every ounce of control that I possess not to look in her direction, debating on cutting my workout short. A nice cold shower should do the trick, or I can just jerk off for the thousandth time—not that it's been helping.

"Ugh!"

Her frustrated groan snaps my attention back to her, and I immediately regret it. She stands up tall, turns her back to me, and then rips her sports bra off up over her head, throwing it to the ground.

Fuck. Me. Sideways.

"Um, is everything all right?" I manage to choke out as she covers her breasts with her forearm and turns around to face me. But why does she bother? I already know what those rosy, pink nipples look like and how they feel in my mouth.

"I think that top is just too small. It's digging into me and I couldn't take it anymore." She grabs her water bottle and then walks right up to me, an innocent smile on her face. "Thanks for trying to adjust it for me, but I guess I just need to get rid of it."

Swallowing down my frustration, I say, "You could've waited to take it off in your room, Cashlynn."

She blinks a few times, dips her eyes down to my crotch, and then lifts her eyes back to mine with a pleased smile on her lips. "Yeah, I could have, but I just couldn't take it for another second." She shrugs and then moves to the door. "I'm gonna hop in the shower."

As soon as she's gone, I look down and see my cock standing at full attention, straining against my shorts. Yeah, there's no way she didn't see that—or feel it with how close she was standing to me.

I drag my hands through my hair and place them on the top of my head, looking up at the ceiling, asking God why I'm being punished when I was just trying to help the woman out.

But it seems karma is hell-bent on making herself known, and Cashlynn is a lot more to handle than I bargained for.

***

"Where's Grady?" I ask as I walk into Catch & Release for our Thursday lunch, finding my brothers already in their usual spots—Dallas behind the bar and Penn on his stool, shoving a burger in his mouth—but no sign of our friend with his daughter strapped to his chest like normal.

"Callie had a doctor's appointment," Dallas says, filling up a glass of Coke for me and sliding it down the bar.

Penn looks at our older brother. "That's going to be you soon. Have you and Willow discussed cutting back your hours at this place once your son arrives?"

Dallas looks out over his restaurant, the business he takes immense pride in. One day, I hope to do the same with Carrington Cove Animal

Hospital. "We have. I'm promoting Sara to manager and hiring a few more servers. I won't be working night shifts anymore, gentlemen. And I'm not sure what will happen to our Thursday lunch dates."

The chime above the door rings out as Grady strolls in. "Sorry I'm late."

"I thought you weren't going to make it," Dallas says.

"Callie's appointment was quicker than expected, so Scottie took her home for some one-on-one time since she has the afternoon off."

Grady slides onto a stool to my left and Dallas pours him a drink. The kitchen bell rings, signaling that my lunch is ready, so Dallas grabs it and asks the cook to throw down another burger for Grady.

"Jimmy's gonna get you a burger going," he says to Grady, setting my plate in front of me.

"Appreciate it." Grady tips his chin to Dallas and then leans back on his stool. "So, what did I miss?"

"We were talking about how Dallas's life is about to change once the baby comes and he has no fucking clue what he's in for," Penn replies.

Grady huffs out a laugh. "There's no preparing for it, man. Life and all of your priorities shift."

Dallas nods. "Yeah, I was telling them I'm not going to be working nights anymore."

Grady nods. "Probably a good idea. Evenings are the witching hour. One night Callie's easy to bathe and put to sleep, then the next, she screams for an hour before bedtime."

Dallas blinks. "Joy."

Penn chuckles. "You'll adjust." Dallas nods, taking a deep breath.

Penn looks to me now. "Speaking of adjusting, how's living with Cashlynn?"

I finish chewing my food and wipe my mouth with my napkin. "It's...interesting."

Dallas laughs. "How so?"

"Well, I swear the woman is trying to drive me nuts. Otherwise, she just has weird fucking habits and I'm not sure I'll make it through the timeline we agreed to."

Penn laughs as he pops a fry in his mouth. "Women are fascinating creatures, that's for sure. What did she do?"

I spend the next few minutes telling the guys about the unplugging of the appliances, her giving me shit about ironing my socks, the kiss, and this morning's little bra-removal incident.

"You iron your fucking socks?" Grady asks from beside me as Dallas hands him his burger.

Penn and Dallas throw their heads back in laughter. "You have to understand something about our little brother," Dallas says. "Parker is what they call anal-retentive." Grady nearly chokes on the bite he just took. "He has a system for everything. And if you mess with them, he blows a fucking gasket."

"I'm not *that* bad," I mumble around a french fry.

"Um, yes you are," Penn adds as he clasps a hand on my shoulder. "But we love you in spite of it."

"Gee, thanks." I look up at the ceiling. "I'm so glad I took time out of my day to have lunch with y'all just to get roasted."

Dallas flicks me in the forehead. "Oh, calm down."

I blink up at him. "Did you just...flick me?"

Grady chuckles and pats me on the back. "I'm sorry. That little segue was my fault. Back to Cashlynn. You said she kissed you and stripped off her bra in front of you?"

I shoot him a glare that I wish could singe off his chest hair. "Yes, and if you haven't noticed, the woman is fucking gorgeous. I'm in quite the predicament."

Grady shakes his head. "I'm wondering if maybe...she's *trying* to drive you crazy?"

Dallas furrows his brow as all three of us look over at Grady. "What do you mean?"

"I could be way off base here, but I remember Scottie telling me about this romance novel her mom and grandma roped her into reading. The guy and girl were roommates for some odd reason, and she knew he liked her, but he wouldn't act on it. So she did all kinds of shit to push him over the edge."

I stare at the half-empty Coke in front of me. "Do you really think she'd do that?"

Penn clears his throat. "I mean, none of us know her as well as you do, but at the gallery that day, she had this look in her eyes when she was speaking to you." He darts his eyes to Dallas and then back to me. "And I hate to say it, but I saw it from you too."

"What kind of look?' Grady asks.

"The kind that if Willow and I weren't in the building with them, they probably would have been naked and fucking up against the wall."

I shake my head. "You didn't see shit," I grumble, even as my mind unhelpfully replays that exact fantasy.

He shoves my shoulder. "Parker, it's okay to fucking like her."

I turn to face Penn. "This isn't grade school. This is my fucking life."

Dallas decides it's time to chime in. "Yes, it is, and you've been wallowing and stomping through it for four fucking years, Parker."

Penn shoves my shoulder again. "You have a woman living under your roof who you've already slept with, you know you have a connection with, and who is genuinely trying to help you while helping herself. You'd be a fool not to explore more with her."

"She does give you those googly eyes," Dallas adds. "I bet she fucking *wants* you and is trying to get you to make a move."

"Then why not just tell me?"

All three of them laugh. "Oh yeah, because you're so open to talking about your feelings," Penn says mockingly.

"Let's be real—none of us are. The only way Willow can get me to open up is if we have sex first," Dallas admits.

Grady turns to him. "That's weird. I always feel like talking about my feelings and shit after Scottie and I have sex too."

"Fuck, me too," Penn says as all three of them stare at one another.

And then a lightbulb clicks on in Dallas's eyes. "Holy shit. Has Cashlynn been hanging out with the girls?"

"Uh, she had a meeting with Willow the other day at Astrid's bakery. She said Scottie and Hazel were there for a little bit..." I grow more anxious the longer this conversation continues.

Dallas snaps his fingers. "That's gotta be it."

"What's gotta be what?"

Grady smacks me on the back of the head. "They're plotting, dipshit. I thought you were a doctor?"

I shove him away. "Fuck you, Grady. My mind is a fucking mess, okay? Between my roommate's Jedi mind tricks and battling Seth at work, I'm barely keeping my own name straight these days."

"Well, I think your fake fiancée knows exactly what she's doing, and step one is making you give in to your attraction to her," Penn says.

My face is starting to hurt from squinting at my brother as I try to wrap my head around what he's saying. "What would possess her to do that? I already agreed to help her with this charade..."

"Yeah, but what if she wants more than just a fake engagement?" Dallas asks.

I rewind the last four weeks in my mind—all the little moments, touches, and conversations we've shared. The confident woman I slept with a year ago definitely wasn't shy about her body then, but to think that she'd be trying to use it against me? I just don't know if I believe it.

Getting involved with each other beyond our agreement opens up a can of worms I've kept secret for a reason. But I can't deny that Cashlynn makes me want to set those worms free. She has this softness about her that makes me feel like I can let my guard down, even though sometimes when I'm around her, I feel like I have to keep it up just so I don't feel too much.

"I don't know that I can offer her anything more," I admit.

Dallas leans over the bar, looking me straight in the eye. "But do you want to?"

I look into the eyes of my older brother, trying to remind myself that he faced his demons, and so did Penn. If they could do it, maybe I'm not destined to be alone forever. Maybe every relationship isn't doomed to fail.

"Is it worth the risk?" I say, my voice so low I'm surprised they hear me.

"Fuck yes," Dallas says, without hesitation. "Willow is the best fucking thing to happen to me, Parker. But if I hadn't dealt with my shit, who knows what would have happened between us?"

I toss my glasses onto the bar and drag my hands down my face. "I don't know if I can handle this right now. With Robert retiring, I already have so much going on and—"

"Let me ask you this," Penn says, cutting me off. "If Robert chooses Seth instead of you, then what?"

My stomach twists as I turn to look at him. "I—I don't fucking know."

"So you're willing to take a risk with your career, but not with your heart? Your job isn't going to keep you warm at night. Your job won't give you a reprieve from the bullshit of life. Your job won't show you what it really means to live." His tone softens, but his next words hit harder. "I hate to say it, Parker, but you're replaceable at your job. We all are. But you can't replace the people who matter, and being with Cashlynn might just help you put that all into perspective."

I can't deny that Penn is right.

I have a woman right in front of me that makes me feel something for the first time in years. But can I let go of the past so I can move forward with her?

Or will I always be waiting for the other shoe to drop?

***

"Cashlynn?"

When I step through the front door, I expect to see Cashlynn on the couch working on her laptop or in the kitchen making a cup of tea. Over the past couple of weeks, that seems to be her evening routine. But the house is eerily quiet and my chest tightens as a flicker of unease creeps in.

Maybe she went out drinking?

She's not Sasha, Parker. She's not out drinking. That's not her.

As I try to talk myself down from a spiral, I hear her voice down the hall. I let out a breath of relief, but then my stomach churns with fresh nerves as I remember the conversation with the guys earlier.

I had a very hard time concentrating at work after I left Catch & Release, warring with myself over what to do about my growing feelings for this woman. I know what my body wants, that much is clear. But my mind is still having a hard time catching up.

Before I can second-guess myself, I make my way to her door, hand raised to knock. But the words I hear come out of Cashlynn's mouth stop me dead in my tracks.

"Yes, I did yoga in my fucking underwear, Hazel. Ripped off my bra and threw it on the ground in front of him, and nothing. He let me walk away without even grunting or cursing under his breath."

Holy shit. She is *trying to get me to snap. And my fucking sister is in on it.*

"I don't know. I think he's determined to keep this platonic." She goes silent, which I can only assume means she's listening to Hazel on the other end of the line. "No, I'm not going to do that."

What the fuck would my sister suggest she do now? Sit on my face so I have no choice but to lick her pussy? What a hardship that would be.

"I just don't know if this is worth it," Cashlynn says, her voice laden with defeat.

The sound of it guts me. Is she talking about bailing on this entire charade? Or is she giving up on me altogether?

"He's just so…" But she doesn't finish that sentence, probably because my sister cut her off. She's really good at that.

In that instant, I take a step away from the door, the heat rising in my chest shifting into irritation.

So, they *have* been conspiring. All of them.

Well, two can play that game, ladies.

You know what they say: Payback's a bitch.

Chapter Thirteen

Parker

"Someone's here early today."

I look up from my desk to find Beth standing in the doorway of my office. I did come in about an hour ahead of schedule because I needed space from Cashlynn before I said or did something I couldn't take back. That's the last fucking thing I need right now.

"I couldn't sleep, and I had some paperwork to get caught up on, so…" I shrug, averting my eyes back down to the file in front of me.

"You know, showing up early isn't going to sway his decision."

That catches my attention. I sit back, crossing my arms. "That's not why I'm here."

"Oh, I just assumed."

"I mean, I can't deny that I'm trying to prove myself, Beth. But honestly, I didn't sleep well, like I said, and I needed to get out of my house."

Her eyebrows raise from that remark. "Is everything okay?"

"Everything is fine. I'm just having a hard time adjusting to living with a woman," I say with a laugh, which thankfully Beth takes as the joke I intended it to be.

"Ah, yes. There are always a few speed bumps when you start living with someone new, but you'll adjust."

Yeah, not so sure about that, especially when my new roommate wants me to have a permanent case of blue balls unless I do something about our growing sexual tension.

"We are, but it's just been a lot of change recently, and I don't handle change very well."

Beth scoffs. "No man does, Parker. Especially Dr. O'Neil."

Her mention of Robert makes my mind flash to the conversation I overheard a few weeks ago, so I seize the opportunity to ask about it. "Is everything okay with Robert?"

I can visibly see her swallow. "Yes, of course."

"You sure? There's not something going on health related that is making him consider retirement?"

"No, Parker. He's fine, at least as far as I know. Why do you ask?"

"I just…" *Do I tell her I heard their conversation?* "I'm just concerned is all."

Beth flashes me a smile that seems a little forced. "I'm sure if there were something going on, Cashlynn would be the one to ask, wouldn't she?"

"Perhaps. But you know Robert. He's stubborn. I could see him hiding a diagnosis from Cashlynn just so he didn't have to argue with her about what he should do."

She nods. "That sounds like him, but as far as I know, he's in perfectly good health. In fact, his doctor said he's looking great after his fall."

"Well, that's good to hear."

She smiles again before she starts to retreat. "Okay, dear. Well, I'll let you get back to work."

"Thanks, Beth. Let's have a smooth day, shall we?"

She rolls her eyes. "That's always the goal, Parker, but you and I both know how crazy this place can get."

I nod, chuckling. "That's true."

"Honestly, once Robert retires, we may need to look into hiring another doctor, so neither you nor Seth have to be here all the time. That's no way to have a life."

I scoff. "This job is my life, Beth."

"No, it *was*. Now you have Cashlynn, and your life together needs to be your new priority." She arches a brow at me before leaving my office and putting me right back into the tailspin I was in last night as I was trying to find sleep.

Hearing Cashlynn on the phone with Hazel was eye-opening, and not just because it confirmed she wants more from me, but because it forced me to ask myself if I can be the man she deserves if I decide to pursue something more.

I've only been in two serious relationships in my life—one in high school and then Sasha. But when I claim a woman as mine, I'm all in, and the thought of doing that again, putting myself out there like that and opening myself up to the possibility of being hurt again makes my stomach turn and my jaw hurt from clenching it.

Growing up, my father preached about being dedicated to a woman and led by example in the way he loved my mom.

When he returned from the Marines before I was born, I know he struggled mentally. He'd seen and done things that no human should ever have to live with. But my mom has always said that me being born is what saved him and their marriage. And I never took that truth for granted. I guess in some way, I felt a responsibility to live up to the example they set, to prove that I was grateful to them for working through their issues and being an example of what love really is—choosing to love someone through every good and bad thing in your life, dedicating yourself to growing and changing with another human right alongside of you.

But with Sasha, I failed.

I failed to make things work, and that disappointment has buried itself deep in my bones. I've walked around with it for years.

But can I let it go? Am I willing to try again? Can I learn from that and make better decisions moving forward?

Is Cashlynn the woman to take that risk with?

I don't know—and it scares the ever-loving shit out of me.

I go back to my paperwork, still conflicted over how to approach this situation with Cashlynn, but by the time the practice opens, my focus is firmly on work. Today is surgery day, so I lead several spaying and neutering procedures, as well as dental cleanings and lump removals.

Around mid-afternoon, I walk back to my office to finish up some paperwork. Seth corners me inside, standing in my doorway with his arms crossed over his chest.

"Can I help you, Dr. Brown?" I ask, not bothering to look up from my desk.

"How do you do it?"

"Do what exactly?"

"Lie and have no remorse about it."

My head pops up to find him smugly smiling in my direction. "Excuse me?"

"People should be able to trust the doctors taking care of their pets."

"Ha. That's rich coming from you," I reply, folding my arms over my chest and leaning back in my chair. "What are you implying, Seth?"

"That I wouldn't trust a liar with my animals."

My pulse spikes as I internally debate what he knows, but I don't want to jump to conclusions or rat myself out in the process, so I opt for nonchalance. "And what exactly would I be lying about?"

He shrugs innocently. "Why don't you tell Dr. O'Neil what his daughter is *really* doing here?"

My stomach drops, but I keep my expression neutral. "You already know the answer to that, Seth. We're engaged."

"Yeah, I'm not buying it, Parker." He steps further into the room and closes the door behind him. "I do have to admit your acting skills aren't half bad, but something just doesn't add up. The timing of this was all very convenient, considering you *knew* Dr. O'Neil was going to retire soon. I think you just wanted to give yourself an edge."

Slowly, I stand from my desk, resting my palms on the surface and leaning forward to look Seth dead in the eye. "I don't need an edge to beat you, Seth." His jaw clenches tighter. "Have you forgotten who's been here longer? Who has a higher success rate with surgeries? Who gets better outcomes for our patients with cancer?"

"That doesn't mean anything," he snaps.

"Dr. O'Neil doesn't see it that way. And here's the thing—you can have the practice, you can have the title, hell, you can have the damn corner office. But you'll never be the better doctor. Not because of the reasons I've already listed, and not because I'm smarter, which I am. But because I fucking care about people and their pets. All you care about are dollar signs."

He grinds his teeth together as he steps back. "I'm going to figure out what's going on, Parker."

"Have fun. Meanwhile, I'll be focusing on what truly matters—my patients."

Without another word, Seth stalks out of my office. As soon as I know he's out of earshot I let out the breath I was holding.

I haven't figured out what I want to say to Cashlynn about what I overheard yet, but this is something I absolutely have to talk to her about—because Seth could ruin the chances of either of us getting what we want.

***

When I walk through the front door after a tumultuous shift, I'm disappointed yet again to see that Cashlynn isn't in the living room or kitchen, so I head to her room, but she's not there either. Her car is in the driveway, so she has to be here somewhere. My frustration simmers as I look around, trying to figure out where she could be. Then it hits me—the garage.

Sure enough, I find her walking on the treadmill, her earbuds in and her laptop balanced on the small desk attachment.

"Cashlynn?"

She holds up a hand without looking at me and speaks aloud. "Sure, I think that'll work. I like the blue, but it's a little one dimensional. It needs more color."

Since she's preoccupied with a call, I head back inside to change out of my work clothes. By the time I return in red gym shorts and a plain black T-shirt, my frustration has only deepened.

"Are you done with your call?" I ask as I step back into the garage.

"Yeah, sorry about that. It was the branding manager I've been working with."

"Isn't it a little late on a Friday for business calls?"

She furrows her brow. "She had a doctor's appointment earlier today and asked to reschedule. I was being accommodating."

"Well, I need to talk to you."

She glances back down at her computer. "I'm almost done with everything I need to do here. Can it wait?"

"No, it can't." My patience with this woman and our situation is razor-thin, and if I don't get the Seth issue off my chest, I'm going to explode.

Cashlynn looks at me again, visibly irritated. "It'll only take fifteen, twenty minutes tops, Parker. Can't we—"

"I need to talk to you right now, Cashlynn." My voice reverberates through the garage, signaling the urgency of the matter. It's enough to make her pause, studying me for a beat before letting out a sigh.

"Fine," she mutters, pressing stop on the treadmill. Once it slows down, she hops off and walks over to me wearing another sinful workout outfit. "This better be important."

"It is," I say sharply.

Her head rears back and her eyes narrow. "Why are you being an asshole right now?"

I arch a brow. "An asshole? Don't even start on my attitude, sweetheart, when you're the one responsible for it."

"What the hell is your problem?"

I hold a hand up. "Not now. I told you there's something important we need to discuss."

"And I told *you* that I'm busy." She plants her hands on her hips.

Fuck, this woman is driving me insane. Where did *her* attitude come from all of a sudden? But then, an idea hits me. "How about I play you for it?"

Her mouth falls open, but then she shakes her head at me, irritation filling her eyes. "I'm just going to use the water balloon again, Parker."

I close the distance between us, adrenaline coursing through my veins. My gaze drops down to the purse of her lips, the challenge in her eyes, and the way her breasts are heaving and straining against her sports bra, the same one she ripped off her body yesterday morning.

Every second we stand here in this stare off only adds fuel to my desire for this woman.

And that's when I make the decision.

This woman wanted me to snap? Fine. She's about to get exactly what she asked for.

I might be smarter than the average bear, but intelligence doesn't always win out over animal instinct.

And right now, my instincts are in full fucking control.

"Why bother with the water balloon, Cashlynn…" I say, dragging her bottom lip down with my thumb as I tilt her chin up. "When I could have you dripping for me instead? Then we both win."

Her jaw drops. "What?"

I don't give her a chance to process.

Smashing my lips to hers, I haul her against my body, pressing my erection into her stomach as all of the blood racing through me travels straight to my cock. But Cashlynn doesn't hesitate—she dives into the kiss with just as much ferocity, clawing at my shoulders, pulling me as close as she can, swirling her tongue with mine. Weeks of tension boil over, and I pour every ounce of frustration into claiming her mouth.

Breaking our kiss, I spin her around and bend her forward so her elbows are resting on the weight bench. My palm connects with her ass, and she yelps, jerking forward.

"Parker!"

I smirk as I grip both of her ass cheeks before I deliver another sharp smack. This time, she doesn't chastise me, but moans loudly, the sound a soothing balm to the demons I keep inside.

"You don't want to talk? That's fine. There's no need for talking."

"Parker, I…"

I lean over her back and cup both of her breasts through the thin fabric of her sports bra. My erection slides right between her ass cheeks. "Do you not want this?"

"Yes," she whispers breathlessly. "I do. I just…"

I nip at the sensitive skin on her neck, making her shiver. "I know you do. I know all about how you've been scheming to drive me crazy, Cashlynn. And now you're about to find out what happens when I lose control."

Before she can say another word, I stand up and yank her leggings down her legs, revealing the smooth, bare skin that makes my pulse thunder. She lifts her feet to help me rid her of the fabric, her socks and shoes hitting the floor. I smack her bare ass this time, the sight of her pink skin making my cock twitch in anticipation. Then, I pull her back to my chest and shove her sports bra up her body, tossing it to the floor like she did the other day.

"Get back down," I command, my voice rough with need. And she obeys without hesitation, bending over the bench again. I rip off my shirt and shove my shorts and boxers to the floor, stroking my cock as I take in the sight in front of me. Damn, Cashlynn's ass is exquisite. I didn't get to fuck her this way our one night together, but you bet your ass I'm about to remedy that right now.

"I don't have a condom, Cashlynn. Are you on birth control?"

She nods, looking at me over her shoulder. "Yes, and I'm clean. I—I haven't been with anyone since you."

"Fuck. Me too, baby." I smooth my palm over her ass, giving it a gentle squeeze.

"Then fuck me, Parker. Please…"

I line my cock up to her entrance, testing her wetness to make sure she's ready for me. And fuck, is she ready. As I slowly push inside, I say, "Oh, I fucking plan on it, sweetheart."

The moan of pleasure she lets out as I bottom out inside her makes my dick swell even more. And then I move, pushing and pulling out of her slowly so she can adjust to me before I pick up the pace and drive into her with deep, relentless thrusts.

The metal bar on the weight rack clinks with each thrust, but it doesn't even phase me as I grip Cashlynn's hips and fuck her harder and faster, wondering how on earth sex can feel like this—this out of control, this full of need. This. Fucking. Good.

I smack her ass again, loving the shriek that leaves her lips as the feeling of her bare makes me feral. Her skin gets redder with each swat of my hand, and I can't get enough.

"Is this what you wanted?" I growl as I pound into her from behind, gripping her hair and tugging gently until her head tilts back and her back bows. Fuck, she looks flawless, better than any of my fantasies. "Is this what you've been teasing me for?"

"Yes, Parker. God, yes..." Her voice comes out breathless and needy.

I lean over, my lips brushing her ear. "All you had to do was ask, baby." Picking up my pace, I pound into her harder, still holding onto her hair for leverage. Her legs start to shake, her moans grow louder, and then she screams, squeezing my cock as she comes all over me, wetness seeping out of her core and dripping down my balls and her legs. I fuck her hard through her orgasm, and when I feel her start to relax, I pull out and help her up, spinning her around so I can crush my lips to hers.

Our kiss is frantic, messy, and all-consuming. Holding her head in my hands, I fuck her mouth with my tongue as my slick cock slides against her stomach.

"Lie down on the bench," I say roughly.

She blinks up at me but doesn't say a word as she moves to lie back underneath the bar. I grab her legs and lift them up, pushing them into her chest and then hooking her feet under the bar, exposing her glistening pussy to me. "Looks like that yoga has paid off."

Her breathing grows faster. "Parker…"

I dip my head down to her pussy and lick her from her core to her clit, swirling my tongue around her bundle of nerves and sucking gently. Her gasp is sharp and her hips buck, but I press against the back of her thighs, holding her in place.

"Oh God!" she cries out as she comes undone again.

"This," I murmur, licking up every drop of her release, "is *my* orgasm." I savor the taste of her before standing tall again, straddling the bench and lining my dick back up to her entrance. I slide back into her wet heat, her legs still up by her ears. "Fuck, Cashlynn. This pussy is going to be the death of me."

"Parker! Oh fuck, you're so deep like this," she moans as I lean forward, grip the bar for leverage, and thrust my cock deeper and deeper inside of her until her legs are shaking and I feel my orgasm building at the base of my spine.

"Your greedy pussy is squeezing my cock like it can't get enough." Cashlynn tightens her pussy around me again, making my release build so quickly, I know I'm only seconds from coming. "Like it remembers how good you take me, how fucking perfect you feel." Cashlynn cries out each time I hit her end, and the faster I go, the closer my release gets. "Fuck, I'm gonna come, Cashlynn," I grate out as I circle my thumb around her clit, trying to get her to burst right along with me.

"Yes! Oh shit, I'm coming!" Cashlynn screams as I roar out, both of us coming undone together. My legs go numb, my hands white from knuckling the bar so hard, and my lungs are out of breath by the time I finally reach the end of my release. When the last drop leaves my body,

I slowly pull out of her and help free her feet from the bar, but she continues to lie there, chest heaving, staring up at the ceiling.

I'm not even sure what to say at this point, since I pretty much just let my dick do the talking. Reaching down to the floor for my clothes, I grab Cashlynn's too just as she starts to sit up.

"Parker..."

I turn away from her, already warring with myself over what just happened. Do I regret it? Absolutely not. But is that how I imagined our conversation tonight was going go? Also a big, fat no.

I lost control just like she wanted me to, just like *I* wanted to.

Then why do I feel like shit—and like I want to do it again?

After I slide my shorts and briefs back on, I feel Cashlynn's hand on my shoulder. "Parker, please talk to me."

I spin to face her, finding her dressed as well. "Seth is on to us," I say, because even though I know there are a thousand things we should be talking about right now, this is the easiest one to discuss.

"What?" Her hand flies to her chest.

"That's what I needed to tell you. He cornered me in my office today, says he doesn't believe that our engagement is real, and he's set on exposing us."

"Do you think he will?"

I drag a hand through my sweat-soaked hair. "I honestly don't know, Cashlynn. I know the guy is scum, but I'm not sure what lengths he would go to in order to make me look bad."

She nods nervously. "I'll talk to my dad, talk you up a bit more then the next time I see him, and try to get more information about who he's leaning toward."

"But what about Seth?"

"There's no proof for him to find. We wouldn't have a marriage license yet since we haven't even picked a date..."

"Yeah, true."

She takes a few steps forward, getting so close that her breasts graze my bare chest. And even though I just fucked her, my dick is eager for a second round. "We can handle this."

"Sure."

"Is there anything else you wanted to talk about?" she asks, her eyes roaming all over my face, her hand shaking just slightly.

She's giving you an opening, Parker. She's asking for you to be honest with her.

"No, that was it."

Her shoulders fall with defeat. "Oh. Okay."

"I'm going to go shower," I say before turning away from her and heading inside. And as I scrub my body and prepare for bed, the self-loathing I've been dealing with for the past four years magnifies tenfold.

I fucked up. And I have no one to blame but myself.

Chapter Fourteen

Cashlynn

"Thank God you're here. I'm starving."

Hazel opens her door, peering at me with one eye barely open as I stand on her doorstep with bags of food in my hand from Astrid's bakery and coffees from Keely's Caffeine Kick.

"Sorry it's so early, but I'm freaking out. I snuck out before Parker woke up."

Hazel yawns loudly as I walk past her. "Well, your text last night said this was an emergency, so as soon as the caffeine kicks in, I'll help put out the fire."

Walking into Hazel's apartment reminds me a lot of my place back in Philadelphia. There are tons of framed photos on the wall, mostly of her family, but some of the Carrington Cove beaches. Everything is decorated in browns and greens, very earthy tones with pops of white and blue for color. It's welcoming and homey, but still very modern.

"Did you take all these pictures?" I ask as I set the bags of pastries on the kitchen counter and move closer to admire the display.

"I did—except that one." She points to a photo of her entire family. "This is the last one we took before Dad passed."

The frail man in the middle of the photo catches my attention instantly. "How long ago did he pass?"

"Almost two years now," she says, melancholy in her voice.

I turn to look at her and see tears welling in her eyes. "I'm sorry. I didn't mean to upset you, I just..."

She brushes a tear from her cheek. "It's okay. I prefer talking about him instead of trying to pretend like he never existed. It keeps his memory alive, and I was lucky to have him as my father. In fact, if you ask my brothers, I got the best version of him, so I won the lottery in that respect." She turns away from me and goes over to the coffees, plucking one out of the tray for herself.

"Parker doesn't talk about him."

Hazel huffs out a laugh. "Yeah, well, I think we can agree that Parker isn't big on talking, period."

I join her at the counter, holding the other coffee like a lifeline, and then blurt out, "Parker and I slept together last night."

Hazel spews her coffee all over the floor. "Hot damn! You did it? You got him to snap?"

"Yes, but I think he knew what I was up to."

Her brows draw together. "Why do you say that?"

"Because he told me as much—while he was fucking me."

Hazel nods her head slowly. "Nice."

I throw my free hand up in the air. "Nice? This is not nice! He came home from work, all pissed off about something, saying he needed to talk to me. I was busy and asked him to wait, but he wouldn't. So we argued, and then the next thing I knew, he was fucking me on his workout bench."

Hazel holds a hand up. "I know this may sound shocking given how invested I've been with this plan since the beginning, but I do *not* need to know details *about* the sex. Just knowing that it happened is enough information for me, all right?"

"What do I do, Hazel?"

She takes another sip of her coffee while she mulls it over. "What did he do afterward?"

I think back to how he acted, and I think that's what has me so confused. One minute, he was whispering dirty things in my ear and contorting me into a human pretzel, and the next, he acted like nothing had happened. Shocker.

"He went right into the conversation he wanted to have before the sex."

"And what was that about?"

"Seth is convinced that Parker and I aren't a real couple, and he's threatening to expose us."

Hazel purses her lips. "Expose what?"

"That's kind of how I feel, like what could he possibly find to prove that our story isn't real, but still…Parker was freaked out about it."

"And then after that? After you talked about Seth?"

"He walked inside, took a shower, and went to bed."

Hazel face-palms herself. "God, my brother is an idiot."

I wrap my arms around my body. "I don't know what to do, Hazel. What if this was all a mistake? You said he would open up once we had sex, and—"

"I didn't say that, the other girls did," she corrects me. "But knowing Parker, he was just as up in his head as you are right now."

"I feel like I'm trying to crack a freaking walnut with my bare hands," I say, exasperated.

Hazel laughs. "Yeah, sounds about right. And as for Seth? That guy is a maggot that needs to be torched."

I cringe. "Wow. That was a vivid image."

"I've never liked him and, given how he's reacting to your dad retiring, my gut was right on the money."

"Parker said he's never had a good feeling about him either. I wonder if my dad sees it."

"You should definitely ask him the next time you see him."

"We're supposed to have lunch this week."

Hazel nods. "Then do your due diligence and hold up your end of this bargain. Make sure that Seth has no chance of your father choosing him."

"I will. Now, what do I do about Parker?"

She gestures for us to sit on the couch and as we do, I notice a sliver of ink on her forearm that wasn't there before. "Wait. Did you get a tattoo?"

She looks down at her arm, pulling up her sleeve to reveal a hummingbird. "Not exactly." Her cheeks turn pink, which makes me press further.

"Why are you blushing?"

She sighs dreamily. "Let's fix your problem and then I'll tell you about mine."

"Okay..." I flick my eyes back and forth between her face and arm, but then Hazel pulls me back to the topic at hand.

"As for my brother, I would have asked you how he was this morning, but you said you snuck out before he was up, so I don't have much to go on here. So, my advice is...just play it cool, and act like nothing changed."

My jaw falls open. "That's it? That's your advice?"

She shrugs. "I don't know what else to say. The other option is to corner him and make him talk. There's only two ways he can react."

"Which are?"

"He caves and finally addresses the tension between you two. You can be truthful with him about what you want, and then hopefully when your business is up and running, you two will agree to give this a real shot. Or, he walks away from you again, at which point I'd say cut your losses."

"But…but I don't want to cut my losses." I clasp a hand over my heart. "I want your brother."

Hazel eyes me over the rim of her coffee. "Congratulations, you just passed the test."

Laughter spills from my lips. "What?"

"I'm just making sure you're not giving up on him, because Parker needs someone who won't stop fighting for him."

"Then what do I *actually* do?"

"You go home, jump his bones, and then right before he's about to come, grab him by the dick and make him talk to you."

I blink at her slowly. "Maybe I should have called Willow."

She shrugs. "It's early and my brain isn't firing on all cylinders yet."

Shaking my head, I consider whether Hazel is right. I've followed her advice thus far, and look where it's gotten me. But I know I'm so close to getting Parker to see what's right in front of him. If I give up now, I'll never forgive myself.

No regrets, Cashlynn. Remember?

"I'm going to corner him today."

Hazel nods approvingly. "I think that's the right move."

"I'll let you know how it goes. If things blow up…" I glance around her apartment. "Do you have space for a roommate?"

She laughs. "I don't think that will be necessary. My brother may be stubborn as all hell, but he's not stupid—though he has his moments. Don't all men?"

I take a sip of my coffee just as my eyes fall to the hummingbird on Hazel's arm again. "Okay, so back to you and this hummingbird."

Hazel's smile grows instantly. "I'm still trying to wrap my head around what happened, Cashlynn, but...do you believe in signs from the universe?"

"Absolutely."

"Well, I think my dad was giving me one."

Goosebumps break out over my skin. "Oh my God..."

"Yeah." Her eyes glisten, but she blinks away the tears. "I was sitting at Keely's, doing some editing and responding to emails because sometimes working outside of my studio makes me more productive," she says as I nod in understanding. "And all of a sudden, this man walks up to me, and I swear, if I had a picture in my mind of what my perfect guy would look like, he would have been it. Tall, lean but muscular, covered in tattoos, and I'm pretty sure I saw a tongue piercing."

My eyes widen. "Ooh, nice."

"Right? So he strides up to me and sits down in the seat across from me. When I took my earbuds out, he asked me if he could draw on my arm."

"What?" I laugh in disbelief.

"Yeah, it was really bizarre, and for a moment, I thought it was his version of a pick-up line. But he explained that he was fulfilling a bucket list item of sorts, and noticed I had beautiful, bare skin."

"Oh my God. My stomach is all tingly right now."

Hazel giggles. Full-on *giggles*. "Believe me, as I watched him draw on me, I couldn't fight the way my body reacted. It was like his touch flipped a switch connected directly to my clit."

I bark out a laugh. "I bet."

"But when he was done, he just stood from the chair, thanked me, and left."

"He didn't ask for your name? Or number?"

"Nope. He was gone before I could even process what the hell happened."

"Do you think he's local?"

She shakes her head. "I've never seen him around here before. He was probably a tourist—this town is full of them, as you know. But it was one of the most exhilarating moments of my life."

"I can't believe that. It's so romantic and..."

"Unreal, right?"

"Yeah... Why do you think it was a sign from your dad?"

Hazel stares down at the bird. "When he was dying, I asked him if he would visit me, and he told me I was stupid to think he wouldn't. He said he would come to me as a hummingbird because he knew how much I love them. So now, whenever I see one, I like to think he's here with me."

I blink away my own tears threatening to fall. "I love that. I definitely believe it was him, Hazel."

A tear slips down her cheek. "Maybe. But now the question is, what was he trying to tell me?"

"I wish I had an answer for you."

She looks up at me and shrugs. "And I wish I had an answer for you about my brother. But I think you're on the right track. If worse comes to worst, I can go over there and slap him around a bit," she teases.

"Oh, I'm sure he would love that."

We both laugh and Hazel moves to the kitchen for the pastries. As I share the progress I'm making on my business and she tells me more about her photography business and her brothers, I realize for the first time since I moved here that I feel like I have a friend.

Hazel is the type of girlfriend you could only dream about, and her brother is the man I *have* dreamed about.

It's time to be honest with him. I know what I want, and I'm tired of us dancing around our feelings. Shit is about to get real. I just hope that Parker can handle it.

**

When I walk into Parker's house a few hours later, I find him in the kitchen making a sandwich. He's in a plain white T-shirt and black athletic shorts, his hair a sexy, disheveled mess. I have to say, I love the way he looks in his button-down shirts, slacks, and ties when he goes to work, but this version of him—relaxed, raw, and unguarded—is my favorite.

When I shut the door behind me, his eyes flick up to meet mine. "Good morning," I say because it's barely after ten, yet I feel like an entire week of agony has passed since last night.

"Morning. I was surprised to find you gone when I woke up. I'm nearly always up before you."

"I—I couldn't sleep." Crossing the living area, I move to stand on the other side of the island, facing him head-on. "I think we need to talk."

Parker inhales deeply, exhaling slowly and looking back down at his sandwich, holding a butter knife. But then his jaw tightens as he squares his shoulders. "What do you want to talk about?"

The way he acts as if *I'm* the frustrating one has *me* snapping now. I slap the counter with my hand. "Damn it, Parker! Enough is enough!"

The knife he was holding clatters against the marble, the sound echoing around us. "What's gotten into you?"

"What's gotten into *me*?" I shout as I round the island and stand right in front of him. "You! You got into me. You fucked me last night and then walked away like it meant nothing." His jaw tightens but he still doesn't say anything. "I can't do this anymore. I can't keep denying what's between us." Placing my hands on his chest, I move in closer to his body. "I need you to talk to me. Please."

"You've been pushing me, Cashlynn," he says, his voice gruff and low. "Torturing me, taunting me with your body, and I gave in. Isn't that what you wanted?"

My heart races as he confirms what he said to me last night in the heat of the moment. And even though I'm regretting the decision of messing with him now, there's no going back. "Yes, I did. But I figured you'd open up to me afterward." I reach up, cupping his face, forcing his eyes to meet mine. "You hurt me when you just walked away."

"Fuck," he mutters, closing his eyes. "The last thing I want to do is hurt you."

"Then what do you want?"

His eyes snap open, locking on mine as I wait with bated breath for him to speak.

Say something, Parker. Tell me what you're feeling.

He hesitates, his throat bobbing as if he's swallowing words that refuse to stay down. And then he snaps.

"I fucking want you, woman! There! Is that what you wanted to hear? That I can't stop thinking about you? That having you in my house makes me consider something I haven't let myself think about in years? That wanting you scares the ever-loving shit out of me?"

A sigh of relief escapes my lips because, even though I can hear the turmoil in his words, he said exactly what I needed to hear—that these feelings racing through me aren't one-sided.

"Yes, that's exactly what I needed to hear, Parker. Now shut up and kiss me."

He doesn't hesitate, pulling me into his chest fully and covering my mouth with his. His kiss is possessive, desperate, and luxurious, the kind of kiss you feel all the way down to your toes. When his hands move to the back of my thighs, I jump into his arms and wrap my legs around his waist as he turns and sets me on the counter. Being back in this position reminds me of the night I stole a kiss, but this time, I hope to God he doesn't shut down again.

"You've been driving me crazy, Cashlynn," he mumbles against my neck as his tongue and teeth mark me.

"I'm sorry," I say softly, threading my fingers through his hair. "I didn't know how else to get you to let your guard down."

He rears back and looks at me. "You make me feel shit, Cashlynn...shit I've buried for years and vowed never to feel again."

"And what happens now?" My voice is barely audible, my heart pounding against my ribs.

"Now..." he says, leaning forward and biting my bottom lip before licking the sting away, "Now I'm going to fuck you again."

"God yes," I moan as he tugs my shirt over my head, throwing it across the room before doing the same with his own. He shoves his shorts and underwear to the floor as I shimmy out of mine. Then, he drops to his knees and pulls me forward on the counter so my pussy is right in front of his face.

"I can't get enough of the taste of you," he says before licking me from bottom to top, giving my clit the attention it needs, swirling his tongue around the bundle of nerves expertly.

I bury my hand in his hair as he feasts on me, exploring every inch of my pussy, spearing his tongue in and out of me as my entire body clenches and prepares for my release.

I feel two of his fingers circle my entrance, and then he slowly enters me, flicking his tongue over my clit while his fingers curl deep inside of me.

"Oh God. Yes...right there." My fingers tug on his hair, my stomach tightens as every stroke of his tongue sends me careening higher and higher toward the pleasure I know he can give me—because he's done it before and nothing has even compared.

"Fucking come on my face, Cashlynn." His words are muffled, but his command is clear. And with a few more strokes of his fingers, I see stars. Screaming out, I pull Parker's face into me, soaking up every last tremor.

As my body trembles in the aftermath, he stands up, lining himself up to my core, and slides right in without giving me a second to recover.

"Jesus, fuck," he groans. Our eyes meet and then we both look down to where we're joined, watching him glide in and out of me. "Look at you take my cock, Cashlynn. Such a good fucking girl and such a greedy pussy."

His words send a rush of heat through me, my nails digging into his shoulders as I gasp, "God, Parker... I need you. Don't stop."

He smacks my clit, sending a jolt of biting pleasure through my body. I cry out, the sound caught somewhere between a moan and a gasp, as he soothes the sting with slow, circular strokes.

Holy shit.

If grumpy Parker always fucks me like this, I have an entirely new problem to deal with when it comes to resisting this man.

He speeds up, thrusting deep and hard as I hold onto his shoulder with one hand, and put another behind me for support. Throwing my head back, I soak up the feeling of every inch of him pushing in and withdrawing from me. It's incredible—so flawless that I almost feel like I could come again.

But suddenly, Parker pulls out, helping me down from the counter before spinning me around and pushing my torso down onto the cool marble. Sliding back inside me, he grips my hips for leverage, his fingers digging deliciously into my skin.

My hands are splayed out above my head on the countertop beneath me, my hips digging into the counter with each thrust. Leaning down, Parker presses his chest against my back, lacing his fingers with mine, pinning me to the marble as his lips brush my ear. "Take my cock, baby. Take every fucking inch."

"God, yes, Parker!" My voice trembles with raw need.

"Wearing my ring while I fuck you...How does that make you feel?" he growls, nipping my earlobe as goosebumps bloom over my skin. "How does that make you feel?"

I moan as his cock hits something deep inside of me. "Wanted," I pant. "Needed." I groan as he swirls his hips behind mine and drags his tongue up the curve of my neck. "Owned."

"Damn right." Parker's hand comes down on my ass with a sharp smack, the sting radiating heat and sending a jolt straight to my core. "But you own me too, sweetheart. That's what you don't realize. You've owned me since the second our eyes met on the plane."

His words make the wetness between my legs intensify, and with a few more thrusts, I feel my orgasm ready to detonate. "I'm close," I say breathlessly.

His hand reaches around my hip and then he's circling my clit, giving me that perfect friction that I need to explode. "Come on my cock, Cashlynn. Make a fucking mess for me."

God, his mouth. "Yes...I'm—I'm coming!" I shout as my entire body tightens and then snaps like a rubber band. Parker picks up his pace, chasing his own release, and finds it on a groan that makes my whole body shiver.

When we've both recovered, he pulls out of me, spins me around and cups my face in both of his hands. "You're going to be the death of me."

I can't help but giggle—because not only did this man just fuck me better than I could have imagined, but a sense of relief comes over me when I realize that now we can finally decide how to move forward.

Parker pulls me into his chest and breathes deeply. "Let's get dressed and then meet in my room."

"Okay," I reply, grabbing my clothes from the floor and then hurrying to the bathroom as I feel his cum dripping down the inside of my thigh. That's an unfortunate side effect of not using condoms I was blissfully unaware of.

Once I clean myself up and throw on a more comfortable outfit, I head to Parker's room. The door's open and he's sitting on the edge of his bed, his forearms resting on his knees.

"You okay?" I ask softly.

He lifts his head and his eyes soften almost immediately, but there's still a pinch in his brow. "Yeah. Come here, Cashlynn."

Nervously, I close the space between us. He reaches out and pulls me between his legs.

"I'm sorry," I murmur.

"For what?"

"For not just sitting down and asking you how you felt."

He grins. "You didn't have to torture me to get me to fuck you again."

Heat rushes to my cheeks. "It wasn't my idea."

"I know. I heard you talking to Hazel on the phone the other night."

I groan, smacking my forehead. "I hate this. I hate that I've even put us in this position."

He tilts his head. "And what position is that?"

I push his hair back from his face. "Did I want to sleep with you again? Yes. But not just for sex. I just…I care about you, Parker. I feel like that night last year wasn't just a fluke. Call it fate or serendipity, or whatever you want, but I couldn't get you out of my head." I let out a shaky breath, searching his face. "And being here, pretending to be engaged, I… I guess I just wonder if there's something real here, and I wasn't sure if you felt that too. And then when I talked to the girls about it, they suggested focusing on the physical connection we have because you'd be more likely to open up to me that way."

Parker chuckles. "Well, they weren't wrong."

"You're locked up tighter than Fort Knox. Every time I think I've found a way in, you shut me out again and we act like nothing happened. I'm tired of that." I pause, taking a steadying breath. "I've been in serious relationships, but none that make me feel an ounce of what I feel for you and with you."

His brows draw together as he stares up at me. For a moment, I fear he's going to push me away again—like he always does. But then he swallows hard and says the words I've been longing to hear. "I don't know what I'm able to give you, Cashlynn. But fuck if I can keep pretending I don't want you too."

I breathe out, five weeks of tension leaving my body as I do. "All I need to know is that we're on the same page. The rest we can figure out later."

"Is that really enough for you?"

"Yes," I say without hesitation.

He reaches up and pushes a strand of my hair behind my ear with a tenderness that makes my chest ache. "How on earth did we find each other a year ago in this big, messy world?"

"I don't know, but don't you think it means something?"

"All I know is that when I met you on that plane, it was the first time in a very long time I felt drawn to someone. I hadn't even entertained the idea of dating anyone. But when we slept together and you left so abruptly, I told myself that was it—just a one-time thing. But then you walked back into my life. So yeah, I do think it means something."

"I honestly had no expectations coming to Carrington Cove, Parker. But the instant I saw you again, all of those feelings came rushing back. You made me feel something I didn't know existed."

He smiles up at me. "And what was that?"

"Safe. Calm, which I really needed in that moment." He nods, urging me to continue. "Fascinated because I wanted to know everything about you. Optimistic, like maybe there really are good men left in the world." Laughter escapes his lips. "But most of all...powerless. Like something bigger than me was pulling me toward you, and I couldn't fight it even if I wanted to. That's why I slept with you that night. I needed to know if my intuition was right, and it was. But when it was over, I panicked. I left because I didn't know how to admit I already knew who you were—or how much I'd started to care."

I run a hand through his hair, my voice softening. "I thought it was just one night too, but it stayed with me, Parker. It made me think about what I really wanted out of my life, what I'd been settling for, and what I could change. That night with you... it made me believe that I could have more, do more, feel more than I ever let myself before."

"Fuck, Cashlynn." He pulls me down to him, pressing our lips together. I show him with this kiss how honest my words are. When he releases me, conflict lingers in his eyes. "You scare the shit out of me."

"I'm scared too, Parker. I feel like you have the potential to destroy me."

"I've been destroyed, baby, and I swear, I'd never do that intentionally. But you have to be patient with me, okay?"

I nod, rubbing my nose against his. "I can do that."

"So, what happens now?"

"Well, for starters, I'm starving, and it looked like you were making some lunch before I interrupted you."

He stands from the bed and cradles my face in his hands. "I was making a sandwich."

"If memory serves, you make a pretty good one. Mind making one more?"

"Yeah, I think I can do that for you, as long as you promise me one thing."

"Okay..."

"No more unplugging the appliances."

I throw my head back with laughter. "Oh my God."

Parker's jaw clenches instantly, and the surly man I've grown to adore returns in an instant. "I'm fucking serious, Cashlynn. That was some next-level, tortuous shit."

I swat him on the chest and press up on my toes to kiss him. "You can thank Willow for that little move."

He grumbles under his breath, "I should have fucking known. First, it was her videos that got me into this mess, and now she's trying to drive me insane through you."

I take his hand, leading him to the kitchen. "You have to admit, it was pretty funny."

"No, Cashlynn. It was ridiculous. Seriously, I was questioning your sanity there for a minute."

Still laughing, I hop onto the stool at the island as Parker moves back to the kitchen counter. That's when we both notice the flattened pieces of bread on the counter.

He looks up at me. "Probably shouldn't use these."

"I think that's my ass print."

Parker chuckles. "Well, I was hungry. I just found something more satisfying to eat." He waggles his eyebrows at me.

A shiver runs down my spine, igniting my need for him again even though we just had sex. Will that ever fade? Doubtful. No one has ever fucked me like Parker does.

"Yes, you did. And I'm happy to serve that up anytime you want."

Chapter Fifteen

Parker

I prop myself up on my elbow, staring down at Cashlynn snuggled into her pillow. She's in my bed, and after yesterday, I have a lot of feelings about it.

Mostly good ones, some I'm avoiding altogether.

It's been years since I've woken up with a woman in my bed. Hookups have been quick, convenient, and forgettable—at their place or a hotel, much like that night with Cashlynn.

But this? Watching her sleeping peacefully next to me, thinking back to our conversation and how she gave me total control of her body last night?

This is making me wonder if I can have this again—a relationship, a person to devote myself to, but this time doing it right. The fact that I'm even thinking that way tells me that Cashlynn is different, even though deep down I already knew that.

Cashlynn stirs next to me, her eyelashes fluttering as she wakes. When her eyes meet mine, a smile appears instantly, and my chest tightens.

"Good morning," she says quietly.

I lean down and press my lips to hers. "Good morning, sweetheart. How'd you sleep?"

"That was the best night's sleep I've had in a while. You wore me out."

I brush her hair away from her face, focusing on those amber eyes that never fail to draw me in. "Pretty sure it was you doing the wearing."

Cashlynn rode me three times last night—once as I leaned up against the headboard, another time while I was flat on my back, and then the last time she rode my cock in the reverse cowgirl position, and I swear, I saw fucking stars when I came.

She giggles, and the sound makes my already hard dick twitch in interest. Now that she's awake, my cock knows he can get his fix and is ready to go.

"You have a nice cock, Parker. What can I say?" she teases.

I arch a brow. "Just nice?"

"Fine." She rolls her eyes and sits up to mimic my position, her head propped up on her hand. "It's amazing—a unicorn cock, if you will."

"A unicorn cock?"

"The mythical being that you want to believe exists, but you're not sure if it's actually real. A unicorn cock, the ultimate cock of all cocks."

With a laugh, I roll on top of her, pinning her to the mattress. Her smile is blinding, her eyes so full of joy that my heart kicks into overdrive. Fuck, I had no chance of resisting this woman. Her sense of humor makes me want to keep her talking for hours, just to see what she'll say next. Her mind is incredible, a perfect blend of creativity and intelligence. And her body? Fucking irresistible. Well, I think we all know how I feel about that now, don't we?

"Did my cock make you believe in magic, Cashlynn?"

She nods slowly, biting her bottom lip. "I'm a true believer now."

Laughing, I pepper her neck with kisses. "Good answer."

She lets out a breathy moan as I rub my cock on her hip.

"But it's mostly your mouth I'm enamored with," she murmurs.

I lift my head. "My mouth?"

"Oh yeah. The filthy things you say to me..." She bites her bottom lip. "It's so fucking hot."

I thrust my hips harder into her side. "Fuck, Cashlynn. You have to be sore, and I don't want to hurt you, but when you say shit like that, I want to see if there are new words to add to my dirty vocabulary."

Her laughter reverberates against my skin. "Tonight. Give me a chance to recover and then it's on."

Reluctantly, I roll off her, giving my dick a chance to calm down. "So what's on the agenda for today?"

"I don't know. It's Sunday. You usually work out and then there's dinner with your family, right?"

I nod. "And you're coming with me."

She bites her bottom lip again. "What are we going to tell your siblings?"

I blow out a breath, not having thought that far ahead. "We don't have to tell them shit. But you know they're going to ask questions."

She nods. "Hazel is going to drill me the second she sees me. In fact, I'd be surprised if she hasn't already sent me several text messages."

Leaning back against the headboard, I stare at the blank TV screen across the room. "Sometimes I hate how involved my siblings are in my life."

She stares up at me, searching my face. "They just care about you, Parker. Especially Hazel. Do you know what she told me when she was pushing me to keep pushing you?"

"What?"

"That she just wanted her brother back."

I peer down at her as my heart twists. "Fuck, she said that?"

Cashlynn nods. "She hates how much your relationship with Sasha changed you. You can't be mad at her for that."

"I can be mad at her all I want," I retort, but I know that Hazel's heart was in the right place. That girl has a way of driving all of us boys nuts, but our lives would be dull without her.

She gives me a knowing look. "Parker…"

I sigh, rolling my head on my neck. "I know she means well —they all do. But when you're drowning in anger and resentment, it's hard to appreciate that kind of attention."

"You have no idea how lucky you are to have them, and your entire family for that matter. It's only been me and my dad for so long, and I've barely seen him since I moved up north for school then settled in Philly." Her eyes start to fill with tears. "Everything between us changed when my mom died, and I'd give anything for him to support me and encourage me the way your family does for you."

"Fuck. I'm sorry, sweetheart. Come here." I pull her into my chest.

"The longer I keep this from my dad, all of this, the more afraid I am to tell him the truth. He's going to blow up either way, and I—"

I place my finger over her lips, silencing her. "We'll cross that bridge when we get to it, okay? That's all we can do since we've already committed to this plan." She nods but doesn't speak. "For now, let's just enjoy this little shift in our relationship."

"Oh believe me, I am enjoying it," she mumbles against my finger, making me smile.

"Me too." I bury my face in her neck again as I roll over on top of her. "Fuck, I can't get enough of you."

"I feel the same way." I lift my head and look down into her eyes as her hand comes up to stroke the side of my face, a look of hesitation in her eyes. "Can I ask you a question?"

"Yes, we can fuck now if you've changed your mind."

She tries to shove me away, but I'm immovable. "Jesus. It wasn't that!"

"Sorry. My mistake." She rolls her eyes. "What do you want to know?"

Her thumb rubs over the scar above my eyebrow. "How did you get this scar?"

I know exactly which one she's talking about because I look at it every day in the mirror, remembering the moment I thought my life might have turned out very differently if it weren't for my two older brothers.

"I took a steel pole to my face."

Her eyes widen. "Oh my God! How? Why?"

Sighing, I prop my head on my hand. "My brothers and I were playing on our jungle gym in the backyard. Me being the youngest, they always tried to get me to do stupid shit. That day, we were pretending to be firefighters, sliding down a metal pole we'd leaned against the side of the monkey bars. It wasn't secured, obviously."

"So how did it end up hitting you in the face?"

"Dallas was arguing with Penn about moving the pole, and I was standing too close to him at the top of the equipment while Penn was down on the ground. Dallas yanked the pole to his side and the top of it hit me right above the eye." The memory floods my mind. "I just remember seeing red and then screaming. When my mother came outside, she thought my eye was gone. It wasn't until I took my hand off of my face that she realized the cut was on my eyebrow, but it was deep and needed stitches." Chuckling, I continue, "My brothers were in so much trouble after that day. I think that was the first time I realized that I really shouldn't listen to anything that they tell me to do."

Cashlynn shakes her head. "Stories like that make me think maybe it was better that I was an only child."

"The two of them were always ganging up on me, but as I've gotten older, I've realized that life would be boring without them. However, I have this nice scar to remind me that I should always look out for myself."

"Do you still exercise caution around them?"

"Uh, hell yes," I say with a laugh.

She giggles. "Can't trust them, can you?"

Her words slam into me. "I would trust them with my life."

Her smile softens "You're lucky to have them."

It's in that moment I realize that I don't appreciate my family enough. Instead of leaning on them, their involvement in my life has made me irritated and jaded. I've let my anger build walls between us, but she's right—I'm lucky to have those stories to tell. She'll never have that privilege.

"What about you? Any scars I should know about?"

Her eyes bounce back and forth between mine. "None you can see," she whispers, and fuck if I don't understand that.

I trail my finger down her arm, watching her skin pebble. "I grasp that all too well, sweetheart."

When she reaches for me and pulls my lips to hers, I fight with myself to open up my mouth and bury myself in her, to smother the bad memories with everything good that this woman represents.

"You know, I read a quote once that reminds me a lot of you and me." I lift my head so I can see her face again.

"Really? What did it say?"

"It said, 'You can't force chemistry to exist where it doesn't, the same way you can't deny it when it does.'"

She sucks in a breath. "I love that."

Something shifts inside of me in that moment, something that urges me to be honest with her. "When I'm with you, Cashlynn... I feel like I can breathe for the first time in years. I want to know everything about you—what you think, what you feel. And then I want to fuck you in every position imaginable."

Okay, there were some feelings in there, Parker. That was a good start.

She laughs. "I'm not opposed to that."

"Thank you for pushing me," I say sincerely, trying to show her that even though I'm a surly grump most of the time, I do appreciate her. I don't deserve her and I'm afraid she's going to fucking realize that before I can get my shit together.

I put my palm on my chest. "Fighting *with* you—fighting *against* you—was making my chest ache."

She cups the side of my face. "I know you've been hurt, Parker, but the last thing I want to do is hurt you again. And one day, I hope that you'll feel ready to share your past with me, your whole past."

My pulse spikes just thinking about it, but deep down, I want that too. I'm finally ready to try to let go, to move forward, and to open my heart again. Maybe Cashlynn can help me see that it's okay to have scars, as long as I can learn to live with them.

***

"There you two are! I was beginning to wonder if you were coming at all." My mother greets us as we step through the front door, pausing just long enough to hug us before returning to the kitchen.

I lean down and whisper in Cashlynn's ear. "Someone was coming, all right."

Cashlynn swats at my chest as I laugh out loud.

"Did I just hear Parker laugh?" Hazel appears from around the corner, wine glass in hand, and eyes us both suspiciously.

We're late because when Cashlynn came out of her room in tight jeans and a black sweater hugging her curves in all the best ways, I knew I wouldn't make it through dinner if I didn't fuck her one more time before we left.

I feel like a sex-crazed teenager right now, but neither one of us is complaining about it.

I narrow my eyes at my sister. "Yes, I laughed. Is that such a shock to you?"

Hazel looks at Cashlynn. "Did you two finally figure your shit out?"

"We did," I say before Cashlynn can respond, wrapping my arms around her shoulders to keep her close to me. "And no thanks to you. Thanks for conspiring to drive me insane, by the way. I'll be sure to repay the favor tenfold."

My sister rolls her eyes, waving me off. "Look, it was for your own good."

Cashlynn places a hand on my chest. "Don't be mad. I'm the one that chose to go along with it, remember?"

I look down at Cashlynn with an arch in my brow. "Oh, I remember. And I'm still not done punishing you for that."

Hazel gags dramatically. "Yuck. Okay, you two. I get it. You've bumped uglies, but spare me the details."

I lean closer to my sister, lowering my voice. "Look, Mom still doesn't know that this was all fake to begin with, all right? So keep your voice down."

She mimics zipping her lips. "Got it. Your secrets are safe with me."

Penn steps into the room. "What secrets?"

"Who has secrets?" Astrid echoes, trailing behind my brother. "Hi, Cashlynn." She leans in to hug my fake fiancée.

Is she still a fake fiancée? Now that we're sleeping together and seeing where things are going, are we technically dating? Engaged? What the hell are we?

Fuck. I don't even know how to answer that.

Penn stares at me. "You look like you're trying to do calculus."

"I'm fine," I mutter, turning to Cashlynn and pressing a kiss her temple. "I'm gonna head outside and catch up with my brothers. Will you be okay?"

"Of course." She presses her lips to mine. "Have fun."

I grab beers from the kitchen and step out onto the deck, where Dallas leans on the railing. Handing beers to both him and Penn, I pop the cap off my own.

"So," Penn says, taking a sip. "What secrets was Hazel talking about in there?"

I sigh, unsure where to start. As solid as I feel about my decisions over the past twenty-four hours, I do need to process everything out loud. "Cashlynn and I are…seeing where things could go between us, but Mom thinks we've been together this whole time, so I told our sister to keep her mouth shut until we figure it out."

Dallas's brows draw together. "When you say seeing where things could go, you mean…"

"You guys were right." I take another sip of my beer. "Cashlynn was doing shit to try to get me to snap and sleep with her. And it worked."

Dallas and Penn both shake their heads, then Dallas speaks first. "These women, I swear they will be the death of us."

"You're telling me," I mutter, taking a long pull from my beer. "But honestly, it needed to happen. After we…you know…."

Dallas nods. "After you had sex. You can say the word, Parker. You are a doctor, after all."

I flip him the bird as Penn stifles his laughter. "After the sex, we had a good talk and…" I blow out a breath and shove my hand through my hair. "I can't deny what's between us anymore. And even though I'm scared shitless, I want to see what can happen between us."

Penn wraps his arm around Dallas's shoulder, resting his head against our brother's. "Oh my gosh, Dallas. Our baby brother is growing up."

"All right. I'm going inside," I say, taking a few steps toward the door, but Dallas pulls me back by the collar of my shirt.

"Relax, Parker." He elbows Penn in the ribs and then turns back to me. "I think what Penn is trying to say is that we're proud of you."

"Yeah, well, let's not get ahead of ourselves, okay?" I take another swig of my beer. "There's still a lot of shit I need to work through."

"Have you considered therapy?" Dallas asks.

"I did a few sessions a couple of years ago, but I don't think I was ready to let go of shit then. I might be more open to it now…"

Penn nods. "I think it could help you a lot, Parker. Honestly."

I turn and face the two of them. "I'm fucking scared, you guys. I never imagined wanting another woman again, and now the stakes are even higher because I'm already pretending to be engaged to her *and* she's my boss's daughter."

"That feeling is valid." Penn props a hand on my shoulder. "I was fucking terrified when I decided to pursue Astrid. But I promise you, it was worth it. From everything you've said, it sounds like Cashlynn is worth it to you."

"I wouldn't be willing to work through my shit if she weren't, dumbass."

"I'm just making sure your head is in the right place," Penn replies. "Well then, where do you go from here?"

I exhale deeply, running a hand through my hair. "I just want to get to know her better," I answer honestly. "I know we have a connection, and it's time to explore that."

Dallas nods. "I think that's a good plan. Take things slow."

I raise an eyebrow. "Um, did you forget we're already engaged?"

"*Fake* engaged. Just because your feelings are real, doesn't mean that the engagement has to be."

An ounce of relief courses through me. My brother is right. This only has a label if we put one on it. And Cashlynn assured me that she'd be patient. I'm almost positive she's not expecting an actual wedding when this is all said and done—at least not right away.

Fuck. Could I imagine marrying Cashlynn? Her walking toward me in a white dress, her hair down in waves around her face, me peeling back a veil to kiss her and promise to love her for all eternity.

"Yoo-hoo," Dallas says. "Earth to Parker. Where'd you go just now?"

I shake off the mental images flooding my mind right now and remind myself to breathe. "Sorry. My thoughts are fucking racing."

"You're so up in your head, man," Penn says. "I know it might seem impossible, but stop overthinking, and instead, just do what feels right. The other shit will work itself out in due time."

Dallas's face lights up as Willow steps outside with Cashlynn trailing closely behind her, effectively ending our conversation. "Hey, Goose," he says.

"Hi, boys. Whatcha doing?" she asks, walking over to Dallas. He pulls her in as close as her growing stomach will allow.

"Just guy talk," Dallas says before he leans down and kisses his wife.

"Hey, you." Cashlynn comes up to me, wrapping her arms around my waist, and fuck, the way she fits against me feels so right.

I tip her chin up, looking her in the eyes for a moment before pressing a soft kiss to her lips. "Hey, sweetheart."

"Oh my God, you guys are too cute!" Willow coos. Then she leans forward and says, "Don't be mad at Cashlynn, but she told me about you two." She waves her hand between us.

Dallas chuckles. "Yeah, we were getting the guy version of what happened."

Willow rolls her eyes. "Sounds riveting. Well, we came out here to tell you guys that dinner's almost ready and… Cashlynn has set the opening date for her gallery!"

I turn to look at the woman in my arms, surprised. "You have?"

She nods, her eyes sparkling. "Willow and I were talking, and given how things are progressing, it looks like everything will be ready by the first week of May!"

Fuck. So that means I have even less time to get my shit together now.

"And as long as I'm not in labor, Dallas and I will be there."

"I'm ready to put in the shelves and cabinetry this week too," Penn says.

"I can't wait to see it all come together. The tables and chairs are getting delivered this week too." Cashlynn squeezes my waist tighter.

"Have you started reaching out to artists yet?" Willow asks.

"Yes, and the flyers you suggested printing will be here tomorrow. Astrid said I can give her some to put in the bakery, and several other businesses also agreed to hand them out too."

I look down at Cashlynn, in awe of her, memorizing the look on her face—the pure joy, pride, and excitement. Her dream is becoming a reality, and I'm proud that I played even a small part in that. Even though I wasn't exactly thrilled about this arrangement at first, the closer we get to the opening of her gallery, I realize it's been worth every minute.

Fuck. I think I'm in deeper than I realized.

***

My knees bounce uncontrollably as I sit on the couch in the waiting room. It's been years since I've sought out therapy, but after the talk with my brothers yesterday, I know this is what I need. Cashlynn deserves a man that doesn't have baggage, a man that can learn from his mistakes and do his best not to repeat them.

But waiting for the door to that office to open is making me more anxious by the second.

I left work and came straight to my appointment, grateful the doctor had a last-minute cancellation. But now that means it's truly time for me to face the music.

"Parker?" A woman's voice breaks through my spiraling thoughts. I look up to see a woman in her late fifties with short, gray hair and glasses standing in the doorway.

I stand from the couch and nod, adjusting my glasses. "Yeah, that's me."

She smiles warmly and gestures for me to follow her inside, shutting the door softly behind her. "Welcome. I'm Dr. Jensen, it's nice to meet you."

"Likewise." I stand awkwardly, not sure what I'm supposed to do. I see a brown leather couch along the far wall, a matching chair to the right, and a few potted plants beside the large, mahogany desk that fills the corner to my left.

I gesture toward the couch. "Do you want me to lie down on the couch, or…"

She smiles. "Whatever makes you comfortable. Some people like to lie down, some prefer to sit—it's up to you." She waves her hand toward the furniture.

Nodding, I head for the couch and opt to just sit on it, clasping my hands between my knees as I lean forward.

"You seem nervous," Dr. Jensen says as she settles into her chair, a clipboard poised on her lap, legs crossed.

I slowly release a breath. "I am. I've been to therapy in the past, but I wasn't really open to it. But now, some things in my life have changed, and I—I'm ready to move forward."

"Okay. I appreciate your honesty. What brought you in before?"

"I was engaged, and it...ended badly."

She jots down a few notes. "Okay. What brings you in now?"

"There's a woman..." The corner of her mouth lifts as she waits for me to continue. "After my failed engagement, I said I would never get involved with anyone again—swore off relationships completely. But then Cashlynn came into my life, and now..."

"Now what?" she prompts gently.

"Now I want to get over this fear of it ending badly too."

She places her pen down on her pad and looks directly at me. "What is it that you're afraid of, Parker? What happened that had you swearing off relationships?"

I shift uncomfortably on the couch, my hands clasped so tightly that my knuckles ache. "I'm afraid I'll fail again," I finally admit, my voice low. "That I don't know how to be the kind of man who can really... be there for someone."

Dr. Jensen nods slightly, her pen poised but not moving. She waits, and the silence stretches long enough for my heart to start pounding.

I take a deep breath and push through the lump in my throat. "Because Sasha..." My voice falters, and I look down at my hands, forcing the words out. "I failed her as a partner. And because of me… she died."

Chapter Sixteen

Parker

"Cashlynn?"

It's after nine by the time I get home, and the front half of the house is pitch-black. The only light in the space is the overhead lamp on the stove where I see a plate covered in tin foil sitting along with a note.

I sit my bag down and head for the kitchen, picking up the paper to find Cashlynn's handwriting.

I made dinner and was hoping we could eat it together, but I got tired of waiting.

Put it in the microwave for two minutes if you're still hungry. I'm going to bed early.

"Shit." I tear the foil off the plate and find chicken and rice casserole. It looks and smells amazing. Cashlynn went out of her way to make this for me, and I let her down.

Covering the plate again, I slide it into the fridge since I grabbed something on the way home. Making my way down the hall to her room, I'm already running through what I'll say—how I'll explain without oversharing. After my session with Dr. Jensen, I know I have a long road ahead, and until I'm sure I won't bail this time, I want to keep my therapy private.

The door is cracked just enough for me to see her lying on her side, scrolling on her phone.

I push the door open gently. "Cashlynn?"

She doesn't turn over. "I'm not in the mood, Parker."

"This isn't a booty call. And if it was, you're always in the mood. What's wrong?"

She shoots me a glare over her shoulder. "Just leave it."

I bristle at that. "Not happening. Tell me what's wrong."

She turns over to look at me. "Nothing. I just thought..." She shakes her head, pressing her lips into a tight line. "You know what, just forget it."

"Cashlynn, I'm sorry I missed dinner. I didn't know you were waiting."

"You know, there are these things called phones," she snaps.

I drag a hand down my face and make my way over to the bed, sitting on the edge so I can see her. Her face is red and blotchy, like she's been crying. *Shit.* "You're right. I could have texted you, but..." She blinks at me, waiting for me to continue. "It's been a long time since I've had to check in with anyone, okay?" Her face softens slightly. "I have to get used to that again, but I *am* sorry."

She lets out a sigh. "I appreciate that, but I don't know, Parker... My mind was spinning when I realized you weren't coming home and then I wondered..."

"Wondered what?"

Her eyes search mine. "If I read this weekend all wrong." Sitting up, she pulls the blankets around her waist. "If maybe I was the only one thinking this was more than just...pretend."

Her words land like a punch, and I don't even hesitate. "You weren't wrong," I say, reaching for her hand. "Look, I should have texted or called to let you know I was going to be late. I messed up. And I'm sorry for making you doubt me."

"Okay... But where were you?" she asks, and I hate the trepidation in her voice.

"I had an appointment," I answer simply, hoping it's enough.

She nods. "Okay."

"But I did already eat, so I'll take the casserole for lunch tomorrow. It looks amazing. Thank you."

I get a small smile from her this time before she slides back under the covers.

I lean down to press a kiss to her forehead. "Goodnight, Cashlynn."

"Goodnight, Parker."

I stand and leave, headed to my bedroom to sleep alone because I can tell Cashlynn's still upset and my mind is racing from my therapy session.

But I pause right outside my door as I realize that I don't want to sleep alone tonight. I don't want to be away from her.

So, after I change and brush my teeth, I return to her room.

"Parker?" she asks, sitting up as I make my way toward her bed.

"Got room for one more in there?"

She looks at me, confused. "Um, sure."

I slide in behind her and prop my head up so I can look at her.

"Why are you in here?" she asks, looking up at me.

"Because I want to wake up next to you."

Her eyes fill with hope. "Oh."

I lean down and press my mouth to hers. "Yeah, oh. Now go to sleep, woman."

The smile she gives me this time is far more reassuring than the last one. She shifts closer, and I wrap my arm around her waist, holding her against me. I fall asleep with the woman I'm finally ready to let in, even as the one from my past haunts my dreams.

***

I reach up and wipe the tartar sauce from my lips, watching Cashlynn with fascination as she takes another bite of her crab cakes, closing her eyes and moaning in approval.

"I told you they're the best," I say with a grin.

"I can't believe I haven't been out here yet." She glances out toward the water that surrounds us. We're sitting at a table outside of Franny's Crab Shack on the pier as people bustle around us. This place is a Carrington Cove hotspot. "But I'll be coming back at least once a week."

"I think we could make that happen." I reach for my drink and take a sip.

Cashlynn finishes chewing and then reaches for my hand. "Thank you again for tonight, Parker. I have to say it was a pleasant surprise."

I lift her hand, brushing a kiss to the back of it. "Well, I think it was about time I took you on a proper date. And after letting you down last night, I wanted to make it up to you."

Her eyes dip to her plate, and her smile falters slightly. "I'm sorry for the way I reacted."

"Hey." I tip her chin up until her eyes meet mine. "You have nothing to apologize for, Cashlynn. I'm the one who fucked up. I'm the one who didn't communicate and made you question things, okay? That is on me."

Her lips twitch into a slow smile. "Okay."

Releasing her chin, I grab my napkin and crumple it up, tossing it into my empty basket. "The night isn't over yet. When you're done, we have another stop to make."

Cashlynn shoves the last bite of her crabcake into her mouth and hands me her basket. "I'm done," she mumbles around her mouthful of food, making me laugh.

"Don't choke." I reach for her hand to help her up from her seat, watching her swallow roughly.

"I'm good. Now, where are you taking me?"

With her hand secured in mine, we head back down the pier toward the sand where I motion for her to take off her sandals. I carry them and mine in my free hand. The feel of the cold sand between my toes instantly calms me, something I'd almost forgotten it has the ability to.

"Well, it's almost sunset, so I figured we could watch it together from the beach. How does that sound?"

She pushes her hair from her face as the wind whips it around. "That sounds amazing."

We stroll slowly, taking in the sound and smell of the water before Cashlynn breaks the silence. "If I lived here, I'd be down by the water every chance I got."

"Uh, newsflash, Cashlynn. You *do* live here now."

She presses a palm to her face. "Oh God. That just came out like a bad habit. You're right. This is home now."

"Are you second-guessing that decision?"

She shakes her head instantly. "No. Not at all. In fact, I've never felt more sure of anything in my entire life."

"Damn. What's that feel like?"

"Certainty?" I nod as she stares out at the water. "I guess it just feels a lot like the opposite of regret."

"Like you're afraid of regret more than taking chances?"

"Yeah. I told you before that my mom always reminded me not to live with regrets, so I guess in those moments I'm unsure about something, I think of her, try to hear her voice speaking to me." She closes her eyes and I watch as she lets her memories take over. I know what that's like. I do that sometimes with my dad—try to hear his voice, remember his smile, what he smells like, or a memory that comes over me at unexpected times.

Cashlynn's eyes pop back open as she looks at me. "So instead of being afraid, I leap—even if I hesitate at first. Lord knows, I've put off this gallery idea for a while, but then something just clicked for me."

"What was it?"

With our eyes locked, she says, "Meeting you."

Fuck.

I stop walking and pull her into my chest. Cupping her cheek, I lean down and slowly press my lips to hers—because hearing her admit that I'm the reason she faced her fears makes me feel like maybe she's the reason that I can finally face mine.

When we part, her eyes open slowly as she stares up at me. "What was that for?"

"For being you. The way you look at me..." I inhale deeply. "It's unnerving sometimes."

Her lips quirk into a smile. "Right back at you."

I press another chaste kiss to her lips and then tug her forward again. "I've forgotten how much I love the feeling of the sand between my toes."

"Really?"

"Yeah. I hate to admit it, but I haven't been down to the water in ages." I drag my foot in the sand to my side. "You'd think living here for practically my whole life I'd take advantage of it, but work has always been the priority."

"When you have something at your fingertips, it's easy to take it for granted."

I nod. "I agree. In fact, I remember when I was in college in California, every time I came home to visit, the water was one of the first places I'd go. Now I don't come down here nearly as often as I'd like." I cast my gaze out at the water.

"Well, maybe it's time to change that."

I look down at her, feeling a shift in my chest. "Yeah, I'm beginning to realize it's time I change a lot of things."

***

"So, Parker, how have things been in the last week?" Dr. Jensen has her pen and notepad ready to go, eager to make notes as I unload everything that's been going through my mind in the last seven days.

I rub the back of my neck. "Well, I took Cashlynn out on a date."

Dr. Jensen perks up in her seat. "And how did it go?"

I think back to the way Cashlynn made me feel at peace while we walked along the beach and talked about any and everything. We watched the sunset like I planned, and when we got home, I ravaged her body, showing her what my mind and heart won't let me say yet.

"I'm falling fast for her. But…I haven't been sleeping well."

"Still having those dreams about Sasha?"

Leaning back against the couch, I run my hands down my thighs. "Yeah."

"Were the dreams the same as the ones you described to me last time?" she asks.

"Two of the nights they were, but the other night...it was different."

She jots something down. "Tell me about it."

"Well, it wasn't the morning I asked her to go to rehab. It was the week after—when I got the phone call that she had checked herself out." She nods, urging me to continue. "But this time, I actually got to see her before she skipped town."

"Did she say anything to you?"

I run a hand over my face. "She kept saying, 'You're the reason I'm dead. You killed me.'"

She purses her lips. "Is that what you believe?"

The question punches me in the gut. My throat tightens as I lean forward, pinching the bridge of my nose. "I don't want to fucking cry," I manage, my voice hoarse.

"Why?"

My knee bounces up and down rapidly.

"Have you cried since Sasha passed away, Parker?" she presses.

When I open my eyes, the first tear slips free. "Not much, no. A little at her funeral, but then her parents started screaming at me, so I left. Then I drank until I couldn't see straight."

"I see." She writes a few more notes on her paper. "So, here's how I see it. You never grieved the woman you thought you were going to spend the rest of your life with, and you blame yourself for her death. Does that sound about right?"

"Aren't I paying you to tell me that, Dr. Jensen?"

She smirks at me. "Just answer the question, Parker."

"Yeah. That sounds about right."

"And how has it felt carrying around all that guilt?"

"Uh, not fucking great. Hence why I'm here, Doc." It's this kind of questioning that irritated me about therapy in the first place.

"And who is the one in control of carrying around the guilt, Parker?"

I tilt my head at her. "Let me guess...me?"

She chuckles. "Very good."

"Okay, so how do I let go of it?"

She shrugs her shoulders. "There's no magic solution, Parker. But there's usually a moment when you realize it's time to let it go. Until then, lean into the discomfort. Push yourself to do the things that scare you." I look down at the floor. "I, uh...Cashlynn's been sleeping next to me for the past week."

Dr. Jensen's eyebrows lift. "That's a big step. How does it make you feel?"

"Not so alone," I admit.

She nods, setting her notepad to the side. "Sometimes we think that isolating ourselves will prevent us from hurting, but it can actually do the opposite and leave us alone with all of the pain we are holding onto."

I lift my eyes and find hers again. "When I'm with her, my chest feels lighter. There's something about this woman that pulled at me from the moment I met her. But..."

"But what?"

I let out a long sigh. "It's always so easy in the beginning of a relationship, right? Like, I never thought Sasha was an alcoholic when we first started dating. Is that because I was naïve about it and didn't want to see it? Or can people really change on you like that?" I snap my fingers. "What if I'm blinded by Cashlynn right now and I repeat the same mistakes? What if I ignore her, don't give her the time she deserves, or..."

"Let me stop you right there," Dr. Jensen says. "That's a lot of 'what ifs.'"

"You should hear what goes on in my head most days, Doc."

She smiles and then continues. "When you say you didn't see who Sasha was, did she ever share her struggles with you?"

"No. She actually hid it from me."

Her eyebrow lifts. "And when you say that *she* changed, did *you* change as well?"

"I mean, yeah. Things shifted when she moved to Carrington Cove with me."

"So would you say that your relationship was strong from the beginning, Parker? Did you two communicate effectively, grow and change together, and speak honestly with each other? Or not?"

A million memories slam into me all at once. "Fuck," I mutter as I lock eyes with Dr. Jensen.

She scribbles something on her notepad with a grin. "I think we're done for today."

***

"Cashlynn?"

It's Wednesday night and I'm getting home just after nine, but I made sure to text Cashlynn this time.

See? I'm fucking learning.

The practice was insanely busy today and an emergency surgery kept me there late. Seth stayed late too, like he was afraid to leave before me. *Jackass.* I seriously can't wait until Robert makes his decision and I can put this whole thing behind me.

"I'm in my room!" Cashlynn calls out, instantly making me feel more at ease. I set my stuff on the kitchen counter and start unbuttoning my shirt as I make my way down the hall. The tie comes off too, and as I step into her room, my shirt already hanging open, I'm ready for her to rip it off since that's been the routine the past few days.

But what I see stops me in my tracks.

She's painting.

Holy shit.

Sitting on a stool in nothing but her underwear and an over-sized T-shirt, she's completely focused on the canvas. Her hands move expertly, blending strokes of dark blue and white, accented by a few hints of yellow. Her hair is piled in a messy bun on top of her head, and she's biting her bottom lip as she assesses each stroke of her brush, contemplating where the next will go.

She's so consumed by what she's doing that she doesn't register I'm behind her until I wrap my arms around her waist. I plant kisses on her exposed neck and collar bone, watching her skin pebble right before my eyes. "You're painting…"

She glances over her shoulder at me. "I am. Why are you so surprised?"

I brush her hair back, studying her work. "You haven't painted since you moved in. I was wondering if I was ever going to see you in action."

She nods, staring back at her canvas. "Honestly, I've been so busy getting ready for the gallery to open and figuring out how to get you to admit that you wanted me, I haven't had the energy. But today, this image came to mind and I got the strongest urge to mess around with some paint, so I did." She shrugs.

"It's beautiful. What inspired it?"

"It was just the colors that kept coming to me."

"Blue and yellow?"

"A mix of calmness and optimism."

I stare at the canvas. "I guess I can see that."

"Each color symbolizes different emotions, and I think those two are the most dominant in my life right now."

I point at the single streak of black in the corner. "And that?"

Cashlynn tilts her head as she stares at the spot in question. "Fear."

My stomach lurches as I clear my throat. "Yeah, I get that too."

She turns her head to look at me. "A little fear is okay, Parker. It means you have something to lose, remember? But see how the other colors are more prominent?" I nod. "Those are the ones you tend to focus on, right?"

I stand back and push a hand through my hair, but Cashlynn doesn't let me get too far. When she reaches out to pull me back into her, her fingers graze my chest and leave a trail of blue paint in their wake. We both stare at the streak of color on my bare chest, my shirt still hanging open. And then I see the hint of mischief in her eyes.

"What's that look for?"

She licks her lips and then dips her finger into the light blue paint this time, rubbing it on her palms and then slapping them to my chest, running them down my stomach, her nails scraping lightly as she does.

"Fuck, Cashlynn. Seriously?"

She nods, pushing my shirt off my shoulders. "God, I love your body, Parker. It's like its own work of art."

My stomach tightens as she backs me up against the wall, running her fingers through the divots in my abs and then traveling up my pecs and over my shoulders, dragging the paint with her as she moves her hands all over my body.

And even though this woman is making a mess, turning me into her own human art project, her touch ignites desire in my veins like it always does.

Before I can contemplate her next move, she drops to her knees, placing her palms on her thighs. Looking up at me, she says, "Drop your pants, Dr. Sheppard."

My cock grows even harder in an instant as I obey. I pop the clasp on my slacks and shove them and my underwear down my legs, leaving me standing there in nothing but my socks—my ironed socks, that is.

"Dr. Sheppard, huh?" I ask as I reach down and stroke myself, using the precum leaking from my tip to coat my length.

She smirks, dipping her hands into red paint this time. "It's like a naughty *Grey's Anatomy* fantasy come to life."

I laugh, but it quickly turns into a groan as Cashlynn presses her painted hands against my thighs, making me tighten all over again just as her mouth closes over the tip of my cock.

"Fuck, sweetheart. Were you thinking about my cock while I was gone today?" I ask her as she hums around my length.

Her eyes flutter closed as she nods, taking me as deep as she can before gagging and repeating the process. When she reaches up to cup my balls, I don't even think about the fact that she's marking me with her paint. In fact, I fucking love it. Me—the guy that hates messes—is so fucking turned on right now as I watch Cashlynn leave her mark all over my body.

"Your greedy pussy needs this cock too, huh?" This time she nods and sucks me harder, swirling her tongue along the underside of my dick while gently rolling my balls in her hands. She slaps one hand on my stomach as she bobs up and down, faster and faster, making my orgasm rush forward.

"Fuck, you're gonna make me come, Cashlynn."

She nods again, looking me in the eyes and telling me without words that she's ready to take my release down her throat.

"Jesus. Fuck, yes. Like that." She moves faster, tugging on my balls this time and pressing against the skin just behind them, and that's what sets me off. "Fuck!"

I watch her intently as she swallows every drop of me down her throat, and when the last drop leaves me, she licks me clean, swirling her tongue around my tip one more time for good measure.

The smile she has on her lips as she stares up at me from the floor, the pure look of pleasure on her face from making me come undone has me eager to return the favor. I lift her from the floor, tear her shirt over her head, and crash into her, covering her mouth with my own, paint going everywhere.

But I don't fucking care. I need this woman. I need to bury myself inside her so deep that she never wants another man to fuck her—because I'll be damned if that thought ever crosses her mind again.

With our mouths still connected, I lead Cashlynn into my bathroom, turning on the shower as we continue to run our hands all over each other. She breaks the kiss for just a moment, long enough to look at us in the mirror, our bodies smeared with blue and red paint.

"What does red represent, Cashlynn?"

She turns back to me. "Passion. Desire. And love."

Our eyes bounce back and forth between one another, but I don't say a word. I push her underwear down her legs, walk her into the shower, and run my hands all over us, cleaning the paint from our skin, and then fuck the woman who has taken ownership of me in a matter of six weeks—because let's be honest, I want her to own me too.

***

"Good thing you had a tarp down in your room, otherwise there would have been paint in the carpet."

Cashlynn laughs as she lies next to me in my bed. We're freshly showered, she's freshly fucked, and now we're talking a bit before we go to sleep. "I'm very surprised you let me do that. I was waiting for you to freak out."

"Not gonna lie, my anxiety flared for a minute, but then you told me to drop my pants, and, well…" I shrug and she laughs, nestling in closer to me.

Then I think of a question I had earlier but never got to ask because nakedness took over. "Do you ever paint people? I know you said you paint mostly scenery and abstracts on the plane, but I was wondering if you ever tried people?"

"Not really."

"Why not?"

She sighs. "It's so hard to get the shadows right. I feel like my mind just can't pay tribute to the lines of the body the way they deserve to be seen."

"Funny. You were paying tribute to the lines on *my* body just fine."

She smacks my chest and then lays her head back down on it. "That was cheesy."

"Sorry if I'm lacking sophistication right now. I'm exhausted."

Trailing her fingers through the short hair on my chest, she hums. "Was the practice crazy today?"

"Yeah. Your father and Beth were gone, so everyone had to step up a bit. I swear, when Beth retires, the whole place might burn to the ground."

"Do you think she might when my father does?"

I think back to the conversation I overheard between the two of them, still not sure of what I heard, so I keep it to myself for now. "I don't know, honestly. I know she's worked there for almost thirty years so I can't imagine her staying for much longer."

"My father had to reschedule our lunch date for next week. Something about an appointment that he was able to get because of a cancellation."

"An appointment for what?" I ask, my nerves activating from this information.

"I don't know. He didn't say and I didn't ask. Sounds like someone else I know," she teases, but my pulse spikes. I still haven't told Cashlynn about my therapy appointments. It's only been two weeks, and I know I have a ton of shit to work through. I want to wait until there's something more productive to tell her, or at least until I'm sure this is going to stick.

"But he's good about going to his regular checkups and stuff, so it's probably something like that. If it was something serious, I'm sure he'd tell me," she continues, pulling me from my thoughts.

I nod, but don't say anything in response. Instead, I decide to change the subject. "What's your favorite color?"

She chuckles, looking up at me again. "Where did that come from?"

"I'm just trying to learn more about you, and that's one of the basic questions I think I should know the answer to."

She rolls her eyes, but she's smiling. "That question is impossible to answer because it changes for me. I go through moods." She glances down at my now clean chest, dancing her fingers along my skin again. "But after tonight? I think blue is *definitely* my favorite right now."

I roll on top of her, cupping her jaw in my hand, and get lost in her amber eyes—a place I would be happy staying lost indefinitely. "Yeah, I think blue just moved to the top of the list for me too."

Chapter Seventeen

Cashlynn

"Hi, Dad." I lean down and kiss my father's cheek before sliding into my side of the booth. I suggested we meet at Catch & Release for our rescheduled lunch date, partly because I've been craving their onion rings. I'm not sure what Dallas puts in his batter, but they're out of this world.

"Hey, June Bug. How are things?"

I push my hair back from my face and set my purse on the seat beside me. "Things are great!" I say a little too enthusiastically.

His eyebrows rise. "That good, huh?"

"I mean, I'm slipping into the small-town life pretty seamlessly, I think. I really love it here." *And my fake fiancé is now treating me like his real one, so my giddiness is beyond my control most days.* "I can see why you were eager to stay when you found out grandpa left you the practice all those years ago."

My father nods. "Yes, well, part of that was a sense of obligation, but I've been very happy here for the past eleven years."

"I think I'm gonna be happy here for at least that long too," I say, growing more optimistic about the idea every day. Every day I can more clearly see a real future here—and that future is quickly including Parker in hopefully a real engagement. But that's a conversation for us way down the road. Right now, we're living in the honeymoon phase, which includes endless amounts of sex—a detail I am *not* complaining about.

"So, things are going well with Parker then?"

"Yes, why wouldn't they be?" I ask, a little too defensively.

"I don't know." He shrugs but there's concern in his eyes. "I was wondering if you two had driven each other crazy yet. Last time we talked, you were unplugging the coffee machine."

Laughing, I reach for my water. "I was messing with him, trying to see how he reacted to certain situations, you know? It was, uh…something I read in an article about moving in with your significant other, a way to see if you're really compatible." That sounded convincing to me, but the look on my father's face is unreadable.

"Well, he sure seems more focused lately. He's been putting in a lot of time at the practice. I hope that hasn't caused any issues."

"Not at all," I say. Those mysterious Monday night *appointments* he still hasn't explained, on the other hand… I don't want to think the worst, but the truth is, I don't know a lot about the man still. I want to trust him, and deep down, I think I do. He said he was going to try to let me in, but then why won't he just be honest with me about where he's going?

Ugh, I'm driving myself nuts with thoughts of what it could be.

"And what about work for you?" Dad's question lands squarely in the pit of my stomach.

I knew this topic was coming. "Work is…slow right now. I finished up a few cases I had open before I left Philly, but right now I'm just processing a lot of paperwork."

"I don't understand how you're supposed to practice law in a different state than the one you have your license in."

"Actually, North Carolina has reciprocity with Pennsylvania, so my license is good here."

He nods, but then his eyes dip down to my hand, that's covered in spots of green paint. "Have you been painting?"

"Um, yes…" The truth is I just came from the gallery and was working on the mural of the coast of Carrington Cove that is going on the wall behind the reception. I thought I'd scrubbed off all the paint, but clearly, I missed some. *Shit*.

He scoffs, shaking his head. "You shouldn't be wasting time painting right now, Cashlynn. Honestly." His voice takes on that familiar tone of judgment. "This community could really use a lawyer of your caliber." He clears his throat before continuing. "I think you should talk to Timothy MacDonald. He's the town lawyer, and I'm sure he could give you a referral. It's been six weeks now, and it's time to start putting down real roots."

Emotion crawls up my throat, but I swallow it down. "I appreciate the thought, Dad, but I'm trying to take my time adjusting here. Parker even encouraged me to do just that."

He shakes his head. "I just don't understand, June. I'm trying to, but…"

"Is this what Mom had to deal with?" I snap, anger fueling me now.

His head rears back. "What on earth are you talking about?"

"Did you berate Mom for every one of her choices too? Try to push her into doing what *you* wanted?" I can feel my hands shaking under the table, but I try hard to keep my composure.

His eyes narrow. "Watch your tone, Cashlynn June."

"Or what?" I shoot back, leaning forward, ready to press the issue. But the waiter arrives right then. And it's probably a good thing. I take that time to get control of my heart rate.

Once the waiter leaves, I lock eyes with my dad. "I honestly want to know if this is how you've treated every woman in your life, or if I'm just the lucky one who gets all of your criticism."

He leans back in the booth, studying me for a moment. He doesn't speak and, for a second, I wonder if I've pushed him too far. But he shocks me when his reply is in an even tone.

"Your mother was the love of my life, June. And yes, there were times I expressed my concerns about her work, but I knew it made her happy, so I supported her the best I could. But losing her..." His bottom lip begins to tremble, and in an instant, I reach for his hand. "I'm sorry. I just..."

The crack in my heart widens as I look at him. "You're so lucky to have experienced a love like that, Dad," I say softly, feeling remorse for going off on him, but fuck, I'm so tired of answering to him. "I miss her every day. Sometimes I wonder what life would be like if she were still here. And sometimes I wonder if you're trying to control me because you think it will stop something from happening to me too."

He stares down at our joined hands and nods. "That might be plausible."

"I love you, and I always will. I'm just asking you to trust me. Let me live my life and own my mistakes if I make them, okay?"

His eyes lift and meet mine again. "I'll try, June. I just—"

"Want what's best for me," I finish for him, repeating the words I've heard countless times over the years.

His lips quirk into a faint smile. "I always have and I'll never stop."

The waiter comes by with our food, breaking our moment. Relief washes over me because as much as I hate seeing my dad upset, this conversation needed to happen. I just hope when he sees what I do with my gallery, he'll be able to accept that my happiness *is* the best way for me to control my life, and that's what matters at the end of the day.

"So, how did your appointment go last week?" I ask as I pop an onion ring in my mouth, salivating as the flavor hits my tongue.

He stares at me quizzically. "What appointment?"

"The one you canceled our lunch plans for."

He nods, clearing his throat. "Oh, yes. It was…good."

"Is everything okay?"

"Yes, June. Everything is fine," he says, his voice clipped.

I tilt my head, not convinced. "Are you sure?"

"Yes, okay? If I had something to tell you, I would."

I lift my hands in surrender. "All right. No need to get snippy."

"Well, you're interrogating me and I don't like it."

Funny—he doesn't like a taste of his own medicine.

"I'm just curious. Parker said you were gone for the rest of the week."

"Yes, I just…went away for the weekend," he finally says. "It was a trip I'd had planned for a while."

"Oh." My surprise is difficult to hide, but my father never leaves work for trips. Or at least, not that I was aware of. "That sounds nice. I'm sure you're looking forward to more trips like that once you pass along the practice, aren't you?"

He arches a brow at me. "Is that your way of digging for information about my decision?"

I lift both of my shoulders. "Not particularly, but you know…if you *had* anything to tell me, you know you could."

He scoffs. "Not when you're engaged to one of my candidates, I can't."

I debate pushing the topic, but then I remember my deal with Parker. Even though our status has changed, I still need to hold up my end of our bargain. "You know, Parker has so many plans for the practice, Dad."

"He does, does he?"

"We talk about it all the time." *We don't, but he doesn't know that.*

"Like what?"

Shit.

I pop an onion ring into my mouth, shaking my head. "I think you should ask him yourself. As much as I try to understand everything he talks about, I don't speak veterinarian."

My father scoffs, but there's a smile on his lips. "Okay. I will."

"Really?"

"Yeah, I think a conversation about the future of the business might help me make my decision."

"Are you honestly considering Seth?"

My father's brows draw together. "Seth is a fine doctor. He does a decent job."

"Just decent? You want your legacy to be carried on by someone that is *decent*?"

He narrows his eyes. "There's more that goes into this decision than you realize, June."

"I can't imagine how difficult this must be for you. One chapter of your life is closing, and a new one is beginning, but I hope you're thinking about the big picture, Dad. I can't see Seth being the best choice. Beth has told me some stories about him."

"Beth needs to keep her opinions to herself." He drops his eyes from mine, reaching for another french fry. "But this is a new chapter, indeed. Nobody likes change, especially me."

A laugh escapes me. "You don't say."

Rolling his eyes, he reaches for my hand. "I must say though, being able to have lunch with you on a random weekday is a nice change." *Yeah, something I wouldn't to be able to do if I was still a lawyer.*

I squeeze his fingers, cherishing the moment while we have it. "Me too, Dad. Me too."

***

"That mural is turning out amazing."

I stand back and assess the portion I just finished as Willow stands behind me to get the entire effect. "I'm actually really happy with the way it's turning out so far.

"And the white walls with those blue circles are going to be perfect for displaying the artwork."

"I'm glad you like it. Most galleries stick with all-white walls, but I wanted to tie in the mural more. I think the little bit of color did that."

Willow nods, moving toward the back of the space through the opening that separates the studio from the gallery. "The cabinets turned out great too."

"Penn put those together so fast that I felt like I blinked and they were done."

Willow laughs. "The man is a whiz with power tools. Believe me, I know from personal experience. He practically renovated my entire house."

"I would love to see it sometime. I can't imagine having the ocean as my front yard."

She sighs. "It's incredible and never gets old. In fact, why don't you and Parker come over for dinner this week? You can see the house, and while he's there, he can check on the geese for me."

My eyes light up. "The viral geese?"

Willow clasps her hands together over her chest. "Yes, and I *love* that you saw those videos."

"It was part of the reason I got him to agree to be my fake fiancé—to deter his new admirers." I wink at her.

"And now I like you even more."

A knock on the front door pulls my attention. Through the brown butcher paper still covering the glass, I see the silhouette of someone waving like a lunatic. Stepping closer, I peel back a corner of the paper and laugh when I see Hazel's grinning face. I open the door, and she shuffles in, balancing a tray of coffees. "Hello, ladies!"

"Hi." I shut and lock the door behind her.

Hazel takes in the mural as she walks over to one of the high-top tables I have strategically placed around the room, setting the tray of drinks down before turning to admire the wall in its entirety. "I fucking love this, Cashlynn."

"Thank you. It's coming together slowly but surely. I honestly still can't believe that this space is mine."

Willow reaches for her decaf coffee and takes a sip. "Oh believe it, because in about a month, this place will be open to the public."

I sigh. "Yeah, and then I have to come clean to my dad about everything."

Hazel hands me my coffee. "How did lunch with him go the other day?"

I take a sip before answering. "The usual. He had a lot to say about my job, or lack thereof. He still thinks I'm working remotely, but he insisted that I speak with Timothy McDonald to try to practice law here."

Willow flashes me a look of understanding. "I'm sorry, Cashlynn. Hopefully, when he sees what you've created, it'll all be worth it."

"I hope so. He saw paint on my hands and instantly chastised me about it." Hazel shakes her head as I continue. "It made me so angry that I snapped at him."

"What did you say?" Hazel asks.

"I asked him if he criticized my mom the way he criticizes me."

Willow's eyebrows shoot up. "Damn. What did he say?"

"His mood shifted instantly. He told me that there were times he expressed his concerns about her work but tried to support her as much as he could. So, I asked him to do the same for me. I almost told him right then and there what I've been up to, but I can't. Not yet. There's still too many unknowns and I don't want to jeopardize my side of my deal with Parker."

Hazel steps toward me, placing her arm around my shoulder, her eyes moving around the room. "Just keep making this place the best it can be and hope that he can see all of the love you've poured into it. If not, then maybe the man needs reminding about what it means to be a supportive father, and I have no problem giving him that with a knuckle sandwich on the side."

Willow rolls her eyes. "You beating up an old man isn't going to solve anything, Hazel."

She turns to face her sister-in-law. "You don't know that."

I squeeze Hazel from the side. "I appreciate the offer, but physical harm isn't necessary. He'll either accept it or he won't, but either way, at least I'll have what I've always wanted out of this, and hopefully Parker will too. I talked to my dad about his decision a bit during our lunch and told him he'd be stupid to pick Seth." I chew on my bottom lip. "I might have also told him that Parker has plans for the practice if he takes over though, and I'm not exactly sure that's true."

Hazel rolls her eyes. "If I know my brother, I'm sure that it is. But you might want to give him a heads-up."

"I'm going to talk to him about it tonight. He got home late last night, and we uh, didn't exactly do a lot of talking before we went to sleep." My cheeks flush as the girls gawk at me.

Hazel gags. "Didn't need to know that."

Willow takes a step closer to us. "So things are going well with him?"

"Yes, but he still hasn't opened up about certain things. And he uh...has these appointments on Monday nights that make him come home late."

"Okay..."

"But he won't tell me what they're for."

"Have you tried sex again?" Hazel asks as I shove her off me, her laughter ringing out.

"No, and that's not how I want to get him to open up. I'm hoping that, with time, he'll want to tell me. But if he doesn't... How can I trust him fully if he's keeping secrets? And how can I avoid triggering him if I don't even know what he's dealing with?"

"Any idea what it could be?" Willow asks, turning to Hazel.

"Maybe he's getting his balls waxed," Hazel says with a shrug.

Willow and I stare at her in disbelief. "What the hell is wrong with you?" Willow demands, shaking her head at her sister-in-law.

Hazel holds her hands up. "Hey, it's something a guy wouldn't want to share with someone!"

"Don't you think Cashlynn would know if Parker gets his balls waxed, though?"

Hazel's hands drop to her side. "Good point."

"Not that we should even be discussing this, but I know for a fact that's not it."

Willows blows out a breath, still shaking her head. "Okay, well... I'm sure it's not something bad. I mean, all the man does is work and exercise. Is he going to a gym?"

I shake my head. "He has pretty much every piece of equipment you could think of in his garage. That wouldn't make any sense. And he doesn't come home sweaty. But, his hair is always a mess when he walks in, like he's been running his hands through it, or someone else has," I say, my stomach churning at the thought.

Hazel takes a step toward me. "He is not cheating on you, so don't even think it." I nod as she continues. "My brother is a lot of things, but a cheater is not one of them."

"I think so too, but I'm just in the dark, and he won't talk to me about it. Everything feels very surface-level right now—except the sex. That's still amazing."

"Men are so fragile when it comes to feelings," Willow says, running her nails absently across her stomach. "I can tell you this—my son won't be afraid of talking about his emotions, not after the roadblocks Dallas and I have both overcome in that department."

Hazel wraps her arm around Willow's shoulders. "And women everywhere will be thanking you for generations to come."

Chapter Eighteen

Cashlynn

"Hey, you two. Welcome!" Willow greets us with a big smile as she opens her front door. Parker's hand rests possessively on my lower back as we step inside, something I'm growing ridiculously fond of.

"Thanks for having us. This property is gorgeous," I tell her as I take in the open layout and the beautiful view of the ocean just a small stretch of sand away.

Dallas walks up behind Willow, wrapping his arm around her waist, admiring the view himself. "Thank you. This is our own little slice of heaven in Carrington Cove." Then he turns to Parker and claps him on the shoulder. "How's it going, little brother?"

Parker reciprocates the gesture. "It's going. Busy, but making progress."

I wish I knew more about what he's making progress with, but alas, my fake fiancé is still locked up pretty tight. After my talk with Willow and Hazel earlier this week, I decided to continue to wait on him to open up to me, but he still hasn't said any more about his mysterious Monday night appointments.

It's seriously making me question if they're a figment of my imagination.

"Hey, before I forget," Dallas says, turning to his brother, "I wanted to know if you had plans next weekend."

Parker turns to me for silent confirmation, and I shake my head, loving that he thought to check with me about our plans—even if I'm not entirely sure where our relationship stands. Just the thought of asking him about it has my anxiety building again.

"Not that I'm aware of," he replies.

"Would you be willing to help me build a shed out back?" Dallas jerks his thumb over his shoulder. "I want to get it done before the baby comes, and Penn is tied up with a few jobs.."

"So, I'm second choice?" Parker quips. "The brotherly equivalent of a second-string quarterback. Got it."

Dallas rolls his eyes. "If that's how you want to take it, sure."

Parker smirks. "Of course I can help you. I'm just giving you shit."

Dallas blinks at him. "Wait a minute. Did you just crack a joke?"

"Jesus, don't make a big deal out of it," Parker grumbles. "I said I'd help you, didn't I?"

Dallas turns to me. "Keep up whatever it is that you're doing. I like the effect it's having on my little brother."

I laugh under my breath. *If he only knew.*

"So, how are the geese doing?" Parker asks Willow, changing the subject as we head toward the kitchen. Willow has a bottle of wine chilling for us and a sparkling water with lime for herself.

Willow smiles proudly as she pours the wine. "Mallory and Gary have been patrolling the yard, watching over the eggs for the past week. We started with two and now we're up to five."

"Mallory and Gary?" I ask.

Dallas groans. "Willow's named every bird that comes within fifty feet of this house, like they're her pets. Later, I'll tell you how they started out as mortal enemies."

Willow shoots her husband a glare, and then motions for us to follow her outside. We step onto the wraparound porch and head toward the side of the house, where a narrow path of tall grass separates their property from the neighbor's. Near the edge of the grass are two geese—one sitting on the ground, covering the eggs, I'm assuming, and another patrolling the area.

The second we get too close, the one standing begins to voice his concern.

"Honk!"

Willow places her hands on her hip as she stares down at the bird. "Easy, Gary. Parker is just here to make sure you and Mallory are gonna hatch healthy little babies."

Gary shifts his head, eyeing her, and then takes off toward his partner. "Honk!"

I giggle, watching the interaction. Parker takes a few steps closer. "I need to wait for Mallory to move to check them."

"How exactly are you going to do that?" I ask.

He pulls a flashlight from his pocket, clicking it on and off. "I shine the light through them to check that they are viable. If Mallory has been sitting on them thus far and doesn't move, they're probably good to go. But if several aren't viable, she might abandon the whole nest, and then the ones that could have survived won't, so that's what we want to be careful about."

I look to my side to find Willow recording Parker on her phone. "Don't mind me, just documenting him in action." She winks in my direction, and suddenly, I think I know exactly what she's up to.

"What if she doesn't move?" I ask.

"She should. If she only laid the eggs this week, we still should have a few days before she starts to incubate. Once she does, she won't move at all."

"Not even to eat or drink?" I ask, stepping closer to him.

"Nope. Her sole purpose becomes making sure those eggs hatch." As he senses me near, he pulls me into his side and looks down at me.

"I hate to admit this, but all of this bird talk is actually kind of hot."

He arches a brow at me as he laughs. "Hot, huh?"

"Yeah. Seeing you in your element, talking about something you know so much about…it's really sexy." I reach up and straighten his glasses.

"Well, taking care of animals is my job." He presses a kiss to my nose, and then one on my lips before moving his mouth to my ear and whispering, "But glad to know that it turns you on."

I can feel my cheeks grow hot. I glance over at Willow, who is still recording us, and she flashes me a thumbs up.

"You know, watching you paint has the same effect on me," he says to me, his voice still low.

When I lean back and look up at him, I can see the reverence and heat in his eyes. "Maybe I'll just have to start another painting."

He pulls me tighter into his body where I can feel just how much he likes that idea. "You should start it tonight."

Dallas clears his throat, breaking our moment as Willow puts her phone away. "All right, you two. Dinner is almost ready. Let's head inside and you two can continue to eye-fuck each other in there."

Parker flips his brother off, grabs my hand, and leads me back toward the house. But before we go inside, I pull on his hand, holding him back.

"Everything okay?" he asks.

Cupping his jaw, I lock onto his eyes, wanting to make sure that he sees the honesty in mine when I speak. "You're amazing, you know that, right?"

A pinch in his brow appears, making him seem confused. "Okay…"

"The way you care for others, the way you care about animals. You act like your brothers irritate the shit out of you, but I'm starting to understand that's part of your love language." He scoffs but lets me continue. "You're an amazing man, Parker Sheppard. And I'm proud to call you my fake fiancé."

I want to continue with, *"How can you not see how perfect you are for me, how much I want to make our relationship real and how wonderful I know it could be if you'd just let me in?"*

But I don't.

I'm too afraid of telling Parker the truth, and the irony that I'm keeping my true feelings from both of the men in my life is not lost on me.

With intense speed, he yanks me into his chest, cupping my jaw this time and stroking my skin with his thumb. The intensity of his gaze makes my pulse climb. "You have no idea how much that means to me, Cashlynn." He seals his lips over mine, slowly moving his tongue along mine, kissing me with a passion and reverence that is brand new, something I haven't felt from him before.

This feels like more.

This feels like *love*.

***

Later that night, after Parker and I clawed at each other the second we got home, I'm lying in bed next to him as he sleeps when my phone buzzes on the nightstand.

I pick it up and see a message from Willow. It's a link to a new video she uploaded to her social media—the video of Parker at her house earlier.

The video opens with just him in the frame as he explains what would happen with the geese, but when he pulls me into him, she made sure to capture the two of us during our intimate conversation. Luckily, you can't hear everything that we're saying, but that's not what's holding my attention anyway—it's the way Parker is looking at me. And then I read the caption.

"He's off the market, ladies. What's that look on his face? Oh, that's love."

My heart thrashes in my chest. My eyes keep watching us interact on the screen.

And in that moment, I know I'm in love with Parker Sheppard.

I just hope that my heart doesn't end up broken because his might still be too damaged to love me back.

***

The front door opens, startling me from my focus. I was having trouble concentrating in my room earlier, so I moved my laptop and notebooks out to the dining room table, planning to get in another hour of work before starting dinner.

But when Parker walks in just after five, the look on his face immediately sets off my alarm bells.

Standing from my chair, I walk over to him as he sets his bag on the floor by the door. "Parker, is everything okay?"

He blows out a breath and heads in my direction, wrapping me in his arms and burying his face in my neck. "Just a shitty day."

Rubbing his back as he holds me tightly, I give him a moment and just soak up his warmth. I hate that his day was awful, but part of me is enjoying every minute he's finding comfort in me. "Do you want to talk about it?"

"Sometimes I really hate this job," he says, surprising me.

"Never thought I'd hear you say those words."

He releases me and drags a hand through his hair before removing his glasses and setting them on the kitchen table. "I had to euthanize four dogs today, two of which were emergencies that were too late to fix."

I can almost feel my heart crack. "I'm sorry." Gently taking his hand, I lead him toward the couch. I take out my phone and order some food for delivery, deciding neither of us is going to want to cook tonight.

We settle into the couch, Parker resting his feet on the coffee table in front of him as he leans back and stares at the ceiling. "It never gets easier," he says as his voice cracks. "I feel like a failure when I can't save them."

"I can imagine."

"And watching the owners have to say goodbye fucking sucks."

"My dad used to say that was the hardest part of the job too."

He shakes his head, his eyes still directed above us. "It's not fair that dogs don't live as long as people."

"Yeah, I agree. We always had a dog growing up, and our last one died right after my mom did. I think between the two, my father and I agreed we couldn't handle another loss, and I was about to move away for college, so he didn't want to take on that responsibility again by himself."

He finally turns to me. "I felt that way as soon as I moved back home. I was focused on work, and then with Sasha…" he starts, but stops almost instantly, as if he caught himself talking about something he shouldn't.

Adrenaline races through me. "What about Sasha?"

He shakes his head, darting his eyes away from me. "Nothing."

"You know you can talk to me about her, Parker," I say, hoping he'll use this moment to break through this wall that's between us. I know we both can feel it, but there's something still holding him back. "Are you ever going to tell me about her?" I ask, trepidation in my voice, but once the words are out, I'm curious as to what he'll say.

He lets out a heavy sigh, his shoulders slumping. His hands clench as he wars with himself, every ounce of frustration visible in his body. But he finally turns to me, his gaze full of vulnerability. "I want to do right by you, Cashlynn. I don't want to carry my issues into another relationship."

"Then why can't you tell me what's going on?" I ask softly, optimistic that his admission means he does want a relationship with me. "Or what happened—so I can try to understand."

"*I'm* still trying to understand it, Cashlynn." His eyes close as he contemplates what to say next. "But I'm working on it."

Well, that's both promising and vague. "All right…"

He turns to me again and reaches for my hand. "I'm just asking you to trust me."

"I do."

"And be patient."

"I—I told you that I would."

His gaze drops down to our hands. Silence hangs between us, and honestly, I'm not sure what else to say.

I trust him, but I also feel like I'm being kept in the dark.

He lets out a groan as he rubs his temple. "I think I need to just close my eyes for a bit."

"Okay."

I expect him to head to the bedroom, but instead, he grabs a throw pillow and pushes it into my lap. Kicking off his shoes, he stretches out along the couch, resting his head against my stomach.

"Is this okay?" he murmurs.

"Of course, Parker," I whisper, stroking his hair softly as his breathing evens out. Watching him drift off, I wonder what demons haunt him in his sleep—and whether he'll ever let me help him face them.

Chapter Nineteen

Parker

"How have the past two weeks been, Parker?"

Dr. Jensen is sitting in her usual chair, notepad balanced on her knee.

I wasn't able to see her last week because she went on vacation, but honestly, I think that was what I needed, time to process how we left our last session.

"Interesting."

"How so?"

"Well, for starters, I didn't like that little cliff hanger thing you pulled last time." I wave a finger at her. Her smirk tells me she knew exactly what she was doing. "But it definitely made me think."

"And what conclusions or realizations did you come to?" Her pen is poised on her pad, ready to capture my thoughts.

I clench and unclench my hands in my lap. "That maybe the way I remember my relationship with Sasha makes me place blame on myself, but she was responsible for the deterioration of it too."

Dr. Jensen smiles. "Okay. Tell me more."

"Well, it's like you suggested...she didn't share her struggles with me about alcohol, and even though I know that we both changed, we didn't change together. Both of us played a part in our relationship dissolving, something I think I was forgetting to acknowledge."

"And how does that make you feel?"

"Like my chest is a little lighter," I say honestly.

She nods while jotting down a few notes. "Okay, so I love that you've had some time to think, and now I want to go back to your 'what if' game that you said your brain likes to play with you all the time." Setting her notepad to the side, she uncrosses her legs and then leans forward in her chair. "A lot of times when our minds generate 'what if' thoughts, they are rooted in fear and helplessness."

"Uh, yeah that sounds about right. Those are two things I hate fucking feeling."

"And it's completely normal. But the good thing is, we can shift those thoughts by changing just one word."

I lean forward, mirroring her position. "Okay..."

"Instead of thinking 'what if,' change it to 'even if.'"

"Even if?" I repeat, my brows knitting together.

She nods. "Yes. For example, instead of saying, 'What if I get hurt again?' you say, 'Even if I get hurt again...'" My brows draw together, but she continues. "By changing one word, we give our brain the affirmation that even if something happens, we can figure it out and get through it."

"Yeah, but how do I know that?"

She straightens in her chair. "Well, let me ask you this: Have you gotten through everything you've dealt with in life so far?"

"Well, yeah..."

"So, if you've gotten through one-hundred percent of your hardest days so far, doesn't that feel more empowering to remind yourself that you can survive anything else that might come your way?"

I sink back into the cushion on the couch as multiple lights start to flicker on in my brain. "Huh."

She smirks, knowing once again what she just did to my mind. And for the first time in four years, I don't dread the idea of thinking about a future, and most importantly, a future with Cashlynn.

"Here's what I want you to sit with this week. One, people will always reveal themselves to you, you just have to give them time. Part of the reason you didn't see Sasha's struggles was because she hid that part of herself from you until she couldn't anymore. What happened to her is *not your fault*," she says, punctuating the last three words. "It is entirely unfair of you to hold responsibility for her choices."

My eyes start to sting as she continues.

"And two, love isn't perfect, and it doesn't always come easy. It's about working together to overcome challenges and face obstacles, choosing to keep fighting for each other over and over. Love takes effort, but it's worth it when you find someone who's willing to fight just as hard for you." Dr. Jensen becomes blurry as I look at her now. "What you need to ask yourself is, is Cashlynn that person you want to fight for?"

"I want her to be."

"I want that for you too, Parker. But ultimately, the decision is yours."

***

"You're really engaged to that woman?" Christy—I think that's her name—waltzes up to me as I make my way into the animal hospital Tuesday morning. I got the best night's sleep I've had in months last night, and I think it was because of my session with Dr. Jensen yesterday.

Who knew therapy could do such wonders?

But now, my joyous morning is being interrupted by one of my female admirers, thanks to Willow posting another video.

Next time I see her, I'm taking her goddamn phone away.

"Good morning," I say to Christy, trying to walk past her, but apparently that was a mistake.

She pulls on my shirt sleeve, stopping me in my tracks. "How long have you been seeing her? Why would you keep something like that from me?" Her eyes are wide and unnervingly intense.

I fight the urge to roll my eyes at this woman who clearly could benefit from a little therapy herself.

I take a deep breath to keep my calm. "Christy? It is Christy, right?" She nods, still holding onto my shirt. I peel her fingers from my clothing and take a step back. "With all due respect, you and I have never had a relationship, nor will we ever. Yes, I am engaged to the woman in the video, and she, unlike you, is respectful of personal space. I'm going to kindly ask you to refrain from showing up here again, or next time I will call the police to escort you off the property."

She shakes her head at me. "She'll never make you happy," she says as she stomps over to her car.

I grumble under my breath, "Yeah, well, at least she isn't giving me a headache first thing in the morning."

Stepping inside, I'm greeted by the sight of the receptionists chuckling behind their hands. "Glad I could provide early morning entertainment for everyone."

Cassandra holds up her phone. "Hey, I had 9-1-1 ready to call in case she pulled out a pair of handcuffs to bind you two together."

"Good to know." I reply dryly.

"Mrs. Kingston is your first patient today," Cassandra says, trailing me to my office.

"Great. Get the room set up and I'll be in there in a minute."

She leaves and I take a minute to look myself over in the mirror, grab my lab coat, and then make my rounds on a few overnight patients. But as I pass Beth's office, voices draw my attention.

"I just don't know what else to do, Beth," Dr. O'Neil says.

"You can't do anything, Robert. She's going to make her own mistakes, and you just have to let her."

"Why would she lie to me?" he asks, his voice heavy with disappointment.

My heart starts racing. *Fuck. Does he know about the gallery? Does he know about our fake engagement?*

"Well, can you blame her? You overreact to everything."

Ha. Good for you, Beth.

"I react the way a father should."

"Yeah, maybe if she were sixteen. But she's going to be thirty next year, honey. This is where you have to let the baby bird fly whichever way the wind blows her."

Honey? Did Beth just call Dr. O'Neil honey?

"I need to tell her that I know—bring it up and see what she says."

I reach up and drag my hand down my face, growing more nervous the longer I listen. If Dr. O'Neil knows about our arrangement, that means he's going to come for me too.

Fuck. We're just one week away from Cashlynn's gallery opening and a few weeks away from him making his decision about the practice, and I still couldn't tell you which way he is leaning. But this? If he knows the truth and confronts Cashlynn about it before she's ready, it could be catastrophic.

I walk away, even though every part of me wants to keep listening, but the receptionists just unlocked the doors, and I have patients to attend to. If I can avoid Robert for the rest of the morning, perhaps I can talk to him at lunch, gauge how much he knows, and maybe head him off before he speaks with Cashlynn.

Or maybe I just tell him the truth myself?

But Cashlynn wanted to wait. She's been adamant about it.

"Dr. Sheppard?" Cassandra calls me, pulling me back to reality.

"Yeah?"

"Mrs. Kingston is ready in room two."

"Thank you."

Knowing I have to put my personal life on hold right now, I enter the room to check on one of my favorite patients.

The rest of the morning goes by so quickly, I barely have time to dwell on the conversation I overheard this morning between Dr. O'Neil and Beth. But as soon as lunchtime hits and I head toward my office, I hear Dr. O'Neil yelling from his.

"Why did you lie to me?" his voice echoes down the hall as I make my way in that direction. "I'm so disappointed, June."

Fuck. He's talking to Cashlynn.

Before I can think, I'm standing in his doorway and when he turns around and sees me there, he bristles. "We'll talk more later." He ends the call abruptly, shoving his phone in his pocket and standing tall. "Can I help you, Parker?"

I don't take a second to overthink what I'm about to do, I just act.

"All Cashlynn wants is for you to believe in her and trust her enough to make decisions on her own about her life. Is that really too much to ask?"

His eyebrows raise, surprised by my confronting him, I'm sure. "I don't like my daughter keeping secrets from me."

"Ha. That's rich coming from you."

He takes a step closer to me. "What did you just say to me?"

I lower my voice, but stand my ground. "I think it's ironic that you're upset with your daughter for not being honest when you're keeping secrets from her too."

He narrows his eyes at me. "I'm not sure what you think you know…"

"I know enough," I say, debating if I should reveal my hand or wait.

"You'd better watch your tone with me."

"Or what? You're not going to hand the practice over to me?" I say a little too loudly. "At this point, that's a risk I'm willing to take."

Something comes over me in this moment, rage fueled by a protective instinct mixed with optimism and purpose. I've bent over backwards for this man for the past six years, but right now, I've lost so much respect for him that I'm prepared to handle the consequences of speaking up.

What kind of man doesn't support his own daughter? What kind of man chastises her so much in her life and pushes her to do what he wants so much that *she* feels the need to lie to him about something she's been working toward and dreaming about for years?

I refuse to let him treat her like this anymore, and if that means that I have to sacrifice what I've been working toward, then so be it.

"You would risk the practice for my daughter?"

"In a heartbeat," I say as clarity takes hold in my chest.

Cashlynn is mine to protect now, mine to cherish, mine to *love*. And in that moment, it hits me—I'm in love with her. I never stood a chance from the moment her amber eyes met mine.

You could tell Robert right now why Cashlynn is really here though, Parker—how everything she did was because of him, and hopefully that might get him to admit what he's hiding and see what an ass he is.

But I won't betray her. The foundation of our relationship has been built on lies. She deserves honesty and trust.

When the truth comes out, it will be a mutual decision like we've discussed. I want that kind of relationship, the one Dr. Jensen described—one where we fight for what we have, not against each other. That's the fresh start I want.

"You can leave my office now, son."

I take a step back, but keep my eyes locked on his. "If you're not careful, you're going to push her away for good, Robert. And if that happens, you'll have to get through me the next time you want to talk to her."

Spinning on my heel, I leave his office and stride down the hallway, so much energy running through me that I feel like I could run a fucking marathon right now.

But when I get to my office, I see Seth sitting at my desk, waiting for me with a slimy smirk on his face.

This douche is the last fucking person I want to see right now.

"Get the hell out of my chair," I snap.

He shakes his head at me. "Now, now…that's no way to speak to me, Dr. Sheppard."

"You're in my fucking office, so you're the one who should be watching how you speak to me."

He stands from my chair slowly, straightening his lab coat as he makes his way around my desk. I circle my desk from the other side, choosing to remain standing in case I feel the need to leap over this thing and beat his ass to a pulp.

"Sounds like you're *actually* in love," Seth says, confusing me with his choice of topic. But the last person I'm going to talk to about that is Seth Brown.

"What's your point, Seth? Need tips on how to get a woman to like you? Newsflash—even a professional wouldn't be able to help."

"I just don't see it. Parker Sheppard in love with Cashlynn O'Neil."

"I'm engaged to her, aren't I?" I quip.

"That wasn't an answer to my question."

"You didn't ask one." We stay in a stare down for a few seconds before I huff out a laugh. "Look, I don't owe you an explanation about my personal life, all right?"

"You're right. You don't. But the more I think about it, the more things don't add up. it just doesn't make sense that *you* would date Robert's daughter and never say a word to anyone. So I did a little digging..." My heart rate is borderline alarming right now, but I'm not going to freak out yet. "According to her former employer, she no longer works there. I asked around, and funny thing...nobody from her former job even knew she was dating anyone."

This fucker.

"And then there's you," Seth continues. "I heard about your previous engagement and how tragically it ended. Anyone who's been through something like that would surely be more cautious when it comes to marriage, don't you think?"

I step up to him so we are face to face. "Choose your next words carefully, Seth."

"Or what?"

I clear my throat. "Cashlynn and I are engaged. We are getting married. And the last person who should have anything to say about that is you."

Seth's smile grows. "You'd better watch yourself, Parker. This practice is mine, and I think I just found the key to making sure it works out that way. I can't wait to see the look on Robert's face when he finds out the truth."

When Seth leaves my office, I stand there, realizing that my fists are clenched so tight at my sides that my knuckles have turned white. I release my hands and turn my back to the door, pushing a hand through my hair as I debate what to do.

Just a few moments ago, I was set on keeping the truth about our arrangement to myself and waiting to tell Robert together like we planned. But now?

Do I tell Robert before Seth does? Will Seth tell him or is he just hanging this over my head to make me back out of the running for the practice?

Didn't I already kind of do that when I told Robert that I'd choose Cashlynn over the practice anyway?

My mind is racing, my heart is pounding, but there's one thing for certain: Robert will find out the truth, one way or another. The question isn't if he'll find out—it's when, and how. And that will determine the rest of my future, especially the one I hope to build with Cashlynn.

Chapter Twenty

Parker

"I'm trying to run a restaurant, and you call an emergency meeting?" Dallas walks into the back room of Catch & Release, hands on his hips. Penn and Grady are already seated, waiting for me expectantly.

"You know I wouldn't if it wasn't important. Cashlynn has enough to deal with right now and Seth's my mess to clean up."

My oldest brother sighs and sits on the edge of a table, crossing his arms over his chest. "All right. What's going on?"

The second I left work, I texted my brothers and Grady, knowing I needed some advice before I went home to Cashlynn. I let her know I was going to be late, and then headed to the restaurant, hoping that hearing some different perspectives on the matter would help me decide what to do because I'm fucking torn.

"Seth knows that Cashlynn quit her job," I say, getting straight to the point. "He's threatening me with the information, basically saying he's going to tell Dr. O'Neil and use it as a way to get the practice."

Penn growls. "Do we know his address? I have quite a few power tools on me that could do a lot of structural damage."

"Fucking up his house isn't going to solve anything," Grady says. "But I could have Chase throw a baseball through his window accidentally."

"Focus, please," I say.

"So, what if he does tell Robert?" Dallas asks. "Do you think it'd be enough reason not to give you the practice?"

"I don't give a fuck about the animal hospital anymore. I'm worried about Cashlynn."

My oldest brother smiles proudly at me. "Looks like you've finally figured some shit out."

I stare down at my hands clasped between my legs. "Yeah, therapy will do that to you."

Penn slaps me on the shoulder. "Proud of you, little brother."

"It was time," I say, not wanting to focus on that revelation right now. "Back to the problem, please."

"What if *you* told Dr. O'Neil first?" Grady asks.

"That's my dilemma. I feel like if I do, I can give him the real story, not the one that Seth is going to fabricate. But Cashlynn wanted me to wait. She's been adamant that her dad was not to know anything until the gallery is open."

Grady shrugs. "That's this Saturday though, right? What's a couple of days?"

Dallas clears his throat. "Sorry to say this, but you have to look out for everyone's best interest here, Parker, and I think telling him before the opening could be the best option."

"Even if it means breaking Cashlynn's trust?"

"She might thank you in the long run," Penn says.

I bury my head in my hands. "I just don't want to fuck this up. Do you know what it feels like to fail at love?"

Dallas's brows pinch together. "A failure in love? Is that what you think you are?"

I peer back up at my oldest brother. "It's the one thing I've never been able to get right. Everything else in my life is a piece of cake, but loving Sasha was the one thing I failed at. I don't want to fail Cashlynn too."

"Are you fucking kidding me?" Penn chimes in. "God, you're naïve if you think that one failed relationship means you are a failure, Parker, let alone that one."

"Two relationships, actually," I correct him. "Don't forget about Ashley in high school."

"Okay, two relationships. You've *only* had two and you think that makes you a failure because neither of them worked out? Do you realize how many times people start dating someone only for it to end up…ending?" Penn scoffs.

"Well, it's not like you two have failed at it. And Mom and Dad…"

"Do you know how badly I messed up with Willow in the beginning?" My older brother asks me.

"Yeah, but that was just because you were mad about the house."

He points a finger at his chest. "It wasn't just the house. It was *my* fucking feelings that I didn't know how to manage, especially when I found out how we were connected. I fucked up royally, and I still do shit wrong sometimes, but loving someone isn't about being perfect, and it isn't about saving them."

Penn shoves my shoulder. "Look at me and Astrid. We tiptoed around each other for years because we were afraid of getting things wrong, and as a result, we lost time together, but transitioning from friends to lovers was still difficult. And we still argue. It's never going to be perfect, but it's worth it with the right person."

Grady clears his throat. "Need I remind you that I was too chickenshit to tell Scottie that I liked her back in high school, and it took seventeen years and a surprise pregnancy for us to get it right?"

"Well, I mean—"

"You are not a fucking failure, Parker," Dallas adds, cutting me off as I focus back on him. "You loved Sasha and did everything you could to help her, but she was never yours to save. You two were not meant to be, that's the truth of it all. And it's time you let that relationship go." He stands from his seat and walks over to me, placing his hand on my shoulder.

"You're right, and I'm starting to understand that," I say as the ground below starts to grow blurry. "But I just want to get this right with her, do this relationship differently. Three months ago, I was hell-bent on keeping this platonic, but this woman...she's this light I didn't know I needed, and now I want *her*." I lick my bottom lip. "I don't want to live without her and it's killing me that I could potentially fuck it all up with one wrong choice." Burying my hands in my hair, I groan. "I should have never agreed to this. I should have just pushed her to be honest from the beginning and then I wouldn't be in this predicament."

"Do you love her?" Penn asks, and I pop my head back up.

"What?"

"You heard me." His jaw is tight as his eyes remain locked on mine. "Do you love her?"

But I don't get the chance to respond because shouting from the other side of the room startles us all.

"Parker Eric Sheppard!"

All four of us spin toward the entrance of the back room to find my mother standing there with her hands on her hips, her face contorted in that look she gave my brothers more than me growing up because I was the good one—but it seems it's my turn now.

"Mom?"

She waves her phone in the air as she walks into the room.

"Hi, Mom." Dallas kisses her on the cheek, but she waves him off and comes to stand right in front of me.

Fuck. This can't be good.

"Do you think I'm stupid, Parker?"

"Absolutely not," I answer quickly.

She smacks me upside the head. "Did you forget that your mother also has a phone and social media?"

"Uh, no," I say, rubbing my head in the spot where she just smacked me. "But I guess you're about to remind me?"

"Then why did it take me this long to figure out that my son is a liar and Cashlynn O'Neil was just a cover to get these crazy stalker women away from you?"

Dallas leans in toward us both. "Uh, Mom. You might want to lower your voice a bit."

She spins around and points a finger at him. "Did you know about this?"

"We all did," Grady says just as Penn shoves him. "What?"

"Not fucking cool, man."

Needing to put an end to this madness, I stand from my chair and spin my mother back to face me. "Mom, it's not exactly what you think."

"You lied to me."

"I did, but Cashlynn was the one who came to *me* about being her fake fiancé, not the other way around. The arrangement just gave me the added bonus of getting my admirers to back off."

She sighs, seeming to calm down slightly from that information. "I had to find out during my gardening club that my son was an internet sensation. And then to discover that it was Willow that was posting these videos..." She glances back at Dallas.

He holds his hands up in the air. "Hey, I had nothing to do with this."

"You're gonna tell me that you had no idea what your wife was up to?"

"Mom." I reach for her hand and motion for her to sit. Dallas grabs her a glass of water and then urges Penn and Grady to leave the room with him, leaving me and my mom alone.

"Yes, the engagement was fake, but my feelings are real."

Her eyes start to soften. "Really?"

"Yeah, Mom. Cashlynn is it for me, and it's taken me a year and three months and lots of therapy to realize it, but our situation is a lot more complicated than you think."

Her bottom lip trembles. "You've been going to therapy?"

I huff out a laugh. "Yeah, and it fucking sucks, but it's time to let go of Sasha."

Her hand molds around the side of my face, sending her warmth and understanding through me. I know that deep down I never wanted to let my father down, but on some level, I think this woman is the one who always let me fall so I knew that I could and things would still be okay.

"Someday you learn that it's not the *wrong* person who makes you question what you want in life. It's the *right* one, Parker." Goosebumps break out on my arms from her words. "I'm glad that you finally figured it out."

My vision gets cloudy again, but I blink away the moisture building in my eyes. "I'm working on it, but I'm still scared, Mom. I don't want to fuck this up. I really thought after Sasha that my chance was gone. I felt like I let her down, and...

"I wish I understood where you got this idea that you only got once chance at love."

Shaking my head, I glance around the empty room. "I've been thinking about that the past few weeks and I guess I never really struggled or failed at things in my life until that moment. Like, school was easy for me, and I stayed out of trouble unlike my brothers." My mother rolls her eyes at that comment. "And I guess I just wanted a love like you had with Dad. I wanted to make you two proud of me. I loved Sasha, Mom, but the more I process everything, the more I realize I was young and naïve, and she was responsible for her choices. That relationship was a stepping stone for me to figure out how to be a better partner. I just wish I could have helped her more."

"I know you do, but it wasn't your job to fix her, Parker. She pulled away from you just as much as you did to her. She needed help, and you gave her that chance when you encouraged her to go to rehab. But she made the choice to leave, to drink, to drive. None of that was on you. You loved her enough to let her go, Parker, and that love gave her a second chance at a better life—for her and for you. She's the one who chose not to take it."

I pull my mother into my chest, inhaling deeply and exhaling guilt and lies as I breathe out. "I love you, Mom."

"I love you two, son. I'm so proud of the young man you are and that you're dealing with your past to have a chance at a better future."

"Thank you." When my mom releases me, a pinch in her brow develops. "What?"

"If this whole engagement was Cashlynn's idea, what was in it for her?"

"Let's just say that not everyone's parents are as understanding as you," I reply. "But make sure you don't have any plans on Saturday. We have a gallery opening to attend."

And then I tell my mother everything, and she helps me figure out exactly what I need to do next.

***

"Parker?" Cashlynn sits up on the couch as soon as I walk in the house later that evening. She rubs the tiredness from her eyes and blinks, focusing on me as I make my way over to her.

"Hey, sweetheart." I take a seat next to her on the couch, pressing a kiss to her forehead. "Sorry I kept you waiting tonight."

She sits up, covering her mouth as she yawns. "It's okay. I can't believe I fell asleep out here."

"Well, you've been working yourself hard these past few weeks getting ready for the opening on Saturday."

"I know, but I barely closed my eyes and the next thing I knew you were walking through the door." She glances at the clock on the wall. "It's after eight already?"

"Yeah." Pushing a hand through my hair, I take my glasses off and set them on the coffee table, preparing to tell her everything I've been holding back.

"Uh oh. The glasses are coming off," she teases. "Is everything okay?"

I look her straight in her amber eyes, hoping like hell that what I'm about to say doesn't destroy us. "I just came from your dad's house."

Her spine straightens. "What? Why?"

"I told him everything, Cashlynn."

She leaps from the couch and clutches her hands to her chest. "Are you serious? Please tell me you're joking!"

Looking up at her, I say, "No, sweetheart. I'm being completely honest with you."

Her hands cover her mouth, and her eyes are wide as she stares down at me. "Why on earth would you do that without even talking to me about it, Parker?"

"Because if I didn't, Seth was going to."

She squints at me now, her expression hardening in an instant. "So to save yourself, you jeopardized everything that I've been working toward for the past three months?"

I stand now, not wanting her to run from what I'm going to say. Reaching out to her, I place my hand on her upper arm, but she swats me away. "Cashlynn…"

"No, Parker." Her voice cracks as tears fill her eyes. "How could you?"

"I know you can't see it right now, but this was the best thing to do. Your father deserved the truth, not the half-assed version that Seth was likely to give him, and now he won't make a scene on Saturday if he shows up."

A tear slides down her cheek. "I thought…"

I reach out to her again, hating to see the pain and betrayal filling her eyes, but she steps away from me this time, putting even more space between us. "I'm sorry. I know you asked me not to, but I did what I thought was best."

"Yeah, what was best for you."

"No, for *us*. He knows everything, and now he can decide if he will support you in this decision. In the *real* decision. I couldn't stand by while he kept hurting you, Cashlynn. I told him because I refuse to watch you crumble under fear of his judgment any longer. I'm asking you to trust me, sweetheart. Please..."

"You're asking me to trust you, but you won't even trust me enough to tell me what the hell happened in your last relationship!" Her words sting, but they're true. "Telling my dad was *not* your choice to make, Parker." She starts to walk away from me, down the hall to her room, but I follow her because we are *not* done talking. I'm not done convincing her that this was the right choice, that I only had her best interests at heart.

"I'm involved in these lies too, Cashlynn." She steps inside her room, and I trail her closely. Reaching inside the closet, she grabs a duffle bag and starts stuffing it with clothes. "Where are you going?"

"I don't know. I just...I can't be around you right now."

I grab her arm and turn her to face me. "Look at me, Cashlynn."

Her eyes are brimming with tears and her face is starting to turn red. Fuck, I hate seeing her like this, so hurt, so torn up because I wanted to prevent her from hurting further.

After I talked to my mom, I decided to tell Robert immediately, to give him time to process everything before the gallery opening on Saturday. That way, if he does show up, he'll have had time to cool down so maybe he can be open to what she's created for herself. Hopefully Beth, who was at his house when I showed up, can smack some sense into him. The two of them have some things to admit to Cashlynn themselves, but now's not the time to bring that up.

"I heard your father on the phone with you earlier today." That gets her attention. "I heard him telling you that he was disappointed that you lied to him, so I ambushed him when he ended the call and sort of went off on him without knowing exactly what he was talking about." I smooth my hand down the side of her face.

"He found out I never talked to Timothy McDonald about a job like I said I would..."

I nod, also knowing the truth about that now. "Regardless of what you were talking about, the fact that you can't tell him anything without fear of his reaction is bullshit, Cashlynn. I told him that he should be supporting you, not tearing you down. He didn't like it, of course, but I told him that if standing up for you meant losing the practice, so be it. I don't want it if it comes at your expense."

Her lips part, stunned. "You said that to him?"

"Yes." My voice is steady, though my heart is pounding. "I don't give a shit about the practice anymore, Cashlynn. Truth be told, I've been questioning it for a while."

"What made you come to that conclusion?"

I swallow roughly and say, "My therapist."

She takes a step closer to me. "You've been seeing a therapist?"

"Yeah. Those Monday night appointments? I was seeing her." I release her as she steps back from me again, her eyes bouncing all over my face.

"Why couldn't you have just told me that?" she asks as more tears build in her eyes. "I've been wondering for weeks what you've been keeping from me, convincing myself that you wouldn't cheat on me, or..."

Cupping the side of her face, I say adamantly, "I would *never* be unfaithful to you. I didn't want to tell you until I could work through some shit. Because I knew you'd have questions that I wouldn't have answers to yet. But I do now. I've realized a lot..."

"But you lied to me, and then you betrayed me by going to my dad when I asked you not to!" Turning her back to me again, she grabs a few more pieces of clothing from the closet and then moves to go around me, but I block the door, holding my hands out to cross the door jamb. "Move, Parker."

"Don't leave. We need to talk about this."

Her lips are trembling. "I'm leaving because I trusted you. I was patient these past three months, and I told myself that your actions spoke louder than words—that you'd open up to me when you were ready. But now?" She shakes her head. "Your actions are making me question everything." When I still don't budge, my heart thrashing in my chest as I stare at her, she clears her throat. "Please move, Parker."

"This can't be over, Cashlynn."

She takes her ring off of her finger and holds it out to me. "It was over the moment you betrayed my trust."

I swear I can feel my heart crack as I stare down at the ring I knew belonged on her finger the moment I saw it.

When I don't reach out to take it, she puts it in the pocket of my shirt and ducks under my outstretched arms, marching down the hall to grab her purse.

And I should go after her. I could try to plead my case some more. But maybe she just needs some space and time to see that my heart was in the right place. My mother warned me that this might be her reaction, but I just hate feeling like history is repeating itself.

When I hear the door shut, I heave out a sigh. "Fuck!"

Pulling my phone from my pocket, I dial my sister. Luckily, she answers on the first ring.

"Hello?"

"I think Cashlynn might be coming to you," I say as I head back to the living room, trying to rewind the last twenty-four hours and decide if any decision I've made was the right one.

"And why would she be doing that?"

"I told her dad everything tonight."

"Oh, Parker," she sighs. "Why the hell would you do that?"

"I was trying to help, Hazel." I plop down onto the couch and feel a sense of déjà vu come over me as I explain the day to my sister.

This isn't the first time I've tried to help a woman I love. And last time it didn't end well.

Let's just hope this time is different. It has to be.

Chapter Twenty-One

Cashlynn

"I already have wine and ice cream on standby, but if you need something else for wallowing, let me know and I'll order it."

As soon as Hazel opens the door to her apartment, I feel like I can breathe. But then I process what she just said and instantly become irritated again.

"Did your brother call you?" I ask as I walk through her door and drop my bag on the floor before heading to her couch and throwing myself on it, burying my face in a pillow.

"He did."

I lift my head just long enough to speak. "I know he's your brother, but I really hate his guts right now."

Hazel tilts her head at me. "No you don't. You love him. But he hurt you, betrayed your trust, and you have every right to feel the way you do."

"But..."

"No buts. I'd be pissed too if the man I was seeing did something like that to me."

I lean back and stare at the floor. "I just can't believe that he did exactly what I made him promise me he wouldn't."

"Usually, it's the people we care about the most who hurt us the worst. Because we let them in—we show them our weaknesses, what we value most. It's like handing them the bullets to load the gun."

"You sound like you're speaking from personal experience."

She shrugs. "I think we've all had jackass ex-boyfriends we've contemplated making Voodoo dolls for."

I chuckle. "You're not wrong about that."

"But Parker isn't a jackass."

"Then what would you call him?"

"And idiot. But probably an idiot in love."

I focus back on the floor. "He told me where he's been going during his late-night appointments."

That has Hazel perking up. "He did?"

"Yeah. He's been seeing a therapist."

Her eyes widen. "No shit."

"Yeah. Can you believe he was hiding something like that from me?"

"Why does that surprise you?"

I contemplate her question for a moment. "I guess it doesn't, but still...that's not some life-altering secret. If he would have just been honest with me about it, I would have told him how much I supported that."

"See, that's where you're wrong, Cashlynn. Going to therapy *is* life-altering for Parker. My mom, my brothers, and I have all tried to convince him for years." I start picking at my nails as she continues.

"The fact that he's finally going tells me that he's serious about your relationship. It sure as hell wasn't me who pushed him to go this time."

"Oh."

"And I'm not trying to point any fingers or place blame here," she says, "but you're the one who started all of these lies, and he went along with it. The fact that he ended them before you did might be a good thing."

"Why?"

"Because then he looked like the bad guy to your father, not you."

My eyes fill with fresh tears as I stare across the room at her. "He said he stood up to my father, told him that he didn't care if it meant losing the practice."

Hazel raises her eyebrows. "I think that's pretty amazing, but again, I might be biased because it's my brother we're talking about."

I shove my face back into the pillow and let my emotions wash over me.

All the work, all the time I've put in over the past three months feels like it was for nothing because *I* wasn't the one to reveal it to my father. I'd been imagining that moment, hoping his reaction would be one of awe and understanding, but after hearing Parker defend me and challenge my father, it just reminds me that I was probably living in a fantasy.

Was Parker right to tell him? Will he hopefully be less angry by the time the opening comes in a few days? Will he even show up?

And what about me and Parker?

"My chest fucking hurts," I say through my tears.

"That's understandable."

Sniffling, I continue. "I gave Parker back his ring before I left."

She closes her eyes, exhales loudly, and then stands heading to the kitchen. "Yeah, I'm busting open the wine. No way are we getting through this without some alcohol."

***

An hour later, I'm three glasses in and my brain is feeling quite fuzzy.

"I fucked up," I blurt, hiccupping as the words leave my mouth.

"Pobody is nerfect, Cashlynn."

I lean forward to focus on Hazel as wine sloshes around in my glass. "Are you drunker than me?"

She shakes her head. "Girl, I'm still on my first glass."

"Then am I *that* drunk that I heard you say pobody is nerfect?"

"No, you heard that correctly."

I can literally feel the wheels in my brain turning. "Care to explain?"

A soft smile spreads across her lips. "My father used to say that to me when I was growing up. He learned it from a Vet that he worked with at the Carrington Cove Veteran's Center, but he said it was a great reminder that nobody is perfect." I still stare at her, trying to process. "It's a play on words, Cashlynn. You just switch the beginning letters, and…"

I hold up my hand and nod. "I get it now."

"So, the point is, you and Parker both made some mistakes here, but now you need to decide what you want to do about it."

Staring down into my wine glass, I feel my eyes sting with tears again. "I really love him, Hazel. I fell in love with your stupid brother and I don't want to live without him."

She laughs. "Then tell him that. Just…not tonight."

I shake my head. "No. I'm way too intoxicated to apologize."

"I don't know. I always believed that alcohol is like a truth serum. It gives you the courage to say things that you wouldn't normally."

"I don't need it to help me. I know what I need to do. I need to apologize, kiss him with my tongue, and then suck his dick."

Hazel spits wine all over the floor. "Jesus, girl. Warn a person before you start talking about sucking their brother's dick to them, all right?"

I laugh so hard I snort, but then my laugher turns into tears. Hazel leaps from her spot on the couch and rushes over to me, taking my wine glass from my hand and pulling me into her chest. "Hey, it's going to be okay."

"I really messed this up, Hazel—with my dad and Parker. I'm almost thirty. Shouldn't I know better than this?"

"Hey. We all learn at our own pace, right? Some of us take longer to learn important lessons, some of us need experience to gain that knowledge, and some of us get really lucky and find someone who wants to learn right alongside you."

I peer up at her, trying to see her through my tears. "I wanna learn everything with Parker."

"Then tell him that, and promise to never lie about anything, especially to each other, ever again."

Chapter Twenty-Two

Parker

I squat down one more time then re-rack the bar, stepping away as I try to get my heart rate under control.

But even lifting weights can't burn off the nerves racing through my body after Cashlynn left my house last night. My sister texted me as soon as she arrived, and about two hours later after Cashlynn fell asleep, letting me know that she was all right and they had a good talk.

My heart tells me that sounds promising, but my head is still reeling with everything that could go wrong.

"Not what if, *even* if, Parker," I say out loud to myself, practicing the tip Dr. Jensen gave me.

Even if Cashlynn decides she can't get past my betrayal, at least I feel in my heart that I did the right thing. I told the truth, stood up for the woman I love, and finally realized what was truly important to me in all of this.

That's not something I could have said three months ago.

Fuck. I've done a lot of growing lately, and there's only one person I can give credit to.

As I hang my head in my hands, hoping that this wasn't all for nothing, that Cashlynn can see past my imperfections and understand that all I wanted was what's best for her, the sound of a car pulling into the driveway pulls me from my thoughts.

I called out sick today, something I haven't done in almost a year, and I took tomorrow off as well, giving me through the weekend to hopefully get my life on track.

At least, I hope.

A car door slams and then I hear footsteps on the other side of the garage door, so I head inside. When Cashlynn walks through the front door, my heart tries to leap out of my chest.

"Hey," she says, setting her duffle bag on the floor by the door as we stare at each other.

"Hey, sweetheart."

She licks her lips, takes a couple of hesitant steps toward me, but then runs at me, jumping up into my arms as I open them to catch her. "I'm so sorry, Parker," she cries into my neck as I hold her against me, breathing her in, hearing my heartbeat in my ears.

"Fuck, I'm sorry too, Cashlynn." Needing to take a moment to believe this, I stand there holding her in my arms, rocking her from side to side as she falls apart. When I finally feel her sobs start to subside, I head over to the couch and sit down with her still wrapped around me. "Talk to me, baby. Tell me what's going through your head."

She lifts her tear-streaked face, her skin blotchy and red, yet she's never looked more beautiful. She's never looked more like *mine*.

"I shouldn't have left last night, but I'm glad I did. I needed a chance to wrap my brain around everything and for your sister to smack some sense into me."

"Yeah, she's pretty good at that."

She laughs, wiping under her eyes. "Yes, and the wine helped. Until this morning, that is, when I woke up with a splitting headache." Then something dawns on her. "Wait, what are you doing home right now?"

"I called in sick. The last thing I wanted was to be at work when you decided to come home." Stroking the side of her face, I continue. "Because this is your home, Cashlynn...at least, if you still want it to be."

She nods. "I do, but first, there's something I need to say."

"Okay."

I rub my hands up and down her back, as she glances up at the ceiling, gathering her thoughts. "I know you thought telling my father was the right thing to do, but next time, I would appreciate you coming to talk to me about it first."

I nod. "I promise. But I want you to know, the only reason I didn't is because Seth forced my hand, which made it feel like my mess to clean up. And time was of the essence."

"I understand, and I would have fought you on it, but I still would have liked to be given the choice and the chance to say no."

"Okay. You got it. I will give you all the chances to say no in the future."

Her smile helps the fist wrapped around my heart loosen slightly. "Second, I'm sorry that I reacted the way I did about you going to therapy. That was insensitive of me."

"I swear, Cashlynn, I was going to tell you everything, but—"

She holds up a hand to stop me. "I get it. Talking about your feelings is not something that comes easy to you, but know that if you had told me, I would have respected that and not pushed you to talk about things until you were ready, like I said in the beginning."

My head bobs up and down. "That's fair. I assumed how you would have reacted again."

"Yes, you did. I've been doing the same thing with my dad for years," she says, tears filling her eyes. "It's a bad habit to break, but I'd like to work on it with you, if you're still interested."

Her bottom lip trembles as I reach up and cup her jaw. "I want nothing more than that, Cashlynn."

"Good. But before we have life-changing make up sex, I think you need to tell me about Sasha."

The sigh that escapes me feels like dropping a brick I've carried the weight of for the past four years.

"Okay, but I'm going to start at the beginning so you know everything."

"Okay."

Her hands rest on my shoulders as I prepare to share the long-buried story with the woman I hope to write a new one with. My palms grow sweaty and my mind races, but I know this is what I need to do to truly move forward.

"Sasha and I met my senior year at UC Davis. I was twenty, ahead on credits, and she was two years older. I fell hard and fast for her. I was studying to be a veterinarian, and she wanted to be a pharmacist—it felt like a perfect match. But by the time I started the DVM program, Sasha wasn't sure she wanted to pursue pharmacy anymore. She got a job in a medical office while I focused on school." Cashlynn keeps her eyes locked on mine as I speak.

"I was honest with her that I planned to move back to Carrington Cove to practice. I wanted to give back to the community that I was raised in, and I had been in contact with your grandfather before I left for college. We had even discussed me returning to work for him. But you know how that turned out."

She nods. "Yeah… So my father hired you?"

"Yes, and Sasha moved back with me because I proposed to her before I finished the veterinary program. She was leaving her life in California, but we were in love, and she seemed excited about small-town life. But that changed the longer she lived here."

Cashlynn's brows knit together, concern in her eyes.

"It started small, now that I think back on it. She got a job at a medical office here and made friends, and started going to happy hour with them after work. And I thought it was great. She was building a life in a new place, and I was focused on proving myself at work. Honestly, it made me feel less guilty for being gone all the time. But I was so focused on work, I didn't even realize we were drifting apart until it was too late." I swallow roughly before I continue.

"Years passed and we both just slipped into a routine. I got up and went to work, and she did the same, but didn't come home until late most nights. It wasn't until I smelled alcohol on her breath one morning that I started to become concerned. Then I was watching her more closely, looking for signs that it was a real problem. She was an adult, right? If she wanted a few drinks after work, who was I to stop her? Then one night, I got a call from the police. She'd run her car into a telephone pole—while intoxicated."

"Oh my God," Cashlynn whispers, her hand covering her mouth.

"Yeah. So that was my wake-up call. I sat down with her and told her I was concerned, all the while wondering how this got so out of control. But I wasn't focused on her, I was focused on myself and my career, so she found another form of attention and entertainment. I asked her if she'd get help, and she told me she didn't have a problem. I let things go on for a few more weeks until I had to pick her up from Ricky's one night and take her to the E.R. for alcohol poisoning."

"Jesus," Cashlynn whispers.

"The next morning, I packed her a suitcase and told her I was taking her to rehab, or we were done. She was scared, but I honestly believed that she just needed help. If she got clean, we could start over and I would do better—give her more attention, watch over her, make sure she was healthy."

"Oh, Parker..."

"She only lasted a week in rehab before she checked herself out," I say, my voice cracking now. "When she called me from a payphone, I was shocked, and even more by what she said."

"What did she say to you?"

I pinch the bridge of my nose, trying to keep my composure as all the memories and emotions flood my body, most of all the rage I feel reliving this moment. "She told me that she hated me, that she never should have moved across the country with me. She admitted to being unfaithful to me multiple times. And then she told me she wasn't coming back." I lift my head and look Cashlynn in the eyes as I say the last part. "Two days later, she died in a car accident. She was under the influence and swerved into oncoming traffic. They say she died on impact."

Cashlynn's eyes well with tears, her hand trembling as it moves to cover her mouth. "Oh, Parker."

"I have carried around the guilt of what happened to her for years," I say hoarsely. "Convinced myself it was my fault. That I should've done more, been better. That if I hadn't dragged her here, she'd still be alive. But then I met you," I say, brushing her hair from her face as she drops her hand from her mouth.

"And you made me feel shit I'd been avoiding. But honestly, I don't think I would have been willing to face my past if it weren't you that I wanted in my future." Her eyes bounce back and forth between mine. "I love you," I say simply, watching as a smile breaks through her tears.

"I love you so much. You brought me back to life, and I want to get this right with you. That doesn't mean we won't make mistakes, as we've already learned. But God, I want to make them with you... If you'll give me that chance."

She leans forward, pressing her lips to mine, and whispers, "I love you too, Parker Sheppard."

"Fuck, baby." Relief washes over me as her words sink in.

"Thank you for telling me everything. I understand you so much better now. You are such a strong man for having gone through something like that and still striving to be the best version of yourself that you can be."

"You coming back into my life showed me what I would lose if I wasn't willing to let go of my failures."

She cups the side of my face. "You are not a failure. You're human. And I love you for every scar you carry, on the inside and out." She reaches up and strokes the scar above my eyebrow.

"I love you too, and I know that your relationship with your father is complicated, and I may have made it even more difficult, but I promise, I won't let him treat you like anything less than the incredible woman you are."

"As much as I don't want to admit it, I think you were right to tell him."

"Can I get that in writing to have on record for the future?" I tease.

She narrows her eyes at me. "Watch it. I just got over being mad at you."

"Yeah, but anger leads to some pretty incredible makeup sex, so I think I'll take my chances." She shakes her head at me. "But I think you need to give us a chance to get this right."

"Oh really?"

"Yup. But to make it fair, I say we play for it."

"And what shall we play?"

"Oh, I think you know."

Her laughter coats my soul, easing some of the remorse I feel every day, but then she grows serious again. "When you left my dad's house, how did he seem?"

"Well, he'd stopped yelling at me, so that was a plus."

Her jaw clenches. "God, his temper..."

"Honestly, I think it was what Beth said to him that really got through to him."

She tilts her head in confusion. "Beth was there?"

"Yeah. Your dad and Beth...they uh..." I scratch the back of my head.

"What aren't you telling me, Parker? I thought we said no more lies."

I sigh. "Your dad and Beth have been dating for six months."

Her eyes widen. "What?"

"Yeah. You're not the only one who's been keeping secrets." She barely blinks while she processes this information. "But just know, he's been struggling with how to tell you about it. Seems we all need to work on our communication skills."

"Does he know that you planned to tell me?"

I nod. "I told him that giving you time to process this would be just as important as the time I gave him."

"Oh my God...all this time."

I stroke her arms gently. "Are you okay?"

"Yeah, I just..."

"The past twenty-four hours have been a lot to take in."

She lets out a sigh. "Yeah, they have."

"But I know that I feel better."

Her smile instantly makes me feel more at ease. "Me too. There's one more thing I didn't get a chance to say to you, though."

"What's that?"

"I'm sorry for giving you the ring back," she whispers. "I shouldn't have, but I was so angry and—"

I press a finger to her lips. "Don't apologize. You had every right to feel that way. But if it's okay with you, I'd like to give it back to you when our engagement is real. How does that sound?"

Her lips spread under my finger. "I like that idea a lot."

"Me too, sweetheart. Now kiss me, please. I need to taste you because I feel like it's been way too fucking long."

She doesn't hesitate, leaning in to press her lips to mine. When our lips meet, I feel like a piece of me snaps back into place.

It took a lot of strength and work to get here, but I wouldn't trade a second of it—not when the woman I'm holding is the one who taught me how to love again.

The stranger from the airplane who turned out to be the one person I'd realize I couldn't live without.

Chapter Twenty-Three

Cashlynn

"To Cashlynn, and Carrington Cove's very first art gallery!" Willow holds up her glass of sparkling apple cider while everyone else holds their flutes of champagne, toasting to me and the official opening of my gallery.

Somebody please pinch me.

"Here, here!" Everyone echoes around the room.

Astrid speaks first as Scottie opens the door, letting in people who have been lined up outside all morning. "I think I speak for everyone when I say that we are so proud of what you've created here. The artwork is phenomenal, and I, for one, can't wait to buy a piece for my house."

Sally, one of the waitresses from Catch & Release, stands at the door to greet people and hand out the flyers for the classes I have scheduled for the next month. Dallas said she was eager for another job, so I jumped at the opportunity to hire her as my first employee.

Penn snickers. "And I'll be the one figuring out someplace to put it."

Everyone laughs as Astrid glares at her husband. "But not only that, you've brought an artistic outlet to our community. Lilly has been asking me every day for the past month about when she can come here to paint."

"I told you not to tell her about it," Penn mutters.

"I was just too excited! You know how I get," she says as Willow approaches.

"I'm very ready for this little boy to leave my body, but part of me is very grateful that I got to be here for the opening."

Dallas rubs her belly. "Me too. But we aren't going to stay long. Doctor said I need to keep this woman off her feet until my son is done cooking."

Willow rolls her eyes at her husband. "Oh, he's done all right. And if he keeps kicking my bladder, I'll be waking him up every night for *years* to pay him back."

I can't help but laugh, though part of it is from nerves. My eyes keep moving to the door as more and more people trickle in, but none of them are the two men I'm longing to see.

"Well, I can't wait for you to come to the school in a few weeks to do the squirt gun painting with my class," Scottie says as she bounces her daughter in her arms. "The kids are so excited. I also made the mistake of telling them, so I get asked about it at least five times a day."

Grady shakes his head. "And then I get to hear about it just as many times."

"You all sound so happy in your wedded bliss," Hazel quips before taking a sip of her champagne. "You really make a person want to get married over here." She points to herself.

Dallas chuckles. "Oh, I can't wait for the day you get married, Hazelnut, so you can eat your words and vent about all of the annoying things your husband does, and we can all just laugh about it."

Hazel scoffs. "Yeah, well, you have to actually date someone in order for that to happen and do you see a man for me around here?" She twists her head around the room. "That would be a no."

But it's at that moment that the man I'm in love with walks into the room, with my father trailing right behind him.

"Oh my God, I think I'm gonna throw up."

Scottie places her hand on my shoulder. "Just breathe. This is neither the time nor the place you want to do that. But just in case, do you have a trash can under your desk? Because that saved my life when I was pregnant with this one." She waves her daughter's hand around.

Grady pulls her away from me. "Not everyone is as interested in the topic of throwing up as you are, babe. Let's give Cashlynn some space, shall we?"

When I turn around, the entire Sheppard family has dispersed, leaving me alone as Parker and my father approach.

Parker leans forward and kisses my cheek. "Congratulations, sweetheart."

"Thank you," I murmur, smoothing his shirt nervously.

"Cashlynn," my father says, pulling my attention toward him. And when our eyes lock, I see the remorse in his that I've wanted to see for years. His eyes move around the room. "You created this, June Bug?"

Parker takes my hand and stands to my side, grounding me. "I did, Dad."

He blinks away tears as he looks around. "It's beautiful. Your mother would have loved this."

I suck in a breath as I fight to keep my emotions under control. "That means a lot."

When his eyes land on the framed picture on the wall by the main counter, he walks over to it, leaving Parker and me behind.

"Are you gonna be okay?" Parker whispers to me as I watch my father study the painting on the wall that my mother made for me when I was a little girl. It is the one piece of art in the gallery that isn't for sale. It's a reminder of what my mother gave me—a piece of her that I'll always cherish.

"Yeah, I'll be fine."

"He assured me he wouldn't yell."

I sniffle through a laugh. "Well, that sounds promising."

"I'll be around if you need me, okay?"

I turn and look up at him. "Thank you. I love you so much."

"Ditto, sweetheart." With a chaste kiss, he leaves me, and I head in the direction of my father, who hasn't moved from admiring the picture on the wall.

"I remember the morning she painted this for you," he says as soon as he senses me. "You were obsessed with the color pink, so we slathered the canvas in every shade she could find and began putting lines in it, turning it into a collage of flowers."

"I had it hanging up in my apartment in Philly, but I knew it belonged here, where everyone could see it.

When he turns to me, I see unshed tears in his eyes. "Can we talk?"

I look to Hazel, who agreed to help if I needed her, and she gives me a nod with a thumbs-up when she silently understands I'm in need of that favor.

"Sure. Let me take you to the back."

I have my father follow me down a small hallway to a storage room where it's quiet enough that we can speak but not be overheard by potential customers. "Look, Dad—"

He holds a hand up, cutting me off. "No, Cashlynn. I have a lot to say and I need to get it off my chest, please."

"Okay."

A tear slips down his cheek. "I have been a terrible father to you."

"What?"

He swipes away the tear and clears his throat. "I took the past few days to really think about everything that Parker said to me the other night, and he was right. I haven't supported you the way I should have." My eyes begin to sting, but he continues. "Losing your mother nearly killed me, June. And I wanted to find someone or something to blame, so I blamed her passion for art. If she hadn't been in the car, driving to that gallery, she wouldn't have died."

"I know, Dad."

"But if she hadn't gone, she would have regretted it for the rest of her life. It's taken me a long time to get past the guilt and anger of losing her, and on some level, I don't think I'll ever be over it. But I wasn't the only one who shut down when she died. So did you."

"What do you mean?"

"You stopped talking to me, stopped sharing your life with me. I knew you were still painting, but you never showed me."

"I thought it would hurt you. I didn't want to make you angry or sad..."

"And that's my fault for ever making you feel that way," he says. "But seeing the parts of your mother in you doesn't hurt me, June. It fills me with love and pride that she lives on in you."

The tears start to fall right then and there. "Dad..."

"What you did here, what you've created? It's incredible—such an accomplishment. I'm so disappointed in myself for making you feel like you couldn't share it with me and let me be proud of it with you."

He steps forward and takes my hands. "I'm so sorry, June Bug. And I promise to do better."

I lunge for him, holding his as tightly as I can. "I love you, Dad."

"I love you more than you'll ever know, Cashlynn."

"And I'm sorry I lied to you."

He releases me and wipes the tears from under my eyes with his thumbs. "I know that now. And I know that it took a lot of guts for that man to stand up for you the way he did."

"I love him."

"I know that too. He told me that he feels the same way, and asked for my permission to marry you when the time is right for you both."

I'm so relieved to know that he still wants that with me. "Please don't punish him for what happened, okay?"

"If this is about the practice…"

"It's not just that," I say, interrupting him. "It's for *our* future too. I don't want you to hold this against him."

"I won't, June. But there's something else we need to discuss."

I nod, knowing what's coming next. Placing my hands on my hips, I tilt my head at him. "You and Beth?"

He sighs, glancing down at the ground while shaking his head. "I was so hurt when your mother died, I never thought I'd love again, June. In fact, I had no plans for it. But Beth broke down my walls, she made me see that true strength doesn't come from pushing people away, it's from letting them in again knowing the risk of being hurt is still there. I'm retiring so she and I can enjoy the rest of our lives together, and I hope you can accept that."

"You deserve that, Dad." I reach for his hand this time. "And I adore Beth. She's good for you, keeps you in line."

He laughs. "That she does. She threatened to leave me if I didn't make things right with you."

"I think we would have gotten here eventually." I smile, feeling more relieved with each passing second. "Parker and I got through our own issues too, so you weren't the only one that was having relationship disagreements."

"It's normal for couples to have conflict, to hurt one another intentionally and unintentionally. What matters is how you solve your problems, rebuilding that trust, and whether you can compromise to make sure it doesn't continue being an issue."

A thought crosses my mind. "How did you and Mom handle disagreements?"

He grins, thinking back over his memories for a minute. "Well, if it wasn't something we could agree on, we'd play for it."

"And what did you play?"

He laughs and leans toward me. "Rock, paper, scissors."

***

"I really need to get back to the gallery and balance the drawer, Dad," I say, trailing after him into his house, eager to finish up my day after a whirlwind of emotions.

"This won't take long. Parker said he'd wait for you there, but I have to drive you back with this stuff, so your day isn't over yet." He smirks at me over his shoulder.

"Wait a minute…what stuff?"

The whole day has been a blur—I lost track of how many people I spoke to and how many paintings I sold. It felt like the entire town made an appearance throughout the day, and I had so many people eager to submit their artwork or request certain types of art they were looking for. My classes are also entirely booked for the month, and I already have a waitlist forming for the summer.

I was sitting at my desk, trying to wrap my head around the day, when my father came into my office and asked if he could take me somewhere. I turned him down initially, but he insisted and then Parker encouraged me as well. Now, I'm more than curious about what *stuff* he has for me.

When we step inside, he leads me to the basement, unlocking the door and urging me to go ahead of him.

"Are you sure it's safe? I mean, this is where you fell and hurt yourself, isn't it?" I tease him as I head down the stairs.

"Hey, watch it, young lady. I'm still your father," he grumbles, though a smile pulls at his lips.

Laughing, I make it to the bottom of the staircase just as Dad flips on a light switch. The moment the room comes into view, I gasp. "Oh my God."

"This is what I was coming down to see when I fell that day, June Bug."

Rows of canvases line the walls, stacked neatly on top of each other. I know who the artist is before I even take a look.

"Did she paint *all* of these?" My voice cracks as my eyes move at lightning speed.

My father nods. "Yep. She had most of them in storage before she passed, and when I moved to Carrington Cove, I forgot about them. A couple of years later, I got a call from the storage unit in Florida saying the bill hadn't been paid and they were going to auction it off. I knew what was in there, so I drove down immediately and brought them back here."

I move around the room, looking at every painting my mother kept over the years, ones I'm sure she wanted to sell or keep for herself instead. Memories flood my mind of watching her at work, and even those times when she would set up a canvas next to her for me to paint right alongside her.

"I come down here when I want to be close to her, June. She was so talented, so beautiful and carefree. So wise and funny," my father says, emotion clogging his throat. "You remind me of her so much, and I think she'd want you to have these. I think they would look beautiful in your gallery."

I move toward my father and envelop him in my arms. "I think so too."

"You can sell them or put them on display, whatever you choose."

"There's so many of them. There's no way I can take them all today," I say as I lean back a bit, but he keeps me tucked into his side.

"I know, but I imagined we could take a chunk back with us tonight and start figuring out where to go from there. No rush, sweetie."

"I still can't believe this." My skin is covered in goosebumps, almost like I can feel my mother with us at this very moment.

"I miss her so much, June, but my biggest regret is how I've treated you since she passed. I'm so sorry that you were the object of my grief when I didn't know what to do with it," he croaks out as I feel his tears hit my shoulder.

"It's okay."

"No, it's not. But I'll do better. I promise you that."

And right there, in my father's basement with my mother surrounding us, the two of us begin to heal in ways we both desperately needed.

Chapter Twenty-Four

Parker

The sound of the key turning in the lock pulls me from my sweeping. I've been trying to clean up as much as I could while Robert took Cashlynn back to his house to show her her mother's paintings.

Our eyes meet as she walks inside the gallery, Robert trailing behind her.

"What are you doing?"

My eyes drop down to the broom in my hand, my shirt sleeves unbuttoned and rolled up. "I'm sweeping."

"You didn't have to do that," she says as she crosses the room to me.

"I know I didn't, but I was trying to make myself useful." I place a chaste kiss on her lips as soon as she's close enough, and then look up to find Robert carrying two canvases, one in each hand. "Robert," I greet him with a nod.

"Parker," he says before turning back to his daughter. "Where do you want me to put these, June?"

"In the storage room for now." She leads him back there as I finish cleaning up the pile of dirt I created and discard it in the trash. When they return, Robert asks me to help him unload the other paintings from his car, so I follow him outside.

"So, how'd it go?" I ask once we're alone.

He blows out a breath. "Well, I know what matters now is that my actions back up my words, and I'm going to do everything I can to right my wrongs with my daughter."

I nod in approval. "You're a good man, Robert."

"I've made plenty of mistakes, Parker, but there's always time to correct them." His words resonate with me more than he realizes. "Just promise me that you'll live up to your intentions as well."

"I love your daughter, Robert."

"I know you do." His voice cracks. "I've never been more sure of anything in my life, and I couldn't have asked for a better man for her." My own throat grows tight as Robert gestures back to his car. "Now, let's get these inside so we can all go home and rest after an incredible, yet exhausting day."

Once Robert and I have moved all of the canvases into the storage room and he says goodbye to Cashlynn, I lock the front door behind him and turn to find Cashlynn crunching numbers at the front counter.

Her tongue peeks out from the side of her mouth, and her eyes are moving so fast, I wonder if she's getting dizzy. "So, how'd you do?"

Her eyes light up as she lifts her head. "I just might make my first month's rent from today alone!"

Crossing the room to get to her, I wrap my arms around her and pull her into my chest. "That's incredible, sweetheart. You fucking did it." I give her a chaste kiss. "And how do you feel about your talk with your dad?"

"Relieved," she says as she exhales. "Hopeful too. I don't know what you said to him, but he definitely had a change of heart somewhere along the way."

"I don't think it was so much the words I said as the reminder that if he wasn't careful, he was going to push you out of his life for good. When you realize you could lose something you care about, it definitely puts things into perspective," I say, leaning back to cup her jaw.

"Yeah, I know that feeling too."

"I'm glad you two talked. And today was insane, baby. The energy in here was amazing. Everyone was so impressed with what you've done with this space, and I can't wait to see how this only grows over time."

Her smile is electric, but her eyes are brimming with tears. "I can't believe it, Parker. This is actually going to work. I get to do this for a living now."

Feeling a rush of need run through me, I take her by the hands and back her up to the wall behind us, holding her hands above her head as I slant my mouth over hers. "Believe it, baby. You did it, and I'm so fucking proud of you."

"I couldn't have done this without you," she says, her breathing growing more shallow.

"Yes, you would have. But I'd like to think that everything worked out the way it was supposed to."

"And how is that?"

Thrusting my cock into her stomach so she can sense where this conversation is headed, I say, "With you and me—together." Our eyes remain locked. "I love you, Cashlynn June O'Neil."

She giggles. "I love you too, Parker Eric Sheppard."

No other words are spoken as we celebrate all we've overcome to get to this moment: lessons learned and pasts healed, with nothing but our future in front of us.

***

"When do you think they hatched?" I close my car door behind me, holding the phone between my shoulder and my ear.

"Must have been early this morning."

"And has Mallory left the nest at all?"

"Nope. I've been peeking through the blinds all morning and she's remained there."

I blow out a sigh of relief. "That's good. I'll stop by on my way home from work just to double check everything myself, but it seems your geese problem won't be going away anytime soon, Willow."

My sister-in-law chuckles through the line. "I'm learning to embrace it, if you haven't figured that out yet."

I end the call and open the door to Carrington Cove Animal Hospital, eager to get my day started. But the look on Cassandra's face when I enter tells me that Robert has already called everyone to the back for his announcement.

When Robert and I talked last week before Cashlynn's gallery opening, I told him I wanted to remove myself from the running to take over the practice. He was curious, of course, especially since he had always planned on handing me the reins.

But, after many hours of therapy, I realized there was more to life than just work. I love my job, don't get me wrong. But I don't want it to consume me, and Robert respected me for that.

"I don't want you to make the same mistake I did—making life all about work. You should be able to have it all, Parker, and that includes a life with my June Bug that you can both enjoy."

I guess he took my choice to heart—because the other thing we discussed is about to go down.

"What's going on?" Cassandra whispers as I breeze past her and toward my office to collect my coat.

The sound of her footsteps following me echoes off the walls. "What do you mean?"

Cassandra scoffs. "You know what I mean, Parker." She grabs my shoulder, forcing me to stop. "He still has a month before he's set to retire but he's called an emergency meeting today. That's not a good sign."

"You don't know that," I say, looking her dead in the eyes.

"What I do know is that if he doesn't name you the head doctor, I'm going to quit."

I close my eyes and let out a breath. This isn't how I wanted to have this conversation with her, but she's going to find out in about ten minutes anyway. "Cassandra..."

"Parker? Cassandra?" The two of us spin around to find Beth lifting an eyebrow in our direction. "We're waiting on you." She walks away just as quickly as she summoned us.

When Cassandra and I turn the corner, I find Robert standing at the head of our staff right next to Seth, and I'm instantly giddy.

"Now, I'm sure you're all wondering why we're gathered here today," Robert starts as my eyes dart over to Seth, his arms crossed over his body, his smug smile so slimy that it almost makes me feel bad for what's about to happen.

I said almost, okay?

This guy is about to get everything that's coming to him.

"It isn't like me to make announcements before the time is right, but after an eye-opening weekend, I decided there was no time like the present to take care of something."

Seth slaps Robert on the shoulder. "I think that's smart, Dr. O'Neil."

Robert turns to Seth. "You do, do you?"

"Absolutely. I mean, if your gut is telling you something, you should listen to it."

God, I wish I had some popcorn for this.

Robert flashes Seth a placating smile. "I'm so glad you think so, Seth." Seth puffs out his chest as Robert continues. "Which is why I wanted everyone here to witness me firing you."

You could hear a pin drop with how quiet the entire room grows, but then Cassandra stifles her laugh behind her hand.

It takes a minute for the words to process in Seth's mind, but when his slimy smile falls and his brows knit together, he turns to Robert with the most bewildered expression on his face. "I'm sorry. What did you just say?"

"I said you're fired, Seth."

Seth scoffs, glancing around the room filled with eyes all pointed in his direction. "You're—you're firing me?" He points a finger to his chest. "On what basis?"

"Lying, manipulation, extortion, and fraud. I think everyone deserves to know how you tried to blackmail Parker and my daughter, and how you've been taking cuts from the suppliers we partner with. No wonder you've been pushing the one brand over the others."

Seth huffs out a laugh, but it's uneasy.

I, on the other hand, am having the hardest time keeping my composure.

But when Seth's eyes land on me, his entire demeanor changes. "You…" he seethes before taking a step toward me.

The technicians beside me scatter as Seth heads in my direction, a menacing glare on his face.

"Seth!" Robert calls after him, but there is no stopping the determination in his body right now.

"You did this!" Seth shouts before cocking his arm back and taking a swing at me.

Luckily, I duck before his fist connects with my face, but when I pop back up, he's rushing me, shoving me back into the wall behind me.

He cocks his arm back again, but before he can swing, I clock him from the left, sending him crumbling to the ground.

Blood rushes from his nose as he stares up at me. "Fuck you, Parker!"

"Right back at you, Seth."

Robert hobbles over, standing between us. "You okay?" he asks me as I realize my chest is heaving.

"Yeah, I'm fine."

"Good." Turning to Seth, Robert hovers over him. "I think it's rich that you have the audacity to blame Parker for your termination."

"He's lying to you! His relationship with your daughter—"

"Is none of your concern!" Robert bellows as everyone continues to stare at the shitshow unfolding before them.

Cassandra comes up beside me with an ice pack for my hand. "Thank you," I whisper to her as we continue to watch Robert put Seth in his place.

"You honestly think that I wouldn't have done my research?" Seth continues to wipe under his nose. "Not only did you threaten Parker and my daughter, but you've been stealing from the practice!"

"It's a lie," Seth mutters.

"Do you even know what's the truth anymore, Seth? Now, I suggest you leave my practice before I have you removed by the police."

Seth scrambles to his feet, but before he gets too far, I reach out and tug him back by his shirt, wrapping my hand around the back of his neck and leaning in toward the side of his face. "And let me make one more point." My voice drops to a deadly whisper. "If you ever come near Cashlynn again, I will break every bone in your hands so you won't be able to practice medicine ever again." I watch his Adam's apple bob. "Have I made myself clear?"

Seth nods and I release him. The staff watches him scurry toward the front of the practice, where Beth lets him out and locks the door behind him.

"Holy shit," Cassandra says loud enough for everyone to hear before turning to me. "So does this mean that you're taking over the practice?"

I take a deep breath, meet the eyes of my boss and future father-in-law—who nods at me to answer the question—and then brace myself for the reactions I'm sure will come. "Well, not exactly…"

***

"So, everyone took the news pretty well then?" Cashlynn strokes my forehead, pushing my hair back as I stare up at her from my position on the couch. My head is in her lap, and she's upside down from where I'm lying, but this has become our new routine when I get home from work and we catch up on our days.

"Everyone except for Cassandra, yeah."

"You knew she wasn't going to like your choice."

"Yes, but now she has motivation to go back and get her DVM."

Cashlynn smiles as she strokes my jaw with her index finger. "Are you really sure about this decision, Parker? I mean, a few months ago, you wanted nothing more than to own the practice, and now…"

I push myself up and turn to face her, framing her face in my hands. "Now I have you." She swallows roughly but keeps her eyes locked on mine. "My job has been such a focus in my life for so long, baby. But if this whole thing has taught me anything, it's that the right people in your life will help you learn lessons you need to at the right time. You've helped me see that there is more to life than work."

"But—"

"And I'm so fucking glad." I press my finger to her lips. "Your job from before didn't fulfill you, right?" She nods against my hand. "Well, the truth is, mine hasn't fulfilled me in a lot of ways for a very long time. And now, I know why."

"Why?"

"Because my life was missing you." Her eyes begin to well with tears. "You've helped me see what matters, that there is so much to experience outside of work when you have a partner that makes you feel alive. I want to plan things with you, travel and have lazy days in bed together where we never wear clothes." Her giggle goes straight to my dick, but I maintain my composure. "I can't have that if I'm the boss, Cashlynn. I realized I'd rather just be your boss in bed."

Her laughter rings out. "I guess I can't argue with that."

I nuzzle her neck. "You know what fighting with you does to me though, baby. Want me to show you?"

She pushes me away playfully, and then her smile falls. "I just want to make sure this is what you want, Parker. I don't want you to resent me down the road because you didn't follow your dreams."

"I could never resent you for making me realize that my dreams could change. I didn't think there was anything else I could want more than being the boss, but there is."

"So what are your dreams now?"

I cup the side of her face. "Anything that involves you, baby."

Chapter Twenty-Five

Cashlynn

Six Months Later

When I unlock the door to the Paula O'Neil Art Gallery of Carrington Cove—named after my mother—all the lights are off except for one in the very back of the space where I usually hold my paint nights. I know I shut off every light last night before locking up, so the faint glow and the text Parker sent earlier, telling me to meet him here, piques my curiosity. We're celebrating the six-month anniversary of the gallery being open, a milestone that still seems unreal. I honestly thought we'd be celebrating at home—preferably in bed—but Parker seems to have other plans.

My father and Beth are taking us out to dinner in honor of the milestone tomorrow, and Willow, Astrid, and Hazel have something planned on Sunday at the Sheppard family dinner.

But the two of us? We tend to celebrate in our own messy way, and I love it.

My life has turned an entire one-eighty since I moved to Carrington Cove, and I don't regret it for a second.

"Follow the light!" Parker calls out as I lock the door behind me and shove the keys in my pocket.

Over the past six months, we've made a habit of meeting here when he gets off work. Usually, he picks up some dinner for us to enjoy together while he helps me balance the books or unload supplies. But I've hired two more employees, so those nights have dwindled in frequency recently.

The faint smell of chocolate hits my nostrils as I get closer to the man who's become a permanent fixture in my life, the person I feel completely free to be myself with. When I embarked on this adventure of chasing my dream in Carrington Cove, I never imagined it would lead me to this kind of contentment. Between the improved relationship with my father, and the safety and peace I feel with Parker, it makes me wonder if I really am living in a dream sometimes.

But when I see what Parker has on the table waiting for me, I'm convinced that this has to be a dream and I'm going to wake up any minute.

I glance back at the chocolate fountain before meeting his eyes, trying like hell not to focus on the fact that my boyfriend is shirtless in board shorts because that's a distraction I wasn't anticipating at all. "I'm...confused."

He takes a step toward me. "Well, I knew that if I wanted to make this happen, we had to do it here. If chocolate got on the carpet at home, you know I'd freak out."

I cover my mouth as a snort escapes me. "Sounds about right."

He takes my hand and leads me over to the table with the chocolate fountain, reaching for a white bikini lying next to it. "You need to go get changed, though."

"You want me to wear that?"

"Honestly, I'd prefer you naked, but I thought trying to prevent chocolate from getting into places it shouldn't would be smarter."

I glance over at the floor, noticing the tarp under the easel holding up a canvas under a white sheet. "We're painting with chocolate?"

"We are, but not in the way that you think." He pulls me into his chest, and as soon as our torsos touch, I can feel his erection building against my thigh. "Now go change so we can get to the best part of the evening."

With a grin on my lips, I head for the bathroom, changing into the bikini. I could've changed in front of him, but this feels like part of the mystery, so I play along.

When I return to the room, soft candlelight illuminates the space from electric candles. Parker has two glasses of red wine poured for us, holding one out to me.

"Red wine and white clothing don't mix," I say as I take the glass from his hand.

"Neither does chocolate and white fabric, but that's kind of the point."

I take a sip from my glass. "This isn't how I anticipated celebrating."

Parker takes a deep breath before replying. "I've been driving myself insane for the past few weeks, trying to think of a way to show you how proud I am of you, how much you've changed my life in the past six months, Cashlynn—"

"You show me that every day, Parker," I say, cutting him off.

He shakes his head. "Not enough." Setting his wine glass on the table, he takes mine as well and places it down, then moves to cup my face in his hands. "When I tell you that my world was black and white before you came into it, I'm not just trying to use a pun that you'd understand and appreciate." The corner of my mouth lifts up. "You've truly helped me see color again, beautiful—the beauty and complexity that life has to offer. I'm in awe of the way you view the world, of how you inspire others to find the glimmers that make life truly incredible."

My eyes begin to well with tears. "Parker..."

He takes a deep breath and releases me. "So, to show you how much you inspire me, to prove that what you are doing in our small town does make a difference, I painted something for you."

My mouth falls open. "You...you what?"

He moves to the sheet covering the canvas and removes it, revealing a picture that I can't help but turn my head to the side to admire.

"You...you painted the clouds."

"I did." He reaches for my hand and takes me closer to the canvas. "I know it's really simple, but I thought I couldn't possibly fuck it up."

I giggle. "It's actually quite beautiful," I say, admiring the small flecks of yellow and pink he added to the sky.

"It reminded me of the sunrise I saw from the sky on the morning I returned from Philadelphia all those months ago."

His confession renders me speechless. "What?"

"That morning as I sat on the plane back to Raleigh, I couldn't stop thinking about you, wishing you hadn't run away, wishing I had the courage in that moment to stop you." He glances at his painting and then back to me. "You changed my life that weekend, Cashlynn, and even though I wonder what would have happened if I had acted differently that night, I can't regret where it put us now."

His face glistens behind my tears. "I don't regret it either."

He holds my face in his hands again. "I'm so damn proud of you—for leaving your life in Philly, for coming back here to chase after what you wanted, and as much as I hated it in the moment, I'm so damn grateful that you made me be your fake fiancé, because I can't imagine my life without you."

I don't even have words to respond, so I lunge for him, smashing my lips to his. Parker consumes me, holding me to his strong chest, swirling his tongue with mine. "I love you," I whisper breathlessly when we part, our foreheads resting against one another.

"I love you too, baby."

After a moment of silence, I ask, "So... What is the chocolate for?"

He leans back with a mischievous grin on his face. "That's for us to make our own art together."

"Is that why there's a tarp down?"

"Uh, yeah. You know I love you, but I still can't fucking stand messes."

Laughing, I reach for his painting and place it off to the side so it doesn't get ruined. "I guess we can figure that out later, but I don't want this to get ruined in the process."

"Are you gonna sell it?" he asks. "I actually don't think it's half bad."

Spinning to face him, I say, "Never. This one gets added to my personal collection."

With his hand outstretched, he commands me toward him again. "I like that idea."

"Me too."

"But you know what sounds better?"

I close the distance between us and wrap my arms around his neck. "What?"

"Me slathering you in chocolate and then licking you clean."

I moan. "Yeah, I like the sound of that too."

Chapter Twenty-Six

Parker

Six Months Later

"Oh god. It's happening." Cashlynn squeezes my hand as the flight crew closes the cabin, preparing for takeoff.

"Cashlynn, you've got this. Remember, once we land, we'll be in Greece."

"Yeah, but then we have to fly back, and—"

I shut her up with my mouth, swallowing her fear and her moans as I use my tongue to distract her from her biggest fear.

It's been one year since she opened her gallery in Carrington Cove, and I told her that to celebrate, we both deserved a vacation. Her instant argument was no flying, but I pushed her to agree to it if I took her to one of her bucket list places, and she did. I honestly don't know if she thought I was joking or not, but when we played rock, paper, scissors (with no fire or water balloon involved) to decide, I won fair and square, so I booked the trip and have been coaxing her through each step, knowing that this trip will be cause for more than one reason to celebrate.

We just need to get in the air first.

When I break our kiss, her eyes flutter open. "If you want to distract me like that for the whole flight, I wouldn't be opposed to it."

"That's thirteen hours of kissing. You think you can handle that without taking it any further?"

She groans at the idea. "Okay, maybe not."

I lean toward her ear and lower my voice. "Maybe once the sun goes down and they turn the lights off in the cabin, I'll try to feel you up."

She smacks my arm. "You wouldn't dare."

I stare right into her eyes as I say, "You should know me better than that by now, Cashlynn. When I want something, I make it happen."

"Except for owning the animal hospital. You gave that up pretty easily."

"Yeah, because you are more important to me."

A few months after Robert fired Seth, he found a suitable replacement for him as our new owners—a couple from Georgia who were looking to relocate to a smaller town. Turns out he'd had offers to sell over the years, but never entertained the idea because he wasn't ready. But when Sheryl and Theodore Monroe approached him about the practice for the second time, he jumped at their offer, and the couple have been incredible to work with. Between the three of us, we've managed our patients extremely well.

"I still can't believe you took two weeks off."

"You're one to talk. I thought I was going to have to pry your fingers off the door jamb of the gallery to get you to go on this trip."

"Well, Sally and Erica have it under control, I just need to trust them. Plus, Willow insisted she would stop by and help them if they had any questions. Hazel offered, but she has too much on her plate right now."

I let out a sigh. "I know. I can't believe that Mrs. Kingston left her Blueberry."

Diane Kingston sadly passed away a few weeks ago, and she left her dog to my sister. They already had a bond and she was familiar with his care, but it's been a lot for Hazel to manage her business and a dog. Not to mention she has to meet with Timothy McDonald this week to go over the rest of Diane's will.

"I think it will be good for her to have a little companion."

Cashlynn sighs. "I've tried to convince her to start dating again, but she's fed up. Says there's no available men in town and she's contemplating becoming a lesbian, but she's not sure if she could handle a life without dick."

I give Cashlynn a deadpan stare. "I could have gone my entire life without hearing that."

She laughs, but then the plane starts to move, heading for the runway. "Oh God. Hold my hand, please."

I surround both of her hands with my own. "Just breathe. Remember, taking off and landing is the worst part."

She nods, closing her eyes and taking deep breaths. "I don't know if you'll ever be able to talk me into this again."

I smirk before dropping my first hint to her about the reason for this trip. "Really? Not even for our honeymoon?"

With her eyes still closed, she scoffs. "We aren't even engaged, Parker. I can't think about a honeymoon without a ring on my finger."

I take her ring out of my pocket after waiting more than one year to give it back to her. "Well, we'd better fix that, then." I take her left hand and slide her ring back on her finger just as her eyes snap open.

"Parker? What the..."

"I figured celebrating our engagement in Greece might make you reconsider flying for a honeymoon."

Her eyes well with tears. "Are you saying..."

"Since we met on a plane, it only seems fitting that I bring our story full circle this way." I take a deep breath as I prepare to recite the speech I practiced. "You, Cashlynn O'Neil, are the love of my life. You have taught me so much about myself in such a short time, and if we weren't flying right now, I'd take off my seatbelt and get down on one knee, but the flight attendant told me that I couldn't."

She laughs as I hear people start to murmur and peek their heads around to listen to us. I imagine someone must be recording, and since I'm already an internet sensation—yes, Willow continues to post videos of me—it only seems fitting that this gets broadcasted to the world as well.

"Will you be my fiancée for real this time, sweetheart?" I ask just as the pilot sends the plane up into the sky. But Cashlynn isn't even focused on that, and my distraction tactic for takeoff is working perfectly.

"Will you marry me, make mistakes with me, and learn everything else that life has yet to teach us...*with me*? I want to have babies with you, grow old with you, watch you paint in your underwear and help you with inspiration when you need it," I say, waggling my eyebrows. "I want to spend the rest of my life with you. What do you say? Care to make it official this time?"

She nods, her lips trembling. "Yes, Parker. Yes, I'll marry you!"

When I pull her into me and seal my lips over hers, I hear applause ring out around us. We part and Cashlynn buries her face in my neck as my pulse thrums in my ears.

"I can't believe you did that while we were taking off."

"Well, it took your mind off it, didn't it?"

Her eyes meet mine when she lifts her head. "Yeah, it did."

"Then I'd say I'm being the best flight companion yet again."

She holds my face in her hands. "And you're the only one I want for the rest of our lives."

***

Not ready to say goodbye to Parker and Cashlynn? Click here for a sneak peek into their future.

***

Hazel's book is next in the final book of the series. Somehow You Knew releases July 1st, and you can pre-order here.

Chapter Twenty-Seven

Sneak Peek for Hazel

"There are a few stipulations to the will, of course."

"Like what?"

Timothy McDonald, our town lawyer, lets out a heavy sigh. "Let me just say, I was opposed to this idea, but your aunt was insistent."

When Diane Kingston died, it was a hard pill to swallow. We'd all known her COPD was worsening, but it still felt like a gut punch when it finally happened. And it reminded me of watching my own father pass away from cancer.

But then she left me her dog, and apparently an inheritance of some kind. To say I was shocked was an understatement because my friendship with her was completely authentic and sometimes, I'm not sure who benefited from it more—me or her.

But now I'm sitting next to her nephew, waiting to hear about what comes next as her estate is settled, but the man sitting next to me is making me extremely *unsettled* because I've seen him before—*when he was drawing a hummingbird on my arm almost a year ago.*

"What are you talking about?" Gage—AKA hummingbird guy—asks, and suddenly the urge to throw up comes on pretty strong. I still can't believe that *he* was the man who made me question my sanity and singledom. Too bad he disappeared and I never saw him again—until now.

Timothy takes a deep breath. "Your aunt had amassed a total wealth of 10.2 million dollars."

I can feel my eyes threaten to fall out of my head. "Holy shit."

Gage blows out a breath. "I knew she had money, but not that much."

"Yes, well she was smart with her investments and lived well below her means. She made a good living as an engineer and wanted to be able to pass down her wealth to the people that meant the most to her."

Gage and I share a look before I speak. "So what's the issue?" I ask. "I mean, even if we split it, that's still a substantial amount. I still can't believe that she included me in this."

"Oh, that was her intention—for the two of you to split the money, but only after you satisfy a set of conditions." Timothy shifts through a stack of papers.

My stomach tightens. "Conditions?" Gage echoes, beating me to the question. "What kind of conditions?"

I wait with bated breath, wondering what crazy idea this woman could have possibly come up with. I mean, I know Diane was quirky, but this is taking it to another level.

Timothy shakes his head. "In order to inherit the money, the first thing you two have to do is...get married."

The words hang in the air like a live wire. Gage and I turn to each other, identical expressions of shock plastered on our faces. For once, it seems like we're in complete agreement—this was the last thing we expected to hear.

But as the weight of the stipulation settles over me, I know I have a decision to make.

I just hope I don't make the wrong one.

Somehow You Knew is available for Pre-Order TODAY!

Also By Harlow James

Carrington Cove Series
Somewhere You Belong (Dallas and Willow)
Someone You Deserve (Penn and Astrid)
Sometimes You Fall (Grady and Scottie)
Someday You Learn (Parker and Cashlynn)
Somehow You Knew (Gage and Hazel)

***

The Ladies Who Brunch (rom-coms with a ton of spice)
Never Say Never (Charlotte and Damien)
No One Else (Amelia and Ethan)
Now's The Time (Penelope and Maddox)
Not As Planned (Noelle and Grant)
Nice Guys Still Finish (Jeffrey and Ariel)

***

The Newberry Springs (Gibson Brothers) Series
Everything to Lose (Wyatt & Kelsea)
Everything He Couldn't (Walker & Evelyn)
Everything But You (Forrest & Shauna)

***

The California Billionaires Series (rom coms with heart and heat)
My Unexpected Serenity (Wes and Shayla)
My Unexpected Vow (Hayes and Waverly)
My Unexpected Family (Silas and Chloe)

***

The Emerson Falls Series (smalltown romance with a found family friend group)
Tangled (Kane & Olivia)
Enticed (Cooper & Clara)
Captivated (Cash and Piper)
Revived (Luke and Rachel)
Devoted (Brooks and Jess)

***

Lost and Found in Copper Ridge

A holiday romance in which two people book a stay in a cabin for the same amount of time thanks to a serendipitous $5 bill.

Guilty as Charged

An intense opposites attract standalone that will melt your kindle. He's an ex-con construction worker. She's a lawyer looking for passion.

McKenzie's Turn to Fall

A holiday romance where a romance author falls for her neighborhood butcher.

Acknowledgements

Parker and Cashlynn were one of those couples that left me giggling after I was done writing them. Their banter, the way Cashlynn drove him nuts, and getting to explore Parker's wounds made this story one that was almost effortless to write.

This book was also the last book I wrote while my dog, Daisy, was still alive. She sat at my feet and kept me company like she always did, and I'll never forget that. That's why this book is dedicated to her.

As much as I know that readers aren't ready for the series to end, I think Hazel's story is the perfect way to say goodbye to this town and these characters that have changed my life.

And I hope you stay along for the ride until the very end.

To my husband: Thank you for believing in me and cheering me on every step of the way. Thank you for traveling with me, investing in my success, and being my person, my best friend, the man that inspires all of my book boyfriends, and my official Book Bitch. I love you.

To my beta readers: Keely, Emily, Kelly, and Carolina: you four are the best voices I have in my corner. Each of you gives me the advice, feedback, and support that I need in your own way. I'm so grateful to have the four of you on my team still after all this time. I love you all and appreciate you more than you'll ever know.

To Kait, my P.A.: Hiring you has been one of the best decisions I've ever made. Your friendship and professional support have helped me so much this year. Thank you for being my newest cheerleader!

To Jess, my social media manager: You have single-handedly made my life better! I have so much more time to focus on writing and other aspects of my business thanks to you. Your time and creativity is appreciated SO much. Thank you from the bottom of my heart for doing what you do for me.

And to my readers: thank you for supporting me, whether you've been here since the beginning, or you're brand new. I LOVE this hobby turned business of mine. It's an amazing feeling to be able to create art for someone to enjoy and forming a relationship from that. I never take my readers for granted and know that there would be no Harlow James without you.

So thank you for supporting a wife and mom who found a hobby that she loves.
And a future career that I'm working toward with each passing day.

Connect with Harlow James

Follow me on Amazon

Follow me on Instagram

Follow me on Facebook

Join my Facebook Group: https://www.facebook.com/groups/494991441142710/

Follow me on Goodreads

Follow me on Book Bub

Subscribe to my Newsletter for Updates on New Releases and Giveaways

Website

Printed in Great Britain
by Amazon